John Drake trained as a biochemist to post-doctorate research level before realizing he was no good at science. His working career was in the television department of ICI until 1999 when he became a fulltime writer. He is married with a son and two grandchildren.

PRAISE FOR JOHN DRAKE:

"Broad comedy, high drama, plenty of action, a pinch of sex . . . the genre has room for this cheerily debunking outsider" – *Daily Mail*

"Swashbuckling adventure on the high seas doesn't get much better than this. [. . .] John Drake writes beautifully, and you'll be torn between savoring the words and quickly flipping the pages. Any favorable comparison to Stevenson or Patrick O'Brian is totally justified." – Nelson DeMille, #1 *New York Times* bestselling author

FLETCHER'S GLORIOUS 1ST OF JUNE

JOHN DRAKE

ENDEAVOURINK

AN ENDEAVOUR INK PAPERBACK

First published by New English Library under the pen name
J C Edwards in 1993

This paperback edition published in 2017
by Endeavour Ink

Endeavour Ink is an imprint of Endeavour Press Ltd
Endeavour Press, 85-87 Borough High Street,
London, SE1 1NH

ISBN 978-1-911445-51-7

Typeset by Palimpsest Book Production Ltd, Falkirk, Stirlingshire

Printed and bound in Great Britain by
Clays Ltd, St Ives plc

www.endeavourpress.com

In fond memory of
David Burkhill Howarth

------------ DBH ------------

1946 - 2009

PATRIFAMILIAS AMATISSIMO
MAGISTRO DOCTISSIMO
INGENIOSISSIMO TECHNITAE
OPTIMO AMICO

Table of Contents

Introduction

The lewd and depraved substance of much that the ogre obliged me to set down, must ever be a source of shame to one whose aspirations inclined towards holy orders.

(Samuel Pettit, 5th June 1877.)

*

Following the success of *Fletcher's Fortune* I have been asked to say a little more about the Journals from which the Fletcher series is drawn, and about Mr Pettit, the clerk employed by Jacob Fletcher to take down the story of his adventures.

As regards Pettit, the above quotation from a letter to his second cousin Ariadne sums up his attitude to Fletcher and the memoirs better than anything I can say. Pettit was eventually ordained into the Anglican clergy some time during the latter half of 1877. He became a parish priest in Liverpool where he devoted himself to good works among the city's poor, especially indigent sailors. He married Ariadne in 1881 and they had four children.

As in the first book, I have left Pettit's footnotes as he wrote them, without comment. Also, at the beginning of Chapter 12, I have left his quaint warning of what follows next. What Pettit found so objectionable in this section is hard to fathom since the passage which presumably upset him is far from being the only piece of erotica in the Journals. Furthermore, it is obvious that the passage was a favourite with somebody, and the volume falls open at that place. One can only speculate as to who this person might have been.

The memoirs themselves are in twenty-five volumes, uniformly bound in dark blue leather, embossed with the word "Fletcher" with a roman numeral and the Admiralty's "fouled anchor" emblem. The paper is of imperial quarto size.

The first twelve volumes are in Pettit's own immaculate hand, but the rest are typed on one of the early Remington typewriters, specially imported from the U.S.A. for this purpose.

The present binding dates from the early 1900s since the originals were badly damaged when a determined effort was made to destroy them by that early feminist and founder of the Empire League for Female Suffragism,

Lady Evangeline Hyde-Fletcher, who in March of 1900 ordered her head gardener to burn them on a bonfire. But somebody, probably Lady Evangeline's husband, Rear-Admiral Sir Jacob Hyde-Fletcher (Fletcher's great-great-grandson) rescued the volumes and had them re-bound in the present binding.

As in *Fletcher's Fortune* I have improvised chapters between the run of Fletcher's narrative, drawing for my information on the papers in my growing archive of Fletcher memorabilia. I stress that these third-person chapters are my invention, though based on careful research.

John Drake, Cheshire, 2015

Chapter 1

Hubert Spry. 28th August. Five minutes and thirty seconds.
Only moderate sport.

(From Victor Coignwood's *Book of*
Extra-ordinaries for 1793.)

*

The sun beat down, the birds sang, the sky was blue and the crowds were out in their thousands. Voraciously Lady Sarah Coignwood drank in the sights and sounds of the merry multitude, surrounding the expensive hired carriage where she and Victor were seated. It was late August of 1793 and in one short month Lady Sarah's entire world had turned on its head. But today she was happy, enjoying a holiday from hiding in the shabby, grubby house in Greenwich, owned by her brother Admiral Lord Williams.

She smiled happily as balladeers bawled out the latest songs, jugglers juggled, piemen clanged their bells, old women hawked gin at a penny a nip, red-faced musicians fought to outplay each other and the dear innocent little children wrestled in the dust, pummelling each other's faces.

Of course, she had to keep somewhat in the shadows of the carriage interior as her disguise as a lady's maid might not stand close inspection. She'd already recognised several faces among the fashionable ladies and gentlemen in nearby carriages, so they might well recognise her if they got too good a look. But this was a small price to pay and even added to the thrill of the occasion.

She turned to her Victor, her younger son, whose disguise was more elaborate than hers, since he was attired as a lady of fashion – a little pleasure of his that he loved to indulge.

"Victor," she sighed, "you are so good to me. You know that nothing so lifts my spirits as a day such as this."

"My pleasure is to serve," said he.

"You really are my dearest boy," said she.

"Thank you, Mother," said he, "but it is the Good Lord to whom we owe the sunshine."

"Yes," she said, "but I do hate to see an occasion spoiled by bad weather. Everyone is so miserable." Impulsively she threw her arms around her son and kissed him, and they laughed and giggled together like the innocent girls that they were not.

At that moment, there came a sudden hum of anticipation from the crowd.

"Dearest!" said Victor. "It begins," and mother and son turned to the day's sport.

The small procession came out through the gate in the walls which gave access to the high wooden stage erected in front of the building to keep everything above the crowd and yet in plain sight. Victor, the aficionado, pointed out the various dignitaries to his mother and explained their part in the proceedings.

"Ah!" said she. "What a fine thing it is to see these ancient customs upheld."

Then came a deep roar from the mob. A huge, bestial, upswelling howl of delight and derision as, here at last, came the principal performer, pale and grim, bareheaded in an open-neck shirt, and with a turnkey leading him by either arm. He shrank at the hostility of the crowd and the spattering of missiles that curved up towards him. The height of the platform protected him from stones and clods, but nothing could save him from the ghastly sight of the gallows crossbeam with its dangling noose, for that stood boldly in front of him on the scaffold outside Newgate Prison.

"Watch most carefully now," said Victor pointing at the doomed figure. "There!" he cried and a shudder of unholy pleasure ran through Lady Sarah as she saw the sick horror overwhelm the victim. He staggered visibly and his head sank upon his breast.

Close beside the condemned man strode the Chaplain-in-Ordinary of the prison. His was a most important part in the proceedings and he was fully conscious of it. He held up his Bible for the condemned to see, and thundered out scripture as if Lucifer were in the very act of clambering upon the scaffold to rob the hangman of his meat.

As they came beneath the very shadow of the great beam, the Ordinary gave the Twenty-third Psalm. He always did at this juncture. For one thing he was fond of it and for another it was exceedingly apt.

"Yea though I walk through the Valley of the Shadow of Death," he boomed, "I shall fear no evil!" He shook his head emphatically, "For THOU art with me!" He jabbed a finger at Heaven, "Thy rod and Thy staff they comfort me . . ." The mob knew the Chaplain and gave him the cheers that this fine performance deserved. Afterwards, he would acknowledge them, like the great actor Garrick (whom he'd so much admired in the '60s) taking his applause at Drury Lane. But meanwhile, the good Chaplain concentrated upon delivering spiritual comfort to the condemned man. And he delivered it at the top of his voice. That way, if he couldn't save a soul, at least he could drown out the hoary old favourites that the crowd so loved to shout at his wretched one-man congregation.

"Tired, old cove? We'll soon take the weight off yer feet!"

"You'll find it comfortabler going back inside, cocky: you'll be lying down!"

"Hang on yer legs for a shillin', mister?"

"Mind the rope don't break, cully. You could have a nasty fall!"

Unfortunately, these efforts of the Chaplain and mob were all wasted, for at this stage in the game, the victim's senses were obliterated by terror and he'd not have noticed anything short of King George himself riding up, in crown and coronation robes, waving a pardon in his fist.

And so to the business itself. The turnkeys stood back. The hangman stood forward. The crowd bawled its approval and the hangman gravely acknowledged them. The condemned was placed upon the trap and the hangman pinioned the hands and feet. He asked for a dying confession and a massive silence fell as thousands strained to hear. But no words came as strength died in the victim's limbs. The turnkeys held him up and the hangman covered the head with a white cap. The hangman set the noose and stepped back and his assistant knocked out the prop beneath the trap.

And so, the victim fell the few feet of the short drop and began to choke as prescribed by law. The legs kicked, the shoulders wrenched and the chest heaved to suck air through the crushed windpipe. The white cap, clumsily put on, rode up, revealing the contorted and purple face with its throttling, slobbering mouth. The tongue flapped and the eyes bulged as if they'd pop. The body spun on the end of the swaying line like a hooked fish. It jerked and bent and shuddered.

In her comfortable carriage, so conveniently placed for a good view (thanks to Victor's foresight and the expenditure of a large sum of money) Lady Sarah watched, transported in fascination. She could not believe how long it took a hanged man to die. In point of fact, however, and by Victor's watch, all movement ceased after five minutes and thirty seconds.

"A modest performance," he said, jotting down the details in a pretty little notebook kept for the purpose. "I've seen them last fifteen minutes."

Lady Sarah sighed and shook her head.

"Why have I never seen this before?" she said.

"You'd never come!" protested Victor. "I've told you a thousand times what sport it is. And it was even better in the good old days at Tyburn, with the cart and the procession." He shook his head in sorrow, "But alas those days are gone for ever." He gestured at the dangling figure. "A hanging isn't half the fun it used to be."

"None the less," she said, "never doubt that I shall come again!" She smiled happily. "What happens now?" she asked.

"Nothing really," said Victor. "He'll stay up a while, until they're quite, *quite* sure he's dead. The town's full of tricksters claiming to have been cut down alive and . . ."

"Who is that man?" she said, interrupting, "there, addressing the hangman." She pointed at an immaculately-dressed man, all in black with a tall round hat, who had come forward from among the officials on the scaffold to shake hands with the executioner. What caught the eye was the air of authority about him. The hangman was behaving like a schoolboy brought before his headmaster, and the turnkeys doffed their hats in deepest respect.

"He?" said Victor, in great surprise. "Surely you know him, my darling? Everybody knows him."

"Everybody who moves in these circles," she said, indicating the mob with an elegant hand. "But I lack your familiarity with such society, my dear."

Victor winced. The smile on his mother's lovely face was like the flowers of spring, but he knew a sneer when he heard it.

"It's Slym, the thief-taker," he said. "He is a most remarkable man."

"In what respect is he remarkable?" she asked, and as Victor explained, she listened with growing interest.

*

Later that evening, back in her brother's safe, dull house in Greenwich, Lady Sarah's imagination was running hot and running down dangerous channels. She was elated by the day's freedom but eaten with fury at what circumstances had done to her in the last few weeks.

Instead of enjoying the vast fortune left by her husband, Sir Henry Coignwood, she'd had to fight (unsuccessfully as it turned out) to keep the money – money that was hers by right – out of the hands of Sir Henry's bastard son, Jacob Fletcher. And all she'd got for her efforts was the death of her favourite son Alexander and a charge of murder that had caused her and Victor, her younger son, to flee Coignwood Hall one jump ahead of the law. She and Victor were now fugitives and but for the charity of her elderly brother they'd even now be hiding under a hedge in some field or other.

Fortunately, the old man doted on her and when she and Victor arrived on his doorstep, late one night, she'd easily persuaded him to hide them here in the Greenwich house, safely outside the busy heart of London. She'd thought it better to keep him under her own hand too, and so she made him turn out his servants and close his town house to come down here to Greenwich. The old fool was sunk in illness and senility and couldn't be trusted to hold his tongue.

She looked about the decayed sitting room, poorly lit by its dirty windows and mouldering curtains, and sighed with the irony of it. She had plenty of ready money, thanks to her brother, and yet she had to live like this!

Certainly there was no question of moving to her own magnificent house in Dulwich Square. Even without the fear of being recognised and arrested, she couldn't go there. Since London learned she'd got nothing from her husband's Will, Dulwich Square had been besieged by creditors. The place was buried in debt.

As a woman of active appetites, she was driven to desperation by being locked up in this miserable house, with only Victor and two servants for company – them and her bedridden brother. Above all, it was the loneliness of it that she could not bear. She'd always been surrounded by admirers and comforters, by lovers and hangers-on. It was more than she could bear and the more she thought over the day's events and the temporary return to the real world, the more there grew within her a mad desire to send for her coach, to dress in her finest gown and go through London for all to see. It would be worth it for the pleasure of being among the things that she knew and cherished.

It was only by the narrowest of margins that she chose to do something else instead. Something that would more directly begin the fight against those who had wronged her, and against one of those in particular. But first, she spoke to Victor and asked his advice.

Chapter 2

I like Americans and I like their country. I like the people for their enterprise and their energy and I like the country because an Englishman can step ashore there and not be surrounded by bloody foreigners gibbering nineteen-to-the-dozen, smelling of garlic and waving their arms about. Foreigners are a curse and there should be a law against 'em. But Americans are kindred folk and not at all to be considered as foreigners, within the meaning of the word. Consequently if, God forbid, I couldn't be English, then I should certainly want to be American.

Let that stand as my natural attitude towards the Yankees. But since I turned my back on the Coignwood inheritance in order to make my own money, I've had a special dislike for anybody who tries to take it from me. So when an American privateer chases me across the high seas with intent to do precisely that, then I may take a different view. Especially I may when he gives me grape and roundshot from a British-made carronade 18-pounder and the best gun on my ship is an old brass nine, drooping at the muzzle from over-firing.

I date my career as an independent merchant from 3rd August 1793 when I signed on as Second Mate aboard the West Indiaman, *Bednal Green*. She was a Blackwall-built, ship-rigged vessel of 350 tons; 98 feet long in the hull, with 27 feet at the beam, and an 18-foot depth in hold. Smaller and cheaper to run than a massive East Indiaman, you could sail her round the world with fifteen hands and bring her home with a cargo worth a fortune. She was as fine an example of an ocean-going merchantman as you'd find on the seven seas.

She was fitted out as a slaver, for the triangular trade with Africa and the West Indies, and so she had to be able to defend herself. To that end, she had 10 gun-ports a side and mounted a mixture of 4- and 6-pounders, with a single 9-pounder brass gun in the bow. And to give enough hands to work the guns, if need be, she left London with a crew of thirty-nine, counting two boys, the ship's cat and a dago savage from the Brazils.

The deal I made with Captain Horace Jenkins, the master and owner of *Bednal Green*, was that I should buy a £100 share of his outward-bound cargo for an equiv-alent share of the final profits at London prices. As a fringe benefit, he promised to instruct me in celestial navigation.

He did too, by lunar observation as well as by chronometer. Not many merchant ships had chronometers aboard in those days because of the high cost of the instrument. But old Horace was worth a pound or two, and had invested in one for the greater certainty it allowed of an accurate landfall. But what a puff it all was, this "Art and Mysterie" of navigation! A trained monkey could take angles with a sextant. And as for the calculations, why, they're tedious certainly, but there's nothing difficult about them. I used to do them in my head. I don't know what all the fuss was about.

[I must reluctantly confirm Fletcher's boasting by the admission that he was startlingly adept at all mathematical operations. S.P.]

Horace was amazed at how fast I picked it up because he'd made the mistake of looking at my six feet three inches and sixteen stone and thinking that since I was so big, then I must be stupid. I'm sure he took me on because he thought I'd keep his crew in line. Mr Tadcaster, his First Mate, had sailed with Horace for years, and had used to be his bruiser, but Tadcaster was beginning to show too great an interest in the rum.

Horace was an odd bird in many ways. He knew his job all right or he'd not have lasted five minutes at sea. Not off the African coast, he wouldn't. And he knew how to pick a crew of good men, even with the Press Gang sweeping London. But he was an old woman in some ways and looked tireder and greyer than his years. And he worried too much. His worst peculiarity, however, was a constant protestation of solicitude towards the men, which meant no starting, flogging or beating. I don't know how Tadcaster had ever gone about his work. Presumably he'd done it when Horace was looking the other way.

In the event, I had to find my own way when, two days out and running down Channel, one of the men gave back an oath in exchange for an order. He was a Manxman named Jervis, an active and sinewy fellow, hard as nails, who was the fist-fighter among the fo'c'sle hands. He'd been spoiling for trouble ever since I came aboard. Now, I didn't mind that. It's perfectly natural for a ship's crew to sort itself out so as to see whose arm cracks the walnuts. The trouble was, under Horace's rules I wasn't sure how to deal with the dark looks and surly mutterings I was getting from Mr Jervis.

But on this occasion he pushed the thing too far, and I had to make my own arrangements. *Bednal Green* was rolling along steadily, with a fair wind, lines coiled down and with little for the watch to do. Most of the other hands were on deck idling, since the weather was fine. Horace was on the quarterdeck, by the wheel, and Tadcaster was down below with another bottle. Jervis was sitting cross-legged by a companionway sewing a shirt when I told him to shift before somebody tripped over him.

"Garn, ye bugger!" says he, and every conversation instantly stopped. The men looked on eagerly to see what would happen next, and Horace affected not to have heard, although he was barely twenty feet away. Knowing his views, however, I felt it best to be careful, so I turned, and went down the companionway to the lower deck, and beckoned Jervis to follow me.

Jervis got up with a leer and swaggered after me, making lewd signs with his fingers at my back for all his mates to see. There was a lot of laughter but that didn't matter 'cos once he was below decks, the swab was mine.

I swept him off his feet by the collar and the seat of his breeches and, swinging him like a sack, I cracked his head smartly two or three times against a nearby oaken bulkhead. I wasn't angry and was seeking to correct rather than chastise. When I thought he'd had enough, I dropped him on the deck. But Jervis bounced up like a jack-in-the-box! And the rascal caught me a blow on the jaw with the full swing of his arm. I shook my head. That hurt. And it roused my temper too, such that I put my own fists up and let Mr Jervis have what he'd been asking for since first I came aboard.

Later, when he resumed his sewing, his well-blacked eyes, his thick lips and his tapped claret told their own story to the whole crew. And do you know, I never had the least trouble out of any of them after that? Most especially not from Jervis.

And so I learned a most important lesson about the running of a ship. Had I dealt with Jervis at once, as I should have, then I'd not have had to batter him quite so hard. Ever afterwards, I made it my practice on joining a ship, immediately to seek out the "Jervis" among her crew and to thrash him on the spot. I have found this to be a kindly and efficient way to run a ship, and to prove it, every vessel I have had the unhindered mastery of has gone like clockwork with the hands jumping to obey. Oh by George they did, just you believe me!

So in fact Horace got exactly what he wanted out of me. That is, he got his enforcer and bruiser. At first that's all he thought I was good for. But I soon put him right and in return got back something that I wanted out of him. For Horace had the virtue that he knew talent when he saw it, and once he saw where my real gifts lay, he let me exploit them. Needless to say, this was in the area of trade and commerce.

The first time we came to the transcendingly important matter of bargaining for price was with a Portuguese Hebrew named Pareira-Gomez who was chief factor of a West Africa baracoon.

[A baracoon was a fort where wretched negroes were confined awaiting sale to slavers. What follows establishes Fletcher's involvement in the slave trade, of which enterprise his only opinion was enthusiasm for the vast profits to be made. S.P.]

Pareira had a face like a razor and doubtless made

his own children pay for their mother's milk. Horace started the dealings but I soon edged him out and he had the sense to leave me to it, where he might have let his pride get in the way. What clinched it was Pareira-Gomez himself. When he and I finally shook hands on the deal, he put his head on one side and grinned like a cobra.

"Boy," says he, "you sure you not a little bit of a Jew, eh? You pretty damn bloody good bastard!" I shall always treasure those words as the sincere compliment of one expert to another. After that, old Horace left me to make all dealings for the ship. So all went well apart from the fact that we lost a third of our crew from some filthy African pox that also sent Mr Tadcaster deeper into the bottom of a rum cast, and turned Horace into a grey old man.

None the less, Pareira-Gomez got us a fine cargo of blacks in exchange for our trade goods. A splendid piece of business this, since our goods were cheap trash, strong gin and rusty muskets (it being disputable as to which of the two latter commodities was the more deadly to the user). Pareira took quite a shine to me and invited me to go up the coast with him to meet the local king that he dealt with. There, I was feasted and entertained with every imaginable kindness while the king's warriors gathered in the last of our slaves.

By February of 1794 we were bound for America on the second leg of the triangular trade. We sold our cargo at Charleston, Carolina, at a second healthy profit and took on a third cargo of cotton and tobacco for the homeward voyage. Once we sold that cargo in London we would have made a profit on every penny originally invested in *Bednal Green* three times over! Do you see the beauty of it?

But first we had to get our cargo home. And while we were in Charleston, we heard some very bad news. The whole town was holding its breath waiting for the Yankee Congress in Washington to declare war on England.

Today, people have forgotten the American war of 1794, for it was overshadowed by events in Europe and it didn't involve much more than a few single-ship actions at sea. It was all due to the Yankees securing their business interests following monstrous great purchases of American wheat by the Froggie Government. When *Bednal Green* anchored in Charleston on 10th March, an enormous French convoy of 117 ships, under Rear-Admiral Vanstable, with a couple of 74's and assorted frigates, was busy loading wheat, up north in Norfolk, Virginia. The wheat was to feed Mossoo the common Frog, since thanks to La Revolution, and all the benefits of liberty and fraternity, the Frogs had so comprehensively buggered the '93 harvest that they were facing starvation in '94 (serve 'em right too).

Unfortunately, all that French gold spent in America had tipped the balance of Yankee opinion in favour of

Mossoo. So Congress worked itself into a passion, observed that the Royal Navy had for years been pressing Yankees into the King's service, and suddenly decided that this was cause for war. Of course, what Congress was really doing was keeping the Frogs sweet for next year's wheat sales.

And a nice little war with England was good business in its own right. It meant that the Yankees could let loose their privateers in legalised piracy against our merchantmen. It had to be privateers since they had had no navy since 1785. But they'd plenty of armed merchantmen ready and waiting, and all Congress had to do was issue Letters of Marque to these ships and a swarm of them would be out into the Atlantic sniffing for British merchantmen – that is, for ships like *Bednal Green.*

It was a dire prospect, for the Yankees were fine seamen and fought like Britons. Faced with this, all we could do was try to get out of Charleston as fast as we could in the hope of being gone before the game started. And there we were lucky, for Charleston was split in its loyalties. Some of the people supported a war, but the tobacco and cotton merchants, who traded mainly with London, didn't want their markets shut down. So in fact we had every assistance in completing our business, taking on cargo and getting to sea again.

In the event, we very nearly did it. We left Charleston on the 15th, with a fair westerly in our sails, on the very day Congress took the plunge, but before news had reached Charleston. Before nightfall we were out of sight of land. All next day we were on tenterhooks, and every man of us searched the horizon for strange sails. But those we saw made no approach and by the second day we felt ourselves safe.

The only event of note was Mr Tadcaster's sudden appearance on deck and his epic ascent of the mainmast to escape the blue goblin that had chased him out of his cabin. He was going strongly, calling all hands to his aid in a loud voice, and had reached the t'gallant shrouds, when he let go his grip, all the better to pull something off his back. And so he returned to the deck, hands clenched tight about an invisible neck which he exerted himself to strangle, while bellowing the triumphant words, "Got ye, y'little bastard!"

He landed in the longboat, where it lay in the waist, with a thump that shook the vessel, and once the sail-maker had sewn him snug in his hammock, we put him to rest in the deep. The crew stood bare-headed, the Captain read from The Book, and Matti the Braziliano, mumbled some prayers of his own to such gods as he honoured. I mention this episode as it confirmed my position as First Mate "de jure" as well as "de facto" and I was now a watch-keeping officer immune to the Navy's impressment.

Then, about mid-day on the 17th February, our main-mast lookout spied a ship bearing down from the north-west. She came on steadily and Horace began to chew his hat with anxiety. North-west was just the direction a Yankee privateer might come from. Horace squinted at our sails and turned to me.

"D'ye think she'll bear more sail, Mister?" says he. I went through the pretence of looking.

"She'll take fore, main and mizzen t'gallants, sir," says I. As usual Horace was running under easy sail. It was typical of him. That way he'd have all the less sail to take in should the weather blow up. It was craven, if you ask me. True, he hadn't the huge crew of a warship, where a single word would send hundreds of men running to obey. In fact, after the African fever, we'd only a handful of real topmen. But other merchant skippers were bolder than he. Look at the way they drive the tea clippers home from China, nowadays, and with only twenty men in the crew.

But he listened to me on that occasion 'cos he was frightened, and so *Bednal Green* shook out her extra sail and plunged along that much harder.

"Heave the log, mister," says Horace. "See what she's making." That was pointless. It wouldn't make her go a knot faster, but it kept Horace quiet, so I whistled up the two boys and had one turn the sand glass while the other cast the log over the stern and held up the great spool of line for it to run out as the ship left the log behind. I counted the knots in the line coming off the spool. She was going seven and a half knots, which wasn't bad for a bluff-bowed trader in a heavy swell.

If you ask me, *Bednal Green* was a grand little ship and was doing her best for us. She wasn't built for speed, after all. Her hull was squarish in cross section to pack in the maximum bulk of cargo. She was a good, sea-keeping vessel but not fast. You'd never choose to race her against a New England ship with its fine lines, broad spars and deep sails. Unfortunately, that's exactly what we were tying to do on that occasion.

"Seven and a half knots, Cap'n," says I to Horace, but he knew already. He'd been right at my elbow. He looked at the pursuing sails, now visible from deck level, and he took the brim of his hat out of his mouth for a second.

"Put her before the wind, mister," says he. "We'll run for it."

"With respect, Cap'n," says I, "we're already on our best point of sailing. She'll not do better than this."

"Perhaps they're harmless," says he, nodding at the distant sails. "Mr Fletcher, take my glass and have a look from the masthead." He gave me his glass and I made the climb up to the mainmast cross-trees.

Now you won't know what that means, so I'll tell you. Take a pencil and snap it in half. Lay the stumps side by side on a table, as if they were two sides of an imaginary square. Now take three more pencils and lay them parallel to each other, at right angles across the two stumps, to form a grid, with the long ends of the unbroken pencils sticking out on either side of the two stumps.

Now look at what you have made and magnify it so it's made of oaken spars, with the longer ones six feet long and six inches thick. Then bolt it all together and place it one hundred feet over a ship's deck at sea, with the peak of the topmast sticking out of it, and the t'gallant mast lashed to the topmast and rising another fifteen feet above. And that is the cross-trees of a ship – the thing into which I was climbing. Not a piece of work, incidentally, that my bulk makes easy for me.

Once up there, there's no shelter, no comfort, and the height of the mast exaggerates the movement of the ship so you're swung like a conker on a string. You need a monkey's grip and a leather arse just to stay up there five minutes. God knows how the lookouts stand it for hours on end, but then they ain't humans like you and me, they're seamen.

The lookout on this occasion was a Londoner named Welles, with a red woollen cap that he always wore. He knuckled his brow respectfully. "Mr Fletcher," said his lips, but I couldn't hear him. That far above the sea, the wind was howling so loud that speech was impossible. And there was far more spray about than at deck level. It stung the eyes and drenched your clothes. Welles pointed and mouthed something. I looked but could see nothing other than the endless, grey-green of the waves.

My God but that's a dismal sight. There's nothing to make you feel so insignificant as to look from the masthead in mid-ocean. The bloody sea goes on for ever, and it rolls and turns and plays with you. But Welles was tugging at my arm and pointing again. I was looking the wrong way. All too easy when you're half stupid with dizzy movement. And then I saw it. There it was. I put the glass on it and tried to hold it in view. It took some time, but I got them in the end.

The first thing I saw was the Yankee ensign, then I counted a broadside of at least a dozen guns and saw the decks alive with men: fifty or more against our dozen. And she was forging along with the spray bursting over her narrow bow like breakers on the rocks. She was a ship superficially like our own, three-masted and about the same tonnage. A landsman would never spot the difference. But I could see that she was faster and better armed than us. She had privateer written all over her, and barring some miracle, she must catch us.

It was a moment of intense disappointment. I remembered the times I'd taken prizes in the Royal Navy and thought what capital sport it was, and never thought about what it was like to be on the other end. Well now I was learning and I didn't like it one bit.

The fruits of months of hard work were about to be taken off me by some damned, greedy, legalised pirate.

I was furious and I decided then and there that they weren't getting my money without a fight. Many times in my life I've had to fight for reasons, and in causes, that weren't mine, but not on this occasion. This time I would fight for myself and in defence of my own profits. They might get the victory at the end of the day, but first I was going to kill some of the buggers.

Chapter 3

CLIENT: *Lady Sarah Coignwood.*
INTEREST: *Find Jacob Fletcher.*
FEE: *Unlimited.*
(Heading from filing card, transcribed from the
shorthand, Samuel Slym's system, 30th August
1793.)

*

Slym was very neat. He was neat in his clothes, neat in his black, crop-short hair, and especially neat in his face, which was shaved to within an inch of its life, and the cheeks and chin of which glowed with a red-black shine.

Everything in his office was neat. His desk was bare but for pen and ink and a stack of white, oblong cards each about the size of a man's hand. The spotless room was furnished wall-to-wall with rows of little drawers: dozens of them, like those for the drugs in an apothecary's shop. But these were not for drugs, though each was labelled with a neat and mysterious hieroglyph.

Slym stood as Lady Sarah entered, and as he did so this better view of him showed up the contrast between the gentleman that he was trying so hard to be and the thing that he actually was: a bully in gentleman's clothes. Thick muscular calves bulged through his silk stockings. Big hands with knobbed knuckles thrust through the narrow cuffs of his tailored coat. And cold eyes glared under black brows with all the God-damn-you confidence of a man who'd sent over a hundred felons to the hangman, and always made a special point of going to watch them dance.

"Mr Slym?" said Lady Sarah.

"*Slym*, ma'am," he corrected, pronouncing the word like "slime". "Mr Samuel Slym, at your service, ma'am."

"Indeed?" said Lady Sarah with a tiny smile at his pretentiousness.

Slym spotted this instantly, and for all his formidable reputation, he proved as susceptible to Lady Sarah as any lesser man. Suddenly he felt the need to explain himself.

"The name used to be 'Slim', ma'am," he said, "but I found it insufficiently particular to a man o' my talents, and so I out with the 'i' and in with the 'y' for the more mellifluous sound it . . . er . . . hmm . . ."

His voice faded away as he realised that he was only making things worse.

"I see," said Lady Sarah, sweetly, "Mr Samuel Slym the thief-taker." She paused for effect, then added, "Known to all London, I believe, as 'Slimy Sam'."

Slym almost managed to control himself, but one side of his face twitched like a horse's flank when it shakes off a fly.

"As to that, ma'am," he said, "I cannot be responsible for the minds of the vulgar. But I'll say this. I may be known as . . . *that*," he could not say the actual words, "but nobody calls me by it." He smiled without a trace of mirth. "Not in my hearing, leastways."

"Oh!" said Lady Sarah with the wondering round eyes and rosebud lips of a virgin. But she believed him, none the less. She held the innocent expression and continued, "You could of course replace the 'y' and revert to Slim?" she suggested, and saw the pulses throb in Slym's neck and the black blood rise up his face.

"Not I, ma'am," he said thickly, "I stands by me guns."

"How noble!" she exclaimed, and fluttered her lovely lashes to such effect that Slym was stopped in his anger, soothed, and nicely poised for the next drop. "And of course," she said, "were you to change the name again, the vulgar might laugh at you even more than they do already."

She observed his reaction with wicked glee but recognised that he was now pushed to the limit of his capacity to be deceived that the hurt was unintended, and so the game was now at an end. Torment of *all* kinds was one of her pleasures and she liked to explore any new acquaintance to find where the tender spots lay. With Slym, there was the added thrill of the danger. It was like jabbing a sharp stick into a tiger.

She reflected on the advantage of being a woman. Slym would never have tolerated this from a man. But enough was enough. She needed Slym's active co-operation and it was time for business.

"Mr Slym," she said with a dazzling smile, "I am told that you are the best man in London at your trade . . ."

She turned the full light of her charm upon him and soon the matter of his unfortunate nickname was forgotten and even the coarsened, barnacled emotions of Samuel Slym the gallows-feeder were stirred with the pleasure of her company. She drew him on and encouraged him to talk, and she listened carefully. Then she spoke.

"So, Mr Slym, you claim to find and catch any man who has run."

"Mostly, ma'am," he said modestly.

"But how," said she, "when a fugitive has all the vast metropolis of London in which to hide, let alone England or the rest of the world?" Slym smiled and leaned forward. He was on home ground. As he spoke, his large, scrubbed fingers with their ferociously manicured nails, played with the white cards, tapping the perfectly aligned stack into a super-perfection.

"No, ma'am," he said, as teacher to pupil, "that ain't the way of it, at all. Let me give you two fresh instances from my work: Izzy Cohen the Whitechapel forger, and 'Big Arthur' Barker the meat porter, what kicked his wife to death while drunk. Two men, ma'am, as different as could be and yet both on the hop from a capital charge." He paused and looked Lady Sarah in the eye. "Now, ma'am," he said, "according to you, Izzy or Big Arthur could've gone anywhere. They could've took ship for China even. Am I correct?"

She nodded and Slym saw that he'd caught her entire attention.

"But where d'ye think I found 'em, ma'am? Eh? I'll tell you: Izzy I pulled from under his mother's bed in the house next door to his own, and Big Arthur I took from a gin-shop not five minutes' walk from where he lived. The only difference betwixt 'em was that Izzy came quiet and Big Arthur didn't. And now, next Friday, they swing together side-by-side."

"But how can this be?" said Lady Sarah, suddenly uncomfortable. "Did they not run? Did they not realise the peril of being caught? Did they not run far away?"

"Ah, but they did, ma'am!" said Slym, relishing the chance to air his knowledge before such an audience. "They all do at first. But do *you* realise how terrible hard it is to run far away?

"Consider if it were you, ma'am!" he said. "How should you live? Where should you go? And how should you bear the separation from all that you esteem?" Slym shook his head. "No, ma'am! 'Tis the loneliness that gets 'em. They can't bear to keep away from home."

Lady Sarah's self-control was better than Slym's. The soft, attentive smile never wavered. So he never knew the heavy effect of his words as Lady Sarah learned three very shocking things all in one instant. First, how common were the emotions that she had thought unique to herself. Second, how close she had come to putting her head in a rope, and third how very much more deadly was Mr Slym than she had imagined. She'd been putting her hand in an adder's nest to play with its pups.

But Lady Sarah Coignwood was nothing if not resolute. She crushed her fear and continued the inquisition.

"So is it then a simple matter to catch them?" she said. Slym smiled gravely and nodded.

"Sometimes, ma'am. The neighbours themselves'll seize a man if they think him a villain – and he ain't a dangerous one like Big Arthur – or they may snitch on him. But what if they take his part, as often they will? In that case he must be winkled out! But then, who's to find his home ground? And who's to watch over it, to spy him out? And who's to get a magistrate's warrant for the entering of premises? And finally, who's to take the knocks should he fight?" He shook his head reflectively. "Five men came with me for Big Arthur, ma'am, which number I thought sufficient. But he broke the bones of three, and left his mark on every man including myself.

I tell you freely, ma'am, mine is a fearful business at times, and it exercises my imagination to wonder what might become of me, some dark night!"

Lady Sarah smiled. "Mr Slym," she said, "I seriously doubt that a man of your abilities will be seen off by common ruffians. And as to fear, I would venture to guess that you are a man of action in whom it strikes no root." Slym smirked at this considerable compliment and bowed in his chair.

"Thank'ee, ma'am!" said he.

"And my imagination is exercised to wonder how you effect the finding of a man who seeks to hide. To me that still seems the principal difficulty. How do you do it?"

"By the careful accumulation of knowledge, ma'am," he said. "You see, ma'am, every man thinks he's special. He fancies he's the only one there is. But he aint!" He slapped the table with his hand. "He's one of a family, and he's one of a trade, and one of a club, or a gin-shop, or a cobbler's clientele. Or he's the Jack-spry-dandy with a doxy-on-the-sly what he meets in the room over a baker's shop! And by all these things he may be known . . . and found!" Slym's eyes were gleaming with enthusiasm. "I goes out a lot, ma'am – a terrible lot. And I talks to people as sees things: ostlers, maids, shopkeepers, tapmen and the like. And what I learns I set down here." He got up and opened one of the little drawers. It was filled with a row of cards. He took one out and gave it to her. "There's your answer, ma'am," said he. "Thousands of these, indexed and catalogued, so's I can dig 'em out as I want. There's all sorts in here and I can start a search in a dozen ways: names, trades, vices . . ." He broke off as he saw her puzzling over the card. He smiled. "No, ma'am, you won't be able to read it. 'Tis shorthand, you see. My own method. A faster version of Samuel Taylor's of 1786."

He sat down again and leaned back in his chair, his hands smoothing imaginary dust off the polished surface of his desk. "*All* my own methods, ma'am, developed by myself. No other man in England works in this way. Maybe none other in the world."

Again, Lady Sarah shuddered inwardly at the risk she had taken in coming here. A risk so much greater than she had known. Victor had described Slym as no more than a superior thug; a tool that she might train to the application of violence where she chose. Certainly she had found a physically dangerous man, but also one possessed of intellectual gifts not far beneath her own. She had not expected the insight into human nature, nor the sharpness and creative originality of mind. But no matter. She resolved to punish Victor savagely for the fright she'd had, and as for Slym himself, he was far too gifted not to be used.

Fortunately, and early on in their conversation, she had identified the weakness in Slym's character that would enable him to be led like a bull with a ring in his nose.

"Mr Slym," she said, "I am come to a decision. I shall employ you to find me a man. His name is Jacob Fletcher."

"Fletcher, ma'am," said Slym. He dipped his pen, wiped it neatly and inscribed a fresh card with a few bold strokes.

"But Mr Slym," she said, "be warned! This matter is so important that you shall devote yourself to it before all else."

"Oh," said Slym, "shall I indeed?" He put down the pen and raised his eyebrows. "Ma'am," said he, "if you know my reputation, you'll know I don't work cheap. Not even for normal services, let alone my exclusive attentions. So might I ask what payment you have in mind?"

Lady Sarah's lips parted and her breasts rose as she breathed deeply.

"Why, sir," she said, "your heart's desire . . ."

*

That evening, Lady Sarah reclined at her ease on a sofa in the sitting room at 208 Maze Hill, Greenwich. The room was shockingly ill-furnished but at least Lady Sarah had her gowns. She was wearing a favourite "Directoire" gown, of white muslin, which clung admirably to her slender legs and swept full-length to her ankles to frame her pretty, naked feet in a web of fabric. Over these feet, her son Victor crouched, where he knelt at the end of the sofa. His coat, waistcoat and shirt lay in a crumpled heap beside him, and the thin white skin of his back and shoulders was crossed with red stripes. He snivelled and sniffed and sobbed his apologies.

"Oh, stop it!" said Lady Sarah, impatiently. "You're steeped in hypocrisy, as all the world knows. I believe you enjoy it!"

"I don't," he gasped, "not when you lay on so hard."

"Hmm," she said, absently, considering the long slender riding-crop swinging from her right hand. "Perhaps not. I do hope not anyway."

Victor stretched one hand awkwardly behind his neck and down the middle of his back. He probed with his fingers.

"Look!" he said, as he drew back his hand. "Blood!"

"Ah, my baby," she exclaimed, leaping to her feet with the most affecting display of remorse. "Show me the place for Mother to kiss it. I did not know." Victor turned himself round for her inspection.

"There," he said.

"Where?" she asked in a voice like a dove.

"There," he confirmed.

And CRACK! She brought the crop whistling down precisely on the spot. Victor screeched and jumped.

"There!" cried Lady Sarah, breathing through flared nostrils. She flung the riding-crop aside. "That's better! Now you're well served, you stupid ninny." She smiled a heavy smile and licked her lips in satisfaction. "Next time, take care what you tell me. Now get dressed and come here. There is much to do."

Victor recognised the change in mood and had more sense than to argue. He struggled painfully into his shirt, stifling his groans, and sat beside his mother on the sofa. She smiled and stretched her gleaming arms invitingly to him. She took his head in her lap and petted him like a baby. She ran her fingers through his hair and gently scratched his scalp with the tips of her fingernails.

Victor watched her warily through half-closed eyes and fought the delicious ecstasy that her attentions were inducing. He could never be quite sure what she would do next.

As anyone who knew him would agree, Victor Coignwood was a sadistic degenerate. But equally, any fair-minded man who learned the full details of Victor's upbringing, would be amazed that the boy had turned out so well.

"Now," said Lady Sarah, "I see the way forward. Three things stand between us and your father's money." Victor stiffened as he guessed what was coming next. He drew breath to protest, and saw his mother's fingers hook into claws, which hovered over his eyes. And he felt the soft arms turn to steel.

He shut his mouth tight and looked up at her in terror.

"Good boy!" she said, and the slim hands stroked him again. "You weren't going to say that we are safe here, were you?"

"No, Mother," he said.

"And you weren't going to say that we should not risk ourselves to seek the Coignwood fortune, were you?"

"No, Mother," he said.

"Good," she said. "It is true that your Uncle Williams's house has served us well. Without it we should have had nowhere to go. And I have it from an expert that we should then have betrayed ourselves." She tapped his nose gently in admonition. "But I have told you many times, that we cannot stay here for ever, reliant upon your uncle's resources."

"Why does my Uncle Williams do your bidding so completely?" Victor asked, to change the subject.

"Because he loves me, Victor, as you do," she said and smiled down at him. Victor was stabbed with the beauty of her face, and it occurred to him that his mother had precisely the expression that popish painters tried to put on to the faces of their Holy Madonnas. He sniggered as he thought of himself as the baby Jesus. She misunderstood his emotion.

"Yes, darling," she said, "your uncle is very afraid of you."

"Is he?" said Victor with much interest.

"Oh yes," she said. "When I go to him, he always asks if you are with me, and always I reassure him that you are not." Victor sat up, intrigued.

"Why do you never let me see him?" he asked.

"Because I am reserving you for a purpose, Victor.

At present your uncle does my bidding. He signs papers as he is told. But if ever he proved difficult, I might let you go to him."

"Why?" asked Victor.

"Because he is so very old and weak, my dear," she said. "He is broken by the death of your brother Alexander, whom he seems truly to have loved, despite all. But his horror of yourself is so great that I think your appearance at his bedside would see him off . . . should ever the need arise."

"Ah," said Victor, "I see. Poor old fellow! And if the fright didn't do it, why, I am sure a helpless invalid might be drowned in his bed with any convenient liquid. One would bind his arms with his sheets, sit on his legs, pinch his nose shut, and fill his mouth." He waved a hand airily. "Soup would do, and would look perfectly natural."

"Bless you, my boy," she said, "I knew I might rely on you." Then the mood changed again and Victor went cold with fright.

"Now listen!" she said. "I shall not sit here and await events. I shall act. We must crush the charges of murder, we must overturn the will that gives everything to the Brat, Fletcher, and we must be rid of Fletcher himself."

Victor was terrified and fascinated all at once.

"But how?" he said. "We were seen doing murder before witnesses. All the world is ranged against us."

"I shall make it clear, my love," she said, "so that even you shall understand . . . Up!" she said, and pushed him to his feet. She clapped her hands like a governess with her charges, "Pen and paper! At once!"

Victor fetched what she wanted and spread them on a small table, convenient for her use. She smiled like an angel, stroked her son's cheek, and inscribed a few lines in her stylish, elegant handwriting. When she was done, she nodded in satisfaction at her work:

> Mr Forster the magistrate
> Mr Pendennis the Polmouth merchant
> Mr Richard Lucey the solicitor
> Mr Taylor the bookseller (& wife)
> Mr Forster's Constable
> The Constable's two brothers.

Victor watched in a thrill of fascination and growing excitement as his mother lectured him upon this list, and her pen moved decisively over it.

"First the threat," she said, "the people who keep us in danger of our lives. You, my dear, were seen by Mr and Mrs Taylor on the night of 19th July when you emerged from 29 Market Street, having murdered Edward Lucey . . ."

"Murdered?" said Victor, shrinking from the ugly word. She laughed.

"What word would you prefer?" she said, and continued, "Having *murdered* Edward Lucey and wounded his son Richard."

"And Andrew Potter," interrupted Victor anxious that no good deed of his should be forgotten. "He also. I did kill him too."

"Of course, my dear," she said, "Potter, your play-mate." She paused and looked at him with a little smile. "A *gentleman of the back door* like yourself." Before Victor could wonder if he were being sneered at, she was talking rapidly. "So, Richard Lucey and the Taylors could give evidence against us for the events of that night. And now we turn to 29th July, and Mr Magistrate Forster's attempt to arrest us. On that occasion, you shot dead one man and wounded another." Victor smirked and shrugged his shoulders modestly. "The following could give evidence of this: Forster, his Constable, the Constable's two brothers . . . and of course, our old friend Mr Nathan Pendennis, Lord Mayor of Polmouth, who came with them.

"Thus the problem," she said. "Now the solution." She drew quick lines upon the page, striking out the Constable and his brothers. "This matter must come to court," she said, "and no English jury will take the word of these clods against mine. They are of no account."

"Come to court?" gasped Victor whose face had lost its colour and whose eyes showed white around the pupils.

"Of course," she said. "How else may things be resolved?" She pressed on, "As to Pendennis and Lucey, I have power over them, as we know. And this power I shall reinforce very soon." She smiled confidently at her son. "Which means, my dear, that this formidable list reduces thus, although the Brat's name must be added at the head." Victor looked down at the list.

> Fletcher
> Mr Forster the magistrate
> Mr Pendennis the Polmouth merchant
> Mr Richard Lucey the solicitor
> Mr Taylor the bookseller (& wife)
> ~~Mr Forster's Constable~~
> ~~The Constable's two brothers.~~

"Now," she said, "this is what I propose. I shall go to Polmouth to deal with Pendennis and Lucey, you shall go north to Lonborough for Forster and the Taylors, and Slym shall deal with Fletcher." Victor shuddered at the thought of what he must do, and even more at the very rare expression of grim ugliness that crossed his mother's face. "We might contest your father's Will in the courts and so refute Fletcher's claim to our inheritance, but I want Fletcher dead."

"But how shall you control Slym?" said Victor, frightened again. "The man is a thief-taker. Why should he not 'peach on *us*? And how will you make him kill Fletcher? He is an honest rogue who never even took a bribe to let a felon escape."

"I shall manage Slym," she said and sank back into

the cushions, stretching her limbs like a magnificent luscious cat.

"Oh," said Victor, "*that way* . . ."

"Not entirely," she said. "I shall need to hold this man for many months. I do not think that this can be a speedy business." She considered the matter and made her calculations. "I think I could hold him for a month or two with the constantly promised but constantly denied glutting of his lust. Naturally, I should delay the consummation for as long as possible . . ."

"I see," said Victor.

"For in that phase a man is most utterly under control."

"Quite so!" said Victor.

"But eventually I must let him have his way, and then the grip progressively weakens. Even I can hold a man no more than a few weeks after that. They come back for more, of course, but think it their right not their privilege. It is the way of all men." She smiled sadly, imparting a mother's wisdom as if to a daughter.

"I know!" said Victor, shaking his head in sorrow.

"But with Slym, there is something more. The creature is obsessed with pathetic ideas of self-improvement. He thinks he can be a gentleman and dreams of finding some patron who will introduce him into society. I can promise him this and so secure a more lasting power over him, though regrettably I doubt I can avoid the former method. The fellow is drooling at the mouth already!" She shrugged her shoulders philosophically, "Ah well, at least he is clean in his person."

Victor smiled at her cleverness, and it was typical of both mother and son that neither even considered that there might be anything other than lust or self-interest to bind one human being to another.

Having faced her peril and declared her strategic objectives, Lady Sarah went on to give Victor the practical details of her plans. Victor smiled at this, and chuckled with enthusiasm, though in giving her son this insight, Lady Sarah told him fully as much as he needed to know, and no more.

Chapter 4

I went down the shrouds like a midshipman at play and shoved Horace's glass into his hands.

"Permission to unlock the magazine, Cap'n?" says I, and his knees began to knock like a marine drummer beating to quarters.

"Ah! Ah!" says he, "is it then an enemy?" and he stammered awkwardly over the two "n" sounds.

"Aye-aye, sir!" says I. "And if we don't do something about it, we'll lose the ship and everything in her." That made him twitch, for he had far more to lose than I.

"Ah!" says he, looking up at me with watery eyes. "Then what would you suggest, Mr Fletcher?" That's what the African fever had done to him. Five weeks in his hammock, knocking at death's door with his skin bright yellow, his bowels in cramps and his mind gone away with the pixies. He'd never fully recovered and he wasn't the man who'd set out from London.

"The keys to the magazine, please, sir," says I. "We must bring up powder for the guns."

"Ah!" says he, and bit a fair chunk out of his hat.

"The keys are in your desk, Cap'n," says I, "in your cabin. I'd better fetch them, hadn't I, sir?"

He looked at me in an agony of worry. There were actually tears in his eyes, and he mumbled as he chewed his lump of felt. In practice, I took command from that moment and didn't refer to him again for any orders.

"Aye-aye, sir!" says I, loudly, and touched my hat to him for the benefit of the crew. Then I darted below and into his cabin. The desk was locked. I hadn't thought of that and I couldn't bear the prospect of going back to get another key off him, but there were cutlasses in a rack on the stern bulkhead so I seized one and levered at the lid of the desk. The polished mahogany splintered easily and I was rummaging in his papers in a second. I remember a half-finished letter in which he addressed his wife as "Little Pigsnee".

Then I had his keys and was opening the arms locker by the cutlass rack. There were a dozen each of pistols and muskets with flints in the hammers and cartridges ready in boxes. They were battered old stock that Horace had bought cheap off an East India captain. Swiftly, I loaded a pair of pistols and stuck them in my belt with the cutlass. Then I took a pocketful of cartridges and ran to the magazine.

This was a proper man-o'-war style magazine, down below the waterline and lit through a little double-glazed casement window jutting in from the lamp room adjoining. It was honeycombed with shelves for the ship's powder: kegs at deck level, filled flannel cartridges for the guns, above. The only way in was down a short, narrow passageway, with doors at each end. In a mad haste, I charged in and found myself in pitch dark. Damnation! There was no light burning in the lamp room. Urgently, I felt for the nearest shelf and groped about. As my hands ran across a row of fat flannel cylinders, I felt a touch of grit beneath my fingers.

"What's that?" I thought, and snatched my hand away as I realised it was loose powder.

Fear shot up my legs and across my belly like cold water. Christ, what a bloody fool I was! This was the most dangerous part of the entire ship. One spark in here would blow her to driftwood and there were strict rules to be obeyed. No naked lights, obviously, but more than that, nothing that could possibly strike fire, hence no tools or implements of iron. In King's ships, the gunner and his mates even wore felt slippers in the magazine in case the nails in their shoes might work mischief. Aboard *Bednal Green* we made do with bare feet – or were supposed to. And here was me blundering in with shoes, cutlass and a pair of loaded pistols! What if one of those pistols slipped out of my belt and went off as it hit the deck? That was perfectly possible as the half-cocks on these old barkers were worn, and they were none too safe.

I made myself stand still, and grabbed a shelf to steady myself against the motion of the ship. I spent a few minutes getting a hold on myself, since I realised that this sort of behaviour wouldn't do. If I'd acted like this in sight of the men, then they'd panic and we'd do more harm to ourselves than the Yankees could.

Now I'd seen the right way to behave, as practised by Royal Navy officers. I'd seen them parading about in action, with their hands clasped behind them and that peculiar affectation of indifference to danger. I knew that I should have to copy them. Christ! Could I do it? I was in a sweat of nerves and my heart thundering merrily. I was a seasoned seafarer by now, and that helped. I'd seen rock and tempest and fire afloat, but leading a ship's crew into action against a powerful enemy is something else.

The trouble was, it all hinged on me. The only times I'd gone into action was aboard H.M. Frigate *Phiandra*, under a set of elite officers and with a crew trained to perfection. All I had to do was follow the orders that these experts gave me. Now, by comparison, I had a Captain who was eating his hat and a crew too small to man the guns properly and, worst of all – would they fight?

They were hard men but it wasn't as if it were the Frogs or the dagoes that were after us, the which were their natural enemies. Nor was it African savages who they *had* to fight because of the ghastly tales of what the darkies would do should they get hold of you. By contrast, most of *Bednal Green*'s crew would as soon serve aboard a Yankee as a British ship, if it came to that. So I would be asking them to face death or mutilation for their pay and such small shares in the cargo as some of them had.

On the other hand, I knew them and they knew me after the months we'd sailed together. Even if Horace hadn't let me train them quite as I'd liked they knew not to disobey any order of mine, as long as I was standing over them. And as I stood in the dark of the magazine the germ of a plan of battle formed in my mind. There was just the possibility that if I were very lucky, I might do better than simply make the Yankees pay: I might save my money.

So I took myself a deep breath, and went carefully out of the magazine, shutting both doors behind me. Then I went up on deck and looked about me. I was looking for Jonas Spry, our gunner (he was also cooper and tailor, but that's what you get in a small crew). There he was, with his messmates, sheltering from the wind in the lee of the longboat, where it was secured amidships. Typical English seamen, you could read their very souls in their faces.

They were sulky. They knew I wanted to fight and they knew we were outclassed. If I didn't put some heart into 'em, I might as well haul down our colours and bid farewell to my money right now, and I was damned if I was going to do that. Clearly the moment had come for me to act out my role. I knew what was wanted, 'cos I'd seen it done dozens of times. All I had to do (God help me) was copy it, and then if I looked confident the men would follow my lead. That's how it was with seamen. So I took a deep breath, and gave the assembled company my representation of one of His Majesty's Royal Navy officers, in command of a 100-gun ship, about to do battle with a cockle-boat manned with Quaker pacifists.

"Mr Spry," says I in a bold voice, "have the goodness to unlock the magazine and send up powder for a full broadside. And you may also send up firelock triggers for the guns, out of your stores. I intend to give the enemy a bloody nose and bring our ship safe home to England!"

By George, you should have seen the change come over them. It worked! They grinned and nudged one another and, as for Spry, he damn near split the planks of the deck as he saluted me, seaman-style, stamping down with his foot.

"Aye-aye, Mr Fletcher, sir!" says he. Greatly encouraged, I gave them some more, putting in a little joke as a good leader should.

"And Mr Spry," says I, "take the boys to run cartridges

to the guns, but mind you keep an eye on 'em. I know I can rely on you, but we don't want to lose the ship through the nippers skylarking in the magazine among the powder!" They all laughed and I handed Spry the keys, as if it had never crossed my mind to enter the magazine myself, let alone do so with an ironmonger's shop clashing at my belt.

Spry ran off like a good 'un and I turned to one of his mates. "Hayworth," says I, "down to the Cap'n's cabin at the double and bring up the small-arms. Issue a cutlass to all hands and load all the firearms. But stack those under the Cap'n's eye by the wheel. No man's to touch 'em without my word." I looked around for the rest of them. "And you others . . . All hands!" I roared. "Rig boarding nets!"

That got 'em moving. Nearest thing to man-o'-war fashion I ever saw on that vessel. I looked at the Captain, standing by the wheel, and raised my hat to him with a flourish. I was swept away by the thrill of the moment. He nodded back, happy to let me get on with things while he concentrated on his hat. It looked as if he'd finished the brim and was about to start on the crown. I wondered how he'd manage the silver buckle on the hatband.

So I swaggered about, roaring at the men and lending a hand to raise the nets, which had to be hoist by lines secured to the tops above and secured below to the bulwarks. That way they covered our decks in a great, sagging tent of heavy netting, to keep out enemy boarders. The men worked well and my spirits rose. I was just congratulating myself on what a man of action I'd turned out to be, and how much better at it than poor old Horace, when I noticed the red-brown face and lank, soot-black hair of Matti the Braziliano, bobbing up and down at my elbow as he chattered at me, bent double with respect and furiously knuckling his brow.

The rogue hadn't a word of English but he understood orders well enough, and he was a hard worker. So why wasn't he rigging the nets with his mates? And then I saw the boys gaping at me, one with a pair of cartridge-cases and the other with a handful of cannon-locks. The mists cleared. Matti was reminding me that it was time to cast off the sea-lashings from the guns and make ready to load.

The gall of it! This from a jungle savage who'd swung through the trees with the monkeys till the Jesuits caught him and put breeches on him! The thing was, he was fascinated by the guns. On the beastly hot nights by the African shore, when only Matti felt comfortable, and those that could sleep tried to do it on deck, I'd seen Matti curl up beside a gun for company, muttering to the bloody thing and clapping an ear to it, for its reply. And on the rare occasions when we'd fired them, he'd leapt and gambolled with joy, snapping his fingers and laughing.

"Yes, of course, you heathen Hottentot!" says I. "Just

as soon as the nets are secured. First things first!" Christ! It'd slipped my mind. But nobody noticed and the instant the nets were rigged I gave the word to load and run out. I saw Matti dash to the nearest gun in delight. He bent over it busily casting off the lashings and I gave him a good kick up the arse for being too damn clever. I clipped the boys' ears too, for good measure. Best thing for 'em.

All the same, I threw off my coat and hauled with the men. *Bednal Green*'s larboard battery was five 6-pounders and five 4-pounders with the same again to starboard. To serve this artillery properly was the work of forty men, so you can see how stretched we were with only twelve men in total.

If Horace hadn't been so obstinate, I'd have had the guns loaded and run out as soon as we left Charleston, and kept 'em that way, against eventualities. But he wouldn't have it. He claimed the spray would damp the powder and rust the firelocks. My answer to that was daily gun-drill with live firing. But he wouldn't have that either for the expense of the powder and shot. Or so he said. But I think he was so terrified of being caught by a privateer that he couldn't bring himself to face the fact that it might happen.

So we had to go through the whole process of unlashing the muzzles, where they were secured to the ship's side, and then haul them in to give room to ply the rammers, and then set to with firelocks and charges from below, and shot, wads, powder-horns, priming quills and all the rest, from the lockers beside each gun. There was no question of all guns being loaded and run out together, so I split the hands into three gun-crews and we did the thing in dribs and drabs, till both broadsides were ready for action.

At that stage, with all prepared as best as could be, and the ship thrashing along merrily, and nobody actually firing into us just yet, I suffered a rush of enthusiasm to the head. I went round slapping the men on their backs, calling them jolly tars and British lions (even Matti) and telling them what a drubbing we were going to give those Yankees, damn-their-eyes-and-split-their-bones.

But then the sight of old Horace with his soggy hat in his hands brought me to my senses. By George but he looked dismal. He saw my face fall, and it must have stirred something within him, he'd been a master mariner over twenty years, after all. He made a pathetic attempt to straighten his back and he stuck his hat on his head, which made him look all the worse considering the state of it.

But it was time to look at the Yankee again. So I borrowed Horace's glass and got up into the shrouds. The privateer's t'gallants, tops'ls and courses were all clearly visible from deck level with the black smudge of his hull heaving in and out of sight between the waves. He was overhauling us without a doubt, though not quite so fast as I'd feared. I estimated he'd be alongside of us in a couple of hours. The idea that had occurred to me in the magazine, leapt out again. The thing looked like being a stern chase, in which case we must make use of our 9-pounder to put the Yankee under fire as she came up astern. It was the best gun in the ship and, with luck, we might knock enough holes in Mr Yankee to slow him down and let us escape. Provided of course that he didn't do the same to us.

First, however, we would have to move our long nine from its station in the bow, and remount it to fire through the solid oak of the taffrail, astern, which was not pierced for gunfire. But this was a simple matter and I did no more than give the orders and stand back while the crew organised themselves to the work. Seamen are most amazingly ingenious at things of that kind, especially when they go at it with a will. And they did too, because it was obvious that remounting that gun astern offered us the chance of shaking off our pursuer without a fight – the best of all possible outcomes.

The gun was seven-and-a-half feet in the barrel and weighed twenty-one hundredweights. But ten men levered it out of its carriage and, taking the load with a rope cradle lashed beneath it, they walked the gun astern. The companionway ladders (down from fo'c'sle to waist, and up from waist to quarterdeck) gave them some trouble but all hands pitched in and they completed in ten minutes a job that landsmen would have spent a week over.

Then, for relaxation, they fetched the gun-carriage and

mounted the gun, ready for use with its wheels chocked
to keep it still, and all its tackles laid alongside. All that
was done well before the carpenter and his mate had
finished hacking a hole through the taffrail, and had
screwed a big ringbolt into either side of it to take the
breeching tackles that would control the gun's recoil.

Then it was up to me. I was in command, and thanks
to my time aboard *Phiandra* there was no better-trained
gunner in the ship. So I chose a full gun-crew, loaded
and ran out, and waited for Yankee Doodle to put himself
in range. In fact it was about an hour before I could
open fire, and during the wait, I had some food served
out for the men, and I trimmed the sails constantly to
try to get another knot out of the ship. Our course was
E S E and the Yankee was closing from the north-west.
The combination resulted in his bearing down from our
larboard quarter, giving the nine-pounder a good view
of him through the new port.

Slowly the Yankee grew larger, till we could see every
detail of her, right down to the men crowded on her
fo'c'sle and the busy topmen working aloft. They too
were squeezing the last drop of speed out of their ship.
She had a huge spread of sail, and every last one appeared
to be drawing. Finally, late in the afternoon, with the
enemy half a mile astern, I looked down the barrel of
my gun, took up the slack of the firing lanyard, and
pulled.

Now, in understanding what I was trying to do, you

must set aside all your modern notions of gunnery. Forget your Armstrong rifled cannon, machined from steel to a thousandth of an inch. Forget your colossal iron steamers to give a steady platform for the gun. Think instead of a brass, smooth-bore gun fired from a little wooden ship, pitching and rolling along across the face of the mighty Atlantic. Why, the gun didn't even have proper sights but needed two aimings.

[I am informed that "two aimings" means peering through a slot in the breech top centre and one at the muzzle top centre, to point the gun at the target. Then a second aiming for range, looking through slots in the side of the breech and one in the side of the muzzle. A tedious and obsolete system even in Fletcher's young day. S.P.]

Under those conditions, a good gunner would hit another ship with every shot he fired, at any range inside fifty yards. At 100 yards he might hit it once in five shots. At 200 yards he'd be lucky to hit it at all. So why was I firing at half a mile?

Well, firstly I was firing for the benefit of my men, because your own ship's gunfire is a splendid thing to hear when the foe is bearing down upon you (Matti certainly thought so). More important, the Yankee was closing on us at about two knots, so I didn't have endless time in which to hit him. Even by opening fire at half a mile, and with the best speed possible from my half-trained gunners, I'd get no more than a dozen rounds out of the gun before the enemy was alongside. And anyway, I was fed up waiting. You just try it yourself, some day, and see how long you can resist having a crack at the bastards.

All hands cheered my first shot (which went God-knows-where) and they were positively elbowing each other aside for the privilege of reloading and hauling her out again, but soon settled into a routine, as the gun boomed out with not the slightest effect on the Yankee's progress. Now I'm not a great gunner, but I studied under one: Sammy Bone of *Phiandra*, *a* man with magic in his hands. So I suppose I'm as good as most, and that afternoon I gave the task all that I had.

On the other hand, the gun was no bloody good. It was drooped at the muzzle, I'm sure: a fault with all brass guns when they're old and over-used. So it was only when the Yankees got really close that the white splashes of my shot started to fall about her. Eventually, though, I saw splinters fly off his bow as I scored my first hit. She was only a musket-shot astern of us by then, and had so far disdained to return our fire. But that hit stung her into manning one of her bow-chasers. I was sweating and tired by then and I remember the busy Yankee gunners setting to with their gun, and me yelling at my men to redouble their efforts to load.

Their first shot passed through our rigging without doing any harm, and then the most extraordinary thing happened. Our brass-9 was scorching hot by now – it skinned your flesh if you touched it – and the shot was going anywhere but where I aimed, so what happened next was by pure chance.

A second after the Yankee fired, I gave them my next shot and my men cheered their heads off as a terrific clang came from the Yankee as our 9-pound ball crashed directly into their gun, knocking it out of its carriage and showering terrible iron splinters in all directions.

I found myself surrounded by grinning faces and that ape from the Brazils threw himself on his knees before me and locked his arms tight about my knees. I had to lever him off with a handspike.

But that was the end of the game. The brass gun grew worse and worse, and there were no more hits that I could see. And the Yankee got his sharpshooters up into the foretop and opened a brisk fire. From the crack and flash of musketry I'd say there were three of them up there, all good marksmen. And in fact it wasn't just muskets that were turned on us, but rifles (Americans being partial to the weapon), so the bullets smacked and splintered into the taffrail and whistled through our gunport too hot to be ignored. We had to leave the gun and take cover.

That is except for Matti. He wouldn't be told to keep his head down and jigged about screeching and howling at the enemy, until one of them put a ball neatly through the centre of his chest. He sat down then, looking tired, and just had time to say his prayers before he was taken wherever it is that such people go.

Worse still, the Yankee had two bow-chasers and opened fire with number two. It was a nine at least and shot began to roar through our rigging. The range was so close now that lines began to part and chunks flew off our spars as they started to make hits. They were aiming high, to avoid hull-damage which might spoil the prize, and soon they'd bring down a mast and have us at their mercy. And there was nothing to do since we'd not a single gun bearing on them.

I tried to think of something to do. The crew were skulking in corners out of the way of shot. Those of them, that is, that hadn't already run below. I could forget about appeals to repel boarders. This crew would never see off a boarding party as it came across slavering at the chops for its prize money. Then I saw Horace, the only man still standing. He was at the wheel, since the helmsman had disappeared. That gave me an idea; I got up and ran over to him.

"Put her about, Cap'n," says I. "Bring her larboard guns to bear. Perhaps we can still knock a spar off 'em!" He stared straight at me with watery eyes.

"If the wind holds, we should make London in thirty days, Mr Fletcher," says he. "What price the bale do you think best Virginia tobacco will fetch?" God and all his little angels! The silly old fool was unhinged! He was raving!

Boom! went the Yankees again. Crash! went the fore-topmast and hung in ruins with its sail flapping and rent.

"Jesus!" says I, and seizing the wheel, I spun it round and shoved it back into Horace's hands. "Hold her steady!" says I, and he nodded absently. I ran to our aftermost gun. The Yankee was very close now, maybe as little as thirty yards. As *Bednal Green* answered the helm, the privateer swum across our line of fire and I ran from gun to gun setting them off. It made a brave show and a loud noise, but none of it was aimed. It was just the best I could do under the circumstances. Or, perhaps, it was the worst thing I could have done. For as the smoke of my broadside cleared, I saw the Yankee coming about to give us the benefit of her broadside, this time aimed into the hull. I had the sense to throw myself flat as his 9-pounder long guns and his four 18-pounder carronades gave us grape and roundshot.

Chapter 5

In a Grand Dinner at his new house in Market Square, Mr Pendennis, Lord Mayor, entertained yesterday, a most elevated company of the nobility and gentry of the county, reflecting the universal estimation in which His Worship is held by all classes of society today.

(From the *Polmouth Monitor*, 13th September 1793.)

*

Mrs Pendennis judged her moment and cleared her throat to attract attention. Heads turned towards her down the long table. On every side, the room glittered with the finest fixtures and fittings that London could supply. And the company glittered to match it. A most gratifying sight to Mrs Pendennis who had stretched her uttermost endeavours to bring together the following persons to dine at her board:

> Her dear, dear husband, Mr Pendennis
> Her dear, brave, son-in-law Richard Lucey
> Richard's wife, her own eldest daughter, Sophia
> Mr Alfred Manning, Lord Mayor of Exeter
> Mrs Manning
> Sir David Manners of Manners Hall
> Lady Manners
> Colonel Sir Arthur Howard of the 9th Dragoons
> Lady Howard
> The Most Reverend Doctor Lincon, Dean of Polmouth Cathedral
> Mrs Lincon
> But best of all, and surpassing all past expectations:
> Lord Cedric Godwin and his wife Lady Carolyn!

It should be explained that a direct and mail-clad ancestor of Lord Cedric had stood loyal to his master King Harold upon the field of Hastings, and had with his own great axe despatched a large number of Norman gentlemen in that lost but noble cause. Consequently, those who traced their titles back to the gift of younger dynasties like Plantagenet, Tudor or Hanover were parvenu incomers compared with Lord Cedric, and consequently any hostess who received Lord Cedric into her house automatically gained entry into any other house in the land – be her connections never so vulgar before.

Mrs Pendennis knew very well that, less than a year ago, the Godwins' immeasurably noble knees would have scorned to place themselves beneath her bourgeois table. But that was before Mr Pendennis (her dear, dear husband) and Richard Lucey (her dear, brave son-in-law) had so mightily distinguished themselves in the Coignwood affair and had become trustees of the greatest fortune in the land. This triumph had boosted Mr Pendennis's business, and his wealth, to the stars and had opened doors like magic.

For all this Mrs Pendennis thanked her husband. She thanked him so much that she had quite forgotten that there had ever been a time when her opinion of him had differed from its current state of worshipful adoration.

"Mr Pendennis?" she said.

"Ma'am?" smiled the great man from the head of his table where he presided in dignity, like the very incarnation of John Bull: solidly worthy, splendidly corpulent, and ruddy of countenance.

"If you will excuse us," she said, "I will lead the ladies to the withdrawing room and leave you gentlemen to your port."

And so, in the splendour of a dress of Moravian worked muslin at three guineas the yard, Mrs Pendennis came down the room like a line-of-battle ship in its glory, with the lesser females keeping station in line astern of her, and Lady Carolyn in company upon her starboard beam. To add to the joy of the moment, Mrs Pendennis noted that Lady Carolyn's gown was of mere French lawn at 8s. 6d. the yard, top price.

As the ladies passed in review with colours flying, Mr Pendennis sighed at the elegance of the sight. Finally, the doors closed behind the last swishing gown and Lord Cedric smote the table with his fist.

"Burn me bollocks!" he cried. "Bloody women! Thought they'd never leave." He turned to Pendennis. "For the love of God, man, where d'ye keep the damn pisspots?" Pendennis's eyes widened and his glance flicked from one to another of his guests. A few mouths had dropped open but he was relieved to see that the Dean had not turned a hair.

In fact, unlike Mr Pendennis, Dr Lincon was used to rural noblemen who, as a species, tended to do and say just exactly whatever they liked. And in any case, Dean Lincon's employment and a living of £2,000 a year lay in the palm of the hand of Bishop Godwin, Lord Cedric's son.

"God in heaven, Pendennis, come to it, man!" groaned the noble lord. "Me damn bladder's about to split! There'll be a bloody tragedy presently if you don't shift sharp."

Pendennis nodded to his butler, who nodded to the footmen, and a series of cupboards, hidden in the panelling of the room, were thrown open to reveal a row of pots-de-chambre ready and waiting. They were of silver and shone like fire in the afternoon sun, for Nathan Pendennis had spared no expense to equip his dining room with every convenience known to the civilisation of Europe, including these invaluable vessels which saved his guests the trouble of staggering to the privy, burdened as they were with food and wine. The withdrawing room was similarly equipped, which is why the ladies had withdrawn in the first place.

"God be thanked!" said Lord Godwin from the bottom of his heart, as a footman handed him a gleaming bowl, with a deep bow. Godwin fumbled with his breeches and proceeded to relieve himself with the strength and noise of a dray horse. "Ahhhh." he sighed with the smile of a Bhudda. With less display, but equal gratitude, the other men did likewise, and the product of their labours was quietly removed by Pendennis's excellent servants, enabling the gentlemen to make their combined assault on the port.

Later, when Pendennis led the gentlemen to join the ladies, he rejoiced in the splendour of his withdrawing room, on display before the finest in the county. And he rejoiced in the beauty of the ladies and in the contentment radiating from his wife. He smiled fondly at Richard, his son-in-law. It was a very happy moment in Nathan Pendennis's life.

Unfortunately the moment was short, for even before he could sit down, his butler approached.

"Sir," he said, "a person is arrived at the door on an errand of urgent importance. He insists that you would wish to be drawn even from this gathering to attend to the matter."

Pendennis looked at his wife. Her smile was straining. He guessed that like himself, she thought this must be some matter of business. If it were, then the quicker it were dealt with the better. On this day when the Pendennis's were passing through the gateway to society, the very last thing that was wanted was any reminder of their connection in trade.

"My Lord, Lady Carolyn, ladies and gentlemen," said Pendennis, thinking fast, "I maintain a number of pensioners from the deserving poor of Polmouth and from time to time I am called upon to settle some crisis among them." He smiled benignly. "Small enough matters though they be, they seem urgent and important to the poor unfortunates themselves."

"A most proper thing," pronounced Lady Carolyn. "Lord Cedric himself maintains pensioners from among the poor of his estates." Pendennis already knew that perfectly well and so was able to leave the company to a glow of approval, particularly from his wife. Pleased with the stratagem he made a mental note to make the lie true upon the morrow. He could easily afford to run a few beggars.

The butler led him into the hall where a man in riding clothes stood waiting with his hat in his hand. He bowed politely as he saw Pendennis. The fellow was clearly a servant. Pendennis was surprised. He had been expecting one of his own people from the counting house, or one of his warehouses. He sent the butler away and beckoned the messenger to come close.

"Now, my lad," he said, "what is it?"

"Mr Pendennis, sir, this is for you . . . The lady . . . she said I was to put it into your hand and no other. I am to await your reply." He held out a flat package wrapped in brown paper and heavily sealed.

Pendennis took it and moved to a sconce of candles for the better light, and to avoid the messenger's seeing what was within, in case it should be private. He raised the package and studied the seal.

"Oh no," he prayed. "Please, please, please, dear God no." The package was sealed with the Coignwood crest, and he recognised the elegant, feminine handwriting with which the package was addressed to himself.

Chapter 6

John Stark's broadside struck home at a range of less than twenty feet. Every shot must have told and at least two more of our men were killed. Poor old Horace was smashed to offal before my eyes, still dreaming of London baccy prices, and Welles with his red woollen cap lost a leg and bled to death in seconds through the great artery of the thigh. He screamed like a pig in a slaughter-house, a dreadful sound and tried to squeeze the ragged stump to save himself, but all in vain. It was awful to see, and my courage wavered. For a second I thought of striking my colours. But then I remembered the £1,500 that the rogues were robbing me of. And so I fought on.

Unfortunately something had hit me when the broadside came aboard, a splinter probably, and I was staggering about stunned when the first wildly yelling figures started hacking their way through our boarding nets. I was so dizzy that I made a bodge of things. The right way to deal with enemies in the nettings is to take a pike and stick 'em with it, one at a time, deliberately. If you keep your head you can kill 'em like flies while they're hanging there trying to cut through the heavy ropes. They can't strike at you and they're practically helpless. But I didn't keep my head. I grabbed a five-foot oaken handspike with its iron head and swung it like a club. I knocked a few of them into the sea, but I couldn't keep them out of the ship. After all, it was me alone against dozens of them.

Soon they were dropping on to our decks and about ten of them rushed me, all at once. There would have been more, since I was the only thing left to fight, and every one of them was thirsting for blood. But there was no room and they came on elbow-to-elbow. They bawled their war-cry, their feet battered the deck, pistols banged and balls whizzed in all directions. But each marksman got in every other's way and none took proper aim.

Then they were on me and I was laying about with the ponderous handspike. The implement is too heavy for hand-to-hand fighting for an ordinary man, but not for me. I knocked down four or five of them in the first few swings, and those left in the front line tried to fall back – I could see the sudden fear in their eyes – but twenty or thirty others were pressing forward from behind and an officer, resplendent in a uniform coat and hessian boots, shoved forward, ducked under my guard and cut at me with his sword. If I hadn't had half a dozen other enemies to deal with, I'd have pulverised the bastard, but I did have. His blow was awkwardly aimed what with him being in a crouch, but he caught me across the forehead and blood streamed down into my eyes and blinded me.

And that was the end of that. The mob swarmed forward, brought me down, and I got my share of kicks and blows as they worked out their anger. But the officer yelled some orders to clear a space, and he called on me to surrender the ship. I think he'd recognised me as a ship's officer, and anyway there was nobody else to ask.

"Do you yield, sir?" says he.

"I do, sir!" says I, after a moment's thought, for I could feel his sword-point hovering just under my chin. He sheathed the blade and bellowed at a couple of his men to take me in charge, and I was roughly hauled to my feet for the blood to be wiped from my eyes and a bandage to be clapped on my head. Then it was across to the Yankee, which incidentally gleamed like a new pin, with snowy decks and shining metalwork that would have graced a flagship.

She was full of men, all of them grinning and reckoning up their shares. They pressed round to view their prisoner, and to have some fun.

"Hey, Limey," says one of them, in his nasal Yankee honk, "how's King Jarrrge? Still tokkin t' th' trees?"

Fletcher's Glorious 1ˢᵗ of June

[Note the incontinent rage which gripped Fletcher when I mentioned that the word Limey stems from the British use of lime juice as a preventative of scurvey, adopted by the Royal Navy only in 1795 and well after the above incident, thus his memory was false. In return I was told to "shut your trap as a know-nothing crawling land-lubber". S.P.]

By George they did laughed. But I didn't. Every Englishman knew that the King was mad but we didn't like it pointed out to us by others. The grinning clown who made those remarks can consider himself very lucky that I was wounded and had a man hanging on each arm. So I ground my teeth and thought myself a much abused man. In fact I'd little to complain about from this sort of treatment. In later years I witnessed what happened to a Colonel of Turkish Police who fell into the hands of Greek pirates. The decks needed hosing down when they'd finished with that beauty.

Meanwhile, the clown got bolder. He stepped right up to me and jabbed his finger into my chest.

"Say, what's the difference between a Limey and a seagull?" All hands awaited the denouement that never came.

"Belay that!" roared a voice; it was the officer who'd downed me, Commander Cooper he called himself, who'd come aboard that instant, "Get about your business, you men! This ship's filthy – it looks like a hog-waller!" And all credit to him, the silly grins vanished and his men snapped to it like lightning (and left me wondering all these years what the answer to the riddle might be). "Get the surgeon to this man," says he, looking askance at the steady drip of blood from me to his gleaming quarterdeck, "and take him below!"

To my surprise, "below" meant the great cabin, in the stern with its span of windows and shiny furnishings, rather than some pokey surgeon's den under the water-line. I was joined in the cabin by the sawbones himself, one of his mates to hold his tools, and by Commander Cooper and Lieutenant Hunt, his second-in-command.

While the surgeon did his work, the officers fired stern questions at me on the movements of other British ships. But with a needle going in and out of my face at regular intervals, I paid them less than full attention. I began to regret not having been left on *Bednal Green*, now on her way to Boston under a prize crew, and I thought I was in for rough treatment, but once the surgeon had done, he took himself off and Cooper called for food and drink, and I had the chance to look about me a bit. I even asked a few questions of my own, and learned the basics about my captors.

In the first place, *John Stark* was something odd for a privateer, as Commander Daniel Cooper and Lieutenant Eustace Hunt both regarded themselves as officers in the newly reformed American Navy (the Yankees wound up their navy at the end of the Revolution, and didn't re-form it until '94) and they ran the ship service-style. For instance, they used their navy titles and they wore their service uniforms. They'd seventy men on board, all prime seamen, they'd provisions for a six-month cruise and they'd twenty-four guns, not counting carronades. *John Stark* was something precious close to being a small frigate.

But she was legally a privateer. Cooper and Hunt might have been officers, but the Yankee Navy had no ships, so both men had joined a venture financed by a group of Boston merchants, who'd taken advantage of the political situation to fit out a private cruiser as an investment. The Yankees had a long-established tradition of privateering, with each merchant receiving a share of two-thirds of the value of any vessel captured by their ship. That's Yankee enterprise for you.

The remaining third, of course, went to *John Stark*'s crew: three shares to each of the officers and equal shares to every other man jack. That's Yankee democracy for you.

So that's the ship I'd come aboard of. And strange as it may seem, I never was better treated in any ship in my career. Once the actual fighting was done, the *John Stark*'s were as merry as could be, and bore me not the least ill-will. Quite the reverse in fact, as I will explain. They kept me aboard because of my wound while the rest of *Bednal Green*'s crew went locked under their own hatches to Boston under a prize crew. The wound ran across my forehead and round to one ear and Cooper said he felt responsible, as the inflictor of it, and thought his own surgeon should have charge of me.

Well, it was a Christian act undoubtedly, and I'd be the last to complain, but I've had worse wounds than that and recovered – with or without a surgeon's aid. So I don't believe that was really why I was kept on board. The truth was more complicated and very interesting too, for it shows how folk will say one thing and believe another.

Commander Cooper and his Lieutenant were two peas out of the same pod. Smart young men, keen as mustard and mightily proud of their ship. They were delighted to have taken a prize so early in their cruise, and as regards myself, at first they were like their men, only more genteel.

They'd got themselves a genuine Limey prisoner and they wanted to tell him what was what. That was the first reason I was in their ship. They were full of defiance of Kings and Tyrants and they drank to the downfall of the "BriDish" Navy and the martyrs of the Revolution (theirs, that is, not the Froggy one).

"I'll tell you, sir," says Cooper, "now I've seen my men stand firm under such fire . . . why, damned if I don't hope the next ship we encounter'll be one of your frigates!"

"I drink to that, sir!" says Lieutenant Hunt and raised his glass.

"Good luck to you both, me boys," thinks I to myself, "and I hope you get your wish."

"By Heaven!" says Cooper, "wait till we tell those

fellows at home," and he grew so benign that he turned his smile on me and raised his glass. "Your health, sir," says he, "for a noble enemy!"

"And to our own noble dead," says Hunt.

So they toasted again and refilled. They were getting happier by the minute. Hunt leaned across and slapped my shoulder.

"Damned if I shouldn't've liked to have shook the hand of your gunner, sir. The man who kept us under such a deadly fire, and hit our bow-chaser with a single shot." He shook his head seriously and I noticed that Cooper did too. "Never seen such a thing!" says Hunt.

I was taken aback. What "noble enemy"? What "deadly fire"? They'd fought a merchantman armed with pop-guns and they were blathering on as if they'd sunk the Spanish Armada. And surely the silly devils knew it was only chance that I'd hit their gun. And then the light shone upon me. I'd been taken in by the uniforms and all the smart seamanship. These were really youngsters like me. But *they'd* never been in action before. It was their first time. They'd seen shot come aboard and men killed, and in their innocence, they thought they'd been in a real battle.

At once, I saw an advantage here waiting to be taken.

"Sir," says I to Lieutenant Hunt, sitting straight in my chair with all the dignity I could assume, "my gunner offers you his hand," and I shoved out my paw.

"Goldarn it!" says Hunt with shining eyes, pumping

my arm with all his might. "Where d'you learn such gunnery, sir?" He'd *won* you see, so he could afford to be gracious. When you praise the skill of your vanquished enemy, you are praising yourself twice over.

"I learned gunnery aboard His Majesty's Ship *Phiandra*," says I, which as you know, was the simple truth. But the effect upon the pair of them was electrical. They nearly shot out of their chairs.

"By cracky!" says Cooper, "not the same *Phiandra* that whopped the tar out of two French forty-gunners at Passage d'Aron?"

"The very same," says I. "I had the honour to serve in that action."

Clip! Clop! Their jaws dropped together.

"You mean you sailed under Captain Bollington, the gunnery genius?" says Cooper, and everything changed. You could see the envy and hero-worship oozing out of them. They'd have given an arm and a leg each to have done what I had. Their navy hadn't fought an action since '85.

And so we passed a most congenial evening together. At first I was amazed at how well informed they were about events on the other side of the Atlantic. But I shouldn't have been. Ships passed to and fro all the time, and carried newspapers in them for all to read who cared to. And educated Americans were following the European war with intense interest. They seized on every scrap of information and chewed it over among themselves. And

Fletcher's Glorious 1ˢᵗ of June

I soon found that Cooper and Hunt were as familiar with the *London Gazette as* any British officer, and they could quote chunks of the despatches on Passage d'Aron. But they were hungry for more news, which was the other reason they'd kept me.

Immediately they had me give my account of *Phiandra*'s battle against *Thermidor* and *Taureus*.

During this interrogation, I realised that they'd assumed that I was a naval officer, temporarily unemployed, earning his crust in the merchant service. Much like themselves, in fact. It would have been a shame to disappoint them with the truth and I thought I'd get better treatment as an officer. So I let this misunderstanding pass as fact, and it serves me right for the troubles it got me into later.

As we talked I was intrigued to see their genuine, as opposed to their pretended, attitude to the British peeping out. Despite the fact that they'd swallowed all the French political rot, and they'd not forgiven us for making them fight for their liberty, they had an enormous respect for the Royal Navy, and an envy for its huge size and limitless opportunities for professional advancement. What's more, they obviously thought the Royal Navy set the standards by which others were judged. In short, they were modelling themselves on the British Navy. Now, of course, they didn't say any of this. Not in plain words, and they'd have spat in my eye if I'd put it to them, but those were the feelings hidden just under the surface.

And then, just when I was thinking that Americans were just like Englishmen, only with peculiar accents, Cooper did something that no English sea officer would have done in a thousand years.

He had me up on deck, mustered his men in the waist, and demanded that I give the whole story of Passage d'Aron right through again, for the benefit of the common hands! Don't ask me how he kept discipline, indulging the men like that. I'm surprised he didn't ask their opinions before giving an order. But that's Americans.

He introduced me as "Lieutenant Jacob Fletcher, late gunnery officer of His Britannic Majesty's 32-gun frigate, *Phiandra*". I let that pass and definitively accepted the lie which led me to so much pain.

On the next day, however, pain of a more immediate kind fell upon me. My wound went bad, as wounds sometimes will. The side of my face swelled up like a red melon, I felt weak and ill and couldn't get out of my hammock.

Cooper and his men made a great fuss of me and I'd not have got better treatment from my mother (if ever I'd had one). But I slipped into a delirium and there I stayed for some time. I suppose I must have been really dangerously ill, but I remember nothing of it.

I came to myself, sickly and ill, and with a fine scar, in the second week of March when *John Stark* was homeward bound for Boston after a rattling fine cruise (from their viewpoint, if not from ours). Cooper had taken no other prizes, but *Bednal Green* alone more than justified the voyage, and his backers would be delighted.

On 15th March 1794, we saluted the fort with fifteen guns as we came into Boston old harbour and tied up at the Long Wharf. Dozens of fishing boats followed us in and the town turned out to greet *John Stark* with flags and music. Which was splendid for Cooper and his men, but not for me. I was taken ashore to the Court House and prison in Queen Street, to be interned by the military authorities. That's what I got for posing as a Naval Officer.

Lesser forms of Britisher the Yankees set free as harmless, and I learned that *Bednal Green*'s crew had all promptly signed on aboard American ships. You can't blame them. They had no money, nowhere to go, and as I've said, it wasn't as if it was the Frogs.

Knowing where I was bound, Cooper supplied me with clothes and other necessities, and some money too. And his men gave me three cheers as they swung me over the side in a bosun's chair, for I was still too ill to climb over the side.

And so I was stuck in a pokey room with barred windows and a truckle bed. It was in fact the best available cell in the prison, for I was their prize exhibit. A genuine BriDish officer. The first they'd caught. It wasn't a bad place for a gaol but for me it was a miserable time. I was so feeble that I had to spend most of the day in bed, which gave me endless hours to brood and troubled nights when I couldn't sleep 'cos I was never properly tired. Also, young as I was, my past was catching up on me.

My conscience was pricking for the men who'd died because I wanted to fight for my money. Much of it was nonsense that I should never have worried about, but not all, and anyway I was alone, and locked up and still sickly. And so I churned it all over and over in my mind: Matti the Braziliano Indian, who'd never see the jungle again; Horace with his chewed hat; and Welles with his leg blown off. None of them had wanted to fight, it was only my greed. Worse still, I started to fret over my shipmates from *Phiandra*. Particularly I did at night, when a black despair settled on me.

I missed Sammy Bone, who'd been a father to me, in place of the real father I'd never known: Sir Henry Coignwood the potteries millionaire, with his bags of gold, the very bags of gold I'd turned my back on. I even wondered about the servant-girl, Mary Fletcher, who'd died giving birth to me.

But worst of all, this got me thinking about Kate Booth (the girl I'd had aboard *Phiandra*) and I couldn't get her out of my mind. And so I fretted and dreamed of her: a tiny, slender, little thing, so sweet and lovely even if she was a Portsmouth tart. I wondered if she'd ever cared for me, other than as a protector.

This happy state of affairs ran on for a week until one afternoon, all unannounced, Cooper came bustling into my room, with the Commandant of the prison and a document for me to read. It was a piece of a Yankee newspaper, some weeks old. Cooper chattered and smiled and apologised he'd not come sooner, but pleaded pressure of work and was friendly as could be. But I was reading what he'd given me and wondering whether to laugh out loud or struggle to my feet to see if I could manage to knock his teeth out.

Chapter 7

The horrible murder of Mr Ivor Jones, a respectable Master Butcher of Old Street, reported in yesterday's edition, is now alleged to have been committed by one Johnson, a meat porter.

(From *The Morning Post* of 9th September 1793.)

*

The thin, rickety door burst into ruin as Slym threw his weight on it and led his men into the room. The place stank of damp and human filth, and it was dark as a cellar. The only light came from a feeble sunbeam that had fought its way in through the grimy scraps of glass in a window that was mainly stuffed up with rags. A few wretched sticks of furniture were scattered about, and the "bed" was a heap of rags against one wall. In other words, the room was a perfectly ordinary example of the accommodation to be found in a Liquorpond Street tenement opposite Meux's Brewery in the Parish of St Giles's, where nine families lived in twelve rooms on four floors.

A thin wail came from the bed and one of Slym's men started forward.

"Wait!" snapped Slym, and thrust him back with a heavy blackthorn stick. The three men blinked in the gloom and the dull forms on the bed took the shape of a woman with a pile of children clutched about her. Slym went to the bed and was confronted with a familiar scene: the old-young face of the woman, marked by regular beatings and starvation, the skinny, half-naked children that had learned not to cry out even in their terror. Slym was used to such things.

"Mrs Johnson?" said Slym, and the woman nodded. "Where is he?" said Slym, and she shook her head, far too frightened to speak. But her eyes flicked upward.

"Ah!" said Slym. "Danny, you search the room; Jimmy, let some light in."

Slym jabbed upward with his stick. "There's a way up top somewhere," he said.

Meanwhile, and with gusto, Jimmy took his cudgel to the window and noisily smashed it out: glass, frames, rags and all. Light flooded in and the search became unnecessary. In one corner was a half-open door leading to a steep, cramped stairway up to the roof space.

"Mister," pleaded the woman, "for Gordsake don't say I told. He'd kill me if he thought I told."

"Huh!" said Slym. "I shouldn't worry about him, missus. It don't matter what he thinks now." Danny grinned, and to interpret Mr Slym's remark for the benefit of Mrs Johnson, he took the end of his grubby cotton cravat, and pulled on it like a noose, making rattling noises in his throat. Strangely, this did not comfort the lady but threw her into floods of tears. "Right," said Slym, taking a grip of his stick, "with me, lads!" and he started up the stair.

"Mister," cried the woman, desperately, "he's got a knife. For pity's sake don't let him do for my Daisy."

"What?" said Slym. "Get back there," he said to Danny and Jimmy and pushed his way back into the room. "What's this, missus?" he said to the pathetic creature.

"It's my eldest, Daisy. He's got her up there and he swears to slit her throat and then his own rather than be took."

"Fire and shite!" said Slym and sighed heavily. He looked at Danny and Jimmy. Good lads, the pair of 'em, for a scrap. But not an ounce of brain between 'em. "Now then," said Slym, "you two stay here and guard that door." He pointed to the stairway. "And if he comes down without me, then he's all yours and I don't care what you do with him."

"No! No!" screamed Mrs Johnson. "Don't hurt him, not my Jacky, he's not a bad man . . ." But the three men had heard that a hundred times from battered wives, and they paid it not the slightest attention.

But Danny edged towards his master and dropped his voice, "Beggin' your pardon, Captain," said he.

"What?" said Slym, with a frown.

"Well, Captain," said Danny, looking anxiously at Slym, and with real concern, "it's dead or alive for Johnson, ain't it?"

"Yes," said Slym.

"Well then," said Danny, "don't take no risks, Captain," and he slid a finger across his throat. "Let the bleeder top 'isself if that's what 'e's set 'is 'eart on. What's the difference if he get's it here or outside Newgate Prison? We gets the gelt either way."

"Yeah," said Jimmy, "an' don't worry about no moll, Captain, no one's paying us for 'er!"

"Shut your gobs, both o' you," said Slym and went up the stair.

"Cor!" said Danny. "What's the matter with 'im?"

"Dunno," said Jimmy. "The sod's bin like that all day. And did you know there's no more work for you and me after this? On account of . . ." he glanced at the stair to check there was no chance of Slym's overhearing the fell nickname, ". . . Slimey Sam's got something special, just for hisself alone." Jimmy sneered, "Sod him, I say!"

The attic was better lit than the room below, as it had a large window let into one end. Mr Jack Johnson, a Smithfield meat porter, was up there with his daughter

Daisy, looking at the bright sunlight and the little grains of dust that floated within it.

Two days ago, Johnson had fallen out with Mr Jones the butcher in the matter of a loan that Johnson could not repay. Words were exchanged, and one thing led to another. Finally, as knives are laid out ready to hand in a butcher's shop, Johnson had selected a large one and thrust it so hard into Jones's belly, that much of the blade came out on the other side.

And now Johnson was sitting cross-legged across the rafters with his back propped against one of the timber uprights that supported the roof. He was facing the stairway, and in front of him was sprawled Daisy, a thin, pretty girl of thirteen, just on the brink of womanhood. Her neck and shoulders gleamed where they had been bared for the razor-sharp, eighteen-inch blade of the knife in her father's hand. His left hand was wound into her long hair, to give a purchase to pull her head back across his knee, to keep her chin up and her throat exposed.

"I know you," said Johnson, as Slym cautiously stepped into the attic, "I seen you at the hangings, you bastard."

"I know," said Slym with careful politeness, "but I'm not here on that sort o' business, Mr Johnson." Slym talked quietly and steadily as he measured the distance to Johnson, taking note of where he might put his foot without going through the flimsy lath-and-plaster work between the rafters.

"Get back," yelled Johnson, and Slym's heart jumped

as the knife waved over the girl's neck. She moaned and said something to her father.

"Shut up," said Johnson, "or I'll do it now this minute."

"Wait," said Slym. "I've got a message from the Bow Street Magistrate's Office. It could mean a pardon!"

"What?" said Johnson, whom Slym had correctly judged not to be one of London's brightest sons.

"A pardon," said Slym with a smile. "I'll sit here and tell you about it, shall I?"

"What pardon?" said Johnson.

"A Royal, warrant-of-arms pardon," said Slym. "Sanctified by the Bishop of London under the Lord Common Seal. It's the way in these cases."

"What?" said Johnson.

"Yes," said Slym, "it means casuistical, sophomorical extinction of the crime, or crimes, under the Yeoman Hearthfires Act of 1345."

"What's that?" said Johnson, mystified and lowering the knife somewhat. "What's it all mean?"

"It means that first you have to have a chimney in the house, Mr Johnson, like that one there," and Slym leaned forward to point with his blackthorn stick.

"Garn," said Johnson, "there ain't no chimbley there . . ." But he turned to look, and the gnarled head of Slym's blackthorn (with the eight ounces of lead that he'd personally filled it with) sliced through the air in an arc that pivoted on Slym's hand, and terminated in a terrific thwack on the blade of Johnson's knife.

"Arrrgh!" roared Johnson, as the knife clattered away into the recesses of the attic corners.

"This way!" yelled Slym and lunged for the girl's legs to pull her bodily out of her father's grasp. He scooped her up and threw her out of the way and she screamed and tumbled over and over, and put her arm through the lath-and-plaster as she tried to get up.

"You bastard!" cried Johnson and leapt to his feet, pulling another knife, the twin to the first, from out of his belt. "Come on then!" he screamed, with mad eyes, "I'll cut you, you fuckin' bastard, I'll cut your fuckin' eyes out!"

But now Slym had no third party to worry about and it was a straight fight: himself with his stick against a maniac armed with a knife the size of a gladiator's sword, with the added refinement that one false step would plunge him hip-deep through the floor.

Down below, Jimmy and Danny followed the proceedings in the attic by the various sounds to be heard, and by the sight of Daisy's arm bursting through the ceiling in a shower of plaster dust. Finally, there came a rumbling on the attic stair, like a load of coals being tipped into a cellar. And a limp form shot through the doorway, head first and deeply unconscious. He was recognisable as Mr Jack Johnson, but only just. Mrs Johnson screamed at the sight of him and even Jimmy and Danny winced.

"Stap me, Captain!" said Jimmy, when Slym appeared, "You didn't half baste him!"

"Shut your gob!" said Slym.

It was dark when Slym finally emerged from No. 4 Bow Street, the most important Magistrate's Office in London and the one with the widest jurisdiction. He had just delivered up the body of Johnson the Knife Murderer, more or less alive and intact. Normally, for Slym, it could never be a simple matter of darting in and out of the Bow Street office. There was too much life there for a man like him to ignore. Too many useful contacts: professional rivals like the Robin Redbreast "Runners", potential customers among the aggrieved victims howling for justice, and shoals of clerks, petty lawyers, and informers of all kinds who might be useful to him. Besides, there was the drama of the place when it was in full swing: the shouting and jostling and arguing.

But tonight he couldn't take pleasure in the spectacle and left as soon as he could. He turned left out of the door and set off at a smart pace along Bow Street.

He turned left into Long Acre, right into Hanover Street, followed it into Belton Street, then left into Broad Street and so on to Oxford Street, and straight on to the junction with Marylebone Lane on the left. A brisk fifteen minutes for Slym who walked by choice, and walked hard.

As he arrived at the Marylebone Watch House, a file of elderly men, thickly overcoated against the night air, was emerging from the big double doors. They were kitted out alike, with lanterns, cudgels and woollen cap with long flaps to cover the ears. They leaned heavily on their cudgels and they looked up at the night sky with the grim pessimism of men who knew how useless it was to complain of what the weather might do to them. They had old, watery eyes, and wind-reddened cheeks, and a single drop of clear moisture hung under the point of every nose, as if it were an officially issued part of the uniform. This body of men was the Marylebone Parish Watch going forward to its nightly duty.

The Watch Men made way for Slym, and touched their caps respectfully at sight of him. "Mr Slym!" they said as he entered the building. It was a combination of a lock-up for such drunks as the Watch might bring in and a police house where the Watch were organised and their stores were kept. Right now, it was still full of shambling wrapped-up figures, swaying slowly towards the door, and the round interior of the room growled with the sound of old mens' voices as they gossiped and got their orders from the Constable of the Night, at his table to one side. He was a superior figure with a wig and a suit of blue clothes, and as well as busying himself with the pen and papers on his table, he puffed at a long pipe and refreshed himself from a quart pewter tankard as he gave his men their orders. This was more of a task than it sounds, as none of them were quick-minded and some were very deaf.

The Constable spotted Slym as he entered, and his eyebrows twitched. Slym went over to him.

"Well, well!" said the Constable, in a bold, clear voice that all present could hear. "Look who's come! Gor' blind me if it isn't Slimy Sam himself."

"Huh!" grunted Slym, dismissing the dreadful words with a wave of the hand, for this was the one man in London from whom he must accept them without complaint: his father, Mr James Slim.

The resemblance between the two men was marked and would have been remarkable but for the fact that James Slim had been a prize-fighter of some note, in his earlier years, and this had developed his features in other directions than nature had planned. But he had the same stark, black hair, untinged with grey, and the same broad, stocky build and heavy hands with red knuckles. True he was thicker about the middle than his son, and he was not so terrifyingly smart in his turnout. But his figure was good for a man of sixty, and as for the latter disparity, no man born could equal Sam Slym for the brutal force with which he blacked and shone his boots.

"Sit yourself here, boy," said Slim, indicating a chair. "When the Watch is out, we'll go into my room to be more cosy." He tapped a forefinger against his tankard, "I'd offer you a wet, but I suppose you'd not thank me?" Slym shook his head. "Tch! Tch!" said Slim. "Can't see how you can be no son of mine, what won't take a drop of drink, nor baccy neither!"

"Tea'll do nicely, Pa," said Slym.

"Tea?" said Slim, raising his eyebrows. "Expensive

tastes you've acquired, my lad!" But later on, when the last noble guardian of the King's Peace had sallied forth, coughing and spitting upon his creaking limbs, Slim led his son into the Constable's room, unlocked his tea-caddy and put a kettle to boil on the patent, cast-iron stove that gave out a steady heat in one corner. The little room was by far the nicest place in the Watch House, with a table and chairs and some sporting prints in frames on the walls. It smelt of tobacco and old leather. Slim opened a cupboard and got out some bread and cheese and a teapot and cups.

"Help yourself," he said.

"I'm obliged, sir," said Slym, sounding the word as "obleeged" in fashionable style. Slim just laughed.

"Are you, indeed?" said he. So they drank tea and munched bread and cheese, and neither spoke.

"Well?" said Slim at length.

"How's Mrs Slim?" countered Slym.

"The Widow?" said Slim, for that's what he persisted in calling her. "She's in robust health, me boy, and I'm sure she sends you her best."

Slym nodded in reply, and looked about him. He waved his hand to take in the whole building.

"Why d'ye bother with this?" said he. "You've married a woman that owns the biggest alehouse in Wapping, and two more down Billingsgate way. You could live at your ease like a gentleman of leisure."

"I do it 'cos a man must have his work," said Slim,

"as well you know!" Slim leaned across the table and fixed his son with his eye. "Now, Sammy-boy," said he, "are we two going to pass the night talkin' about me and the Widow? Or are we to come to the point? It's not twice a year you come to look up your old dad, and when you do it's never for nothing good. And judging from the look on your face now, there's something going forward that's got you wound up like a clock-spring. So tell the truth, my lad, and shame the devil! What is it?"

Slym frowned and played with his blackthorn stick and looked at the highlights in his impossibly glossy boots.

"It's a woman, Pa," he said.

"Well, heaven be praised!" said his father. "There's been times when I've wondered if you hadn't the taste for it."

"Pig-shite!" said Slym. "I've the taste for it, all right, by God I have! But I've never had the time," he sighed miserably and shook his head, "never the time, Pa."

"So what about this one?" said Slim. "You managed to find the time for her, I take it?"

"In the way of business, Pa," said Slym, and fell silent again.

"Talking of business," said Slim to fill the silence, "I hear it was you that took Izzy Cohen" – Slym still gazed at his boots – "and the murmur is," said Slim, "that Izzy offered five hundred in gold for you to look the other way when you found him."

"Three hundred," said Slym.

"Three hundred or five," said Slim, shaking his head in disapproval, "what's the matter with you, Sam? That little Jew-boy was a forger, that's all. Where's the harm in that? I beg to ask. Why didn't you take his money like a sensible kiddy and let the poor cove run?"

"'Cos I can't and I won't, Pa," said Slym, "and that's what it's all about with me and this woman. I've never met any woman like her. Not in all my life. I can't stop thinking about her. I can't sleep properly. And you know me – head on the pillow and off!"

Slym looked at his father gloomily. "She's got me so damn angry, I nearly killed a man today. And I don't do such things. I keep control."

"Well," said Slim, "looks like you're smitten at last, my lad. In that case you may be forced into matrimony. But if you take my advice you'll get your leg across her first, and give her a good rogering to see if that's all there is to it! That's if she'll grant you the pleasure without the price, of course!"

Slym shook his head. "She'll do that right enough," he said, "when she's ready. She thinks she's trapped me with the promise of it. But she hasn't."

"Ah!" said Slim, "she's that sort, is she?"

"No!" said Slym. "She's a great lady. A Society lady. She's got everything that I want, and you should see her, Pa. You should just see her . . ."

"Hmm," said his father, and for the first time he

thought he'd begun to understand his son's problem. It was time for him to give serious advice. "Now look here, my boy," said he, not unkindly, "you always did have ideas above your station, and I'd be the first to congratulate you on what you've made of yourself, but there's limits in this world. There's the likes of *us*, in Wapping and Billingsgate, and there's the likes of *them* in Grosvenor Square. And as far as they're concerned, whatever you do to better yourself, why, you're just a dog-turd stuck with roses! D'ye think this woman'll ever marry you?"

"Yes," said Slym.

"Bah!" said his father.

"Pa," said Slym, and reached across to take his father's arm, "I'm deadly serious! This woman'll give me everything she has, because she needs me to get it back for her in the first place. She thinks she's been very clever and that I don't know who she is. But I do. She's Lady Sarah Coignwood."

"Lady Sarah Coignwood?" said Slim, and frowned. "I know that moll. I know the name . . ." He thought for a moment, then James Slim rocked his chair back on its two hind legs and whistled slowly. "My stars, Sam," said he, "you're fighting out of your weight, kiddy. There's too much money in it. There's lords and dukes'd take an interest in this. *And* bleedin' lawyers: regiments of 'em! And all England knows about that woman and her son, the papers had the story and everyone talked about it."

"That was last month," said Slym; "the public has the

war to think about now, and the fear of a French invasion. And who'd recognise Lady Sarah Coignwood in the
street? Only her own friends, and them she can avoid.
Who else knows what she looks like, unless they've been
to Coignwood Hall to see her portrait! You wouldn't
recognise *yourself* from a picture in a print shop!"

Slim looked at his son and a feeling of great unease
fell upon him.

"You want to throw in with her, don't you?" he said.

"Yes," said Slym.

"She's a bad 'un, Sam."

"I know."

"She's done murder, and worse."

"I know."

"Yet you wouldn't take Izzy Cohen's money?"

"No."

"You never took fourpence that weren't honest."

"No."

"There's a reward out for her . . ."

"I don't care."

"This could ruin you."

"I know."

"You could find a rope round your own neck."

"Yes."

"So *why?*"

"Because I'm in love with her."

Chapter 8

The newspaper article that Cooper wanted me to read, as near as I can remember it, was this:

SPLENDID TRIUMPH AT SEA OVER
THE FORCES OF THE BRITANNIC NAVY
BY THE HEROIC ARMS OF THE
UNITED STATES

The Globe is informed that there came this 24th day of February, into Boston harbor, captive under prize crew, the British Armed Cruiser *Bednal Green* of thirty twelve-pounder guns and one hundred and fifty men. This powerful vessel was seized and taken after the most bloody struggle by the Boston vessel *John Stark*, Captain Daniel Cooper, a ship having but twelve guns of small size and less than fifty men embarked. The prolonged and desperate resistance of the British ship was entirely due to the leadership of her Captain, Lieutenant Jacob Fletcher, late victor of the celebrated battle of Passage d'Aron, whose unsurpassed excellence as a gunnery officer was so recently an example to the world. All the greater, therefore, is the valor and terrible efficiency of Captain Cooper and his band of men whose . . .

I broke off reading to glance up at Cooper. I wondered if he was the source of this rubbish. Perhaps he'd even written it himself? It turned my stomach, quite frankly. It's bad enough when a man robs you. But when he wants to pretend he's a hero into the bargain, that's too much. The seeds of my great disliking for Daniel Cooper were sewn that day, though if I hadn't been feeling so low, I should probably have felt sorry for him, to see a man revel like that in false flattery. And there was more to come yet.

"There, sir!" says he. "See how my exploits are reported for all Washington to see." I looked again at the cutting. It was from *The Globe*, a Washington paper. I'd missed that. "Every member of the Congress will have seen it," says Cooper, turning to Colonel Derby, the Commandant, and a couple of civilians who'd come in with them. They were brothers, by the name of Hart. "Only think what this will mean for the Navy and Boston!" says Cooper and they all three smiled so merrily that first I thought they were a set of toad-eaters crawling for his favour. But they weren't.

"Now we shall get our frigate!" says one of the Harts.

"And our Navy Dockyard!" says the other.

Something was going on, and I couldn't guess what, but I could see this was not the moment to pitch into Cooper for the damned lies in that damned newspaper. So I held my peace and waited for Cooper to get round to me. There had to be more reason for his coming here than to show off his press cuttings.

"But, Lieutenant Fletcher," says he, "you must wonder what purpose brings me here?"

"It had crossed my mind," said I, and everyone laughed like drains and slapped me on the back. This looked good. I'd been right to keep quiet.

"Sir," says Colonel Derby, a red-faced old buffer in a powdered wig and service coat, "Commander Cooper has spoken for you. He insists that the word of a British Naval Officer may be relied upon and he is come to bear you off to more comfortable quarters."

And so he had, by George! Derby took charge and made me raise my right hand and swear by the Almighty not to attempt escape. And since he was a professional soldier, and a veteran of the Revolution, we had all the trimmings too. I had to swear ". . . not to offer harm to the Peoples nor Properties of these United States, nor essay whatsoever act that might undermine its constitution . . . etc., etc.". Which was all harmless fun as far as I was concerned and wouldn't hold me back five seconds if I saw a good chance to run. The only trouble was, where to? I wasn't going into the vast American interior with its murdering, scalping savages, and I couldn't get home to England without a ship and a crew.

But that could wait upon opportunity. The first thing was to get out from behind iron bars. Once we'd completed Colonel Derby's formalities we went out into Queen Street, where Cooper had a carriage waiting, and I began to realise that he was something more than an unemployed sea officer. The carriage was a spanking new landau, German-built and harnessed to a fine team of matched greys. And he had smart liveried servants on the box, both black as my boot. In short, I sniffed the authentic reek of money.

Cooper waved me in with a bow, and he and the Hart brothers got in after me. Colonel Derby raised his hat, the two sentries on the door presented arms, and the carriage moved off.

During the short ride to Cooper's house, the bold Commander chattered nonstop to the Harts, and I looked about me pretending to take a view of Boston while paying careful attention to what was said. In fact it was all of a piece. It was all a matter of Boston and its politics.

To begin with, this was no frontier town with clapboard shacks and hairy-arsed wild men pistolling one another on the street. Boston in 1794 was a real, bustling city of nearly 20,000 people. As you approached from the sea, the skyline was a packed mass of roofs, bristling with church spires and public buildings. There were libraries, bath-houses, coffee-shops, insurance offices, theatres, warehouses, clock towers, ironmongers and fashionable ladies taking tea in their salons.

The city was two miles long by a mile and a quarter wide, and was built on a squat peninsula shaped not unlike a miniature of the North American continent itself, and connected to the Massachusetts mainland by a narrow isthmus at the southern end. At the top end, Boston looked a quarter of a mile across the Charles River estuary, to the Charlestown peninsula and Bunker Hill. So Boston was encircled by water, and the eastward (seaward) side was a mass of wharves and dockyards.

And there you have factors one and two in Boston politics. Number one: Boston depended on seafaring. Number two: Boston had no love for the British, as you may have deduced from the name "Bunker Hill".

For a jolly little battle was fought on Bunker Hill, nineteen years earlier, in 1775, during the Revolutionary War. 2,600 Redcoats marched up the slope in perfect formation, to the sound of fife and drum, and steadily on into the massed fire of American infantry dug in behind fortifications. Our side was heavily mauled, but after two or three dreadful repulses, they broke through and treated the Yankees to the bayonet. It was the bloodiest single engagement of the entire Revolution and neither side ever forgot it. That was the sort of tale that a young Bostonian like Cooper learned at his mother's knee.

Perhaps as a consequence of this, Cooper and his friends, who were of the Republican faction, supported the French and opposed the British in our present war. They also supported the rebuilding of the United States Navy which Congress had sanctioned in March, a fine thing for Cooper and the Hart family, for they had the U.S. Navy's one and only ship fitting out in the Hart yard, and Cooper was pulling every string in sight to get command of it. What's more, President Washington had approved a series of big over-blown frigates to be new built, and the Harts had high hopes of getting the contract for one of them, a forty-gunner to be called *Constitution*. It was my introduction into Boston politics – Yankee politics really – a dish I hadn't the least taste for, but got stuffed with till it made me sick.

Cooper was up to his neck in it, thanks to his father who'd made his pile in shipping, got himself elected to Congress, and gone south to Washington where the power was. Cooper managed the Boston business, played at being an officer, and lived in the family's elegant house in the Tontine Crescent, on the south side of Franklin Street. It was outside this house that the landau stopped on 18th March. One look at it confirmed that the Coopers had money. It was in a graceful white-stuccoed, curving terrace, like the best of Bath or London. Mind you, the north side of the street was a mire, half-drained, with haphazard works under way.

We clambered out, servants grovelled on all sides, all

of 'em black. Doors opened and in we went, Cooper and the Harts yammering nineteen to the dozen. But I hardly got time to notice the elegance of everything in the hall before my feet gave signs of going from under me.

I was over the worst of my wound and getting better, but after three days mainly in bed, I'd used up my strength. The ceiling swung around my head and all the voices got faint. But I didn't quite go over, and Cooper and his chums clapped a hold on me. Then there was someone else there, taking charge and giving orders in the accent of the deep south. Cooper fell back, the servants took over, and I was bustled off to a delightful little room that had been prepared for me in the back of the house so that they didn't have to haul my deadweight upstairs. Someone had used some brain.

It was all warm and snug in that room, with a fire blazing and a big bed made up and aired. They got me inside, extracted me out of my clothes (which hadn't been changed for weeks and were none too sweet), sat me in a chair stark naked, to sponge the dirt off me, and towelled me down, then they put me to bed in a fresh nightshirt smelling of lavender. I was too weak to do much for myself and the whole process was dreamy and pleasant. For one thing they were a damned smart set of servants who went about their business like experts, and for another the one in charge, who did most of the work, was the most extraordinarily fine woman.

She was black as midnight, with a figure like a sandglass,

tall and splendid with brilliant eyes and flashing white teeth. Her name was Lucinda, and she was Cooper's housekeeper. He had a butler too, but Lucinda gave the orders and kept the purse. She was a remarkable creature in many ways. I'd had some experience of women by then, and black girls, too, thanks to the hospitality of Pareira Gomez's African king, but not girls like her. She looked you straight in the eye and was dressed like a lady of quality. What's more, she had the height to stand eye to eye with me.

Once she'd got me tucked up in bed, she sent the others away and did her final bits of fussing about. Tired though I was, I realised that I was very anxious that she should stay a little longer. Just looking at her was working wonders for me, though she had her nose in the air and was acting the perfect grande dame. I was searching my muddled brain for something to say, when she got in first with her lilting southern voice, "Is they anythin' ay-ulse yoo wan, Loo-tenan' Fletcher?" says she, looking down at me. As she said this, she arched her eyebrows and pouted her lips, ever so slightly. Such tiny movements that I wasn't really sure I'd even seen them. None the less, I got the distinct impression that a signal had just been run up to the masthead.

"Ah, yes!" says I. "Something to drink . . . some soup, perhaps?"

"Yezzah," says she, and glided off as graceful as a panther.

She was back ten minutes later with a bowl of broth and a napkin so I could be fed without splashing the bed. She secured the cloth neatly under my chin, which meant her leaning across me with her breasts bouncing an inch from my nose, and the scent of her went to my head like a jug of rum. We'd just settled down nicely, with her alongside, one hand behind my head and the other shovelling soup with a spoon, when Cooper and the Harts came in to see their tame Limey. They stayed too, damn 'em, 'cos I was almost sure Miss Lucinda had looked me over and liked what she'd seen (she'd had a damn good look, after all) but as long as Cooper and Co. were there, they were queering my pitch and there was nothing I could do to try out what seemed the best piece of luck that I'd had since I'd set eyes on *John Stark*.

But the wretches stayed and talked politics over me till I dropped off to sleep, so there was no fun and games that night. Nor was there for some days thereafter, which was probably just as well since it took me that long to get back my full strength. And in that time I was extended every hospitality by Cooper, including as soon as I was up to it, a tour round the Hart shipyard to view the man-o'-war they were fitting out for the infant United States Navy.

This was *Declaration of Independence*, a gift from the Frog Navy, that had started life as the two-decker *Euphonie*, 64. But the Yankees had no use for one lonely ship of the line, so the Harts had chopped away her poop, quarterdeck and fo'c'sle to form a sort of ponderous frigate, known as a Rahzay.

[The word is properly the French "Rasé" but Fletcher would not have it, reacting to my protest with a violent denunciation of the French, their nation, their language, and their disgusting use of garlic in food. S.P.]

Declaration was rated for thirty-eight 24-pounders on the gun-deck (ex lower gun-deck), and twenty 32-pounder carronades, on her flush-decked quarterdeck/fo'c'sle (ex upper gun-deck). A massive armament for a frigate.

Cooper was a familiar figure in the shipyard and you could see the power his family wielded from the way everyone treated him. Americans like it to be thought that they don't have noblemen and so every man may look any other man in the eye and think himself his equal. Well, from what I saw in Boston in '94, that was almost true but not quite. Cooper didn't call himself a lord, but he damn-well acted like one: At least he did where the common herd was concerned. The only real difference from an English lord was the way he kept company with the Hart brothers, who were tradesmen. Of course, this is hardly surprising, since his own father had been in trade, and rich business folk like these were the power in the land. And a damn fine thing too, if you ask me.

So Cooper would link arms with the Harts and go striding round the yard, in the midst of the thumping and sawing, and the tar and tackles, happy as a child, arguing and pointing and always asking questions. One way or another, Cooper's powerful connections were going to get him a ship, it was obvious. As for me, I was led like a bear, half on parade as a trophy and half there to have my brains picked. As I've said, they had a mighty respect for the Royal Navy in technical matters. But it was a hell of a bore. I've never had any real interest in ships. They're a means to an end for me.

But later that day, when Cooper had had his fill of shipyards, we were whisked back to his house in the carriage, and then he excused himself and said he had to go to a meeting of some Navy Society or other. No doubt more politicking to get the command he wanted. So off he went, leaving me alone in the house with the servants. If I'd wanted to, this would have been the ideal opportunity to run. But there was nowhere to run to, and anyway, I had reason to stay.

Over the past few days, I'd grown more and more convinced that Lucinda had her eye on me. A flick of an eyelash here, a backward glance there, nothing obvious, but I was sure she was beckoning me on. Either that or she was the kind that enjoyed tantalising men. In other words, I wasn't sure at all, and I didn't want to make a fool of myself with my host's trusted housekeeper.

That would be the best and quickest way to get myself out of this cosy berth and back into prison. So I was careful to behave myself and resisted the temptation to grab some of the more delectable parts of Lucinda as she swayed past me in the corridors of Cooper's house. Even when she swept past close enough to brush against me when I was damn sure she didn't have to. The trouble was, the woman was so damn self-possessed. Many tall girls will stoop to try to disguise their height, but not Lucinda. She stretched up to the limit of her inches, held her head high and looked down her nose at the world. And that's just dandy as far as I'm concerned. I don't mind a bit if a woman's as tall as me, or taller, if it comes to that – not if she's as slender as Lucinda, and not if she's got her figure.

So that afternoon I strolled into Cooper's day room as the front door banged after him, on his way off to his meeting. He wouldn't be back for hours. I watched him through the window as he got up into the carriage and the coachman drove him away. Then I took a book out of a book case and settled down in a chair by the fire.

By chance I picked a rattling fine book. It was a book of bound pamphlets all about how the Yankee Congress was trying to set up a proper coinage for the country. Gold always was my favourite subject and I was fascinated to learn that the Yankees hadn't near enough coin of their own, and half the world's gold and silver coinage was passing as legal tender. It nearly put other thoughts out of my mind. But not quite.

Where I was sitting, I was close to the bell-pull that summoned the servants. Now a tug on that cord was supposed to bring the butler, but Lucinda was too sharp-eyed not to notice I was alone, so I wondered who might answer if I were to ring.

I tugged the cord, and seconds later was most disappointed to hear the heavy steps of the butler, Joseph, coming to the door.

"Sah?" says he. "How may I serve you?"

"Oh, fetch me a brandy," says I irritably. Perhaps she hadn't noticed I was alone. Perhaps I'd been mistaken after all and she wasn't running the rule over me. It's too damned easy for a man to believe a thing when he *wants* to believe it.

I was busy feeling sorry for myself when the door opened again, and Lucinda entered with a decanter and glass on a silver tray. She had the same, God-damn-you look in her eye as she put the tray on a little table and moved the table close to my hand.

"Yo' brandy, sah," says she and straightened up to her full height, looking down on me where I sat in my chair. "Ah have to send Joseph into the town, sah, on business. Is they anythin' you might want, sah . . . ?" the eyebrows lifted just a fraction, "from the town, that is?" she completed.

Damn the woman! She had me on a knife-edge. I still didn't know where I stood. Was that an invitation or not? I couldn't tell, and I still had to be careful of offending Cooper's damned puritan sensibilities. He wasn't one for the ladies, that's for sure. He'd not passed a remark about women in all the hours I'd suffered his monologues of conversation. Boston politics and the United States' Navy was his world. And he was a strict churchgoer too. One false step and I'd be out on my ear.

"Nothin', sah?" says she, straight-faced. "You cain't think o' nothin' you want?"

"Er . . ." says I, growing hot under the collar, and looking at the curves under her grey gown, but I funked it. "No," says I, "nothing."

Damn it! thinks I. How could this be the "come on"? From the look on her face she could have been a governess scolding her pupils.

"As you wish, sah," says she, and waltzed to the door. Just as she went out, she stopped and looked back over her shoulder. "I hope you won't be afraid in this big house all alone with me, sah. I had to send the maids out too, sah. They's just you and me here, sah. Nobody else . . ."

That was too much. I was out of the chair and across the room in three steps. I seized her by the waist and whisked her off her feet, straight up into the air at the full length of my arms, just to show her what was what. I doubt many men had served her like that before. Tall and splendid she might be, but I was six feet high and turned the scales at sixteen stone, of which not one ounce was fat.

"Now then, ma'am!" says I, "just what game are we

playing?" She laughed most beautifully, a musical sound that made my spine tingle.

"My," says she, "what a big, fine boy you turned out to be. And just when I was giving you up!" Well, that was plain enough. We were done with codes and ciphers at last. I grinned happily and lowered her until her toes were just clear of the ground, and held her there while I kissed her. Or to be more precise, while she kissed me, for she slid her hands around the back of my neck and dug her fingertips into me, urging me to it like a groom with a horse. And she slid her tongue around and inside my mouth like a hungry animal. By George but that woman knew what she wanted.

"Well," she said, pausing for breath, and giving me a slow, wide smile, "*you* got a fine room with a bed in it, Loo-tenant, and *I* got a fine room with a bed in it. So: are we gonna stand here all day, or are we gonna do this thing properly?" It was the longest sentence I'd ever heard her deliver, and certainly the most welcome, so without further delay, I tossed her bodily in the air and caught her again as she came down, to get her comfortably close to me, with her cheek next to mine, her arms around my neck and my arms curled beneath her thighs and the small of her back.

For that's the way a gentleman should carry a lady when she's declared it's bedtime at three in the afternoon. Another thing to remember is always to use your own bed and your own room on such occasions and never hers. That way, should she change her mind at the wrong moment, *you* can't be accused of forcing your way into her room, and *she* has to explain what she was doing in yours.

Lucinda loved this treatment. She was used to men being smaller than her, but all women like to feel dainty in the presence of a man, so a hulking great chap like me that swept her off her feet like a child was exactly what she was looking for. She screamed in mock-fright as I swung her up into the air, and threw her head back in peals of laughter. Why not, after all? There was only the two of us to hear.

The change in her was amazing compared with her usual dour manner, but it was nothing to what she did once I'd got her safe into my room with the door locked behind us.

She was all over me, running her tongue into my ear, pulling open my shirt and digging her nails into my chest and sliding her thigh over mine. It was all I could do to concentrate on the *vital* matter of getting her out of her gown. What with her laughing and my growing excitement and the waves of delightful shuddering passing up and down my back from the games she was up to, it was worse than splicing a parted line in a hurricane.

"Kiss me, honey!" says she, and folded her arms behind my head and brushed her lips over mine. By George, she smelt beautiful and tasted wonderful!

So we staggered around a while with me doing my

best to cast off the lashings at the front of her bodice, and her laughing at my clumsy efforts. Finally she pushed me away and took pity on me.

"You get yourself comfy, honey," says she, "and leave it to me." So that's what I did. I hauled off my things and sat on the bed while she dropped the grey gown to the floor, with a collection of white linen undergarments to follow, and last of all the red head-scarf that she always wore bound tight around her head. And so she stood up stark naked with one hip jutting forward and her arms stretched over her head. By George she was a gorgeous creature. And didn't she just know it, and wasn't she just proud of it?

She shone like satin, with long smooth limbs and a superb shape. I'd assumed she got some sort of tackle underneath to nip her in at the middle and push her breasts up, but no – it was all Lucinda, unaided. Fortunately for the honour of Old England, I could see that Lucinda was as impressed with me as I was with her. An Italian Count once said to me: "Your body, eet ees so beautiful, eet could be ze model for ze sculptures of ze Greek Gods." But he wore pink satin and chased boys, and I had to kick his dago arse for his impertinence. But to see much the same thought in the eyes of a magnificently lovely woman is something else. Especially when the sunlight is playing on her naked skin and she's wriggling her hips at you.

I made a grab at her but she laughed, ducked under

my arms, and seized hold of my shaft which was standing on tip toes to join the party. And damn me if she didn't open her mouth, fasten her lips on it and lick it like a lollipop.

But enough was enough and I swung her on to the bed, got on top of her and folded my arms around her to stop her confounded wriggling. "Now then, madam," says I, "no more of your games. Got you at last!" She laughed, then her eyes widened in horror and fixed on something over my shoulder.

"Oh my Lord!" says she. "Mizzah Cooper!"

I jumped in shock and twisted my head to see . . . To see *nothing*! Lucinda nearly choked with laughter and I took my revenge in the best possible way.

I got my knees between hers, forced them apart and drove deep inside her, kissing her all the while like a thirsty man fresh from a week in the desert. Nearest thing to rape I've ever done, except that she had her legs twined round me and was urging me to it.

Chapter 9

It is with deepest regret that we are obliged to report the death, upon the field of sport, of one of Staffordshire's most prominent gentlemen.

(From *The Clarion of the North* of 15th
September 1793.)

*

In a low, red-brown blur of movement, the fox shot through a gap in the hedge and half-jumped, half-tumbled down the steep bank into Church Lane. The narrow road ran deep-sunken between high-banked hedgerows of immemorial antiquity, and any man or beast coming across the fields towards the road could easily be misled by the tall thick hedge into thinking the road ran level with the field instead of nearly ten feet below it.

But the fox was small and nimble. He gained his feet in an instant and, turning left, he ran for his life down the lane, past St Luke's Church and into the village of Goostrey. One of the mowers, trimming the grass in the churchyard, saw him go and called to his mate to look. But the fox was stretched out at top speed and was gone even as the man turned his head.

"Aye," said the mower's mate giving a full two seconds to the monosyllable in his dull Cheshire burr, "him'll 'ave the 'unt arter him . . . listen." And the two men stopped work and turned towards Church Lane, expecting to see the spectacle of the Tabley Hunt in full flood come pouring out of the lane and into the village. Unfortunately, the curve of the lane hid from them exactly what happened next, or they would have been excellent witnesses at the subsequent Coroner's inquest.

They did indeed hear the frantic baying of the hounds, and the hunting horns and the heavy thunder of charging horses, but they didn't see the hounds pouring through, over and under the hedge, nor the mad jam of animal bodies as they cascaded on top of each other in the totally unexpected trough of Church Lane.

Nor did they see the awful sight of a powerful black hunter, lathered with foam, sailing clear over the hedge with the leading rider of the field low over his mount's neck. The rider was a magnificent horseman, but one whose blood was so fired with the chase that he was riding ahead of the Master of Fox Hounds: a severe impropriety and a deadly error for one who did not know the ground.

In fact nobody saw the last split seconds of the life of Mr Cecil Forster, magistrate of Lonborough in Staffordshire, Master of Fox Hounds of the West Staffordshire Hunt, and riding upon the 15th September 1793; as a guest of Sir John Fleming-Leicester's Tabley Hunt.

Even Forster himself barely had time to perceive his mistake before the horse fell dreadfully into the seething mass of hounds down in the pit of the sunken lane. There was a heavy crunch of flesh and bone as the big hunter came down with an impact that splintered its forelimbs and drove its broad chest into the mass of struggling hounds, crushing the life from three of them and catapulting Forster out of the saddle at a meteoric velocity, and to instantaneous extinction as his head drove into a tree-trunk and smashed like an apple under a sledge-hammer.

Later there were tears and recriminations as the dismayed members of the "Tabley" stood among their steaming horses in Church Lane, telling each other that everyone knew what a death-trap it was, and that it was *impossible* that Forster had not known, and surely it must have been *somebody*'s duty to tell him? And if *only* Forster hadn't ridden ahead of Sir John, and who would tell Mrs Forster?

In the event, kindly man that he was, Sir John himself

rode that very day the long fifteen miles to Lonborough, and broke the sad news to Forster's wife. To his great relief, she took it philosophically and commented that this was just the death that her husband would have wished, had he been given the choice. Her brave sentiments became public knowledge and were much admired locally. All classes of society were united in the opinion that these were the words of a true-born sporting lady and showed real British "bottom".

In due course all this was reported in Lonborough's principal newspaper, *The Clarion of the North*, when it published a long and respectful obituary on Forster. But the Clarion tactfully ignored another snippet which was also public knowledge, namely that the hideous condition of the corpse had caused even Mr Sorrel the undertaker to be sickened to his stomach when he removed the stained cloth that covered the head in the privacy of his laying-out room.

(Neither did the *Clarion* report that, with the hunt abandoned, the fox escaped and dined that night on a large goose, which he liberated from a farm, on his way home.)

*

By 1794, Polmouth, in Cornwall, always one of the principal seaports and centres of trade, had grown to the point where only Portsmouth itself was more populous or important among England's southern seaports.

As well as the town proper, from about 1780 onwards there had grown up a lesser Polmouth, based on the village of Polcoombe, once separate from Polmouth, but now merging slowly into the city, as each grew and advanced its new building towards the other.

But while Polmouth was devoted to commerce, Polcoombe was devoted to pleasure. It had become to the West Country what Brighton was to London and the South-East. Spreading out from the fine sandy beaches of Polcoombe Cove, the village had grown at a tremendous rate and now offered a solid frontage, gazing down upon the bay, of inns, tea houses, pleasure gardens, barber shops, hotels, lending libraries and even a small opera house which staged musical entertainments every weekday of the season and twice on Saturdays. The beach itself offered the latest in bathing machines: huge, high vehicles upon four wheels, drawn by horses out into the deeper waters of the bay. The machines were entirely enclosed, enabling clients to disrobe in privacy, and were provided with collapsible awnings by the use of which young ladies could take their sea-baths naked, and yet not offend propriety.

Tickets for these machines were to be had at one shilling and sixpence for one hour, from the better tea shops. Tickets could also be had, though at two shillings per hour, for the telescopes set up on the terrace of the Royal George Hotel, supposedly to enable guests to view the shipping, but which were more usually employed by gentlemen in a close examination of the bathing machines.

A further attraction of the Royal George, was its large and excellent tea-room. This was the acknowledged centre of Polcoombe and a place of such unquestioned respectability that unaccompanied ladies might enter and take their pleasure and be entirely at their ease.

Just such a lady entered the tea-room from the connecting doors to the George, at two o'clock in the afternoon of 19th September 1793. She was modestly dressed and immediately took a table which put her back to the run of windows which lit the room and gave a view of the bay. There, she could see everybody who came in, while she was little more than a silhouette.

The lady ordered Lapsong Suchong and rout drop-cakes from the waiter, and sat composed reading a book and keeping a steady watch on the door. She was Lady Sarah Coignwood and was taking a calculated risk.

In the first place, there was the possibility of her being recognised from the many prints and cartoons in circulation purporting to represent her. These were the only means whereby the general public might recognise a celebrity's face, and fortunately the likeness was generally poor. The real risk was the chance arrival of someone who knew her. But this Lady Sarah had to accept, for perfect safety was no longer available to her. Even had she locked herself away in the Greenwich house, there was always the chance that some servant might betray her. And more important, simply to hide and do nothing was impossible to a woman of her will and greed for life.

So Victor had been packed off to Lonborough, and the creature Slym set on the trail of the Brat, while she herself took the cheapest public coach to Portsmouth and Lonborough; not a post-chaise nor even the Mail. It had been galling but wiser. To go post-chaise would have been to invite danger. The vehicle was private to the hirer, but postilions had a far better knowledge of the "Bon Ton" than other Londoners, since the high cost of the fares ensured that most of their passengers were the rich and the famous, so the risk of being recognised was too great. Victor, of course, fancied he had the perfect answer in posing as a woman but Lady Sarah had her doubts. Victor's movements were excellently feminine, but even fresh-shaved his skin was too rough and his Adam's apple too prominent. His was a clever effect for night-time or at a distance, but close to he would always be one of the "Bulgarian" persuasion, and not a woman.

For herself she dressed plainly and wore layers of undergarments to alter the shape of her figure. She curbed her natural exuberance, shrank herself mentally and thought herself into the role of a timid widow living on a modest bequest. This she believed was better than an elaborate disguise which could itself attract attention.

Fortunately, Polcoombe itself should be safe enough.

It was a place that previously she would not have gone near for all the gold in the Indies. For Polcoombe was pretentious, middle-class, *noveau riche* and risible. It was a watering hole for vulgar merchants and their fat wives. And if Lady Sarah thought this, then so would the very people who would be most likely to recognise her: her own friends, her own Dulwich Square set.

Above all else, the risk was a necessary risk, for Lady Sarah had not made the long and boring journey to this ridiculous place for nothing. She was here on vital business. Business that justified any risk. She looked at the large long-case clock, shining in its scarlet-lacquered chinoiserie, that decorated the centre of the opposite wall. It was a quarter past two. Her "guest" would arrive at any minute.

She looked down at her book again. Between the open pages was a neatly-clipped piece from a newspaper. It was an obituary. Her lips twitched into a smile which she smartly extinguished. The luck of it! The damned incredible luck of it! In her mind's eye she saw Victor's letter bubbling with joy and amazement. His pen had flown over the page, chattering about his gratitude to "my demonic equivalent of a guardian angel", which he assured her must have been "sent from the Infernal regions to take my part". Her lips twitched again. Victor included a little Satanism among his amusements.

But nevertheless, there was now a list in a drawer of Lady Sarah's room at the George which looked like this:

Fletcher's Glorious 1ˢᵗ of June

Fletcher
~~Mr Forster the Magistrate~~
Mr Pendennis the Polmouth merchant
Mr Richard Lucey the solicitor
Mr Taylor the bookseller (& wife)
~~Mr Forster's Constable~~
~~The Constables two brothers.~~

She was just beginning to wonder how Victor would fare with the Taylors when a heavy, soberly-dressed figure filled the doorway and a little thrill of fear ran through her. This was the most dangerous moment. It was just conceivable that Pendennis would screw up his courage and bring officers of the law with him to arrest her.

Ahhh! She sighed with relief. Pendennis was alone, and wearing a look of desperate worry on his big red face.

He looked so funny that for all her biting her lip and digging her nails into her palms, she could not hold back the laugh and heads turned to the musical, cascading sound. Sarah Coignwood could harpoon men in a hundred ways and one of them was with that laugh, even when she was trying to withhold it.

Fortunately only one person in the room knew whose laugh it was. Standing in the doorway of the Royal George Teashop, Mr Nathan Pendennis, Lord Mayor of Polmouth, was swept with conflicting emotions. There was fear that he should be seen at this business.

There was horror at the prospect of what this woman could do to his reputation – nothing less than utter ruin. And worst of all, with the captivating sound tinkling in his ears was the terrible, guilty desire that he'd tried to uproot and destroy. One look at her, even though he had to squint to see her against the light, brought back the memory of a wonderful half-hour in her London drawing room, on a sofa as soft as a feather bed, when for the first and only time in his serious, respectable life, an exceptionally lovely woman had allowed him the intimacies of her body. And not only allowed, but joined eagerly into the business with such skills that he never knew existed.

He'd had half an hour of that before the Lady cut the cord that dangled him over the pit, and brought in her powder puff of a son and six false witnesses to a trumped-up charge of rape. So now the woman had him in her power like a bull that's led to market by the ring through its nose. He was so enwrapped in his thoughts that he hardly noticed the waiter grovelling at his side. Pendennis came but seldom to Polcoombe – he hadn't the time for such things – but the waiter knew the Lord Mayor when he saw him.

Pendennis allowed himself to be led to a table and ordered tea. Then he followed the instructions that had come with the package of documents that had been delivered to him on the night of his dinner party. The documents were copies of witnessed depositions by six persons that he, Nathan Pendennis, had upon Sunday, 31st March 1793, inflicted the cruel and shameful crime of rape upon the person of Lady Sarah Coignwood, of Coignwood Hall in Staffordshire. They had been sent as a reminder. And they were accompanied with a letter from the woman herself, telling what was required of him.

This was quite simple. He drank his tea and spoke to nobody. He watched as Lady Sarah paid her bill and left the room. He waited ten full minutes by the clock. He paid and left.

He went to the terrace and saw her sitting on a bench reading a book. He went and sat beside her. He made no attempt to speak. Five minutes later she got up and walked briskly off towards Mr Cicero's Pleasure Gardens. Pendennis followed. She paid and entered. He paid and entered. The Gardens were full of little nooks and arbours where private conversations could take place.

Just over an hour later Lady Sarah left the Pleasure Gardens. Fifteen minutes later, by his watch, Nathan Pendennis left the Pleasure Gardens. Anyone who knew him would have said that ten years had fallen from him and some mad joy had entered in its place. It was all he could do to stop himself throwing his hat in the air, and he who never gave a gratuity left Mr Cicero's gatekeeper with a half sovereign in his trembling hands. The gatekeeper earned just ten shillings a week and could hardly believe his luck as he watched Pendennis stumping off up the street, trying to coax his bulk into a boyish swagger.

Later Lady Sarah considered the list and put down her pen. The list now looked like this:

Fletcher
~~Mr Forster the Magistrate~~
~~Mr Pendennis the Polmouth merchant~~
~~Mr Richard Lucey the solicitor~~
Mr Taylor the bookseller (& wife)
~~Mr Forster's Constable~~
~~The Constables two brothers.~~

Chapter 10

Once I'd got things squared with Lucinda, things picked up something wonderful. For public consumption she continued to glide round the house with her head in the air, and looked down her nose at me. She was careful always to address me as "Sah" or "Loo-tenant", but come night-time and the house asleep she'd tap on my door and everything was "honey" and "sugar". Mind you, that wasn't every night. She had to be careful. That's what she told me, anyway.

Things picked up in another way too, and one that I'd never have imagined. The day after Lucinda and I had executed our first squadronal manoeuvres, a letter arrived in the house from one Henry Knox, who was no less than the Yankee Secretary of War, and the very man charged by President Washington to rebuild the U.S. Navy. Knox was an old friend of the Cooper family, and heavily in debt to Cooper's Pa for contributions to the back-handers and expenses that got Knox into his present job in the first place. And this shows two interesting things. First, how very well-conducted was the Clan Cooper, and second, that for all the Yankees' protestations of democracy and equality, the wheels of power in their land turned remarkably similar to those in England.

I say that because the subject of the letter was unofficial confirmation that young Cooper was to get command of *Declaration of Independence* with the rank of Post Captain. All the niceties would follow: a Commission signed by the President, a Warrant to recruit men, cash to pay the dockyard . . . etc. But with Knox's letter, the thing was assured.

Cooper got his letter at breakfast time and danced round the room in his China silk dressing gown.

"Fletcher, my boy," says he, "just look at this! Just look at this!" and he stuffed the letter in my hand with such a happy smile on his face that for a moment I was genuinely pleased for him. Then his tongue ran away with him: "Shan't I just show it to those Limeys now?" says he, and burst into fits of laughter as he realised what he'd said.

"Oh!" says he, slapping my shoulder, "you don't mind do you, old fellow?" Over his shoulder I could see Lucinda making mock of him, by pouting her lips as if to kiss him and wriggling her breasts behind the back of his head. That made me laugh and Cooper thought I was laughing with him, but I wasn't. I hadn't forgotten who'd robbed my ship from under me and I don't see why I should be pleased that he'd got a bigger command to do the same to others.

After that, he got dressed at lightning speed, called for his carriage and was off to the Harts' yard to set everything in motion. Having got his command, he was terrified that peace would be declared before he could get her to sea and achieve something with her. He was still pulling his boots on as he hopped out of the front door.

"Are you really sure you won't come too, Fletcher, old friend?" says he. "I'd truly appreciate your good advice on my guns."

"No, thank'ee, Cooper," says I, "my wound is aching again and I think I'll rest this morning." I winked at Lucinda as he went out. I certainly didn't want to go over his precious ship with him again. On the contrary, I was hoping to go over Lucinda. But I had no luck there. The house was full of servants, and she said Cooper might be back at any time. She was right too. She'd worked for him for two years and she knew his moods.

Cooper was so exulted with his commission and his wonderful ship that he flew into a passion of activity and once he'd lit fires under the backsides of the dock-yard staff and *Declaration*'s standing officers, he organised

a dinner that very evening for the cream of Boston
Society. The one thing I did respect in Cooper, was his
energy. For when he had an objective in mind he went
after it like a greyhound and worried it like a bulldog.

Early in the afternoon he was back in the house and
had his servants running messages to the great and the
good of Boston. He even had *me* at work. I was given
a list of names and pen and paper, and charged with
drawing up the invitations. The cheek of it! He made
me feel like a clerk again. But there was no saying no to
him, 'cos he was too busy to do it himself, and none of
the servants (even Lucinda) could read or write, they
being Southern Blacks, up from the plantations.

He had a good sense of detail too. I suppose I have
to concede that. I was invited, of course – how could
he show to best advantage without his principal hunting
trophy?

But I had no evening clothes, so he lent me an old
outfit of his father's: a Frenchified suit of maroon-striped
silk. But I can't wear clothes made for you ordinary folk
with your little thin legs and your narrow chests. Lucinda
did her best, letting out the old man's coat, but I looked
ridiculous and stitches popped every time I moved.

That evening we gathered in the big, oval dining room
which was a feature of the better Boston houses, and
was no doubt intended as an imitation of the best English
design.

[Not so. The oval dining room was the original Bostonian

invention of Mr Bullfinch the architect whom Fletcher met on this very occasion. S.P.]

It was a fine display of local rank, and was by far the most exalted company I'd ever sat down with in all my twenty years. I was up near Cooper's end of the table with an architect called Bullfinch on one side of me and Cooper's aunt Gabrielle on the other. The table was enormous (vulgar, if you ask me) and what with all the noise and toasting was too wide to talk across. It was boiling hot, and I sweated like a pig. The food was excellent and the wine plentiful and I as nearly got drunk as ever I have. Normally I go careful with the drink 'cos I detest a thick head, but I was feeling sorry for myself again.

The trouble was, Cooper – who'd really let himself go with the wine – couldn't help using me as a but for his tall tales. I'd have thought that by now Boston was fed up with the account of the capture of *Bednal Green*, but no, it got another airing, and all the company smiled upon him. The ladies simpered, and fluttered their fans, and the gentlemen growled and emptied their glasses.

"So we came alongside of Lieutenant Fletcher's command," says he, to enwrapped silence, "and the brave Lieutenant, the victor of great battles in the present European war [I got some admiring looks for that one, and Cooper's aunt who must have been over forty but wasn't half bad-looking an old bird, patted my hand in sympathy. I could have had that one in ten minutes given a quiet corner], the brave Lieutenant himself directed a shattering broadside into my own poor ship. But notwithstanding the heavy damage caused, and the loss of American lives, I . . . etc., etc."

That was Cooper, you see. Not what you'd call a bad man. He wasn't mean or cruel or brutal. But he was so damn obsessed with climbing the ladder that he'd swallowed his own lies (it *was him* that wrote that article for the Washington newspaper, incidentally). I think he probably believed by now that he'd won a real ship-to-ship action. Anyway, it stuck in my craw. I could easily have stood up and denounced him, but I didn't; the swab could doubtless put me back in prison as quick as he'd got me out. But that didn't stop me feeling fed up to the back teeth with him. Him and his charity and his father's suit that didn't fit me. I was raised on charity and had hoped never to need it again.

So he blathered on, and the courses came and went, and the covers were lifted and the ladies withdrew. That was the signal for the gentlemen to close ranks to fill the vacant places, which put Cooper's uncle Ezekiah next to me. He was a decent old stick, a man in his fifties, wearing a powdered wig and a respectable suit of black brocade. He reminded me strongly of Mr Nathan Pendennis, who'd been my employer when I was counting-house clerk in Polmouth. I took to him from the first words he spoke.

"Well, young man," says he, easing himself into the

chair vacated by his wife, "that was some drubbing you took from my nephew!" He smiled at me and reached for the port. "Least-ways, it *was* the way he tells it!"

Then he smote the table with the flat of his hand and called for silence. He was obviously a man of some importance, and much respected among those round the table.

"Gentlemen," says he, "and loyal Bostonians all. We've had some sport this evening at the expense of the British, which is a good thing to do now we're at war with them again." He looked around the table and nodded at the other men of his generation. "Now some of us here, why, we fought against the British in times past. And some of you were beside me at Bunkers Hill at the birth of our nation."

The room had gone utterly still, and they were hanging on his words. Even Cooper was, for this man was talking about things deeper and more sacred to the American mind than some little skirmish at sea. "And gentlemen," says Ezekiah Cooper, "although I wished 'em ruin, and I gave 'em fire from my musket, I know that I shall never again, so long as I live, see any sight to compare with the massed Grenadiers of the British Regiments coming up Bunkers Hill to the sound of the fife and drum. So I give you the toast," says he: "The British Grenadiers!"

Well, that was oratory for you. Every man raised his glass. Some of the older ones had tears in their eyes as they remembered their lost youth. And as for me, I was drawn into their conversation in a way that I'd not been before, which I truly believe was Ezekiah's intention in saying what he did. He turned me from being a tame bear into the representative of an honourable enemy, from a figure of fun to a man with a man's dignity. It was a kindly act, done out of sympathy for a stranger (so I thought, at least). But it brought me more harm than good in the long run, for it greased the slide beneath me that ran me into danger.

For the conversation, at this stage of the evening, turned to trade. These men around the table were the power-holders of their city. What's more, they were representative of the great men of their land, the men who sat in Congress and the Senate, and held sway. But they talked about trade. They talked of trade, and manufacturing and enterprise and business. It was wonderful. Here were men who held the same place in American society as the Noble Lords and Dukes and Earls held in our own. But they spoke of trade, which no British nobleman dirtied his hands with. Furthermore, some of these Boston Merchant Princes had been born poor. They'd made their way by their own work *and nobody thought the less of them for it.* Can you see what this meant to a man like me? A man born poor and orphaned, whose greatest interest in life was . . . trade?

Some powerfully strange and conflicting thoughts were stirring in my mind, when I noticed the most fascinating conversation was under way at my left elbow. Ezekiah

Cooper and another merchant, a man called Blair, were laughingly trying to make some sort of calculation upon the table, with their fingertips dipped in wine. One or two others were leaning across, following the action. All of them were a little the worse for drink or they'd surely have worked out the thing for themselves. I listened a bit and then stuck my oar in.

"No, no!" says Blair. "My son was to go to Canton, as supercargo, and he was to sell the furs that they'd taken on from the north-west coast."

"Ah," says Ezekiah, "but how would he deal with the Chinese? They offer a mixture of coin from a dozen countries. Moidores, talers, Spanish dollars and English sovereigns. You or I could keep account, but he couldn't."

"Yes, of course," said Blair, in a slurred voice, trying to draw pictures on the polished table-top. "That's just my point. I knew the boy couldn't reckon in different monies, so I told him this," and he tapped the table solemnly in emphasis. "I told my boy to weigh the gold, and I gave him the scales and all to do it with. He was to bring back gold to the value of 4,000 United States dollars. That's 18 pounds 9 ounces, sir!"

"Of course," says Ezekiah, "it's easier simply to weigh out the coin. That way there's no need to . . ."

"But!" says Blair, "yesterday my son comes home. And happy I am to see him, after nearly two years away, but what does he tell me? The rascal tells me that he got his weights and scales stolen and so had to borrow from the Captain of the ship."

"Borrow what?" says Ezekiah, losing the thread of the story.

"Weights and scales, sir!" says Blair impatiently. "Weights and scales. D'ye see?"

"No, sir," said Ezekiah, "I do not."

"Bah!" says Blair, exasperated with his slowness to comprehend. "I gave the wretch jewellers' weights to measure the gold. *jewellers'* weights! And he used some damned ordinary weights and scales of avoirdupois measure. He sold the furs for 17 pounds 8 ounces avoirdupois."

"Ah!" said Ezekiah, understanding at last, and the whole table laughed as he summarised Blair's predicament. "So you don't know whether you've turned a profit or a loss?"

"No, sir, I do not!" says Blair, glaring at the smiling faces. "Not till I get into my office tomorrow and have my clerks calculate the matter."

And this is where I joined in. As you know well, these sorts of dealings are meat and drink to me, and it is my great pride and satisfaction that I'm so good at it. So I was only too ready to butt in and show these Yankees what I can do.

"No need to wait for morning, sir," says I. "The thing don't sound so difficult."

"Indeed, sir?" says Ezekiah, and they all looked at me

to see what I would do next. There were some tolerant smiles and some muttering from Cooper and his immediate cronies. But I didn't mind that in the least. I was about to perform on home ground.

"Indeed not," says I. "Mr Blair's son sold his furs for seventeen and a half pounds of gold, avoirdupois measure, and Mr Blair needs 4,000 U.S. dollars for a profit. Is that correct, sir?" says I to Blair.

"Yes, Mr Fletcher," says Blair.

"Well, sir," says I, drawing on my years of experience as a counting-house clerk, "to begin with, let's distinguish jewellers' weight, that is *troy* weight, from avoirdupois. One pound troy contains 5,760 grains, while one pound avoirdupois contains 7,000 grains . . . as everybody knows," says I, looking round. The smiles were gone and the muttering had stopped. Ezekiah laughed. The rest looked on with new respect. "That's better, you swabs!" thinks I to myself, and continued, "Now I presume, Mr Blair, your calculation that 4,000 dollars equals 18 pounds 9 ounces, bases upon the Act of Congress of 3rd April 1792, establishing that one dollar shall contain 27 grains of fine gold." (You'll remember I'd read that in the book of pamphlets in Cooper's library, and I don't have the least problem in remembering facts of that kind.) "That, and the fact that you would naturally have sought to measure your gold in troy weight, which divides the pound into 12 ounces."

"Ah! Hmm!" says Blair and you could have heard a pin drop for the rest of my little lecture.

"So," says I, and calculated the,rest of the thing in my head, which is child's play for me, "assuming you have 17 pounds 8 ounces of gold, avoirdupois. With 7,000 grains per pound, that gives you 122,500 grains of gold. And that, at a rate of 27 grains to the dollar, gives you 4,537 dollars and four cents . . . approximately, Mr Blair."

Ezekiah and some of the others laughed, but Blair still looked blank, trying to catch up. But I wasn't done yet. These Yankees might have thought themselves businessmen, but I was out to make a demonstration.

"But that, gentlemen," says I, to the table at large, "assumes we are dealing with pure gold. Mr Blair," I asked, "in what coin did your gold come?"

"Mainly British and Portuguese," says Blair, "with some French."

"Good," says I, really showing off now, "turning again to Congress's Act of April '92. The Act allows for the fact that different levels of purity, or 'fine-ness' are found in foreign gold. Thus 27 grains of British or Portuguese gold shall equal one dollar, but 27 and two-fifths of French gold shall be needed as it is less fine. So, Mr Blair," says I, "even if all your gold were French, its value would reduce only in the ratio that 27 stands to 27 and two-fifths, say 135/137 times 4,537 . . . that represents 4,470 dollars, and I congratulate you on a healthy profit!"

There was a moment's silence then a roar of laughter from Ezekiah Cooper. He laughed till his face was beetroot red and he slapped me on the back and called me a damn fine fellow. He laughed so much that the others joined in (even those who were thinking I was too damned clever by half, and a smart-assed Limey to boot) and it was smiles and applause all up and down the table. And, to be fair to a man I never liked, Cooper himself joined in and his cronies with him.

"Come and see me tomorrow, Mr Fletcher," says Ezekiah. "Come to my office in King Street. I can use a man like you."

"Hallo," thinks I to myself, "this looks promising." For Uncle Ezekiah was one of the great men of the town, and fully as important in Boston as my old employer Pendennis was in Polmouth. I hardly dared to guess what might be in this for me. But happy speculation kept my mind occupied for the rest of the evening, until the company were taken off in their carriages in the small hours of the morning. I went to bed merry with expectation and tried to keep awake for a while in the hope that Lucinda would tap on my door. But she didn't and the next thing I knew it was morning.

I saw Cooper at breakfast and raised the subject of his uncle's offer, while Lucinda swanned about with a coffee-pot and her nose in the air.

"Of course, it would mean my going forth unaccompanied . . ." says I, looking closely at Cooper. That was something I'd not yet done and I supposed that he had the right to object, what with my being an enemy officer, parolled into his charge. But he grinned like a monkey and waved this away.

"Darn it, Fletcher," says he, "haven't I your word as a gentleman not to run? And anyways, I've begun to think of you as one of the family." He turned to Lucinda, "Isn't that right, Lucinda?" says he.

"Yezzah," says she pouting at me over his shoulder where he couldn't see. She ran the tip of her tongue slowly round her lips. Then froze her face into immobility as he looked up at her. She nodded politely and he turned back to me.

"Just you cut along to King Street, Fletcher, old fellow," says he. "Anyone'll tell you where my uncle's office is to be found." Then he grinned again, all pleased with himself for some reason or other.

I could see that something was afoot and I'm sure he wanted me to ask him what it was. But the man irritated me with his pomposity and posturing, not to mention his robbing me on the high seas. So I kept quiet.

Half an hour later I was walking through the streets of Boston in my Sunday best. Lucinda had found me a decent black coat that fitted (more or less) and with a round hat, clean shirt and stock, new breeches and a pair of top boots, I was quite the gentleman. In fact I'd never been togged up so smart in my life. I'd been an inky clerk and a Jack Tar, but never a man of fashion. What's more, I found that I was a celebrity. The ladies smiled and the gents tipped their hats.

It was all due to Cooper and his big mouth. Boston society was a small world in those days. They all knew one another, and Cooper had plastered them with his tall tales. These, of course, had included puffing up my reputation to enhance his own. And *I'm* too big to hide in a crowd. So when the smart set clapped eyes on me, they nudged one another and pointed me out. Not all of them were friendly, and I got some hard stares from the King-damning Republicanites, but Americans are generous and hospitable folk as a rule so mostly I got smiles. Especially from the ladies, and it went to my head, I can tell you.

So I swaggered about, saluting my public and asking directions for the fun of being recognised and to hear them babble on about Boston, which they were fearfully proud of and childishly eager to show off to a stranger.

"You're BriDish, ain't you, sir?" says an elderly merchant with his fat wife goggling at me. "Would you, by chance, be Mr Cooper's English Lieutenant?"

"Oh, do be sure and see our fine bridges," says a dear little blondie, out shopping with a footman in tow and her sister giggling on her arm. The one sixteen, the other fifteen, I'd guess. Plump and dimpled, with snub noses like pink little piggies. I could've eaten the pair of 'em. "Why," says she, without pausing for breath, "the Charles River bridge cost 50,000 dollars and is fifteen hundred feet long, with seventy-five oak piers, while the new West Boston bridge, opened last November, and one of the wonders of the world, runs three-and-a-half thousand feet and cost 100,000 dollars . . ." By George but American women can talk!

"The builders' works for the new State House, sir!" says a Dragoon officer in a leather helmet and a sabre at his side. "You must see that! A noble edifice to rival anything in Europe. The dome is to be plated in pure gold!"

The fact was that Boston in 1794 was turning itself inside out with new building, with rebuilding and with improvements. They were even digging out the hills to throw them into the bays to make more land! It was an exciting time in an exciting place: like enough to England to make an Englishman feel at home, but different too. And different in ways I approved of. It was a city wide open to business, trade and enterprise – the natural avenues of my talents and inclinations. The buzz and hum of trade in the area around Exchange Street and Market Square fairly made my pulses race. There were banks, insurance houses and companies of all kinds lined up like guardsmen in close order. It was heaven.

Uncle Ezekiah's offices occupied most of a brick-built edifice of five storeys with long, round-topped windows and fluted stone columns between. It stood on the corner of Exchange and State Streets, near the Long Wharf. It was brand spanking new, and there was a huge black doorman outside, dressed in a green livery-coat and bicorne hat with tassels at the corners and ostrich plumes sprouting from the top. It was a damn close thing what looked more ridiculous: him or a General of the Frog Army. He saluted, smartly as I advanced, and threw open the doors. I could see from the look on him that he expected half-a-crown for this, at the least. But it was the General's unlucky day, for I had no money.

Inside, I caught the eye of a little bald-headed chap who occupied a glazed porter's lodge which gave him a commanding view of the approaches. He had a livery coat just like the General's, but no hat. He stood up as I entered.

"Mr Fletcher?" says he, peering through his spectacles. "Yes," says I, by now used to being recognised.

"You are expected, sir," says he, and paused before adding the final word in tones of awe, ". . . Upstairs!"

"Upstairs?" says I.

"Upstairs," says he. "If you would follow me, sir?" So off we went, past lines of clerks and ledgers, lines of ink-pots and high desks. It was like coming home. And onward, up the stairs to the first floor. Onward through ante-chambers staffed by increasingly senior minions, even unto the very door of the big, front-centre office, where Uncle Ezekiah was waiting with a smile like the sunshine.

"Mr Fletcher!" says he, seizing my hand. "Come in, sir! Come in! Will you take port or brandy?"

The door closed behind me, the sunlight beamed through the tall windows to glow upon the polish of

Ezekiah's desk. A thick Turkish carpet was under my boots and silver and brass ornaments twinkled all around. The room oozed wealth and family portraits lined the walls. It was more like a nobleman's library than an office, but that's Yankees for you. It was all too good to be true, and I should have been on my guard. But I was too overwhelmed with the joy of it.

Ezekiah sat me down, and he grinned, and he said what fun we'd had last night, and he said he'd an offer to make me.

"And all the more willingly now that I know you have a head for business, Mr Fletcher!" says he. Actual tears came to my eyes at that, for here was one of the great men of this great trading city, about to make me a business offer. Here, I thought, was the chance to make right the hideous warping of my life that I'd suffered since those God-damned Coignwoods had shanghaied me into the Navy. Just give me any foothold in Boston trade, I thought, and I'll forge ahead like a clipper ship in a gale of wind. In short, it'll be taking up the life I'd always wanted.

Chapter 11

. . . but the singularist thing, my dear Lucy, was a
gentleman and his wife that sat opposite us in the Mail
up from London. I know so little of these things that only
when my dear husband explained, did I understand what
my eyes had seen.

(From a letter of 21st September 1793 to Mrs
Lucy Gardiner, from her sister-in-law Ruth,
staying with friends at 98 High Street,
Lonborough.)

*

Exactly as the clock of St Luke's struck three, the London
Mail turned into the George Inn at Lonborough. The
three "outsides" ducked their heads in fright as they
passed under the low archway and through the short,

dark tunnel that led into the courtyard. The clatter and thunder of four iron-tyred wheels and sixteen hooves bounded up and back from the cobbles below and the brick walls to either side.

"Whoooa!" cried the driver, hauling on the reins, and the huge, high vehicle, with its stamping steeds, shining brass, chocolate livery and gleaming Royal Crest; with its scarlet-uniformed crew, its packed bundles of luggage and its seven tired passengers, rolled to a stop. Ostlers ran from all sides to minister to the needs of beast and machine where they stood in their splendour: the last word in long-range overland travel, according to the very latest designs.

"The George Inn!" bawled the driver for the benefit of the world at large, and he threw off his driving apron and climbed down in swaggering satisfaction. For here was man conscious of his elite place in an elite service. A man in command of a vehicle that had averaged eleven miles in the hour, with twenty-three changes of horses, to arrive slap-bang on time, at the end of the ten-score miles between here and the courtyard of the Swan Inn, Lad Lane, London.

A crowd of domestics from the George stood by to receive the passengers and to see the Mail come in. Sedentary provincials that they were they gazed in wonderment at the god-like, far-travelled figure of the driver as he took a draught from the pot of strong ale held out by one of the maids (a favourite task for the

George's girls). He winked at her and chatted to his guard in the racy coaching patois that even gentlemen affected when they wanted to be thought sporting bloods.

One such gentleman, an inside passenger, was even then dismounting, and turning back to help down his lady: a tall, slim creature, heavily pregnant and wrapped in a cape with an enveloping hood. Having seen her safely into the charge of a maid, and asked after his luggage, he approached the driver.

"Smart whipping, cully!" said he, with a patronising smile. "A bang-up rig and a spanking set of prancers."

The driver and his guard exchanged glances. They were used to gentlemen who fancied themselves as whips and who felt free to pass judgement on their betters. And this gentleman was not quite a gentleman either. More of a flash cove. A youngster in his early twenties, strongly built and good-looking in a coarse fashion, with curly yellow hair and over-dressed in expensive clothes.

But the gentleman's hand was outstretched and it glinted with gold. The driver's reaction was instinctive and the coin sped to his pocket.

"Your health, Captain!" said he and raised his tankard in salute.

The young man grinned, flashing a set of big white teeth. He raised his hat in return. Then he led his lady inside and called loudly for a private room, since her condition forbade that she should bear a press of people. Liberally pressing coins into the hands of all comers, he elbowed his way before the other passengers. "And mind it's a ground floor room," says he, "and one with a good window on a quiet prospect." Thanks to his generosity, the staff took to him at once, and soon he found himself and his lady in a snug bedroom, with a low, latticed window looking out on the green-hedged lane that ran behind the George.

"Now then, m'lad!" said he, to the elderly servant who'd struggled in with his baggage. "A quart of ale for me, sherry for madame, and a double helping of beef, bread and pickles and a pint of shrimps to go with 'em! Quick-sharp, my boy!" Yet another shilling changed hands and the "boy" sped off, closing the door behind him.

The young man turned to his lady, who was examining the window with much interest. He stepped over to her, took her in his arms and kissed her with a lingering ferocity that was entirely unfitting behaviour towards a lady who looked to be in her eighth month.

But the lady sighed with pleasure and returned his advances with an ardour greater than his own, which was not in the least surprising, since the lady was Mr Victor Coignwood who was not in the least pregnant, despite his innumerable encounters with gentlemen who'd done to him every imaginable thing (and some unimaginable) that might have got him into that condition. And so, sadly, the fruit of these many labours was no more than a pair of cushions tied under Victor's gown to add credence to his favourite disguise.

"Impetuous boy," simpered Victor, "but leave me be, dear Arthur, for the servant will soon return." He took off his bonnet and sat himself before the mirror of the dressing table, preening himself and rearranging his wig.

"You're an odd one, you are!" said Mr Arthur Walton. "I've met one or two of your breed, but none that does it so well as you, Victor."

"Why don't you look to our bags, dear husband?" said Victor. "Just to see that all is well."

"Dear husband," mocked Walton. But he went immediately to a small, heavy leather bag with a pair of handles and an iron lock. He produced a key and opened it.

"All safe," said he, looking inside.

"Good," said Victor. "So all's well."

"Huh!" said Walton. "So you say. What if they hadn't got a ground-floor room, eh?"

"But they had one, didn't they?"

"Aye, and what if they didn't . . . ?"

"Oh don't be a bore, Arthur!" cried Victor.

"And don't you play no tricks!" said Walton. He smiled, but there was menace in his voice.

Victor looked at the handsome face and the broad shoulders and shuddered inwardly with an unholy thrill. Victor was addicted to young men like Arthur Walton precisely because they could be dangerous.

But there was no more conversation for a while because a knock at the door announced the arrival of food and drink.

Later, Walton went out. He told the servants not to disturb his wife as she was sleeping, and he made a tour around Lonborough. He paced the length of Market Street, paying careful attention to the instructions he had received from Victor. He found No. 38 Market Street and he noted the building works opposite, where the Phoenix Insurance Company's money was paying to replace the houses lost in the big fire of 19th July.

Walton carefully observed every aspect of the street and its buildings, he even noted the blistered paint on the heavy front door of No. 38, caused by the intense heat of the fire on the other side of the street. The fire that had reduced Nos. 35 to 41 to smouldering ashes. In short, he made the thorough and careful inspection that, in the specialist terminology of his trade, was known as "casing the crib".

However, if Mr Arthur Walton had known precisely who it was that had started the fire, the effects of which were so apparent, and had he known what the fire was intended to hide, he would have been ten times as careful.

When he had gazed his fill at Market Street, Walton made his way back to the George, where his client was waiting in a state of eager anticipation.

"Well?" said Victor.

"Easy!" said Walton. "The front's like the Tower of London, but the back door's thin wood. And it's in a little yard with high walls and not a lamp in sight. Once we're in there we can take our time."

"Good," said Victor. And quite unable to contain his eagerness for what he was going to do, he added, "Then shall we do it tonight?"

"Tonight, old fellow?" said Walton, baring his teeth in a savage grin. "Now wouldn't that be a circumstance, eh?" said he, looking closely into Victor's eyes. "For didn't you, tell me the gold'd not be in the house till the 23rd? And today's only the 21st."

Victor bit his lip. He'd made a nasty slip. Victor knew plenty of young men who were prepared to be obliging for the right price, and some of them lived in the grey shadowland beyond the law. But only Arthur had the skill of slipping through locked doors and windows that was vital to the operation that his mother had entrusted to Victor. Unfortunately, along with this indispensable qualification (and the blue eyes and golden curls that made Victor sink at the knees) Arthur Walton was brutal, sharp and trusted nobody. Victor searched for a way out.

"Dear boy!" said he, and forced a smile. "What a silly little thing I am! It's just that I'm so eager to begin. All this is new to me, remember." It was the best excuse Victor could invent. It was not very good, and didn't work.

"Victor," said Walton, "you're a twisting little rat, and I don't know what it is you're after in that house, but I'll be surprised if it's gold!" He gave his wolf's-head grin again. "But I don't really care. All I care about is you paying what you owe at the end of this, 'cos I'll slice the prick off you and make you eat it if you play me false!"

"Would you do that?" said Victor, round-eyed with horror. "To me?" Walton laughed, pleased with himself at putting Victor Coignwood in his place. But Victor was smiling inwardly. He was play-acting. He didn't care what young Arthur believed just so long as he got the two of them into 38 Market Street where Mr Taylor lived with his wife and their infant son.

So Victor retrieved his mistake as best he could and agreed that he and Arthur would, of course, spend two more days at the George, until the 23rd, when Taylor would take delivery of the money (he said). He comforted himself with the thought that it meant two more days alone with Arthur.

Two days later, after midnight, the two men quietly left the George by the window in their room. Both wore dark clothes and kept to the shadows. Fortunately, shadows were plentiful, as the few lamps employed to light the streets of Lonborough in those days gave little illumination.

Five minutes' walking brought them to the entrance to the yard behind No. 38. It was almost pitch black but Arthur was prepared for that, and found the entry by counting his paces.

"Lamp," said Arthur, softly in Victor's ear. Victor slightly opened the blind on the hot, stinking lantern he had brought with him. In the feeble cone of yellow light,

Arthur considered the lock on the gate leading into the yard. He sneered with contempt and produced a tool from his bag. The lock yielded in seconds and they were in the yard.

Inside the yard, Victor's excitement became so intense that his hands shook and he felt a ridiculous desire to giggle. He smothered this as Walton ran his fingers over the back door, feeling for the best place of attack.

Methodically, Walton drove a centre bit into the woodwork, attached a handle to it and turned the iron steadily. Victor was horrified at the noise of this procedure, which to his ears was like the grumbling of a millstone grinding corn. But Walton pressed on unconcerned, and soon removed a neat disc of wood from the door. Punctiliously, he dismounted his tool, replaced it in his bag and reached his hand in through the hole. After an instant's fumbling, Victor heard the click of a lock and Arthur drew out the key.

"Stupid bastard's left it in the lock on the inside!" whispered Walton, and shook his head. But the door was still fast and two more discs had to be removed to enable Walton to slide the top and bottom bolts. And then they were in.

Victor opened the blind of the lantern fully to examine the room they'd entered. It was a kitchen and the embers of the fire glowed faintly in the grate behind the night guard.

"Where's the cellar?" whispered Walton, and Victor

pointed to the door leading from the kitchen to he knew not where. Walton led the way but as he reached for the door handle, Victor called softly.

"Psst!" said he. "Arthur! Look!"

"Uh?" said Walton and saw Victor examining something. He was kneeling, with the lantern beside him, fumbling at one of the stone flags that formed the floor.

"I was wrong!" whispered Victor. "It's here!" Walton joined him, and for the first time began to believe what Victor had told him about the gold in Taylor's cellar. Walton knelt beside Victor and peered at the floor.

"Get that one up!" said Victor, pointing. "We need a lever – I'll get the poker." He stood up and fetched the poker from the fire. It was three feet long, thick in the shaft and with a heavy, unworn bulge at the business end. Walton was still peering at the floor when Victor swung the ponderous iron rod with all his might. This was an improvisation. Victor had a razor-sharp knife in his pocket, but he thought that the poker would be better.

THUMP! Regrettably, the blow did not quite land true. The light was bad and Victor over-excited. Instead of the skull-smashing stroke he'd intended, the weapon fell partly across Walton's shoulder.

But Walton slumped over, taking the lantern with him and plunging the room into black dark. Victor stood shaking with an exalted delight. His fingers were in his mouth and his breathing short and shallow. He blinked in the darkness and took out a large Spanish clasp-knife, which his trembling fingers opened with an oily snick. He took the knife in his right hand and, blind in the intense darkness, flapped his left hand about on the floor, searching for Arthur's body. At first he couldn't find it, but then all was well and his hand was sliding up Arthur's arm, to the shoulder, to the coat collar, to the shirt, and then fumbling into the soft, warm throat with its pulsing veins.

Victor's teeth chattered with fascination and he brought the blade to the tips of his fingers to cut the life from Walton. The edge would shave hairs from the back of Victor's hand; he'd sharpened it with extreme care. He pressed to make sure of the pulse and sliced with his knife. But he wasn't quite master of himself and took the tip off his own middle finger, right through the nail.

"Ahhh!" he gasped, and in his pain and anger struck at the unseen body again and again, with the point of his knife. Then he sat back on his haunches panting and sweating. Blood flowed steadily from his finger but he was in an uncanny state of mind and hardly noticed it. Striking down Walton had been a pleasure, but that was as nothing compared to what came next.

Somewhere upstairs asleep, unknowing and at his mercy were the Taylors and their child, and a couple of housemaids. Victor understood that Mr and Mrs Taylor must die, for his mother had explained the need.

The Taylors had seen Victor emerge from 39 Market

Street on the night in July when he'd murdered Mr Andrew Potter (Solicitor's Clerk), Mr Richard Lucey (Solicitor) and half blinded his son Edward before starting the biggest fire in Lonborough's history. Thus rational need condemned the Taylors. But much, much more than that was the enjoyment of the act itself.

Victor found his way to the door, opened it and was pleased to find that moonlight, entering from the fanlight over the front door, lit the hallway outside. A thin light, but far better than the stygian gloom of the kitchen. Knife in hand, Victor glided forward and passed up the stairs in search of the family.

On the first floor, three doors opened from the landing. Soft as a vampire, Victor opened the first door and looked inside. The room was unoccupied. A table, some chairs and boxes of books were all its furniture. But the next door gave on to what he was looking for and he entered the bedroom like the foul smell of some unclean thing. He ran his eyes over his victims and experienced all the sensations of sexual arousal as his deepest fantasies were made flesh. He stared and stared and stared and imagined the thing done one way after another.

Man and wife slept peacefully in the big bed while the child occupied a cradle to one side. Taylor's head was thrown back and he was snoring, with his neck ready for one swift stroke of Victor's knife. The man would be first, Victor thought as the greatest threat should he wake. The wife had on a night-cap and was curled forward with her head half under the bedclothes and half buried in the frilled collar of her nightdress. She would need to be helped free of this impedimenta. The child was invisible under its mound of wrappings, and playthings were scattered on the tiny bed. But no matter. Victor could winkle it out and take pleasure in the deed at leisure, once the parents were despatched.

"So," he thought, "Mr Taylor . . ."

But in that instant of supreme delight, even as Victor drew back his hand for the first cut, a noise faintly behind him caught his ear and Victor screamed aloud with fright.

Blood-smeared and horrible, lips curled in bestial hatred, Arthur Walton stood swaying in the doorway. With his left hand he clutched the doorpost in a desperate grip to keep himself upright. Blood glistened in a growing pool at his feet, and ran a trail all the way back to the kitchen. But he held a pistol in his right hand.

"Bastard!" said he and the pistol flashed and roared.

And the room burst into life. The Taylor family awoke as one. The baby screamed instantly, Mrs Taylor screamed a heart-beat later. Mr Taylor roared in terror and grabbed his spectacles from the bedside table before even thinking of the second important object that he kept beside him at night.

Meanwhile, Walton's pistol-ball, aimed with a shaking hand, sped across the room, missed Victor by a yard, punched a neat hole in the floral wallpaper and buried itself in the lath-and-plaster work of the wall. Victor's very hair stood on end at the shock and dismay of the moment, but the poisonous, spiteful core of his being took hold and he leapt at Walton with his knife raised. Had Walton been fit, such an assault would have been suicide for Victor, but Victor's knife had punctured lungs and opened veins and a desperate struggle took place at the foot of the Taylors' bed, even as those unfortunate people struggled to understand what was happening.

But since last July, and the dreadful fire, Mr Taylor had taken certain precautions. Since that fell night when a good neighbour had been murdered and Mr Taylor had seen the murderer come away from his aweful crime, Mr Taylor had reasoned that what had happened across the street could happen here in his own house. Consequently, Mr Taylor had purcaased a large, four-bore, brass-barrelled blunderbuss by Waters & Co. of Birmingham, which instrument was kept primed and loaded at his bedside every night.

The word "blunderbuss" falls quaint upon the ear, and the stumpy, bell-mouthed barrel looks odd beside a musket or a rifle. But the weapon is exceedingly formid-able. Mr Taylor's was a full inch wide inside the barrel. It was charged with three drachms of powder and a nice round dozen of pistol balls, every one of which measured half an inch in diameter and was perfectly capable of killing a man all by itself.

This, then, was the firearm which Mr Taylor levelled

and discharged at the two intruders who obligingly presented themselves as perfect targets for his aim.

Boom! The bellow of the short-barrelled weapon awoke the street. The muzzle-flash turned night into day and singed the bedclothes. Glowing scraps of wadding smouldered all around and rolling smoke filled the room, while the recoil left a deep and livid bruise on Mr Taylor's shoulder.

But the consequences down-range were immeasurably more severe. Mr Arthur Walton received the bulk of the charge and expired on the spot with his upper torso torn to ragged flesh. In addition one ball had broken the great blood vessels of his neck and a couple more, travelling in company, had gone in through one of Mr Walton's pretty blue eyes and out through the back of his head, taking with them large quantities of vital tissue.

For his part, Mr Victor Coignwood was hit three times. One ball removed the middle finger of his right hand, and a second sped glancingly across his chest, ploughing a blood-filled furrow. Both these missiles continued on their way to their terminus inside Mr Walton. But the third ball took refuge in the meat of Victor's right forearm, having passed between the bones without incident. And so, Victor hopped from one foot to another blaspheming in the most foul manner and howling in pain and in fright.

From this agonising condition, Victor was soon delivered. For Mr Taylor arose from his bed in the terrible anger that consumes any man who fights in the immediate defence of the immeasurably precious lives of his lady and his infant son. Swinging the empty firearm by its butt, Mr Taylor smashed Victor senseless with one enormous blow of its smoking barrel.

Chapter 12

TO THE READER – A WARNING.

The grossly improper substance of certain parts of this chapter are such that even the meretricious subordination properly due from an employee to his employer must take second place to the moral duty of one who aspires to Christian standards. The transcriber therefore warns that this chapter should not be attempted except by gentlemen of mature discernment and that ladies should omit it altogether. The transcriber further protests that only the most terrifying threats from the author compelled him to set it down at all. S.P.

*

Uncle Ezekiah took his own good time in getting round to his offer. First he told me all about the iniquitous state of European politics and pitched into the Frogs something powerful. He even had papers to prove it.

"Here is the official French Gazette, sir, fresh arrived in Boston: the *Moniteur* of 4th February." He shoved it at me and jabbed with his finger. "See here, sir, the National Convention of the French Republic has passed a law proclaiming that all French naval captains who surrender their ships, shall suffer death by the guillotine!"

"Shocking!" says I, staring at the page of heathen Froggy gibberish as if I could read it. It could have been a recipe for octopus-bollock pie for all I knew (and probably was, knowing the French).

"Indeed, sir!" says he. "Contrary to all the civilised usages of war. And what's more . . ."

He hammered his point till I was bored silly. I hated the Frogs before he started, as you well know, so he could have saved his breath. Then he went on to say that because of all this then, as he put it, "The long-term interests of the United States are pitched contrariwise against the French. D'ye see that, Mr Fletcher?"

"Oh yes!" says I, all serious and solemn. They could pitch themselves against the Slave Coast Mandinkas for all I cared. "Good!" says he. "Now let's turn to the matter of trade."

"Ah-ha!" thinks I, and sat up straight.

"Cotton, sugar and tobacco," says he, "are nine parts in ten of my trade, by value. Did you realise, Mr Fletcher, the importance of London and Bristol as markets in those commodities?"

I didn't. Not for Yankees, anyway, but he obviously thought so, so I nodded.

"The long and short of it is, Mr Fletcher," says he, leaning close and dropping his voice, "this war between us and the British . . . it can't last, believe me . . ."

"Oh?" says I. "What about the French fleet you're filling with wheat down in Virginia? Wouldn't you Yankees like to sell more next year?"

"Bah!" said he. "Next year the French might bring in a good harvest and then where'd we be? No, sir! The grain sale is an opportunity of the moment and not to be compared with the links forged by trading in materials your country cannot produce for itself: cotton, sugar and tobacco!"

"Mr Cooper," says I, "I'm interested in what you say, but where is this leading?"

"Mr Fletcher," says he, "where this is leading, is to my nephew's ship, *Declaration of Independence* that will sail, very soon now, from Edmund Hart's yard. She will be the first man-o'-war to hoist our country's flag since the Revolution. But she's an expedient, sir! A foreign ship made over to our service while all Boston waits for the confirmation that a *real* American ship, *Constitution*, shall be built here in Boston – built, sir! From the keel up!" He looked at me with the dollars shining in his eyes, and continued, "Now, some of us Bostonians have been trying to persuade our government to purchase Hart's yard and adopt it as an official yard of the United States Navy."

He licked his lips. "If they did that, sir, then enormous sums of money would flow into this city . . . And Hart and his backers would prosper greatly."

"I see," says I. Obviously one of Hart's backers was sitting right in front of me and just itching to get his hands into the U.S. Treasury's moneybags.

"But all this hinges on the success of *Declaration*'s first cruise," says he. "Should she be lost, then our Congress might lose heart and balk at the huge expense of building new ships of war."

He looked at me again much agitated, and clearly exerting all his powers to try to convince me of something. He seemed nervous too, which was surprising.

"Mr Fletcher . . . Jacob," says he, "you're a man of business, are you not? I'm not wrong, am I?"

"You are not wrong, sir," says I, keeping my voice flat, for I felt that soon we would come to the bargaining.

"Jacob," says he, "what would you say if I were to offer you full recompense for your losses in the capture of *Bednal Green*?"

"Oh joy! Oh happy day!" thinks I, and I struggled not to show my feelings as if fighting to rein in a maddened horse. But my reaction was instinctive.

"I'd say that's not near good enough!" says I. "Where's my compensation for my pain and injuries?"

Ezekiah actually seemed relieved at this answer. Even pleased with it, and he leaned back in his chair and grinned at me.

"Jacob, you're the man I thought you were!" says he. "Would five hundred silver dollars ease your pain?" It was too easy. The alarm bells rang in my head. But I played on.

"One thousand," says I. "Not a penny less."

"One thousand," says he, nodding. "One thousand plus full recompense for your losses . . . provided we reach full agreement."

"Have a care!" thinks I. "Here it comes . . ."

"Meaning what, sir?" says I.

"Jacob," says he, "my nephew's ship is fully equipped. She has a fine complement of navigating officers and a volunteer crew of hand-picked New Englanders. But she lacks one thing." He looked at me hard, again. "Can you guess what that thing is, Jacob?"

I shook my head. I was so busy being a man of business that everything else was swept from my mind.

"She lacks an officer with real battle experience. A seasoned naval officer who knows guns and gunnery . . ."

"What?" says I, leaping from my chair. "Not in a thousand years!" The disappointment was bitter. All the time I thought he'd been impressed with my business skill, he'd just wanted me 'cos he thought I was a bloody Lieutenant in the bloody Royal Navy!

It was a hurt to my pride more than anything else.

"Good day to you, sir," says I, and turned to leave.

But Uncle Ezekiah was out of his chair like a shot, and round the desk and grabbing my arm and pulling me back. He'd read the signs all wrong and thought I'd taken his offer as an insult to my honour as a British sea officer. So he blathered on about honour and country and how the war couldn't last and how it would all be love and kisses between King George and President Washington in two shakes of a lamb's tail. You see, he thought he'd made a hash of things and, as folk will on such occasions, he was so anxious to make things right that his tongue ran away with him.

I learned that he and his nephew really believed that I was some sort of gunnery wizard (they'd not only fooled *Boston*, they'd fooled *themselves!*). Well, I'd never denied it, had I? And young Cooper had seen me dismount his bow-chaser with a single shot. More surprising still was the fact that young Cooper stood in great respect of my opinions in all matters of ships and the sea. That was why he'd dragged me round the ship-yard and all over his precious ship – the little swab even had a notebook where he wrote down my comments (God help him). And he wanted me beside him on his quarterdeck when *Declaration* sailed, as some sort of guide and mentor.

The final revelation, and one that brought a blush to my cheeks for the hard opinions I'd had of young Cooper, was the fact that his conscience was pricking him over taking my ship from me. It was he who'd had the idea of recompensing me for my losses.

When I learned that, it sunk through my thick skull that Uncle Ezekiah's offer did in fact contain everything that I wanted. It was just wrapped up a bit fancy. What it amounted to was this: the Cooper family would get me American citizenship papers, and I would serve aboard *Declaration* as Fourth Lieutenant with special responsibility for gunnery.

So all I had to do was agree to this, survive a few months at sea, and I could come back to Boston and pick up the cash – and my life. I raised my hand to interrupt the unabated flow of Ezekiah's eloquence.

"If I were to say yes, Mr Cooper," says I, and his eyes lit up, "it'd be for just one cruise, I take it?"

"Yes! Yes!" says he. "It's only the first cruise that matters. Once the ship's proved herself, all will be well."

And so we shook hands on the matter and we fell to the practicalities. We agreed on a single payment of $5,000, which sum I insisted on receiving in advance. Ezekiah agreed but transferred the cash by a draft payable in three months' time.

"By then, Jacob," says he, laughing, "you'll be sunk or victorious and the matter will be settled." He might have been laughing, but he meant what he said. He was giving me no chance to run off with his money. But I didn't trust him either and I took his draft into a couple of the banks in Exchange Street, and got them to look it over. The way they grovelled at the sight of Ezekiah's signature was very reassuring.

So off I went, dreaming of the days to come. And I left General Doorman happy, for I'd tapped Ezekiah for twenty dollars, ready cash, and so the worthy minion got his piece of silver, after all.

I thought I'd done a good piece of business. If I'd survived our navy on the lower deck, I doubted the Yankee Navy would give me any troubles as an officer. Aside from having to get through the next few months, I was a happy man without a care in the world.

After that, I sauntered around the town a bit, bought some ribbons for Lucinda and toddled back to Tontine Crescent in time for dinner. Cooper was out when I got back and I managed to corner Lucinda to give her my present. She was pleased as Punch.

"What you do a thing like that for?" says she, but she lifted her shoulders, pouted into a mirror and swanned about holding the ribbons against her face.

"Ah-ha!" thinks I, strike while the iron is hot. So I caught her from behind, threw my arms around her and whispered in her ear. "Lucinda," says I softly, "why don't we . . ."

"No," says she, "I got chores to do."

"Ah," says I, "but you don't know what I've got in mind!"

"Huh!" says she in contemptuous dismissal of that. "You be a good boy an' let go, an' maybe I tap on yo' door tonight."

So there were no fun and games just yet. And I had to make do with expectations.

So I had a solitary dinner, served by the butler, and after that I lounged about the library feeling hard done by, and cursing Lucinda, and wondering whether I ought to look for some fun elsewhere.

I'd heard from the men aboard *John Stark* that around Southack Street in west Boston was an area known as Mount Whoredom that was just the ticket for randy sailors. That sounded interesting and I'd decided to look it up when that swab Cooper came in, togged out in uniform and all full of himself. He'd had a grand day chasing *Declaration*'s crew round the decks to get her ready for sea and now he was ready to take his ease. In the careless way of those brought up with servants, he threw his coat and boots in three different directions and flopped into a chair. He was just itching to boast about his day's work, but there was something he wanted to know before he opened fire.

"Well, old fellow?" says he, looking all arch and mysterious. "Did you go to my uncle today?"

"I did," says I, watching his reaction.

"Well?" says he, like a terrier at a rat-hole.

It was amazing how keen he was. Very flattering, in a way. God only knows what he thought I could do for his wretched ship. But I couldn't be bothered to play games.

"I'm your man . . . Captain," says I.

"Hurrah!" says he, in real delight. "I'd come and shake your hand if I wasn't so tired. Good man, Fletcher! If you'd ring for the servant, old fellow, we could have a drink to celebrate. And by the by, you'll have seen that my carronades are mounted with screws at the breech. I was meaning to ask you, what's your opinion on screw elevation as compared with coigns?"

He kept me at it till after midnight, with me looking at the clock every minute and wondering whether Lucinda had given me up as a bad job. Finally, Cooper fell asleep in his blasted chair. It passed through my mind to find something to cover him but I was comprehensively fed up with him by then, so I left him to it and hoped he'd freeze in the night.

Then I went to bed. Just as I'd settled down, and to my great delight, there came a soft tapping at the door. I was up and out of bed in seconds and wrenched the door half off its hinges. I snatched Lucinda off her feet, threw her on to the bed and locked the door behind me. I dragged my nightshirt off, jumped into bed beside her and pulled the covers over us. Eagerly, I seized her and buried my face in her neck, breathing the delicious smell of her and trying to run my hands over her body – which I couldn't, not with any satisfaction anyway, as she was still wearing her nightgown and shawl.

"Wait!" says she. "Give me time, honey!" So I backed off a little, and let her wriggle out of the shawl and get rid of it. Then she slid herself out of the nightgown and sat up straight, holding her arms out for me to see. There was just enough moonlight to show the difference between the shine of her skin and the thin bands of ribbon that she'd tied around her neck and her wrists.

"Here too," she said, and threw the bedclothes back to show more ribbons wound around her thighs.

"Good Lord!" says I, in surprise, "I thought they went in your hair!" She smothered a laugh.

"Huh!" says she. "They goes where they best suits."

And didn't they just suit too? The contrast between the tightly wound bands and the bare ebony flesh was so artful and exciting that it made her ten times more naked than if she'd had nothing on at all. She laughed and wiggled her arms over her head and pouted her lips at me, shaking her body so that her breasts bounced.

I sighed happily and grabbed her again, and pressed her close to me. There's nothing on God's earth to match the feel of a cool, fresh, naked woman: soft and smooth and slippery as silk. Believe me, my lads, half the delight of it is the wonderful feel of their skin against yours. Which is not to say you shouldn't have the other half too, and by that time the lust was roaring within me like a furnace and an intense hot pleasure burned in my loins. If I didn't have Lucinda that second, I'd burst.

So I rolled her on to her back, slid her long legs around my waist and drove forward. But just when I felt that nothing could stop me short of a lightning bolt, Lucinda surprised me once more.

She wriggled out of the line of fire, and nipped my shaft with all her might between her thumb and fore-finger, just where it joined my body.

"Ouch!" says I, it hurt, and the volcano got stoppered up just as it was about to erupt. I wouldn't have given it credence if it hadn't happened to me. By George but that girl had learned some tricks from somewhere. "Dammit, Lucinda!" says I, feeling hard done by and angry. "Why'd you do that?"

"'Cos you is ignorant and you got no manners!" says she. "What you think you are, a hog with a sow?" She shoved me off, at arm's length. "Now listen, honey, I let you have yo' fun them other times, 'cos I like you, unnerstand?"

"Er, yes," says I, "I think so . . ."

"But this time, I dressed up real nice for you, 'cos you brung me a present, like a gennelman should fo' a lady. So if you gonna be some of a gennelman, you better be all of a gennelman . . ."

"What?" says I.

"Tell me, honey," says she, "what sort of girls you had? Tell Lucinda . . ."

"Well, er . . . Well . . ." says I. What sort of girls did she think sailors had, dammit?

"Huh!" says she, understanding well enough.

"Well no woman's said a word of complaint before, madame, I can tell you!" says I. That was telling her.

" 'Course not, honey," says she, " 'cos all them trash said afterwards was 'Where's the money?'"

"Well at least I ain't no bloody virgin, madam!" says I, getting really angry.

"Sure," says she, "but you don't know nothin'! All you know is pleasin' yo'self. What about me, honey? They's two of us here. You think all there is to it is wham-bam-bam-thank-you-kindly-ma'am?"

That made me laugh. And she laughed too. As the Duke of Wellington said, always pursue advantage. He said it in another context but it works with women too. So I swallowed my pique and kissed her instead, and she sighed and softened and slid her hands up my back to run her fingers in the hair at the nape of my neck.

"So tell me, madam," says I, "what does a gentleman do to please a lady."

"Well," says she, "lots o' things. You can start by kissing me." I leaned forward to kiss her lips . . . "Not just there, honey," says she, "everywhere."

"Everywhere?" says I. That sounded interesting, so I pulled back the bedclothes for a fair view of the target and Lucinda stretched her arms over her head, and lay back with her eyes closed.

"Slowly, honey," says she, "make it slow . . ."

So I did, and I learned the rules as I went. I found the best way to go at it was to kneel across her on all fours, and dip my head like a cat lapping up cream. And the lightest touch, the lightest brushing of my lips across her skin, brought the greatest response. That and an occasional nip with my teeth to vary the pace. By George, what a game it was too! Lucinda moaned and gasped and writhed with her nostrils arched and her mouth half open.

So I worked my way gradually over her landscape, getting steadily more excited myself and wondering how long I could hold myself in.

But Lucinda was a damn fine teacher and I think I learned more from her than any other before or since.

"There, honey," says she, "kiss me there," and "Hold me there, no . . . there, and lift me up . . . that's good . . . yes . . . yes." (Damn me if I don't bring me out in a sweat even now, just to think about it.) Finally she had me kneeling between her legs, and raising her up, with a hand under each round buttock, so I could the more easily kiss her full between the thighs. She was a gorgeous-built creature, with the daintiest fuzz of down on the pudendum, round thighs, flat stomach and glossy skin. She was wet inside with desire, and salty when I tasted her. And when I put my tongue inside and worked it all around she suddenly groaned and shuddered fit to bring the house down and then she sighed and lay still and begged me to take her in my arms.

But she was as much a lady as she'd made me be a gentleman. And when she'd recovered a bit, she climbed on top of me and nibbled all round my ears with the tips of her teeth (which she knew I was partial to – it makes me laugh and tingle all over and it's great fun, except that I could hardly breathe for the thrill of it).

Then she eased herself on to my shaft, and swivelled her rump around it. At last, the unbearably delicious wave of ecstasy that I'd been fighting off could wash over me and I fired my broadside with a great force and a clear conscience.

We dozed off after that, locked in each other's arms, and contented as a pair of dormice in a granary. But later, Lucinda woke me up. She had something to tell me: something that put all my tidy plans at risk.

Chapter 13

That one in whom I had come to place such trust should so abuse it can only mean that all intercourse between us must cease. However, you have my new address whereby you may correspond with my wife, your daughter, should she be willing so to do.

(From a letter of 16th September 1793 to Mr Nathan Pendennis from Mr Edward Lucey.)

*

The discussion between Nathan Pendennis and Edward Lucey had been under way for some time. The hour was late, the servants were abed, and the candles in Pendennis's study had burned low. The two men sat in by the dying fire, staring at its white ashes. So absorbed had they been that neither had thought to add fuel to the embers, though a basket of trimmed logs was standing by. Similarly, a decanter of port and two glasses remained untouched on a small table at Pendennis's elbow.

"No, sir!" said Lucey. "In all things ordinarily you know that I respect your judgement. But this time I believe you to be wrong. It is simply the case that we can never, never, trust her."

Pendennis cursed and damned. He'd exhausted his every argument and he'd failed to persuade – an uncommon experience for him. But then, in all truth, he only half believed in the case himself. In desperation he called up his final reserves. With much reluctance he produced a sealed letter from a pocket of his coat. Lucey looked in surprise at this development, but when the letter was held out to him, and he saw his name upon it in a clear and dainty hand, he shrank back as if from a poisoned chalice.

"No!" said he.

"Read it," said Pendennis.

"What is it?" said Lucey.

"Read it," repeated Pendennis. "It is from the lady herself. She said it would explain all should you . . ." he paused, searching for a form of words that enabled him to pretend (even to himself) that no threat was involved, "should you not understand," he said, finally.

"Never!" said Lucey. He got up and paced the room in agitation. "It is some new threat," said he. He looked down at the man whom he had come to regard as a father, and disillusion fell upon him. "If it is from *her* it can only be some foul blackmail. And, sir, I cannot believe that you do not know it!"

This accurate shaft struck Pendennis in the heart and he squirmed in shame, unable to look his son-in-law in the eye.

"She said that you must read it," he mumbled in a petulant, self-justifying voice, "or the contents will be made public. She does not wish it so, but she cannot prevent it. She said it concerns things that you begged her to do and that she did for you."

Lucey's face drained of colour and he sank into his chair like a dead man. It was now his turn to be unable to look his companion in the eye. Pendennis instantly seized his chance and thrust the letter into Lucey's hand. For a while the two sat in silence, each staring at the letter but with widely different expectations.

"Read it, boy!" said Pendennis, at last, and sheer curiosity forced Lucey to break the seal and unfold the single sheet. Shamefaced, he turned his back on Pendennis and held the letter to catch the dim candlelight. Quickly he read the few lines that Lady Sarah had written. She had written them for his most especial benefit and there was not one dull word on the page.

Meanwhile, Pendennis was eaten with the desire to know what the letter said, but even in that extreme his dignity forbade that he should too obviously spy on another man's correspondence. So, quietly he stretched in his chair, tilted up his head and squinted hard over Lucey's shoulder. At first Pendennis could make out nothing. The light was so bad and the paper shook in Lucey's hands. It seemed to be a list. There was a short paragraph of introduction, and then a list of numbered items. For an instant, Pendennis's eyes focused on one of them, and the breath choked in his throat:

"(3) That you turned me on my belly and used me in the manner of Sodom."

Pendennis gulped and in the same instant Lucey tore the letter in shreds, crushed them in his hands and jammed them into the fire where the few live coals would be sure to set them alight.

"May she roast in hell, for the devil she is!" he groaned. He turned to Pendennis, in a dreadful fear and horror. "It was she that drew me on," said he. "You of all men must understand!"

"I?" said Pendennis.

"You, sir!" cried Lucey. "She whispered in my ear. She named things that I knew not were even possible between a man and a woman. She bad me choose what most inflamed my desires . . . and . . ." he faltered as his own part in the matter weighed upon him, "and I was fool enough to . . ." His voice broke and he hung his head. "God help me should this come to light!" he cried and wrung his hands in agony. "And to think she made me beg for it, like a dog!" He turned again to Pendennis, "Was not this how she treated you, sir?"

Pendennis said nothing. For the answer was no. No, it most certainly was not what had passed between himself and Lady Sarah Coignwood. Pendennis's memory surged again with visions of satin thighs and quivering breasts. But no, indeed. His own congress with the lady had been terminated painfully and sharp and well before he could take his pleasure of her. And now, the overwhelming emotion that filled Pendennis's mind was a great envy of Lucey's adventures together with an insupportable curiosity regarding the other, unknown items on that list. There had been four more at the least.

But Pendennis took command of himself with an effort of will, and dragged his mind back to the business in hand.

"Edward," said he, "will you not believe that she is as much a victim as you or I? Have you not attended to what I have said? The true villain is her son Victor. He holds her in fear of her life. She asks only that I testify to her . . ." He coughed and corrected himself. "That is, to the *true* account of the murder of Mr Forster's coachman."

"But, sir," protested Lucey, "how many times have you yourself told me that she was a party to this murder? That she commanded her son to do it?"

"Ah!" said Pendennis, taken aback, "ah! yes, or rather no . . ." He floundered about trying to square the circle. "The truth is," said he, "that is, the *real* truth, the *greater* truth, that she was forced into it." Lucey's sneer gave this argument the contempt it deserved.

"Real truth? Greater truth?" said Lucey. "How many shades of truth might there be, sir? Shall you pick the one that best pleases?"

"Damn your insolence, sir," cried Pendennis, "Victor Coignwood fired the fatal shot and there's an end on it! I shall give testimony for Lady Sarah and you shall keep your long nose out!" Instantly Pendennis regretted this flare of temper and laid his hand on Lucey's arm. "My dear boy," said he, "we are trapped in this mire. If this comes out we are disgraced before the world. But think what she is offering instead." He shook Lucey's arm to rouse him from the despair in which he was drowning. "Listen to me, Edward! She promises that everything shall be kept secret and that she will abandon her claim to the Coignwood estate, and come to terms with us. This will save all parties the vast cost of litigation."

"Those, sir," said Lucey, "are terms which will enable her to drain us of money for the rest of her life. She has only to turn the screw again, whenever she's short of cash."

"Hold your bloody tongue, you villain!" snapped Pendennis, boiling in rage because his nose had been rubbed in the very thing he was trying so hard not to see. For there was a third clause to Lady Sarah's offer. A secret clause that had been offered him in Cicero's Pleasure Gardens, to the accompaniment of fluttering lashes and maidenly blushes. It concerned certain favours that Pendennis would receive in due course, if Lady Sarah got her way. Pendennis was held by this as surely as a dungeoned prisoner is secured by the heavy chain that links his thick iron collar to the ponderous ring-bolt driven deep into the rock of his cell.

Unfortunately, having been reminded of all its prurient detail, Edward Lucey was equally unable to escape the snare of blackmail into which he'd so eagerly stepped.

And so, the two were brought into Lady Sarah's camp and all their brave resolutions overthrown.

Chapter 14

I was enjoying the most beautiful dream when Lucinda woke me. All about building my own counting-house and putting Mr Nathan Pendennis to work as my clerk. So I wasn't a bit pleased to be disturbed.

"Honey," says she, "wake up! I got to go now, and I got somethin' to tell you first."

"What?" says I. "In the morning . . ." and I threw an arm around her and drew her close. But she pushed me back and pulled the bedclothes off me so I couldn't go back to sleep.

"No," says she, "yo'll be gone soon enough, and I got to tell you now."

"What are you doing, girl?" says I. "It's cold." Then I realised what she'd said. "What do you mean 'gone'?" says I.

"Yo' goin' aboard that ship with Missa Cooper, ain't

you?" says she. "That big ship him so almighty proud of, down in Hart's Yard."

"Who told you that?" says I, for I certainly had not.

"Huh!" says she. "They ain't nothin' goes on in this house I don't know. Missa Cooper him been talking to them Navy Captains that come by the house. He been boastin' that he gonna have you fo' to work his guns."

"Well, stap me!" says I. "The little grub! When was this, Lucinda, for I only decided myself today?"

"That what you think, honey," says she. "Missa Cooper, he told them Captain ten days ago, he gonna get you in that ship, 'cos you a man that loves his money."

"Well I'm damned!" thinks I. Cooper was sharper than I'd thought. Except that presumably he thought he'd hooked a Royal Navy Lieutenant. But then, so did Lucinda as I soon found out.

"Why are you telling me this?" says I.

"First you tell me what you doin' here?" says she. I didn't know how to answer that, for I didn't know how many of my little secrets she might already know.

"Honey," says she, "ain't you an Englishman? An' a Loo-tenant?"

"Yes," says I without thinking, for I'd played the role long enough for the lie to come natural. Well, I was English anyway, wasn't I?

"Well, what you doin' goin' on a 'merican ship, huh? What yo' own people gonna think o' that?" I was even more puzzled at that, and said nothing and let her talk to see where this might lead. "Don't you know what that ship gonna do? Don't you know where she goin'?"

"She's bound away on a cruise," says I, "to work up her crew, and prove herself."

"That just what they done told you, honey!" says she. "Listen, boy, when them Captains was in the Li'bry with Missa Cooper, and I brung in the food, why they just talked right on with me there. Missa Cooper, he say," and here she gave the most rattling funny imitation of Cooper's voice, "he say – *Act as you would before me, gentlemen, my girl Lucinda is entirely faithful to me* – his girl Lucinda indeed! He ain't even man enough to try!"

"Ain't he?" says I.

"No, he ain't," says she.

"So what did they say?" says I, intrigued.

"Yo' know that big French fleet down in Virginia, that loadin' all the corn?"

"Yes," says I.

"Well," says she, "them French, they's afraid you English gonna send your ships out to stop the corn ships. 'Cos if you do that, then them French, why they's gonna starve."

"So?" says I.

"So," says she, "them French they gonna send a big, big fleet of man-o'-war ships out in the sea to meet the corn ships, so's they be safe from you English. And the Americans, they gonna send Missa Cooper's ship out with the corn ships to meet the French Navy ships. They even been told where the meetin' place is. One o' them Captains he showed Missa Cooper the place on a map and he try to cover it up with his hands when I come close with the food."

"But why should they send Cooper's ship out with that French Grain Fleet?" says I. "The Frogs have already got a couple of 74's and some frigates with them already. What's the *Declaration* wanted for?"

"It gonna show them French what good, good friends the 'mericans is, so them French'll come back next year an' buy some more corn. That's what that Captain said, him that told Missa Cooper the meeting place."

"Well," thinks I, "so much for the Americans being 'pitched contrariwise' against the Frogs!" I wondered where Uncle Ezekiah really stood in all this, what with his big offers to me, and his toast to the British Grenadiers. Probably the wily old bugger was playing both sides of Yankee politics. But then a more important thought struck me.

"Why are you telling me this?" says I to Lucinda.

"'Cos you a English Loo-tenant, ain't you? So what you doin' on a 'merican ship goin' out most like to fight against the English Navy?"

Just for once I had no good answer to that. For I thought we were discussing loyalties, and I didn't want to say I was doing it for the money.

"Either you is a funny kind o' Englishman . . ." says Lucinda, "or you is somethin' else . . ."

"What?" says I, realising she was off on another tack completely.

"Yo' is a spy, ain't you?" says she in a whisper and I could feel the excitement mounting within her. "Yo' is gonna steal that meeting place and tell yo' Navy where to find them corn ships!" I could see her eyes gleaming: round and wondering. She was breathing faster, and she was soft and trembling beside me.

"Hallo!" thinks I and following Wellington's maxim once more, I folded her in my arms so that her smooth, warm body lay close to mine. "You have discovered me, ma'am," says I in a deep, sad voice. "I am in your power, and my life lies in your hands. One word from you will put my naked breast before the muskets of a firing squad."

(Damn fine stuff, what? Extemporised too. And by George didn't it just work!)

"My love, my love," moans Lucinda, "my darling!" and smothered me with hotter and more passionate kisses than anything I'd known before, even from her. And then she paid me back for those occasions when I'd ravished her, by doing the same to me – comprehensively. But unlike Lucinda, I never complained.

*

Two weeks later I was stood by Captain Cooper on the quarterdeck of the United States National Ship, *Declaration of Independence* as she came down past the North Battery and Long Wharf to salute Fort Hill with fifteen guns. It was a declared holiday for the people of the town, and tens of thousands of them lined the eastward wharves and piers to see their country's one and only man-o'-war go forth in her pride. A shoal of small craft was all around us, crowds cheered, bands played, banners waved and ladies fainted.

I've seen more than my share of occasions like that and they're infectious. Your foot taps to the band and you join in if you know the words. Now that's not surprising when it's a British song that's being sung, but it's odd the way even foreigners' music has the same effect. I must confess I've even cheered the French in my time, when they played the "Marseillaise". But that's the finest march ever written, and too good by far for the bloody Frogs.

It was odd being in a ship again, too. Most of me thought it a mighty bore, and a diversion from the true path of my life. But a bit of me (a bit that I'd have had cut out by the nearest surgeon if only I knew where it lay) was happy with the salt spray, the screeching gulls, and the working of the big ship to the pressure of the wind in her sails. You could see the power of it in the taut lines and bending topmasts.

She came out on the ebb with a good westerly wind, and the town's best pilot in command. For the sea-channel out from Boston in those days was tortuous and shallow, winding between dozens of islands and mud flats. The order of the day was to creep out under close-reefed topsails with the lead going in the forechains. As we passed between Governor's Island and Dorchester Neck, there was less than three fathoms under the keel. But the pilot knew his trade and brought us safe out through the Narrows north of Nantasket Road and so into the main channel where Cooper took command.

Then the hands cheered everything. They cheered the pilot, they cheered the Stars and Stripes, they cheered Cooper and they cheered the ship's pig's mother-in-law too, so far as my memory serves me. For the lad Cooper had got himself a happy ship.

Of the 450 seamen and thirty boys aboard, there wasn't one who hadn't entered her as a volunteer (unless you count me, of course). Even the two companies of Marines and their officers were keen as mustard. And as for Cooper and his Sea Service officers (three Lieutenants and the Master), they were like boys on holiday. God only knows how that man ever maintained discipline among his people. It was as different as could be from the Royal Navy with its pressed men and constant dread of mutiny.

Mind you, he'd got some hard cases on the lower deck and he flogged one of them for fighting, on the second day of the voyage. And grog was issued just like in our Navy. So don't let anyone tell you the Yankee Navy in those days was manned entirely by teetotal God-fearing saints who spent their spare time singing psalms.

But they were keen; every man jack of 'em. And on that morning, as *Declaration* headed out into the North Atlantic, fresh in her new paint and rigged out with the best of gear, it was an education to see how her crew did their work. They were pretty good for a set of newcomers that hardly knew one another. The hands were cheerful and went at it with a will, and the Bosun's Mates hardly had to tickle them with their starters, while Cooper was a good seaman and his officers too. For they'd all of them, officers and men, learned their trade in the merchant service.

And yet, there was something missing. They just weren't man-o'-war's men. Not by Royal Navy standards. Not yet. And I'm not just talking about any ship's need to work up her crew. I'm talking about the standards by which her officers judge themselves and the hands. I could see that they weren't up to the mark, because I'd known the real thing: there's a sharpness, and an edge and a jump-to-it way of doing things on board the King's ships that just ain't to be learned aboard a merchantman. And none of Cooper's officers were aware of this.

Now of course this is not to say that *Declaration* wasn't an impressive ship, for she was. She was big, strongly built and extremely heavily armed. Against another frigate, against the Frogs or dagos, I'd have backed her and her crew any time. But it wasn't *them* she was measuring herself against, was it?

In short, Cooper and his uncle were right. *Declaration*

was in need of advice from the real thing – but all they'd got was me! This made me think over all I'd been taught of gunnery drill aboard *Phiandra* and I fell to worrying if I was up to the job of schooling Cooper's gun-crews. And then I thought of Lucinda, and her tearful farewell, and her whispering in my ear.

"I always loves you, honey!" says she. "I knows you ain't comin' back, 'cos you's a English officer, and you got your duty . . ." By God the thought of that depressed me! Lucinda was the first woman I'd ever known who'd loved me just for myself, when she didn't have to. And now, not only was I missing her, but the thought of all that she'd said made me uneasy.

I fixed my mind on two things, which were a great comfort to me. Firstly, Lucinda was wrong. I'd be back in Boston so soon as *Declaration*'s cruise was done. My American citizenship papers were in my sea-chest below, and Uncle Ezekiah's bill of hand for $5,000 dollars was deposited in my name in a Boston bank. Once back in Boston I'd bid farewell to the sea and make my fortune in trade. Perhaps I'd buy a house in Tontine Crescent, and I'd certainly poach Lucinda away from Cooper and bring her to live with me. That way I could roger her cross-eyed every night of the week, and twice on Sundays.

"Mr Fletcher!" says a voice. It was Cooper with his officers behind him. They were all grinning. "You've not been attending to me, sir!" says Cooper. "Will you join me in my cabin, or not?"

There was a laugh at this, and I realised how intensely I'd been pondering what I was going to do with myself. Cooper had been talking to me and I'd not heard; I'd have got my ears blasted off aboard a King's ship for that. But habit came to my rescue.

"Aye-aye, sir!" says I, without thinking, and touched my hat.

"Then have the goodness to follow me below, sir!" says he, and he led the troop of us to the great cabin, leaving a nervous Master's Mate in command. Down below, he entertained his wardroom officers to a glass of wine; three Lieutenants, the Master, and the Surgeon, Chaplain and Purser – and myself.

My position aboard *Declaration* was anomalous. I was entered in the ship's books as a midshipman, since not even the Cooper influence could get me a commission in two weeks. But I had a cabin in the wardroom with the officers, and was treated in all respects as if I were a Lieutenant. What's more, among my messmates, I enjoyed the prestige of the veteran naval officer that they thought I was. And none of them thought me a turncoat, neither. Americans are like that. They're so almighty proud of their country that they think a foreigner's simply coming to his senses when he wants to become one of them. In any case, there were a dozen or more British or ex-British hands on the lower deck ("berthing deck" they called it), so I was nothing new.

Cooper, in one of his spurts of generosity, had kitted

me out with personal tackle, including a blue uniform coat and a cocked hat. So I looked the part too. And as regards the matelots, I came complete with my own authority built-in: sixteen stones of it, and when I said jump, they jumped.

Down in the Great Cabin, I was reminded of Cooper's money. He had every luxury that the mind of man could conceive: patent silver lamps swinging in gimbals, elegant furniture, rugs, curtains and rows of books in neat little shelves with brass rails to stop the ship's motion from emptying them. In front of the sweep of the stern windows running completely across the cabin, he had the usual long table with a dozen chairs for entertaining, or as on this occasion, for conferring with his officers.

I wondered what would happen to all this when *Declaration* cleared for action. Captain Bollington of *Phiandra* cleared every second day, as a drill, and every stick in his cabin went down to the hold each time. But then I noticed that there were no guns in Cooper's cabin. That gave him more room and left him undisturbed, but it would never have done in the Royal Navy. That sort of cherishing of a Captain's comforts would have been seen as the moral equivalent of mincing down Drury Lane with a lace handkerchief in your hand and an ostrich plume up your arse.

Presumably the Yankees saw things different, because nobody seemed surprised.

*

Once we were all seated, Cooper gave us a speech. All the usual stuff about duty and country and what prodigious things he was going to do with the ship, should only heaven give him the chance. I'd heard it all before and I've heard it since. I've even given it myself, for it's expected on these occasions. But I'd have dozed off if I hadn't noticed that one or two of the company (especially my old friend Eustace Hunt who was First Lieutenant) were getting their first proper feel of the sea, now that *Declaration* was forging out on to the rolling North Atlantic, with a good westerly in her sails.

By God's grace, sea-sickness never bothered me after my first voyage and one of the things that's kept me jolly these many years at sea has been the fun of watching my shipmates succumb: first they sweat, then they go grey, then they go green, and finally they heave up their guts in tribute to Father Neptune. On that occasion Mr Hunt was going through these stages so perfectly that I could barely look at him without laughing. Serve him right, the swab, he had prize money in the bank from *Bednal Green*.

With the formalities out of the way, Cooper revealed that the voyage was no mere cruise to prove the ship but had a specific purpose. I already knew that, thanks to Lucinda, and I think Lieutenant Hunt did too, being a close crony of Cooper's, but his lack of surprise might have been due to the fact that he was hoping he might die in order to be out of his misery. Everyone else, however, leaned forward like dogs who'd sniffed a rabbit, and not a sound was heard as Cooper told them about the Frogs' Grain Convoy, and how *Declaration* was going along with it, to show the Yankee flag.

"In that drawer," says Cooper, pointing to a drawer of a big desk, glittering with brass and polish, "in that drawer, lie my orders with the latitude and longitude of the rendezvous point where the Brest Fleet, under Admiral Villaret de Joyeuse, shall meet the Grain Convoy to bring it in safe to harbour." He paused to let that sink in, then went on: "I have it from Mr Knox, the Secretary of War, that President Washington is much gratified that the French have entrusted us with a secret, the loss of which to their enemies could bring such ruin upon their nation." Cooper swept his eyes around the table. "And, gentlemen," says he, "the President relies upon our actions, aboard this ship, to cement future relations with our European ally."

That made me think, I can tell you. So the French were "our European ally" were they, indeed? But heads nodded wisely round the table and after we'd drunk a health or two in Cooper's port, he dismissed us to our duties. Hunt was away like a jockey given the off, and up the companionway to the quarterdeck like a mountain goat. But anyone could see how imminently pressing were his duties. The others filed out more sedately, but I got called back.

"Mr Fletcher," cries Cooper, "a word with you!" I sat

down again, and as the Marine sentry outside the door pulled it shut, Cooper shoved the decanter across the table.

"Will you take another, Fletcher?" says he.

"No, thank you, sir," says I. I'd had three already and it was still early morning.

"Fletcher," says he, "I hope you will be happy aboard my ship."

"So do I, sir," says I, waiting for him to come to the point. "You are an American citizen now, are you not?"

"Yes, sir," says I. He bloody well ought to know. He was with me in the Mayor's office when I took the Oath of Allegiance.

"And you have much to return home to, in Boston?" Indeed I did. More than he knew.

"Yes, sir," says I.

He bit his lip and chewed things over in his head, and then looked at me with something like nervousness.

"Jacob," says he: *Jacob*, indeed! "I will entrust you with a confidence as great as that given to me." He waved at the drawer with its hidden secrets. "The President wants to sell more grain to the French. It is vital to the farming interest that is his main support in Congress. But he does not want a long or hard war with the British. Do you understand?"

"Not entirely, sir," says I. He strained even harder, like a sparrow laying a hen's egg. Finally he forced it out.

"The war with Britain is finished. Our representatives

will meet the British in Lisbon as soon as diplomatic couriers can carry the necessary messages to and fro. And a peace will be negotiated." He looked at me closely. "This is uttermost secret, Jacob," says he. "No other person aboard knows this."

"You may rely upon me, sir," says I, solemn as a bishop in a buttocking shop.

"My orders, are," says Cooper, "to join the Grain Convoy at Norfolk, to place my ship at the disposal of the convoy's commander, Rear-Admiral Vanstable, and render him every assistance within my power . . . But . . . I must avoid action against the British."

In that moment I could see the burden of worry he was under. He seemed to be a man of more weight than I'd thought, for he'd covered it up very well. I'd not have thought such pressures were on him. Obviously President-Mr-Yankee-doodle Washington wanted to have his cake and eat it. He wanted to be friends with the British and the French, and Cooper was stuck in the middle. What was the poor devil to do if Admiral Frog ordered him to engage a British ship? Mutiny, perhaps?

"I see your problem, sir," says I, "but why should you tell this to me?"

"I am telling you," says he, "because I need the expertise that you bring to my ship, but I appreciate the divided loyalties that must struggle within you. I wanted you to know that I am under orders not to fight against your former countrymen."

Well, it was handsomely said, I suppose. But he was wrong in one respect. There was no struggle going on within me, I was simply looking forward to going back to Boston.

After that he gave me his hand and then leapt up with a grin on his face.

"Now then, Fletcher," says he, "I shall turn out all hands for your first gun-drill. The stage is set! It is time for you to give us your Hamlet!"

Chapter 15

CASE: *Coignwood v. Fletcher*
BODY: *Salisbury, David, Lt. RN.*
CONNECTION: *Witness to actions of Fletcher?*
ACTION: *Strong interrogation required.*
     (From Samuel Slym's record cards, transcribed
                              from the shorthand.)

*

Slym faced three opponents. Three young men with vicious anticipation writ all over their faces. They were what his dad would have called "Grosvenor Square coves" the sort that by money and birth were used to having the world the way they wanted it. Two of them were big, red-faced, stupid louts, fresh in town from their fathers' estates, and looking for a wiser head to show them how to rake hell. The third, who was their leader, was a tall, thin gentleman, dressed in the height of fashion, and with a thoroughly nasty look about him. He was the one to watch.

"What's your pleasure, Davy?" said one of the bumpkins. "Have you your pocket-knife to hand, Toby?" said Lieutenant David Salisbury.

"Aye," said Sir Toby Moore, Baronet.

"Well, then," said Salisbury, "give it here," and a gleam of steel passed from hand to hand. "Now," said Salisbury, "if you and Billy'd just hold the rogue down and stuff a handkerchief in his mouth, for the noise . . ." he showed his teeth in a lascivious grin, "then I'll trim the bastard's ears for his impertinence!"

"It's madness, gentlemen," said Slym, "this is Brooks's of St James's Street, you cannot . . ."

"Get him!" cried Salisbury, and the two louts dived at Slym. Five minutes later a waiter bearing a tray of refreshment for the patrons, passed along the corridor of side rooms just as a door opened and two gentlemen emerged.

Both appeared drunk, and one was supporting the other. The waiter recognised the helpless one as Mr Salisbury, a well-known member of the establishment, who gossip said had recently lost his employment in the Navy through a scandal believed to be connected with the Coignwood millions.

"May I be hov hassistance, sir?" said the waiter with massive dignity.

"No, no, 's'allright!" said Slym. He shifted his hold on the drooping and barely conscious figure of Salisbury who the waiter noticed was somewhat bruised about the face. Slym grinned and found a coin for the waiter.

"Good fellow!" said Slym and the waiter passed on his way. He wished he had a similar coin for every other time he'd seen members go home in that state.

So Slym and his bosom companion made their way through the opulent splendour of Brooks's subscription house. Down the corridor they went, through the Great Room with its glittering chandeliers, and the shaded lights illuminating the big green-baize table tops surrounded by absorbed gentlemen at their whist, picquet and quinze. This elegant chamber with its Adam fireplace surmounted by a huge mirror, and its vaulted ceiling adorned in gilt and white plasterwork relief, was the very temple of London gambling. Fortunes changed hands every night and there was a long waiting list for membership, even at the stiff cost of eleven guineas per year.

Even as he played the part of a drunken toff, even as he chuckled into Salisbury's dazed ear and laughed at his imagined replies, and hushed him with finger to lips, so as not to disturb the silence of the players, Slym looked about him at this epicentre of the world he ached to join. He well knew that the committee would never even consider membership for such as he. Brooks's was for *gentlemen*, which the creature Slym was supporting could claim to be, and which he could not.

Slym had only got inside by hefty bribes to the Chief Steward and the Head Waiter. Greedy for gold but in fear of their employment, they'd sneaked him in through the servants' entrance and into a private room. A message was then sent to Lieutenant Salisbury at the gaming tables that a gentleman begged to see him in the Coignwood interest. That had brought Salisbury quick enough.

But Slym hadn't expected Salisbury's two chums, nor the savagery of Salisbury's reaction to his questions.

As Slym and Salisbury staggered through the Great Room and made their way to the lobby, the Head Waiter and Chief Steward rushed to their assistance, helped them out into St James's Street and hailed a hackney coach.

Only as the coach pulled away towards Piccadilly did these two functionaries relax from the nervous dread that some Committee Member might discover their connivance at allowing a non-subscriber to enter the premises. They stood on the corner of Park Place and St James's Street, outside the Club, for some minutes sharing their relief and good fortune. When finally they went back inside, they found the porter and one of the waiters laughing over the fact that the two young country gentlemen who'd been brought in by Lieutenant Salisbury had obviously fallen out with one another, for they'd emerged from one of the private rooms with blood down their shirt-fronts and all the marks of having given one another a good battering.

*

By the time the hackney reached the Blue Boar Inn on Aldgate High Street, Lieutenant Salisbury had recovered from the clout he'd had from Slym's fist. His head ached and he felt sick, but he was fully aware of what was going on. None the less he remained meekly co-operative and stood beside Slym and waited while Slym paid the coachman. It was two in the morning, but the street was alive with light and noise from the Blue Boar, and the Bull next door. Tarts and drunks followed their callings and raucous singing came from within both establishments.

When the coach rattled off, Slym jerked his thumb at an alley between the two inns.

"In there!" said he. "You first," and gave Salisbury a shove to help him on his way. The alley was well lit by lamps fixed to the walls and contained stables for the Bull's horses. Above the stables, reached by a flight of heavy wooden stairs clapped against the outside of the buildings, was a first floor, with a long run of windows, like those in weavers' cottages. Slym pushed Salisbury up the stairs.

At the top was a small landing opposite a door. Beside the door, a brass plate was screwed into the wall. It gleamed from daily polishing and bore the two words, "Samuel Slym".

Slym handed Salisbury a key.

"Open it," he said and stepped back. This procedure was necessary in order for Slym effectively to continue with the persuasion that was enforcing Salisbury's meek compliance.

The persuasion was a neat little double-barrelled pistol, by Egg, the Irish gunsmith, with exterior lock-springs, one barrel over the other, and a single trigger that fired each in turn. It was a favourite of Slym's where conceal-ment was important, for it was no longer than his hand and slipped nicely into a coat pocket.

"See this?" he'd said to Salisbury, waving the pistol under his nose when he came to himself in the hackney. "Trim my fuckin' ears, will you, you dirty sod? Listen, kiddy, play me false by just one squeak and I'll pop this in the middle of your back!"

So Salisbury opened the door into Slym's offices, gave the key back to Slym and the two stepped inside, into a narrow hallway lit by a low night-light, fluttering in a dish of water on a side table. Slym pushed Salisbury through a door into a room lined with little drawers. Row upon row of them just visible in the dim light of the single candle that Slym had lit. It was the same room where he'd first met Lady Sarah.

"Sit down," he said to Salisbury, indicating a chair.

"I protest," said Salisbury, as anger overcame fear. "I am a Naval officer. I bear His Majesty's commission, and the Law will not allow . . ."

Crack! The blackthorn stick in Slym's right hand rapped against the side of Salisbury's head.

"Ah!" cried Salisbury, jumping back and holding his hand to his head. "You could have killed me!"

"*Sit down!*" said Slym, firmly. "You'd have been dead

half an hour ago, if that's what I'd wanted. I've told you, kiddy, all I want from you is some answers."

"Damn you!" said Salisbury. "I'm a King's officer and I'm damned if I'll answer to the likes of you!"

Crack! The blackthorn landed on Salisbury's elbow, making him yelp in pain. Slym seized him by the arms and forced him into a chair by main force. Then he drew up another chair and sat facing his victim at one yard's distance.

"Now then," said Slym, "you saw me baste them friends of yours, didn't you?" Salisbury nodded. Slym continued, "Did it with this, didn't I?" He held up the blackthorn stick with its knarled, lead-loaded head. Salisbury nodded again. "Now, we've got all night for this, kiddy," said Slym. "It's you, me and this stick. Just the three of us, see?" Salisbury said nothing, so Slym jabbed the stick hard into his belly. "See?" he repeated.

"Yes," said Salisbury.

"Good," said Slym. "So there's only one more thing you should know." He fell silent and cocked his head on one side. "Listen!" said he and Salisbury heard the sounds of the unquiet streets and the boozy music of the two big inns. This interspersed with the occasional distant cry or peal of laughter. "Hear that?" said Slym. "You can bawl your head off in here, and nobody's going to pay the least heed."

"Good God-in-heaven!" gasped Salisbury. "Do you propose to put me to torture, like a heathen Turk?"

"Yes," said Slym, "that is precisely my intention and I thank you, sir, for saving me the trouble of explaining it to you."

A feeling of uncanny horror came upon Salisbury. He felt he was in the grip of a madman. The dark room with its solitary candle added to the horror. Only a dim light came through the windows and of the man in front of him he could see little more than shadows and the fierce, gleaming eyes.

But even Salisbury, sadist and bully that he was, had held command afloat and was not to be subdued without a fight. Especially not by a man who came from a class that Salisbury believed to be innately inferior to his own.

"I'll tell you nothing, you bloody lubber!" said he. "You cannot touch me, you do not know who I am. By God I'll have the law on you!"

"I know who you are," said Slym, "for I've taken an interest in you. You're Lieutenant David Salisbury, a friend of Lieutenant Alexander Coignwood. You were Master and Commander of the Impress Tender *Bullfrog* when Mr Jacob Fletcher was taken aboard. You carried Fletcher and other pressed men to Portsmouth in February. But later you were relieved of your command over something that happened aboard your ship. I want to know exactly what happened, and I want to know everything you can tell me about Mr Jacob Fletcher."

Salisbury was stunned by this and was instantly pricked with quite another kind of fear.

"How can you know this?" said he.

"I ask questions everywhere," said Slym, "even at the Admiralty."

"I'll tell you nothing!" said Salisbury, for he was terrified of past misdeeds coming back to ruin his future.

The first blow from Slym's stick knocked Salisbury clean out of the chair. And so the interrogation commenced.

*

Later, Slym threw Salisbury out through his front door with such vigour that Salisbury had to grab at the stair rail with his left hand (the fingers of which were still sound) to save himself from going headlong down the flight. He managed it by a whisker and hobbled painfully down the wooden stairs to creep away into the night. There was not the slightest possibility of his taking legal action. He was reduced to praying that Slym might hold his tongue.

As soon as Salisbury was gone, Slym filled his favourite office with light. He lit a dozen candles, without regard to the cost, and methodically cleaned the floor of the marks of Salisbury's presence. Fastidious man that he was, he set to with brushes and cloths and water and an oilcloth apron over his immaculate clothes. As he worked he thought over what he had learned and realised that it was easier to get a few bloodstains off his polished floorboards than it was to rid his mind of the filth that Salisbury had poured into it.

Some of what he'd got out of Salisbury merely confirmed what Slym had already learned from a clerk at the Admiralty: namely, that Fletcher had been entered into H.M. Frigate *Phiandra* (the ship that had made herself so famous recently, by beating the French at Passage d'Aron).

Salisbury also knew that Fletcher had for some reason been discharged by Captain Bollington, at Portsmouth. But this was the sort of gossip any Naval officer might pick up in the coffeehouses, and as to where Fletcher had gone after *Phiandra*, and which Slym dearly needed to know, Salisbury was ignorant – or at least Slym hadn't dared ask any harder, for fear of killing him.

What had set Slym's mind whirling was that Fletcher had been singled out for the press-gang and Salisbury's Impress tender, because of a plot laid by Lady Sarah's son Alexander.

She hadn't told Slym that! And she hadn't told him that her precious bleedin', dead-departed, favourite son, Lieutenant Alexander Coignwood, who was supposed to be Sir bleedin' Galahad, that fell in action against his bleedin' country's enemies, had actually been a dirty-minded sod that was up to Christ-knows-what with turd-pokers like Salisbury and his own brother Victor!

Slym was furious and disgusted all at the same time. Furious that she thought she could keep him ignorant of *any* aspect of the matter once he got his teeth into it, and disgusted at the filthy insinuations Salisbury had made about Lady Sarah herself. He couldn't believe what Salisbury said, be he never so good a friend of her sons and up with all their doings. When he thought of her . . .

"Fire and shite!" he said aloud, on his knees, scrubbing-brush in hand. "I won't have it, and that's that!" A singular remark indeed for a man whose entire career had been built upon rigorous sifting of the evidence.

He ground the brush into the floorboards and scrubbed away at the remains of a bloodstain as he fastened on simpler matters. Alexander had set Salisbury to kill Fletcher – actually *kill* the bugger! That was a spry one for a pair of King's bleedin' officers of the Royal bleedin' Navy! But Salisbury hadn't the stomach for the work, and the most he dared do was set his Bosun to make the sod's life a misery, while the *Bullfrog* made the brief voyage from Polmouth to Portsmouth. But then the stupid fool of a Bosun had disappeared – odd that, thought Slym, bleedin' odd – and Fletcher had been off-loaded with the other pressed men into the receiving ship for the Channel Fleet. And that was the last Salisbury had seen of Jacob Fletcher.

Slym forced himself to push all else out of his mind so he could all the better concentrate on finding Jacob Fletcher. That's what she'd employed him for. The thing now was to find where the bleeder had gone next. Fortunately Salisbury had given him the next step. Salisbury knew an officer who'd met an old shipmate, a common seaman discharged from *Phiandra* too ruptured by heavy lifting to be of further use. This kiddy said Fletcher had been sweet on a tart called Kate Booth aboard *Phiandra*.

It seemed Fletcher and his doxy had piped their eyes something sad to see when they parted, and she'd left the ship a day after him, vowing to follow him. It seemed to Slym that if anyone knew where Fletcher had gone, it would be little Miss Booth. Methodically he completed his cleaning, put his bucket and brushes and cloth away, removed the apron, put on his coat, and took a copy of that day's *Globe* from the rack where newspapers were filed. He looked for the column listing prices and departure times for the Mail Coaches. This was a ritualistic action carried out to calm his mind. He knew the Mail Coach times by heart and, on this occasion, price didn't matter. He'd go as an "inside" and damn the expense. She was paying and she could afford it.

Chapter 16

The instant the last man ceased to move, I felt four hundred pairs of eyes on me, as many of them as could see me anyway. Cooper and his officers were clustered behind me, looking down into the gun-deck. The top men filled the fighting tops, the Marines were deployed with ball cartridge, and the gun-crews stood at their stations behind the main-battery 24-pounders, and the squat 32-pounders that lined the quarterdeck and fo'c'sle. I'd taken my stand at the quarterdeck rail where I could see most of the gun-crews. Only those beneath my feet, under the quarterdeck, were out of sight.

The whole ship was waiting for their tame Limey to do his part. Cooper was waiting, the officers were waiting and the men were waiting. The moment had arrived for which Cooper and his uncle had schemed and planned, for whatever motives, to get me aboard their precious ship to train its gunners. I'd not exactly been dreading the moment, for I'd been well enough trained aboard *Phiandra* to know my business, but I'd expected to have no heart for the business. I'd expected to be bored. But I wasn't.

I looked at the wealth of manpower that *Declaration* was blessed with – 216 faces were grinning at me from the gun-deck and another sixty from the carronades. They were men in their twenties, prime seamen, and every one fit as a butcher's bulldog. They'd been hand-picked from the hordes of volunteers who'd come forward, and then fattened up for weeks in harbour, on fresh meat and new-baked bread (Cooper had seen to that). Even Nelson in his glory never had a crew like 'em.

And I looked at her shiny new guns, fresh from the cannon foundries at Furnace Hope in Rhode Island. I looked at all that and shook my head in disgust for the bodge they were making of their drill.

They were slow and they were slack. They laughed and joked as they ran to general quarters and ran out their guns. They were the happiest set of fellows that ever went to sea. They were playing at the bloody thing and it filled me with anger. It's not that I'd any great love for gun-drill in itself, but *I* knew how bad these Yankees were and *they* did not and it galled me to see the self-satisfied looks on their fat faces. So I took a deep breath and let 'em have it fair and square.

"You slovenly buggers!" says I, in a lion's roar. "A choir of bloody schoolgirls could've done it better!" I'd a fifty-inch chest by then and I'd learned to use my voice, so I can promise you that I shook the paint off the figurehead with my bellowing. And I could tell you they didn't like it one bit. You could see 'em twitch as it hit them. They thought they'd done well, you see. They were expecting a pat on the back. On a rolling deck with the spray coming over the bow, and the ship making a good eight knots, they'd run out and secured their guns just as well as they'd done it in harbour. And they were all seamen, who knew how difficult a feat they'd accomplished.

For *Declaration of Independence.was* the biggest ship they'd ever been in, and her 24-pounders were the biggest guns they'd ever seen. Prime seamen they might have been, but all their experience had been in merchantmen and privateers with their fours, sixes and nines with maybe four or five men per gun. But a full navy crew for a 24-pounder was twelve men and a boy to run cartridges. The barrels alone were nine-feet-six long and weighed fifty-two hundredweights even without the yellow-ochred timber carriages.

So they'd grinned and smirked at one another and thought themselves a fine set of fellows for being able to cast off lashings and haul their guns into a firing position without mashing their toes under the trucks or stuffing live matches into the powder horns.

John Drake

But they'd never seen the machine-like speed and precision of a British man-o'-war steadily delivering a broadside a minute. In short, there wasn't a man in that ship who knew what he was up against.

God knows what had happened to the fighting Captains they'd had in the Revolutionary War, for there were certainly none of them aboard *Declaration* in April of '94. John Paul Jones was two years in his grave by then, and he'd have turned in it if he'd seen what I'd just witnessed. The fact was, of course, that the Yankees simply hadn't got the Sea Service tradition with its corps of professional officers that England took for granted, and the appointment to command *Declaration* had been made by the political interest of the Cooper family. At least the Coopers had had the sense to spot their weakness and attempt to make it good. That's what I was for.

So I took my coat off and went at it with a full heart.

"With your permission, Captain?" says I, catching Cooper's eye as I shoved my hat and coat into the hands of one of the middies. I noticed that Cooper was looking distinctly sulky and it occurred to me that I'd been less than tactful in bawling at his men. In criticising them, I'd criticised him. But as Boney said years later, you can't make omelettes without breaking eggs, so I left him in his pet and ran down the companionway on to the gun-deck.

The men were all around me and on either side. They'd run out on both sides with half crews. Up and down the deck, long lines of guns stretched away in perspective. Eighteen guns each side, six men per gun, rammers, sponges, shot racks, lines of firelock triggers, 36 gun-captains with 36 trigger lines. Apart from the fat round masts, the pumps, capstans and gratings over the hatches, the 200 foot by 40 foot deck was nothing but guns, from the bow to the bulkhead of Cooper's cabin.

Sullen faces were all around me. I'd succeeded in making myself highly unpopular. Now I'd thrown off my coat with the aim of demonstrating how I wanted the drill executed, but on impulse I had a better idea.

As I went to one of the midships guns I got a down-right truculent, insulting look from its crew. The lubbers were muttering too, a thing I could never abide from the lower deck. I'd have dearly loved to have shown 'em the error of their ways, but I held back. I didn't know how Cooper would take to my methods. In the Royal Navy, officers weren't strictly supposed to exchange blows with the men, and I guessed Yankee regulations would be the same as ours, but with King George crossed out and George Washington written in. None the less, I needed some gesture to show the lubbers what was what.

So, with two hundred maindeck gunners around me and the rest of the crew peering down from the decks and rigging above, I took hold of the inhaul tackle secured to the stern of the gun-carriage and threw my weight on it.

It was a risky thing to do, for it was six men's work

to drag the gun bodily back eight feet from its snug berth where its long black snout stuck out of the port. For an instant I thought I'd made a fool of myself before every man and boy in the ship, as my shoes slipped and I damn near went flat on my back. But the deck was sanded for general quarters, and I got a grip. Leaning hard back I put my back and leg muscles to work and heaved with all my strength till the sweat burned in my eyes and the line skinned my hands, which had gone soft from living ashore. But the squat trucks of the gun carriage squealed and grumbled and the great black beast came steadily inboard to meet me. Once it was moving the thing was easy and I hauled her out hand over hand.

When it was done I straightened up, pretended my hands and back weren't ablaze with pain and glared at the gun-crew. They'd got the point. They still didn't like me, but the insolence was gone.

(Best thing I ever did aboard that ship, incidentally. It's just the sort of damn fool prank that wins men's respect. But I wouldn't recommend it to you unless you're my size or some large part of it.)

"Now then, you lubbers," says I to the rest of them, "if I can do it, then so can you! Haul 'em inboard!"

And so I put Cooper's gunners through their paces: run out, haul in. Train astern, train on the bow. Do it with full crew, do it with the starboard watch fallen out. Then every crew to race against every other. Finally I sought the loan of Cooper's fancy pocket watch, with its sweeping hand that registered in seconds, and I had every gun load and fire live ammunition in turn as fast as each could, with the prize of double grog for winners.

The deafening thunder of the big 24-pounders set the blood racing in my veins, and the banks of white smoke, reeking and choking in the throat, brought back memories of the men who'd been my teachers: especially Lieutenant Seymour whose drill it was that I was passing on, and whose tricks of instruction I was using. I wasn't being particularly clever. I was just passing on what I'd learned.

Cooper gave me half a watch (two hours), for that first drill, and when it was over the gun-crews were better men than when they started, for they'd had their stupid fat-headed complacency dented, they'd smelt powder smoke, and they didn't hate me so much neither. Double grog for the winning crew (another of Mr Seymour's tricks) was an inspired act. Twelve men loved me for the getting of it, and the rest had something to hope for in the future. Seamen will sell their lights and livers for grog.

When my time was up, I dismissed the gun-crews and reported back to Cooper, who nodded at me with a mixture of respect and irritation. The other Lieutenants leapt on the hands and instantly sent them doubling in all directions to sail-drill, fire-drill, boat-drill and raising and striking the upper yards. It was laughable really; they'd taken their cue from me and every one of them was trying to show what a tartar he was for efficiency.

So the crew got no rest that day in any respect. Meanwhile, as the upper decks ran alive with harassed matelots, with the Bosun's Mates chasing them up the masts, I went below to look up the Gunner. I had a bone to pick with him. But I was tactful about it this time, and sought him out in his store room down on the orlop, below the water line.

In a King's ship, the Gunner is one of the three "standing officers" – Gunner, Bosun and Carpenter – who live permanently in the ship and are not discharged at the end of a commission. Also, the Gunner, Bosun and Carpenter are always selected from reliable seamen with years of experience. The Gunner in particular has to be a man in whom absolute trust can reside, for he has the key to the powder magazine. In time, the Yankees followed in that same tradition and built up their own corps of Warrant Officers. But for the time being, *Declaration* was their first and only warship, so they had to make do. And *Declaration*'s gunner was one Foden, a New Yorker and lately an employee of the Cooper family. He was another bumped-up pollywog from the merchant service, and much like others in the ship: he had the skills of his trade but not the right expectations.

He was a clerkish-looking fellow with a long coat dyed a dull approximation of service-blue and his hair worked into a tail like a common seaman. He wore small squarish spectacles on the end of his nose and was a man in his forties, much older than most of *Declaration*'s people.

"Mr Gunner!" says I, creeping up on him unexpected – I couldn't resist it: I'd seen him locking his store room, too preoccupied to see who was coming down the companionway behind him. He jumped most satisfactorily.

"Mr Fletcher!" says he, with the lantern light of the orlop shining in his lenses. Precious little sunlight got down here.

"I noticed there was but one priming quill per gun in the maindeck lockers," says I.

"One per gun, sir," says he nervously. "Waaal, that'd be the case," says he.

"Only one?" says I. "And how shall the guns be fired once they are used up?" He licked his lips and explained patiently.

"By filling the vents with priming powder," says he. "To convey the flash of the firelocks to the cartridges. Aye," says he, "that'd be the case." By George, I could've throttled the little swab. He was lecturing me like a schoolboy. "Mr Foden," says I, "whenever I want an explanation of the bloody obvious, I'll remember to call on you!" He jumped again and white appeared around his eyes. "And as to priming powder," says I, "you know as well as I that a cannon-vent full of that takes its own bloody time burning down and God knows when the main charge will fire!"

It's true, too – takes ages and the damn thing fizzes like a roman candle with all hands standing back with their fingers in their ears. "But a priming quill's different, is it not?" says I.

"Aye-aye, sir," says he.

"Why?" says I, irritated with the pompous rogue.

"Waaal, sir," says he, "'tis quicker with a quill in the vent. The powder in the quill takes fire in an instant and sends a flash down the vent that ignites the charge at once."

"Well done, Mr Foden!" says I. "So why did not every gun have a good supply of quills ready for use?"

"Waaal, sir," says he, "'tis the work of making of 'em, I guess. And me with only one mate as understands the work."

"Mr Foden," says I, "you will ensure that every gun and carronade in this ship has a plentiful supply of quills. You will do it in time for my drill tomorrow, or I'll have you disrated!"

Foden went white with shock and stood there trembling before me. He was in terror at the prospect of losing his cosy berth. I honestly think I'd have done him less harm with boxing his ears, and I got no pleasure from frightening the wretched little grub. It made me feel too much of a bully. But what if *Declaration* had been brought to action with her guns relying on powder trails, and firing at half the speed they should have?

The result was that Foden made up the quills pretty

damn sharpish and they were in the lockers for gun-drill the following day. Mind you, I found out later that Foden sneaked to Cooper to complain of me behind my back. But Cooper had the sense to back my order. And it's a damn good thing for him that he did. Without those priming quills I'd never have brought his crews up to anything like proper speed. And then Cooper would have lost his ship.

I was aboard *Declaration* for nearly five weeks in all. In that time, I saw her improve as a fighting ship at the most astonishing rate, for all the basic material was there: ship, crew and gear. And despite all that I've said against them, her people were something astonishingly keen.

Cooper took her far out into the Atlantic and practised his ship in every aspect of the seaman's business. He learned how to get the best out of her too.

A rahsay like *Declaration* had her strengths and weaknesses. She was massively strong for a frigate, for she had a line-o'-battle ship's timbers and so could mount such heavy guns. And her sides were near three feet thick of solid oak at the gun-deck, so she was a sea-castle when she went into action. Against that she rolled something awful and she needed four men at the helm even in fair weather. And if it came on to blow, then another twenty men were needed down below on the relieving tackles to help control the rudder.

That's what came of messing about with what the original Frog designer had laid down, for the garlic-breathers built fine ships, there's no denying it, and they were seldom improved by hacking decks off them in a foreign dockyard.

None the less, Cooper drove his crew from the seamanship angle and I drove them for him from the gunnery angle, until my gun-crews began to do their work like real teams.

There's a certain quality that marks out good team-work which is best described, strangely enough, by the musicians' word "attack". It means the wholehearted and simultaneous delivery of every man's effort together at the instant of need. It must come without let or hesitation, nor the least holding back of utmost commitment. Whether it be fiddlers scraping out Mozart, or a gun-team throwing their weight on a tackle, it's the same. And after days of steady drilling, my gunners were beginning to show that quality. It's a hard thing to describe, but anyone who's seen it, knows it. And it can't even begin to develop until the technique of the craft be known. First the technicalities, then speed, then *attack*!

The result of these constant drills in gunnery and seamanship was that *Declaration of Independence* was fast becoming a very menacing and efficient man-o'-war.

The faults I'd seen earlier were fading away and, given another ten days at sea, I would venture to say that, given her weight of broadside, nothing short of a ship of the line could have bested her in single combat. And I, who couldn't give a damn for such things, was the man most responsible for this.

For Cooper got over his sulks as soon as he saw what I was doing with his gun-crews, and his favour smiled upon me. I was never quite easy with his attitude to me, in that I never got to the bottom of it. He was a devious swab, up to his gills in politics, and it's my belief that he regarded me as some sort of magical, talented being: a mixture of Ariel and Caliban, that he'd conjured up by his own special cleverness, and that was now his to command. Certainly, from the way he strutted up and down the gun-deck during my drills, you'd have thought *he* was due the credit rather than me! What's more, he told his other officers that everything else aboard ship must now be run "Fletcher-fashion". This phrase I would point out was his, and *not* mine.

Of course, this meant that I made no friends among the officers. To them I was teacher's pet and school bully rolled into one. And so my time aboard *Declaration* was somewhat lonely. But I didn't give a monkey's fart for that. For I hoped to be out of the ship in a few months and back to Uncle Ezekiah's 5,000 dollars where they awaited me snug and cosy in my bank in Boston. And then, God willing, I'd never go to sea again. That thought kept me far warmer at night than the society of a bunch of Yankee Lieutenants guzzling wine and salt pork round the Wardroom table. Those that weren't chewing tobacco and spitting on the deck, which disgusting Yankee habit they'd brought with them from the merchant service.

The men liked me though. I think they actually enjoyed the drills once they'd got the idea of what was wanted from them. They certainly gave me their best and you could see the spirit in 'em as they stood tensed and waiting, row upon row, lined up by the gun tackles, looking to me for the word of command.

But I never got those extra days. If I had, then the course of my life would have run very different than it did. Even after all these years I still think of what might have happened in that event. But it never transpired and that's all there is to it.

What happened was that on 26th April 1794, *Declaration*'s lookouts spotted a distant sail, and Cooper immediately steered to close with it. By chance it was the first ship we'd encountered since leaving Boston and the American coast. At once Cooper ordered us to general quarters, and my crews broke all previous records in the smartness of their loading and running out. My station was on the gun-deck, so I was not party to any discussion that might have taken place among Cooper and his other officers on the quarter deck, and I stamped up and down threatening doom and damnation to any of the men who dared to whisper to one another, and wondering why Cooper didn't turn away and make for Virginia and the protection of the Grain Convoy's escorts.

The point was that he was running one hell of a risk

in closing with that distant ship, far away under the horizon. Because if she were a British man-o'-war then he'd have to run, which could seriously demoralise his crew just when they were beginning to learn their business, or he must fight, which he'd been ordered not to do by no less than President Washington himself.

I supposed that Cooper's old, piratical habits had reasserted themselves and that he couldn't resist the chance of earning some prize money. The hands certainly thought so, 'cos that's what they were whispering about. They were eager as could be.

That's what I thought at first, and it merely annoyed me. But soon, the lookout hailed the deck again. "British colours! Enemy in sight!" cried the voice, and an intense excitement ran through the ship. A dull growl arose from my gun-crews that swelled into a cheer.

"Belay that!" I bellowed, but they were wild-eyed and thirsting for blood and grinning at me like children whose father has laid a meal before them.

Cooper said something to one of the middies and the next minute American colours were breaking from the fore, main and mizzen topmasts, to keep company with the big banner trailing at the spanker gaff.

I couldn't believe it. There was only one reason for such a display. Cooper was taking *Declaration* into action. The men cheered their heads off and the officers waved their hats. I actually saw the First Lieutenant shaking Cooper's hand and the two of them laughing and chatting, as merry as could be. A great unease came upon me. One of the props that supported my view on the world had just been knocked out. I beckoned the eldest of the six midshipmen that I had under me to control the gun-deck.

"You," says I, "you're in command!" and I ran along the deck and up the companionway ladder to confront Cooper in the midst of his officers.

"Cooper," says I, all protocol blown to the winds, "what in God's name are you doing?" His face was flushed and his eyes stared. He was in a rare mood of exultation. He'd got a big powerful ship under his feet and he was bearing down on the enemy. I could see from the start I was wasting my time.

"Fletcher," says he, "this is just the chance we need!"

"What about your bloody orders?" says I. "From the President?" The Master, the Marine Lieutenant, assorted midshipmen, the helmsmen, the carronade crews and a file of Marines with muskets at the ready, gaped at me in astonishment. But Cooper wouldn't meet my eye. And nor would his First Lieutenant. They looked like a couple of dirty schoolboys caught fiddling with one another.

"Orders?" says he. "What orders? My orders are to render every assistance to our French allies."

I've never been so thunderstruck in all my life. If it hadn't been for the Marines, I'd have knocked Cooper flat on his own deck for the lying, double-dealing, conniving bastard that he was.

"Mr Fletcher," says he, "attend to your duties or go below." He turned to the Marine officer. "See that Mr Fletcher is escorted, if necessary . . ."

The swine! Even then he wasn't straight with me. Was that a threat or not? The Marine laid his hand on his sword and looked confused. I was so angry that I turned my back on the lot of them and went back to the gun-deck. At least there were friendly faces down there.

I don't know how long I paced up and down worrying over what had happened. For that matter I've never yet worked out what Cooper was up to.

Was it all lies about the President wanting to keep on the right side of the British? Or was Cooper swept away in the surge of the moment? Had Uncle Ezekiah been a part of this? Had he been lying with his tales of French wickedness? After all, the Frogs had helped them win their precious revolution. There would have been no United States without French interference. And, most important of all, was my 5,000 dollars safe or was that another deceit? I thought over every word, gesture and inflection of the conversations I'd had in the banks where I took Ezekiah's draft. There was no way I could have checked better than I did . . . but if the whole Cooper family were plotting against me . . . then . . . then what?

The maddening thing was that I was sure that the swab Cooper did actually like me. My final judgement on him and his uncle is this: both of them were so bound up with their bloody politics that they'd feed a man any damned tale that suited their purposes at any particular moment, and therefore it's pointless trying to sift out the truth from the lies and from the mixture of both.

So I stamped about, head on my chest, for a long time, paying no attention to anything around me, until the gun-crews started cheering again and making such a din that it even penetrated my thick head.

The occasion for this was the appearance of the enemy in plain sight, from where we stood on the gun-deck. Sails, masts and hull were visible, still miles away, but she was coming on bravely under a press of canvas. She was a frigate, and a fast one, for her bows cut the waves in a shower of foam.

She was a fine sight to see, but not one that I relished. For the "enemy" ship, bearing down upon us, with the Union Jacks streaming from her mastheads, was His Majesty's Ship *Phiandra*.

Chapter 17

A scheme more crack-brained and incapable of being carried through, it is hard to imagine. So much then for the "deep and deadly cunning" of the Coignwoods!

(From a letter of 25th September 1793 from Mr Hector Gardiner, J.P., to Mrs Jane Forster, Widow of Mr Cecil Forster, J.P.)

*

"D'you mean to tell me the thing must be done here? In my house?" said Mr Hector Gardiner. "Cannot the wretch be taken to the Lock-up? Or to the Charity Hospital?"

"No, sir!" said the surgeon. "Even the bringing of him here could easily have incurred a fatal outcome!"

Gardiner, the new Magistrate for Lonborough and

district, glanced at the heavy bulk of his Parish Constable who had stood with his brother in silence during this discussion between their betters.

"Did you know this, Plowright?" said the Magistrate irritably. He was not in the best of humours, having been summoned from sleep in the early hours by the arrival at his door of his Constable and several others. He now stood in his nightshirt and dressing gown, holding this enquiry by new-lit candles in his drawing room, while his servants hovered in the hall and his wife stood on the upstairs landing listening in fascination.

"We done everything proper, sir," said the Constable, indignant at the implied criticism. "We brung 'un along on a street front door, sir," said the Constable. "Ain't that so, Abram?"

"Aye," said his brother.

"So's he shouldn't shake nothin' loose what had come apart inside, sir," said the Constable.

"Aye," said Abram.

"Could you not have took him to the lock-up, man?" said Gardiner.

Plowright thought that through, frowning at the act of concentration required, and brought forth his answer.

"Well, Mr Gardiner, sir," said he, "we couldn't not rightly ha' done that, sir. Not seeing as who it was, sir. We couldn't put no gennelman in there, sir. So we brung 'un here. Ain't that right, Abram?"

"Aye," said his brother.

"Huh!" said Mr Wallace the surgeon. "A gentleman, eh?"

"Indeed!" agreed Gardiner. Noah Plowright, the Constable (Acting Constable, in fact) was a good man for taking up drunken farmhands or chasing little boys out of orchards, but he had the brain of an ox. Gardiner wished fervently that Adam Plowright, the eldest brother, might soon be fit to resume his duties.

Meanwhile, Gardiner saw that there was nothing for it but to proceed.

"Do what you must, Mr Wallace," said he. "I ask only that you should do it in the kitchen where the floors may the more easily be washed down."

"Thank you, sir," said the surgeon. "I shall need as much light as possible, a good brisk fire to warm the room, and a stout chair with arms."

"A chair?" said Gardiner. "What's that for?"

Wallace started to explain, but a hammering on the front door announced more arrivals. As Gardiner's servant opened the door, voices were heard outside.

"Arr!" said the Acting Constable, "here's our Adam come to see!"

"Aye!" said his brother.

"Where is he?" cried a voice in the hall, and the company in the withdrawing room, led by Gardiner, trooped into the hall to see who had arrived.

With a dozen men crammed into the narrow space, clustered around the comatose figure on its improvised stretcher, where it lay flat on the floor, there was little room to move. Magistrate, surgeon, Constables and servants stood elbow to elbow, and all spoke at once, and Mrs Gardiner peered over the banisters in her eagerness to miss nothing that might happen.

"Ah, you black-hearted villain!" said the new arrival, a big man shrunken and grey-faced from illness, and obviously another Plowright brother. He looked down upon the occupant of the front street door with bitter hatred.

"See what you done, to me, you bastard!" says Adam Plow-right, lately the Parish Constable, and the company looked upon the empty left leg of his breeches and the two crutches that Plowright walked upon. "Half a man I am, thanks to you!" said Plowright, and looked accusingly at his younger brothers. "What you brung 'un here for, eh?" said he. "He don't need no buggerin' doctors! What he needs is throwing in the buggerin' river, the bloody bastard, with a buggerin' great stone tied round his buggerin' neck!"

"Guard your tongue, man!" cried the Magistrate, sharply. "I'll have no such speech in my house! And this man is under the protection of the Law!"

"Shot me, he did!" said Plowright, miserably, looking down at the half-dead Victor Coignwood. "Last July when we went with Mr Forster to take him," he pointed at Victor, "him, and his blasted mother! Deliberate, it were. He ruined me! Where's the use of a man with one leg?"

"Now, now, Plowright," said Gardiner, sympathetically, "brace up! You shall go on a peg-leg as good as any man here!" Gardiner looked to the surgeon. "Support me now, Wallace! Shan't our Constable walk on a wooden leg, eh?"

"So soon as the stump is fully healed, I shall fit him myself!" said Wallace.

"There!" said Gardiner. "And your post awaits you on your return to health." He pushed forward and laid a hand on Plow-right's arm. "But now you shall go home." He turned to the other Plowrights. "See to your brother like the good fellows you are," said he. "Get him home to his wife."

"Leave me two men, at least, if you please, Mr Gardiner," said the surgeon, looking at the broad backs of the Plowright brothers. "I need two resolute men for what I must do."

*

Half an hour later Mr Wallace, the surgeon, was ready to begin. The slumbering kitchen fire had been aroused, candles blazed all around, and instruments sponges, salves and bandages were laid ready to hand on the kitchen table. Victor Coignwood was semi-conscious. He blinked stupidly and moaned to himself. He was propped up in a big armchair with his wrists and elbows firmly bound to the arms of the chair by stout linen tapes.

As a further precaution, one of the Plowright brothers

was holding Victor's shoulders firmly against the chair back, and Mr Gardiner's footman clamped Victor's wounded forearm between his two fists. Gardiner himself and several of his servants stood in horrified fascination as Mr Wallace, the surgeon, stepped forward in his long apron, with sleeves rolled up and a lancet in his hand. Finding himself brightly lit and centre stage, Wallace rose to the occasion and expounded as if to students.

"Having bandaged the chest wound, which is minor," said he, "the first procedure proper will be one of relative simplicity." He displayed Victor's wound with the tip of his surgical knife. "Here the ball entered at the dorsal aspect of the forearm" – he showed the round entry-wound – "and here, on the ventral aspect, the ball may easily be palpated where it lies beneath the skin." Bolder heads craned forward to see the dull blue shape of the lodged ball, clearly visible through Victor's pale skin. "The radius and ulna are unaffected and it remains to remove extraneous matter from the wound track and to excise the ball."

All present watched in fascination as Wallace cleaned and bandaged the bullet-track across Victor's chest. As Wallace had said, this was a simple matter, since the wound was little more than a graze. But then the surgeon took his knife and slit the round, dark swelling on Victor's arm. An inch-long, red-lipped incision gaped open, blood oozed forth, and some lively work with a pair of forceps extracted the blood-slicked ball and a scrap of shirt that it had carried into the wound.

At this, Victor moaned loudly, most of the audience found business elsewhere, and Gardiner's footman fell back in a swoon.

Wallace looked up from his work. "The arms," said he, "I'd be obliged . . ." Only Gardiner and his cook were left. Gardiner strongly wished to be gone, but although he could see that the woman was quite unmoved he'd been a soldier in his time and felt obliged to give a lead.

"See to that man!" he ordered, and the cook pulled the footman clear, while Gardiner took his place at the forearm.

Gardiner found that the trick of it was to stare fixedly at anything other than what the surgeon was doing. And so he managed without great discomfort as the arm was treated.

"And now," said Wallace, "the more serious procedure. I regret that I shall be obliged to trephine the skull, since the patient's comatose state, consequent upon a depressed fracture of the left frontal bone, indicates an accumulation of . . ." Gardiner did not properly hear the rest. He was looking at the blood stains on Wallace's apron. Also he knew what trepanning involved.

Everything became exceedingly unpleasant for Mr Gardiner after that, and had he anticipated that his duties as Magistrate would involve the like, he would never have taken them on.

Wallace had him stand close in front of Coignwood, holding the man's head between the palms of his hands, while Plowright remained as he was gripping the shoulders. That meant that Wallace had to squeeze in somehow sideways beside Plowright to do his work. But Coignwood himself showed how vital were the two "holders down", for he wept and struggled powerfully once Wallace started with his trephine.

But first Wallace cut short the hair of Coignwood's head and set to with lather and a barber's brush and razor to shave the scalp over an area the size of a man's palm.

"Ah!" said Wallace, when he'd dried the area with a towel. "Note the bruising," and he prodded gently with his fingers, "and a palpable fracture . . ." Gardiner nearly went at the knees as he heard a distinct grating of bone.

"And, so . . ." said Wallace slitting the skin of Victor's scalp in a line about four inches long. Victor groaned horribly and Gardiner had to fight to keep the head still. From the corner of his eye Gardiner caught sight of two hideous instruments as Wallace took them up. They were like something from a torture chamber of the Inquisition: long-shafted double hooks of a wicked sharpness, made of twinkling steel on wooden handles.

"Retractors," said Wallace, "to open the wound," and he hooked the ghastly things into the lips of Coignwood's incision and tugged briskly at right angles to the line of the cut to expose as much skull as possible.

Gardiner kept his eyes shut for a while after that, and did not peep again until he heard a steady scraping noise and Coignwood screamed loudly and fought to get out of the chair.

Wallace was drilling into Victor's skull with quick, neat twisting motions of an instrument like a corkscrew, except that the blade was a small, ring-shaped saw designed to cut out a disk of bone. It is a pity that Mr Arthur Walton was not available for comment, else he would have remarked upon the great similarity between one of his burglar's centre-bits and a surgeon's trephine.

One look at the drilling in progress, and the little wall of pink, damp bone-dust building up around the working edge of the tool was enough for Gardiner. So he kept his eyes tight shut and missed the interesting moment of the removal of the plug of bone, and he missed Wallace's careful opening up of the dura mater to release a gush of fluid and semi-solid blood that was building up beneath.

In fact he kept his eyes shut until Wallace had completed the procedure down to closing up the wound and bandaging, and Gardiner realised that Wallace was telling him to let go of Coignwood's head.

"All done now, sir!" said Wallace, prising Gardiner's fingers free. "Well done, Mr Gardiner!" said Wallace. "And you too, Plowright!"

Magistrate and Constable looked at one another and

it would have been impossible to say which of the two was greener about the gills. Gardiner noticed that his imperturbable cook was still there, but the footman had gone, either carried away or got up and gone of his own volition.

Wallace took command.

"Mr Gardiner," said he, "I suggest that you go to the drawing room and take a large brandy. And perhaps Plowright could have a brandy, here in the kitchen?" Gardiner nodded. "If Plowright would then take charge of the prisoner, I will join you, Mr Gardiner, as soon as all is put to rights here."

*

Much later, after a number of large brandies, Mr Gardiner was his own man again, and was ready to discuss the events of the night with Mr Wallace.

"I believe that the rascal will live," said Wallace. "If mortification does not set in, then he will certainly survive. But he may not be moved . . ."

"Damnation," said Gardiner, "is my house to be a prison as well as a hospital?"

"He's a dead man if we move him, sir!" said Wallace.

"Bah!" said Gardiner. "And all this trouble for a villain who'll be hanged three times over when he comes to court. Our friend Taylor did a grand job on the other rogue and it's more than a pity he didn't finish Coignwood too!"

Wallace nodded in agreement. "Yes," said he, "but it concerns me to wonder just exactly what Coignwood and his friend were attempting to do."

"Why, to kill the Taylors, of course," said Gardiner. "Mr and Mrs Taylor are witnesses to Victor.Coignwood's murdering of Mr Richard Lucey."

"Of course," said Wallace. "But Coignwood and his ally Walton were locked in deadly combat when Mr Taylor awoke. And I have seen the knife wounds in Walton's back! Why was Coignwood trying to kill Walton?"

"To silence him," said Gardiner, "so no person could tell of what Coignwood had done."

"In that case," said Wallace, "Victor Coignwood came to Lonborough with the intention of killing Mr Taylor, Mrs Taylor, his own companion Walton and no doubt the Taylors' two servants and the child too! For we must presume he aimed to fire the *other* side of Market Street to cover his crime." Wallace paused and looked at Gardiner. "Does this not strike you as excessively ambitious for one night's work, sir?"

"What are you getting at, Wallace?" said Gardiner.

"Well, sir," said Wallace, "look at the matter of Coignwood's disguise as a woman. So soon as the news of tonight's doings got about, did they not send from the George to tell you of their two bizarre guests? The London 'gentlemen' and his 'wife' whom all the staff believed to be no woman God ever made?"

"Yes," said Gardiner, "Lonborough is too small for such things not to be made swiftly known."

"Then there you have it, sir!" said Wallace. "What sort of crack-brained nonsense was Victor Coignwood engaged in?"

Chapter 18

To be entirely honest, I wasn't sure that ship was *Phiandra*. Not at first. It's true that no two ships are quite the same any more than two faces. But some of the differences are small and most of my time in *Phiandra* had been in her, if you see what I mean, so I wasn't used to looking at her across the ocean.

But as soon as I was sure, I fell to cursing my ill fortune. After all, the Royal Navy had something like a hundred frigates at sea in early '94, so what I wanted to know was: what in God's name were the other ninety-nine doing? Why should the one that came looking for me be the only one that had all my old messmates aboard?

Worse still, I knew the quality of her. As she bore down upon us and *Declaration*'s lookouts reported her to be a 32, there was another great ringing cheer, and every man grinned his Yankee grin and told his Yankee chums that they would have the Limey for breakfast. And why not? For *Declaration*'s people knew that no British frigate mounted 24-pounders like they did.

Well, I knew better than any man in either ship what the match would be, and this is what it was:

Phiandra —
700 tons burden
32 18-pounder long guns
10 24-pounder carronades
   (Weight of broadside = 408 pounds)
Declaration —
1100 tons burden
36 24-pounder long guns
20 32-pounder carronades
   (Weight of broadside = 704 pounds)

So, you'd think the Yankee confidence not unreasonable wouldn't you? But they didn't know *Phiandra*. They didn't know that what was thrashing along towards them, just as eager as she could be, was one of the Royal Navy's elite champions. A ship whose invincible gunnery had beaten more than twice her weight at Passage d'Aron and whose every man was a battle-hardened veteran. So when it came down to it, I hadn't the least idea who might win the coming contest: *Declaration* with her ship-of-the line timbers and -her heavy guns, or *Phiandra* with her greater skill?

Meanwhile, *Declaration* was buzzing with activity and men were called away from the guns to the work of shortening sail for action. Down came the t'gallants and royals: masts, yards and all. Preventer braces and chain slings were rigged and the courses close-furled. Only the topsails were left, swelling in the strong north-north-wester that drove us on. It drove *Phiandra* on too as she came on steadily, close hauled on the larboard tack.

On *Declaration*'s gun-deck the excitement was intense. Hardly a man of the crew had been in a real action and they crammed their heads out of the gun-ports for a view of the British ship as she came closer and closer. Cooper and his officers on the quarterdeck were just the same. They were up on the carronades and hanging in the shrouds – anywhere for a good view over the hammock nettings that walled in the quarterdeck. They waved their hats and slapped one another on the shoulders and laughed and joked. Waves of cheering rose up, died away and rose again. You'd think we were going to a bloody pantomime.

Eventually, with the two ships no more than half a mile apart, *Declaration*'s gunners were called to their duty, and they stood (just as I'd taught them) in neat rows, each gun-captain with the trigger lanyard in his fist, peering eagerly over the huge fat breech of his heavy gun.

Declaration and *Phiandra* were closing upon each other bow to bow, with each ship going five or six knots. With a quarter mile between us, it seemed as if *Phiandra* was steering to get the weather gauge of us, and so shut off the chance of our running away downwind. Cooper certainly thought so, for I heard him cry out.

"Quartermaster," says he to the helmsman, "run on board of her! She thinks we'll try to escape like a Frenchman! Show what an American can do!"

This brought another great cheer. But they didn't cheer a moment later, for *Phiandra* served them a nasty trick.

As *Declaration*'s quartermasters (four of them, remember, plus a crew down below at the relieving tackles) put up the helm to bring her head round to bear more directly upon *Phiandra* the British ship wore and, spinning round like a top, raked *Declaration* by the bow with a rapid and deliberate discharge of her starboard battery.

[When asked to explain the word "wore" Fletcher described me as a "bloody grub landsman who don't know his a***e from his elbow". For those as innocent as I, to wear a ship means to turn her head away from the wind, as opposed to tacking which turns the head into the wind. Wearing is almost certain to succeed while tacking may fail. Thus wearing is safer in battle. S.P.].

I suppose I should say I was privileged to see a Frog's-eye-view of a British warship going about her business, but it didn't seem like that at the time. It was a fine thing to see, but bloody awful too. A steady series of concussions burst out of the deadly black squares in the sleek hull, accompanied by orange flame and gouting white smoke. The noise was deafening, and if you don't believe me then you try standing in front of a troop of artillery as they give a Royal Salute in one of the London parks.

Instantly a ripping, shredding, tearing series of blows struck *Declaration* as *Phiandra*'s roundshot smashed into her bow and tore the length of her decks. Dust and splinters flew and men cried out in pain and terror. I saw two dead men within feet of me and a dismounted gun up by the bow.

But then the tormentor was gone. *Phiandra* was bearing away on *Declaration*'s starboard bow, and two hundred yards downwind. She was out of effective gunshot and shooting ahead on a somewhat convergent course.

A smaller ship than *Declaration* and one with a less determined crew could have had the stuffing knocked out of her by that treatment. There were five or more dead and twice that many wounded. One gun was thrown over and much damage had been done. And the Yankees hadn't even fired. But Yankees are like the British in a fight and *Declaration*'s men stood to their guns and awaited their chance.

Soon enough, they seemed to get it. *Phiandra* by cracking on sail was still drawing away, but as her course converged with ours, the distance between us closed such that by *Declaration*'s maindeck gunners slewing their starboard battery pieces hard on the bow, their broadside bore on *Phiandra* at a hundred and fifty yards. And so they delivered the drill that I'd taught them and none could say they didn't do it well, with each gun firing as its captain judged best. And while they raced to reload, I cringed in anticipation of what we'd get back in exchange. For if *Declaration*'s guns would bear then so would *Phiandra*'s.

But no broadside came and *Phiandra* hauled away from us. Shouts of derision came from the Yankees and it seemed *Phiandra* was running. Then damn me if she didn't play the same trick again! She got herself ahead of us and suddenly she was wearing again so as to place herself across *Declaration*'s bows. By George she wasn't a crack ship for nothing! Somebody on *Phiandra*'s quarterdeck had taken a good look at *Declaration* and decided she was too heavy for a broadside duel and so was out-manoeuvring her.

Once more the British ship ran across the American's bow and riddled her stem to stern with a double-shotted broadside. This time the damage was far worse, though less men were killed (on the gun-deck at least), since the gunners had the sense to throw themselves on the deck between the guns as *Phiandra*'s shot swept their decks. Another three guns were wrecked, the pumps were smashed and to judge from the screaming from up on the fo'c'sle (which I could not see) some terrible hurt had been caused there too.

In the confusion, as men struggled to put all to rights and heave the wreckage and splinters overside, a ship's boy ran past me howling in terror. He threw down his cartridge box and tried to dive down a hatchway to hide below decks. A Marine sentry was on guard at the hatchway with a brace of pistols and permission to shoot any person trying to do that, but the Marine simply caught the child by the belt, heaved him off his feet and slung him along the deck back where he'd come from. *Phiandra* repeated her tactics two or three times more after that.

She was steadily and efficiently whittling down *Declaration*'s advantage in metal. She was the nimbler ship, sea conditions were to her advantage, with a fresh wind and only a light swell, and she was sailing rings around the clumsy rahsay with her heavy helm and teams of poor devils heaving away on the relieving tackles down in the gun-room.

But then at about two o'clock of the afternoon, the British Captain must have decided that enough was enough and now it was time to show the Yankees what a British man-o'-war could do, for he suddenly gave up the running battle, and simply laid *Phiandra* alongside at pistol-shot range to fight his enemy gun for gun. No doubt he thought *Declaration* had been sufficiently battered to be ready to strike her colours.

And had he been fighting the Frogs or some other lesser breed, then he'd probably have been right. But as it was he'd made a bad decision, for no sooner had *Declaration*'s crew seen what was happening, than all the anger and frustration of being hit without being able to hit back, was thrown into working their guns. The result was one of the fiercest single-ship duels I have ever seen, fought at murderously close range and each broadside threw up a terrible cloud of splinters, rent timbers and torn flesh. The noise and the smoke were indescribable. Every man worked deaf and almost blind in the huge banks of powder smoke poured forth by the simultaneous firing of dozens of heavy guns.

It was simply a matter of which ship could throw the greatest weight of shot in the shortest time, and which crew could stand it the longer. And this is why I say that a week's more training of *Declaration*'s gunners would have changed my life. They were good, and served their 24-pounders well, but they were not yet ready for *Phiandra*'s men, and they were getting back two broadsides for *Declaration*'s one. That or something precious close to it: a rate of fire that more than made up for the disparity in guns mounted.

And so it went on. Every atom of *Declaration* trembled to the voice of her guns. Spars, corpses and wreckage jammed her decks. The men were powder-blacked maniacs and the very fabric of her burst and shook as *Phiandra*'s shot came aboard.

For nearly an hour *Declaration* and *Phiandra* were yard-arm to yard-arm. The Stars and Stripes fought the Union Jack and neither gave an inch. If every shot fired in that dreadful contest had struck home then both ships must have been reduced to wallowing, bloodstained junk.

But usually in such cases only the first few broadsides are properly aimed and so the worst is spared. That's why it's so important to hold your first fire till it really counts.

Eventually *Phiandra* began to fall astern from us. Or rather *Declaration* hauled ahead to the point where neither ship's guns would bear. With the guns silent, the great fog of smoke cleared a little and there was *Phiandra* with her foremast over the side and her men swarming over the shambles to clear away the wreckage.

That should have been the signal for another Yankee cheer, but none came, and I saw that *Declaration*'s people were exhausted. There were thirty or more dead on the gun-deck and as for the living, the vast effort they'd put out had drained them, and for the moment they had no more to give. They'd faced the enemy and they'd not given up, but they were in that desperate stage where one more push from the foe would break them.

Cooper did his best. He went up and down the ship calling on them to bring *Declaration* around to engage the enemy once more, but the men were deadly tired and his sail-trimmers moved like old men, clumsy and slow. And soon *Phiandra*'s tars had hacked away the shattered mast and she was under way again. She'd been sorely hammered. Her topmen were still knotting and splicing as she came, to make good her damage aloft. And amidships four or five guns of her larboard battery were knocked to all points of the compass. But she was coming on to renew the fight and British cheers sounded over the water.

At this the Yankees set their teeth and lifted their heads like men. I saw them do it and it was a sight to see. They're kindred folk to the British, as I've said, and they found the will to fight on, just as *Phiandra*'s men had done.

Had battle been joined again by those two ships then I truly believe they'd have sunk one another. For neither would've given in. But we were saved from that extreme by a hail from the masthead.

"Enemy sail in sight!" I saw Cooper duck his head into a gun-port to see what was coming and he stood up with his face sunk in despair.

He passed within feet of where I was standing on his way back to his quarterdeck, and the look he gave me as he went by would have shrivelled flowers and blighted innocence. He never said a word but from the look on him, I knew the swab was blaming me for what had happened. *Me!* I ask those who know of a finer example of rank ingratitude to send me a letter by the next post, for I'd like to hear it! Perhaps he thought I had not worked hard enough on his guns. Perhaps he thought I was personally responsible for *Phiandra* being the crack ship that she was – we'd passed close enough to read the name painted on her taffrail, so presumably he knew what ship he'd just fought – and perhaps he thought I'd personally whistled up the two more British frigates that were bearing up from the south-east, because that's what he'd just seen through the gun-port.

He should have been pleased really, the little toad. That gave him an honourable way out. He couldn't fight three enemies and so he could withdraw with honour, instead of going to everybody's death, against *Phiandra*.

All he had to do was shake out his courses and bear away under a press of sail, and then he could go home to Boston and tell them how he'd fought *Phiandra* to a standstill and was on the point of boarding her when her consorts hove in sight.

"Yes, gentlemen," he could say, "I am speaking of that very *Phiandra* which achieved such fame in her immortal battle against the French, but which when pitted against American valour . . . etc., etc."

Meanwhile, what about myself? I'd been suspended in limbo. I'd been split down the middle and paralysed with divided loyalties. I wanted my $5,000 and Lucinda, and above all the life of a Boston merchant prince.

But against that had been the horrible necessity of firing into a ship that had Sammy Bone and my old messmates aboard.

For a while I just stood and watched as *Declaration* got herself under way, close-hauled with her jib boom pointing due west for the American coast, and *Phiandra* did her level best to give chase. But even with her sails and rigging torn with shot, *Declaration* had three good masts and nothing like the damage aloft that *Phiandra* had suffered. And so, the Yankee began to pull away while the two fresh, oncoming frigates were no more than royals and t'gallants on the horizon.

Declaration's gun-deck was in a shocking state. It was impossible to put one foot before another without treading on some fragment of shattered gear. With the prospect of action gone, the men were sunk in exhaustion and went about their tasks like the living dead. And then, as I looked about me, I saw something that set me thinking. In a single instant, a number of things that had been whirling around my mind suddenly dropped into place snickety-snick, like the cogs and wheels of a watch. And they all worked together to one accord.

What I saw was the bulkhead leading into the stern cabins at the after end of the gun-deck, smashed wide open by *Phiandra*'s shot, and the poor devil of a Marine who was there to guard the sacred portals of the Captain's lair was bits of him in one place and other bits of him in several others. If you left out his musket, the biggest part left of him was his hat.

In that moment, I perceived an opportunity and I realised several things. I was fed up and disgusted with Cooper and his bloody ship and Cooper was fed up and disgusted with me. Consequently, given the prestige of the Cooper clan, the chances of my being welcomed home to Boston to enjoy my money were about as good as the Marine sentry's chance of becoming a colonel.

On the other hand, I recalled that back home in

England I was heir to *a thousand times* 5,000 miserable Yankee dollars (at a conservative estimate) and this fortune I'd been so bloody stupid as to walk away from. In summary, therefore, what in God's good bloody name was I doing in Yankeeland at all? With the money that was mine in England I could be a merchant, an M.P., a Duke or a bloody Archbishop if I wanted, and above all I could chose *not* to be a bloody sailor!

In a trice I was off the splinter-littered gun-deck and ducking through the broken timbers into Cooper's day-cabin. Inside was a shambles of broken furniture, charts, scraps of Cooper's fancy rugs, and the remains of a 300-guinea chronometer crunching in shards of glass and metal beneath my feet. I went straight through into the Great Cabin and shut the door behind me. The Great Cabin was largely untouched and I was alone in there, with nobody to see what I did.

I went to Cooper's desk and tugged at the drawer where his orders were kept. It was locked, so I hauled the whole thing up off its neat little ball-and-claw feet and smashed it down on the deck with all my might. Two or three vigorous repetitions of this treatment persuaded the drawer to see sense, and it broke open, spilling papers out across the deck. I dropped to my knees to rummage among them and found what I wanted, at once. A letter to Cooper with a heavy seal from the Yankee Department of War. As in the British Service it was enclosed in a tarred canvas wrapper with a grapeshot inside, to sink the secret orders if need be. I took the whole thing, closing the wrapper, and turned to the stern windows.

(Now, as you will have gathered, I was not my usual calculating self at this moment. In fact I was worked up into a state of anger, and even today, when I think of that posturing, conniving little swab Cooper, it still raises my hackles. So I make no apology for the mad-brained, stupid thing I did next. But I do advise you youngsters against ever doing the like.) I had resolved to change ships in mid-ocean and I was leaving by the stern windows. But unfortunately, either they were not made to open or I was too thick-headed to find the catch. So I turned again to my friend the desk, and heaved it through Cooper's leaded lights with their diamond-shaped panes of glass.

Then I was up on to a chair and squeezing my bulk through the hole. Somebody came in at that moment, for I heard the discharge of a pistol and felt the wind of a bullet across my backside. But then I was tumbling head over heels into the cold, wet Atlantic.

I came up spluttering, and fought to keep afloat much encumbered with my clothes and shoes. And it *was* cold. By George it was cold! I'd learned to swim in the rivers of West Africa with African maidens for playfellows – another of the little courtesies I'd enjoyed from Pareira Gomez's African king – and there the water was as soft and warm as a mother's breast. But the North Atlantic in

April chilled your marrow and shrivelled your pecker. It was frightening too. The ship towered over me but was pulling away fast. In fact I came dangerously close to drowning myself, alone and quiet and unremarked. For everything depended on my catching hold of the boat that trailed behind *Declaration* like a calf behind a farmer's cart.

This was Cooper's idea. Many ships had a life-preserver towed astern on a line for "overboards" to swim to before the ship ran on and left them. Cooper went one better and had his gig towed astern with lengths of netting hung over its sides for the convenience of those who might need to clamber in. And that's what I was after. But the boat was coming on fast and I was low in the water. It was on me before I knew and only an instinctive grab at the looming black shape, just as it slid by, saved my life.

My hands closed on the knotted ropes of the netting. My shoulders wrenched at the jerk of the boat's pull as it dragged me along and then I was struggling to get myself into it. I don't know if I'd have managed it, even then, for I was numbed with cold and I'd breathed a lungful of seawater as the boat's motion swept a wave over my head. But somebody was helping me! A pair of strong arms was pulling me up and in. I caught the blur of a white face and a blue jacket as I rolled over the gunnel and collapsed, coughing violently into the bottom of the boat.

There was a man in the boat already! He grinned at

me and gabbled in some foreign tongue. He was a seaman, a lower-deck hand.

A big man with black hair and side-whiskers. He pointed at *Declaration* and I took it that he was a genuine "overboard", knocked into the sea during the action.

I vaguely recollected him. His name was Brown or something that sounded like Brown. He was a Swede or a German or the like. There was a whole gun-crew of 'em, but I know not what breed they were. I've neither the talent nor the inclination to classify foreigners by the noises they make.

In any case, I had to act fast. A musket shot came from the stern of *Declaration* and something hit the boat with a fierce WHACK! Brown gaped at that.

I lurched into the bow and cast off the tow-line. The boat lost way and wallowed in the waves. Bang! Another musket shot. Cooper must have guessed what I was up to. I looked back at *Declaration*'s stern. She had two gun-ports there, with 18-pounders behind them, and oh Christ! They were opening! I'd be blown to mincemeat with grapeshot if I didn't get out of range fast.

I seized the oars and clunked them into the rowlocks. I heaved mightily on the right oar – missed the ocean by inches, went arse-over-tit between the thwarts, struggled right up again and heaved once more. The boat spun round and I put the full weight of my strength into speeding the boat away on an exactly opposite course to *Declaration*'s.

Over my shoulder I could see *Phiandra*'s yards above the waves, and occasionally her bows as she laboured onward in the hopeless attempt to catch *Declaration*. By looking back from time to time, I could keep the boat headed for *Phiandra* while my speed and *Declaration*'s speed took me out of cannon shot. But I'd forgotten Brown.

"Jabber-jabber-jabber?" says he, and the look on his face was comical. He didn't know what was happening. His ship was vanishing and I was puffing hard for the enemy. But he was used to treating me with respect – as an officer, in fact – so I suppose he was asking politely what we were doing.

"Shut your bloody trap!" says I, by way of explanation. That silenced him for a bit, but he soon got nervous.

"Jabber-jabber!" says he, turning nasty, and he did a lot of pointing and waving his arms, then he laid hands on the oars so I couldn't row.

I couldn't have that, so I took a swing at him. But it's hard fist-fighting when you're sitting down in a plunging boat. So I missed.

"*so!*" says he, the only word of his I understood, and he pulled his knife. He pointed to *Declaration* and waved the blade under my nose. Obviously he wanted to go back to the ship.

It was an impasse. I wasn't going to turn the boat, but he wouldn't let me row. We sat glaring at one another for a while, then . . . Boom! One of *Declaration*'s stern chasers fired. Luckily they'd not loaded grape or that would have been the end of us, for either by luck or judgement, the roundshot plunged into the sea within yards of us.

WHOOSH! Splatter-splatter-splash! Brown cringed and stared at the angry water. Since he was sat facing me, quite close, with knees spread apart, I took advantage of this lapse of concentration and kicked him in the walnuts with very great force indeed. He gasped in agony and collapsed forward like a folded clasp-knife. I shoved him backwards off his thwart and left him curled up in the bottom of the boat. I considered braining him with the wooden bailing-bucket but it wasn't needed. I never had a squeak of trouble from him after that. It just goes to show that all men are amenable to reason, if only you can strike the right note.

So I went back to my rowing and soon, as I looked over my shoulder, I could see figures looking at me from *Phiandra*'s quarterdeck and fo'c'sle. I was going home.

Chapter 19

It is, ma'am, my firm belief from what the girl Booth has let slip, that some heavy guilt, of cause as yet unknown, lies over Mr Fletcher, awaiting only to be exploited in your cause.
(From a letter of 20th September 1793 from Samuel Slym to Lady Sarah Coignwood.)

*

Slym gritted his teeth and groaned with the effort of mastering his lust. He tried and failed, for the tableau acting out before him was beyond the strength of mortal man to resist.

The two half-naked girls twined about each other like mating pythons, and the soft red-shaded lamplight glistened on the oils that they were kneading into each other's flesh. The costumes were golden, feathered helmets in the Grecian style, with sandals bound up with thin leather thongs that wound all the way up to the rounded thighs. That and about half-a-yard each of transparent muslin masquerading as a Grecian princess's chiton. Plump breasts slithered against each other and slim, sharp-nailed fingers clenched into swelling buttocks. One "princess" was voluptuous and golden-haired, the other slender and graceful with tiny exquisite features and huge brown eyes.

Mrs Simpson had promised something special, and the honour of her house had been upheld.

"The postures you will find most tasteful and exotic, sir!" she had said. "And our girls, while selected for youth and freshness, are none the less proficient in every accomplishment." She smiled artfully and added, "If the gentleman's taste so requires, my girls can, for instance, deliver every identical satisfaction to the experience of the first enjoyment of a pure virgin."

Slym swore fiercely under his breath as the tableau gathered speed. The slender one had the plump girl thrown on her back, pinned down by the wrists and was straddled across her on the couch heaving her rump up and down and round, against the wriggling pink body.

Sam Slym was here in Portsmouth (Gosport in actual fact) on business. And when Slym was on business, nothing other than his client's interests were pursued. No personal pleasures were indulged, however attractive they might be. That was his rule. And fixated, self-disciplined, ruthlessly polished creature that he was, he kept the rule unbroken. This was so even for normal clients, but for Lady Sarah Coignwood, who filled Slym's mind with hopeless desires, there could be no possibility of his deviating from the path of duty. Even though he had no connection with Lady Sarah other than the professional, for Slym to indulge himself with another woman would be, to him, an adultery against his hopes and dreams.

But, by God it was hard! They were kissing now, locked in each other's arms, mouths pressed together, eyes closed, exploring each other's mouths with their tongues. Slym dragged his eyes away and looked at the surroundings. The room was purpose-built. Heavily curtained to close out the daylight, fitted with a miniature theatrical stage with scenery, and with a row of half-a-dozen little opera-boxes in front of the stage, each carefully partitioned off from the others so that gentlemen could view the entertainment in private without being seen from the boxes on either side. Mrs Simpson's was the best house in Portsmouth. Slym had seen better in London, but for the provinces it was impressive. Extremely expensive too.

"The price, sir," the old bawd had said, "includes dinner, an entertainment of five tableaux vivants, and your choice of young lady companion for the evening." She'd smiled a hard-eyed smile out of a face still showing the remains of a past beauty. "It cannot be less, sir, not with the cost of ensuring both a constant supply of fresh young maids, and also of ensuring that only gentlemen shall be admitted." Slym paid up without complaint. His client could afford it and she would be pleased with his rapid progress in finding a needle in a haystack.

The ancient fortress-city of Portsmouth was the first naval seaport of the kingdom, and with its great guns and encircling ramparts it was the most powerful military position too. With England at war with her old enemy, Portsmouth was chock full of sailors, Marines, sea officers, docks, shipyards and all the bustling commerce of trades and professions required to support the enormous maritime effort required of the main base for the Channel Fleet, the nation's shield against invasion. And not the least of the professions which sailormen looked upon as indispensable was that practised by Mrs Simpson. Although, of course, Mrs Simpson practised it at the very top end of the range.

Three days in Portsmouth, by systematic patient enquiries and characteristic hard work, had brought Slym to Mrs Simpson's in Gosport, out on the road to the Haslar Hospital. It was a large, respectable seeming establishment, behind high railings with a porter at the gate to keep out the riff-raff. Mrs S. received new gentlemen in her parlour and served tea like a lady of fashion in a London salon. Slym went through the routine patiently, but he was after something specific which he chose not to mention to Madame. And so he was put to the trouble of sitting through three tableaux vivants before he saw what he wanted.

"Can't miss er, my ducky," his informant had said, an overblown moll he'd questioned outside the Ship Tavern on Portsmouth Point. "Thin as a lath, she is, an' a little face like a fairy. Lord knows how she done it, Mrs S. takes on'y fresh meat as a rule."

"How d'you know it's her?" Slym had said. "There's a thousand girls in Portsmouth."

"Huh!" said the doxie. "Not like *her*, there ain't! Little madam, with her airs an' graces!" She'd smiled and snuggled up to Slym. "What you want her for, my duck? On'y a shillin' for a bit o' real woman . . ."

As the tableau reached its gasping climax, both girls moaned and squealed and contrived to lose what little cover there had been on their glowing bodies. Finally they lay panting in an artfully composed heap and a band of music, hidden somewhere out of sight, struck up a mysterious, eastern-sounding tune. Slym had to admit that the thing was well done, almost up to London standards.

As the curtains fell across the little stage, Slym got up and left his box by a narrow door in the back. He found Mrs S. and made his choice for the evening.

Five minutes later, Mrs Simpson showed Slym into a sumptuously appointed bedroom done out a *la Turque* with a canopy ceiling richly hung with silks, and decorated with gilt-framed pictures of reclining nudes in the diaphanous robes of harem odalisques. On a low Turkish table, intricately inlaid with mother-of-pearl, lay a folio volume of erotic prints to serve exactly as a menu would have done in a restaurant. The prints were beautifully executed, and although unsigned, the style was quite remarkably like that of Rowlandson, one of the foremost caricaturists of the age.

On a sideboard awaited a cold supper with polished silver cutlery, cut crystal goblets and a choice of fine wines, bottled spa water and iced lemonade. On the huge, silk-draped bed, the covers were turned at one corner to reveal snowy linen within.

Mrs S. smirked in professional pride at these thorough preparations, and Slym nodded too, for he liked to see a thing well done, and was impressed by the cleanliness of it all. In fact the two shared a moment of real rapport, and then she was gone and Slym was awaiting the lady he'd come to see.

Mrs Simpson had warned that she would be a little while, since she would need to bathe and prepare herself after her performance with the scented oils. So Slym took a glass of lemonade and helped himself to a slice of excellent beef and some sort of chopped, mixed-up salad that he did not recognise but which tasted delicious.

When she entered the room, she moved so softly that Slym heard no more than the click of the door. He turned in his chair with a fork halfway to his mouth and stared. She was dressed all in white, in a more elaborate version of her stage costume, which clung to her figure and draped full-length to the floor. One shoulder was bare and her slim, round arm bore a thin gold bracelet at the wrist. Her dark brown hair was drawn up in a way that accentuated the slenderness of her neck and the elfin beauty of her face.

Slym's own tastes inclined to more flesh in a woman, but she quite took his breath away for being so lovely in a childlike, vulnerable fashion with huge and glorious brown eyes and long sweeping lashes.

Slym would have guessed her age at sixteen or seventeen. Certainly not much more, and she had such an innocent look about her that he could barely believe the things he'd just seen her doing with her companion.

"Good afternoon, sir," she said and curtsied low, as if to a king. "What is your pleasure, for I am yours to command." She dropped her eyes and briefly Slym's duty fought with his inclinations. Duty won, as always with Slym, but the fight was a damn sight harder than usual.

"Please sit down, my dear," he said, and the two sat facing each other. She sat straight-backed with her hands in her lap and gazed at Slym with a faint, confident smile. She made him feel like a great clumsy ape she was so slim and elegant.

"My pleasure is to talk," said Slym. "So what's your name, child?"

"Katherine," she said.

"Ah!" he said. "Now listen to me, Katherine, I ain't your normal line of client." He noted the tiny shrug of the shoulders and the unwavering smile, which said, whatever you can think of, my dear sir, we've seen it before.

"No," he said, "you misunderstand me. I don't mean that. The fact is I'm here in the service of a principal and not on my own behalf. So I'll be wanting to talk, and no more. D'ye understand me, Katherine?"

She nodded, and her expression did not change. "Now then, Katherine," said Slym and made the effort to pull his features into a friendly smile. But the muscles for this purpose were atrophied through neglect, and all he achieved was a stiff, death's-head grin. "'Tis my belief that your full name is Katherine Booth – *Kate* Booth. Is that correct?"

"What if it is?" she said, and her eyes narrowed.

"Ah!" said he. "So that's settled. Now, Kate, I am making enquiries in respect of one Jacob Fletcher . . ."

Kate frowned and the fingers of her right hand tapped a tattoo on her thigh.

"So," said Slym, "you knew him."

"What if I did?" she said and Slym paused, wondering how to proceed. During their tête-à-tête in his Aldgate High Street office, Slym had learned from Salisbury that Kate Booth and Fletcher had been lovers. Where passions like that were involved, he would have to tread careful. One false word and the girl might slam shut and he certainly couldn't apply the means that had unlocked Salisbury's tongue. Not here anyway.

Slym chose a bland, open question. One that he hoped would not be seen as a threat to anybody.

"How long did you know Mr Fletcher?"

"Why do you want to know?" said she.

"Because powerful interests are involved."

"Whose?"

"Many people's."

"Whose specifically?"

"Yours, perhaps."

"why?"

"Because I could offer you a lot of money."

"Why?"

Slym paused again. Miss Booth was not what she looked. She was sharper and cleverer. She was fully alert, staring him straight back in the eye, and not giving an inch. Slym's every instinct told him that he'd found a gold-mine of information on Jacob Fletcher. But first he had to find out how things stood between her and Mr Fletcher.

"Because, my dear," he said, "things are very awkward where Mr Fletcher is concerned. He has friends and he has enemies, and it's hard to know which is which."

"And which are you, sir?" she said, giving nothing away. Slym settled down for a long and difficult contest. But he had all night, if necessary; he'd paid for it.

"Mr Fletcher stands to inherit a great fortune," he said, "and I act for the lawyers who seek to bring him to his inheritance."

"Oh," said she, "you mean the Coignwood money?" she shook her head. "He doesn't want it."

"What?" said Slym, not sure that he'd heard aright.

"He doesn't want it," she repeated. "He only wanted to make his own fortune his own way."

"But it's hundreds of thousands . . ." said Slym, in disbelief.

"Whoever holds the Coignwood money is one of the greatest in the land."

"He knows that," she said, firmly. "And he still doesn't want it. But why should this concern you? For whom are you acting?"

Slym was thrown over by this unbelievable piece of information, but he did his best.

"For Nock and Manton," said he, giving the first two names that came into his head. Nock and Manton were London gun-makers, but Kate Booth accepted this clumsy effort without comment.

"In what capacity do you act?" she said, glancing at the heavy fists and the fierce, glowering face. "You will not tell me that you are a clerk out of an office!"

"I pursue my employers' investigations," said he, carefully.

Kate sneered. "You look like a catchpole," she said. "Are you an officer of police?" Slym laughed a rare laugh. It was like an animal's bark.

"No, ma'am," said he, "I'm no Bow Street man. I act in a private capacity." But he saw that she'd spotted him, more or less, for what he was, and his professional vanity was aroused. He squared his shoulders and added, with no little pride, "I am Samuel Slym of Aldgate! Perhaps you know the name?"

"Slym?" said she and smiled slightly. "No."

"Oh," said he, and shook his head. This was no time to allow himself to become irritated. He leaned closer to the girl and composed his face as best he could. His intention was to be reassuring and he placed one broad, knuckly hand on her slim white fingers. But she glanced once at the hand and then stared coldly back at him. She managed the remarkable feat of making Slym feel impertinent. He took his hand away and leaned back. "Careful!" he thought. "Careful!"

"Ma'am," said he, "I've no graces for the ladies, and my face would frighten the devil, but I must ask you to trust me." He thought she relaxed a little and so he spun her his tale. "The truth is, ma'am, that it makes no difference to my employers whether Mr Fletcher wants the Coignwood guineas or no." He paused to check an important matter. "What do you know of the law of legacies, ma'am?"

"Nothing," she said.

"I see," said Slym, serious as a judge. "Then I must make a brief explanation. The case is, that under the Integument of Legacy Bill of 1751, without Mr Fletcher either *takes* his rights under the extant Will, or *assigns them away* by Deed of Draft, then the whole vast fortune of riches is bound frozen!" He studied her face to see how she was accepting this nonsense. "Do you see, ma'am? They cannot move without the legal heir, and meanwhile great matters of estate and money are bearing down upon them."

"I see," she said, and to his intense satisfaction, Slym saw the great brown eyes fixed in attention upon him. For all her sharpness, she was so lovely with her white gown and little heart-shaped face that any normal man would have been touched to the core. And even Slym was smitten with a quick pang of guilt for the nasty trick he was about to play on her. But he crushed this sentiment with practised ease.

"Now, ma'am," said he, "may I ask you an important question?"

"Yes," she said.

"'Tis about Mr Jacob Fletcher."

"Yes?" she said, and her hands fidgeted in her lap. She blinked several times.

"Ah-ha!" thought Slym to himself. "That's the way the wind blows is it?"

"Ma'am," he continued, "I take a risk in asking this, but I must know how you stand. Can I take it that you are a friend of Mr Fletcher, that you are on his side, so to speak . . . like myself?" For once Slym's stony seriousness fitted the part. Added to his unblinking stare, it gave a passing good imitation of earnestness and integrity. In any case, good, bad or indifferent, it challenged

Kate Booth to make up her own mind on Mr Fletcher and on the wisdom of spurning the advances of wealthy gentlemen.

"Yes," she said, "I'd count him a friend."

"I knew it!" he said, as if surprised. "And so, ma'am, I can declare to you the full truth of my commission. That is, to find Mr Fletcher and somehow obtain his co-operation to make all right with my principals!" She was hanging on his words, openmouthed now. "So, ma'am, will you help me find him?"

"Yes," she said, "I'll help you. What have I to lose?"

"Then you must tell me everything you know of him, sparing nothing. In my business the smallest detail can be of pivotal importance . . ."

And so Kate Booth told Sam Slym all about Jacob Fletcher. Despite her instinctive caution with a man like Slym, she found she was more willing than she'd thought to talk upon this particular subject. She was careful, of course, and held back certain matters. She tried to, at least.

They talked for hours. Slym took out a pencil and a notebook and made notes in his neat shorthand. He asked a number of questions. He made more notes.

When Slym finally folded his memorandum book and put it away, he did so with a great delight. He was delighted not for what Kate Booth had told him but for what she had *not* told him. As regards Mr Jacob Fletcher he'd learned much that was useful – such as the fact that if ever Mr Fletcher were to be taken, then it would be a job for six men at least. He'd also learned that the girl didn't know where Fletcher was. All she knew was that he'd said he was going to London to make his fortune. All well and good. London was Slym's home ground.

But none of these things had swelled Slym's bosom with delight. What had done that was something hidden behind the girl's words. There was something she'd kept back. He'd nearly trapped her into spilling it once or twice, but she'd shied away. It was something Fletcher had done, and that she wouldn't reveal. In that case, thought Slym, whatever it was, it was no small thing. Slym would have wagered his reputation that there was a hanging in it for Fletcher somewhere.

In fact, fitting that together with what he'd beaten out of Salisbury, Slym wondered whether the formidable Mr F. might not have had something to do with the disappearance of Bosun Dixon of H.M. Press tender *Bullfrog*? Perhaps he'd thrown the bugger over the side? An interesting idea which Slym would pursue. But the immediate problem was to get Miss Booth out of Mrs Simpson's and *safe* back to London where she could be questioned properly.

"Ma'am," said Slym, "you have become a material asset in my investigation and if we are to find Mr Fletcher I shall need your active assistance. Can I therefore ask you to accompany me back to London? My principals, Nock and Manton, will cover all expenses, and there will doubtless be a substantial reward." He paused and chose his next words with very great care. "You'd be well provided for, believe me. You'd be your own, free, independent woman."

Slym was an artful man. He'd hit the mark precisely. Kate was still suspicious of him and still unsure of her feelings for Jacob Fletcher, while here at Mrs Simpson's she was well paid, well fed and protected. But she knew how short would be her future in this house, with its high standards, and she feared the inexorable decay from gilded courtesan to ragged streetwalker, and a nasty death in the gutter from some loathsome disease.

The risk in going with Slym was considerable. But it offered hope, which her present life did not. Even so, many girls would have clung to the temporary security of Mrs Simpson's house. But Kate was a far tougher creature than her fairy looks would ever have led a man to believe.

Chapter 20

"*Phiandra*!" I yelled. "*Phiandra* ahoy!" I took the risk of standing in the boat and waving an oar over my head. It was a vast and empty ocean. *Declaration* was long gone, and I'd been suddenly smitten with the fear that *Phiandra* might pass me by. If she did, it would be a miserable death from thirst for me and my semi-conscious companion.

But I needn't have worried. *Phiandra* altered course towards me and wallowed along under her tattered sails, with spars wobbling like an old man's loose teeth and the water gushing from her scuppers where the pumps were throwing it, as she tried to keep afloat. She looked more like a shipwreck than a man-o'-war and the closer she came, the more obvious it was that she'd been badly smashed by *Declaration*'s gunners.

I looked her over and shook my head in amazement.

Fletcher's Glorious 1ˢᵗ of June

It was hard to believe that *Phiandra* was still seeking battle while *Declaration* was running for home. Soon I could hear the hack and clatter of the carpenter's crew busy at work on battle-damage and even the groans of the wounded. I searched her rail for a familiar face . . .

"Mr Seymour!" says I, with a great shout. "It's Fletcher! Jacob Fletcher! Permission to come aboard, sir?"

Seymour had been First Lieutenant under Captain Bollington, but I knew from the *Gazette* that Bollington had been given another ship after his great victory at Passage d'Aron. So I guessed that Seymour might now be Captain. I was right too and I saw him throw back his head and bellow at his men. He waved at me, too, which I took to be a good sign.

Soon *Phiandra*'s bulk hung over me and she lay to under backed main topsail to let me come under her lee. They dropped a rope and I went up the side as best I could, by the mizzen chains. Somebody dropped into the boat to help Brown, 'cos he wasn't up to climbing on his own. (That'd teach the lubber to point knives at me!)

As soon as I came over the rail on to the quarterdeck I was horrified at the damage *Phiandra* had suffered. She was floating on courage alone, if you ask me. The clank of the pumps echoed from end to end of her, her bulkwarks were beaten flat all down the side that had faced the enemy, guns were thrown over like toys, the mainmast was sprung and secured by a massive serving with heavy cable, and looked ready to go over the side at the first blow of wind, and her decks looked like a farmer's field after the plough. Not a man aboard was idle and furious activity was under way to make right and mend.

"Fletcher?" said Captain Seymour. "Fletcher the Coignwood heir? What the hell are you doing here?"

He was wild-eyed and exhausted. He was an active, busy little man and even at his best he'd looked odd with his scruffy ways and big head on a short-limbed body. But now he looked like a troll from a smoke-filled cavern. His uniform was in rags, he'd lost his hat and one sleeve hung empty from the shoulder where the stitches had parted that normally kept it folded away. He'd left an arm at Passage d'Aron and now he had to cut his food left-handed, like Nelson.

"Sir!" cries a voice, and a Lieutenant was tugging at Seymour's one arm. A new Lieutenant. New to me, that is, and appointed since I left the ship last July. "More men for the pumps, sir!" says this fellow, saluting. "Water's gaining, sir. Breast deep in the hold. Can you spare me another ten men?"

"No!" says Seymour. "We shall lose both masts presently if I take a man from the work of securing them. Do what you can."

The Lieutenant opened his mouth, shut it again, looked helplessly at me, as if for support, saluted and darted away back to his pump crew.

"Fletcher!" says Seymour again, peering at me closely.

"What in God's name are you doing here? I thought you'd gone to make your fortune in London?" Then his eyes narrowed nastily, as he noted my Yankee coat with its shiny buttons. "Have you taken service with the enemy?" says he.

This was a most undesirable turn of conversation, and one I hadn't expected. But I was saved for the moment by a rush of men going past at the double, hauling on a line. Seymour and I had to leap out of their way.

One of the men hauling on that line was Sammy Bone, my old messmate and probably the best friend I had in all the world. He stared at me in amazement as he went past and then he was gone. That's how desperate it was aboard *Phiandra* at that moment. As they rushed past with the Bosun screaming at them, Seymour stumbled and what with his tiredness and his one arm, he'd have gone over, but I grabbed him and set him on his feet, swinging him easily over the stump of spar that had tripped him. He was a quick-thinking man and instantly put his conclusions to the ship's advantage.

"Hmm!" says he thoughtfully. "You have grown big, Mr Fletcher!"

"Aye-aye, sir!" says I, and he glanced again at my blue coat.

"And you look to be a Sea Service Officer of some kind, so you'll recognise the difficulties that face me, and I'll ask you to get below and help with the pumps. At the double now!"

"Aye-aye, sir!" says I. The cheek of it! Ordering me about like a common hand before the mast. But what could I do? *Phiandra* was going down under our feet, anybody could see that. This was not at all what I'd expected when I left *Declaration*, but it was no time for standing on my dignity. There was nothing for it but to take my place at the pumps.

Pumping is the worst job in a ship. It's the worst because it's unremitting and miserable, and because when you really have to go at it, you do so because the alternative is drowning. The main work fell to *Phiandra's* chain pump, the most powerful in the ship. It could accommodate up to thirty men at the cranking handles, to drive a big sprocket-wheel set in a cistern mounted on the gun-deck. The sprocket-wheel drove a continuous chain down to the well, far below, which collected the bilge water. The chain drew water up from the well through a water-tight casing, by means of leather "saucers" fixed at intervals to the chain, and which tightly fitted inside the casing.

If the men didn't tire, and the chain didn't break (as sometimes it did) then the chain pump would raise two tons of water per minute – not bad going before the days of steam. But I hated the work. Unfortunately pumping is one of the many things about seafaring that everybody thinks the Good Lord made me specifically to do.

So I made the best of it. I shoved three or four

ghastly-tired, half-dead matelots aside, rolled up my
sleeves and took their place. Some of them would have
dropped and slept where they lay, but the Bosun's mates
came round and helped them to other duties with the
toes of their boots, while I turned the handles with
the rest, and sent the water foaming out of the pump
dale.

And that was my return to my "home". I'd have been
better off in *Declaration* with Cooper and his long horse-
face and his wicked liberties with the truth. *Phiandra* was
like an ant-hill that'd been turned with a spade. Poor
mad creatures were charging in all directions trying to
offset disaster and hauling gear in all directions. Everyone
was shouting and nobody had time to talk. Another of
my old messmates, Norris Polperro, was one of the
pumping team. I saw him out of the corner of my eye,
but he was too far gone in exhaustion even to notice
me.

I don't know how long I laboured at the pumps, except
that it was long enough to dry my clothes after my
swimming, but eventually, the two frigates that had been
topsails on the horizon, *Endemnon* and *Fydor*, were alongside and sending their boats manned to give assistance.

That brought a respite as hundreds of fresh men
poured into the ship. They swarmed everywhere with
the energetic initiative of British seamen and every man
seemed to do two jobs at once without ever getting in
any other man's way.

And as for me, I got sent for and got my chance to talk. Norris Polperro gaped at me as a little middy bustled me away, and I never even had the time to say hello. I was wanted up on the quarterdeck where Captain Seymour was in conference with Mr Barrow, *Fydor*'s First Lieutenant and another lieutenant from *Endemnon* whose name I never learned. The three of them gave me some odd looks, 'cos they didn't know what to make of me. In early '94 I was a celebrity. All the newspapers of England had told the tale of Jacob Fletcher and the Coignwood inheritance, and how I'd walked away from it. But on the other hand, there I was dressed in a Yankee uniform coat, fresh from the bosom of the enemy. So what they were thinking was . . . was I an officer, a gentleman and a millionaire, or was I a common turncoat without a penny to his name?

So there on the heaving Atlantic, with *Phiandra* rolling like a hog, and hundreds of seamen going hammer and tongs all around us, at the work of keeping her afloat, I got one of the most serious interrogations of my life.

"Fletcher," says Seymour, "you held a good character in this ship when you served aboard her, so I'll give you the chance to explain yourself, and how you came to be aboard an American – and wearing that coat!"

Damn that bloody Yankee coat! A few yards of blue woollen superfine and some buttons with insignia upon them. That's all it was, but if I wasn't careful it would drag me down as sure as if the entire House of Lords had caught me piddling in the King's claret. Already Seymour and his Lieutenants were scowling and beginning to work themselves up into outrage. If I didn't say something damned convincing, then I was sunk. What was at stake was either to be received by my own people as one of them and so go home to England, fame and wealth, or to be dragged back in chains -as that most despised form of human life, a traitor.

On such occasions, when they've got your most precious parts poised before the mangle, and they're wondering whether to run 'em through the rollers, it's absolutely vital to base your tale as close as ever can be upon *the truth* and *nothing but the truth*. Those two, but never *the whole truth*.

"Captain Seymour! Gentlemen!" says I. "Everything I have done these last months, has been for England." I looked at Seymour like honest Jack Oakham attending to the Chaplain's sermon against strong drink. "May I ask what you gentlemen know of Rear-Admiral Vanstable's Grain Convoy, and of its importance to the French nation?"

That made 'em jump, I can tell you! If they'd had hot irons applied to their backsides they couldn't have started more. "The Grain Convoy?" says Seymour. "What of it?"

I'd got them from that instant. I could see it in their eyes (which were out on stalks). But Seymour was babbling on:

"It is the foremost duty of this squadron to locate

the Grain Convoy," says he. "Lord Howe awaits with the Channel Fleet, twenty-six sail of the line to intercept the Grain Fleet . . ." Suddenly he broke off and looked guiltily about the deck. Lieutenant Barrow guessed what he was thinking.

"I shouldn't worry, sir," says he, looking at the men who swarmed all around us, "I doubt there's a man of the squadron who doesn't know what's in our orders. You know how it is!"

"Hmm," says Seymour, biting his lip, but he dropped his voice, none the less. "We must stop that convoy! If we deny the French the food those ships are bringing, then France will starve and we can impose upon them what terms we wish!" He worried a bit more about how much he could tell me, then cast off the last restraint. "Fletcher," says he, "you must tell me anything you know of the Grain Convoy. Lord Howe is waiting to snap them up, but we don't so much as know when the convoy sails." He looked at me. "That is our purpose in being here, Fletcher. If we cannot bring intelligence to his Lordship on the location of the convoy, then the Channel Fleet will have no better course of action open to it than to patrol the Bay of Biscay in the forlorn hope of intercepting the convoy by chance!"

"It's already sailed, sir," says I. "On 2nd April, from Norfolk, Virginia."

"WHAT?" I think the three of them actually leapt clear of the deck that time.

"My God!" says Seymour miserably. "Then we've failed."

"No!" says Barrow. "Lord Howe must know of this with the minimum delay. We must turn for home at once!"

"Gentlemen!" says I, pulling my ace of trumps. I waved Cooper's orders under their noses. Soggy, sticky and damp, but perfectly legible still. "I said that the whole purpose of my actions was for England's benefit. Well, see the results. I have here orders from the American Congress to the Captain of the United States' ship *Declaration of Independence*." They were positively goggling at me now, like landed fish. "These orders contain a great secret entrusted by the French to their American allies – the rendezvous point where the French Fleet out of Brest shall meet the Grain Convoy and so escort it home." I looked down and read out the vital details: "Latitude 47 degrees 48 minutes north; Longitude 15 degrees 17 minutes west of Paris . . ."

Well, nobody could say that Seymour was slow on the uptake. He and I were aboard *Fydor*, the flagship of the little squadron, just as fast as a boat could be manned. Wide-eyed and bursting with importance, he gabbled my news to Commodore Cutler and a conference of the squadron's officers took place in *Fydor's* Great Cabin within the hour.

By now I was a hero again. My story went round the squadron like lightning, and I was the saviour of Old

England, the jolly lad who'd fooled the Yankees and come away with the secret that would set Lord Howe and his Channel Fleet on the Grain Convoy and snuff this war in its cradle. It was very like my early days aboard *John Stark* when Cooper had listened openmouthed to my tales of Passage d'Aron.

But this was different. It was bigger altogether and more serious. For one thing, the audience to my story was not a couple of Yankee "officers" that had been pirates the day before. It was three Post Captains, R.N., a dozen Lieutenants and assorted Sailing Masters and their Mates, not to mention officers of Marines. A sea of red and blue coats, gold lace and white facings, crammed around Cutler's table under the stern windows of his Great Cabin. And there wasn't no nonsense of turning up the hands to hear the tale, neither. I should jolly well think not, by Jove!

And this is where truth and nothing but the truth really came in. I told them a damn fine tale, all about how I'd been taken by a privateer from my lawful employment as First Mate aboard *Bednal Green* and all about my dreadful wounds, and how a Yankee Captain had offered to take me into his ship, which offer I had accepted only for the opportunity it presented of my gaining information on the Grain Convoy. Well – why shouldn't they believe it? Here I was, after all, having undoubtedly abandoned the Yankees on the high seas and having Cooper's undoubted orders in my pocket. I got three cheers and the raised glasses of the entire company.

Finally, Commodore Cutler raised his hand for silence and gave us all our marching orders.

"Thank you, Mr Fletcher," says he, waving at me to sit, like Old King Cole dismissing the fiddlers three. "My friends and brother officers," says he, with shining eyes – he was a balding, wrinkled old man, grown ancient in the service, and given command of these three frigates by some quirk of backstairs influence. He'd been a happy man already to hoist his Commodore's pennant over *Fydor*'s decks, but now the Lord in His infinite wisdom and mercy had given Philip Cutler the chance to do something momentous for his King and country.

"My brothers," he repeated, with the tears brimming in his eyes, "we shall turn for England at once! Our clear duty is to bear this tremendous news to Lord Howe at our utmost speed. My clerk is making copies of the American orders bearing the rendezvous details, so that each ship may carry one." He turned to the Captain of *Endemnon*. "You, sir, shall seek Lord Howe ashore in case the Fleet may be driven to anchor at St H'lens, or Spithead, while I shall carry my copy to seek his Lordship at sea. My own orders tell me where it is to be found." There was a brief silence and all present nodded. It was obvious sense to split our forces since nobody could predict what the weather might do to Lord Howe's plans for his cruise with the Channel Fleet in search of the Grain Convoy.

Only one man looked glum: Captain Seymour of *Phiandra*. I think he already knew what he would have to do, but nobody had told him yet, and he had to ask.

"And *Phiandra*, sir?" says Seymour. "We've stopped most of the leaks and the pumps are gaining . . ."

Cutler produced a handkerchief and blew his nose slowly, avoiding Seymour's eye.

"My dear boy," says the maudlin old gnome, "I am so sorry. *Phiandra is* gravely wounded in all her masts. She will not bear sail and you're working the pumps without cessation." He turned to his First Lieutenant. "Ain't that so, Barrow?"

"Aye-aye, sir," says Barrow. "I doubt she can be saved . . ."

"She can be!" says Seymour instantly.

"No, Seymour!" says Cutler. "She's lost."

"No, sir!" says Seymour. "Halifax, Nova Scotia, is no more than two days' sail and my crew will . . ."

"No!" says Cutler. "You'd be dismasted and on your beam ends in the first blow. That's if the Yankees don't get you first. You've two hundred prime seamen aboard and I shan't let them be lost." He paused, and made his decision. "I shall take off your people and all possible stores . . . and I shall burn the ship."

And that's just what he did. Don't ask me if it was the right thing to do, but at least old Cutler could act when he had to. Maybe he wasn't so senile as he looked.

So there was a great bustling and hustling again, and the squadron's boats were busy transferring men and gear. *Fydor* took *Phiandra*'s larboard watch and half her officers, and *Endemnon* took the starbolins and all the rest. That meant each ship had best part of four hundred men and boys embarked – close packing for a pair of 38-gun frigates. At least it meant we had plenty of hands for the coming race across the Atlantic.

And it did mean that Sammy and Norris were with me in *Fydor*. It should have been a happy reunion, for it was a great pleasure to see them again, and they were grinning all over their faces when eventually we had the chance for a private talk. But then something stopped our chatter and doused the smiles: the smoke rising from *Phiandra as* our last boat pulled away from her.

It's a dreadful thing to see a ship afire, but we couldn't take our eyes away. You might wonder how a ship burns in the midst of all that water, but a wooden ship, built of seasoned timbers and cram-full of tar and rope and sailcloth, burns furiously once the fire takes hold.

Since *Phiandra* still had powder in her magazines there was no question of our lingering to see her go down, even if we hadn't the urgent task of seeking out Lord Howe. So *Fydor* and *Endemnon* filled their sails and hauled away under a strong, fresh blow that drove them eastward at a good ten knots. In the end, with the old ship blazing like a Viking funeral, miles behind in our wake, there came a bright orange flash and she lifted her midships in the water, as her spine snapped and she threw her masts into the air like lances. The heavy rumble of the detonation came later. Grown men stood and wept, and I was one of them.

That was the evening of 26th April. With fair winds the two frigates headed westward, set fair to make a swift passage. As you may know (or even if you don't) the winds of the North Atlantic tend to blow from the west, so a west to east passage is quicker under sail then east to west. In those days, for a reasonably well-found ship, you could reckon on forty to fifty days to America or the West Indies, while the home-bound crossing might take thirty days or less. Rough figures, those, and in later years the clippers made better time, but they'll give an idea of what we were about in the days before the steamers changed everything.

Commodore Cutler decided that I was a gentleman and should mess with his commissioned officers, and I should inhabit a cabin in the wardroom. In fact, I did take my meals in the wardroom, but what with *Fydor*'s own people to accommodate, plus Captain Seymour and three or four of *Phiandra*'s gentlemen, I ended up sharing with the Gunner's Mate down on the orlop. But I won't complain. I was treated like an officer, and was kitted out with shirts, razor and other necessities, at Cutler's own expense. He knew all about the Coignwood money and I suspect he wanted to earn my favour. I'd seen it before with Captain Bollington of *Phiandra*. Once they think you're a millionaire they treat you like royalty. As a result, I kept no watches, slept snug, got my meals regular and had little to do other than cross off the days to England.

One thing I did do, though, was to get rid of that Yankee coat. It was causing me embarrassment. So I dropped it over the side and crammed myself into a respectable, bottle-green coat that I borrowed from *Fydor*'s chaplain who was at least something near my size. But there's no chance of my shoulders going unaided into any coat that isn't tailored for me, so Sammy Bone had to alter it for me. Like many seamen, Sammy was a better tailor than many who called themselves masters of that craft.

With so many hands aboard, there was light work for the crew and finally I did have plenty of opportunity to sit and yarn with Sammy and Norris. I told them everything except my gunnery activities aboard *Declaration*. I thought it would be better for everyone if I kept that to myself. But it wouldn't be kept quiet. That blasted German Swede, "Brown" or "Braun" or whatever, was aboard *Fydor* and learning how to talk English.

One evening, about ten days after the battle with *Declaration*, and just after the turn of first dogwatch, when Sammy had no duties, we were sat by one of the fo'c'sle carronades. Sammy had something to say. I could tell that from the look on his face. But he took his time getting round to it. He asked me about Boston, and the

Coopers and all sorts of things, and then he got to talking about my duties aboard *Declaration*. Now we'd been over all this before, so I wondered what Sammy wanted.

"So you was a quarterdeck officer, then?" says he. "Kept watches an' all, did you?"

"Er . . . yes," says I.

"How about the guns?" says he, fixing me with his eye. That gave me cause to think, but Sammy was waiting for an answer. "What about them?" says I.

"I hear you was teachin' them Yankees our British drill," says he.

"No more than any other officer," says I, natural as I could manage. "You know the Yankees. They fight like we do. We all took turns at gun-drill. All the officers."

"Oh?" says Sammy. "That's not what Johan Braun says."

"Who?" says I.

"That Swede you brung with you, in the boat. They've took him into the ship and he's in with the mess next to ours."

"Bah!" says I. "He can't speak a word of English. He was in a mess where they were all Swedes, like himself."

"Well, he ain't any more!" says Sammy. "Learning English nicely, from his new mates, he is." Sammy looked at me a bit odd. "Braun's got some funny things to say about you, Jacob. He says you're a bugger for the guns. He says you taught them Yankees all they know."

This was very difficult. I didn't want that known. But

I couldn't lie to Sammy. He knew every other secret of mine, in any case.

"Well, perhaps I did," says I. "Sammy, it was the only way I could get aboard that ship. And I had to do it so as to . . ." I faltered as I saw the sneer on his face.

"So as to get the Grain Convoy rendezvous?" says he. "Don't give me that shit, Jacob! Save that for them as don't know you like I do!" says he. "Can you look me in the eye, lad, and say you went aboard that Yankee just to spy for Old England? Are you telling me there wasn't some money in it for you, somewhere?" I felt my face burning red and I dropped my eyes. Sammy just laughed.

"By God," says he, poking me in the ribs with a finger like an iron ramrod, "you're a bugger, Jacob Fletcher, and no mistake! Go on, tell me. How much was it?"

"Five thousand dollars," says I and I laughed too. Not another man in all the world could have got that out of me. But that was Sammy Bone. He should have been in Parliament.

"Right," says he, "now we've cleared the decks, let's have the whole tale, from the beginning."

And so I told him. He laughed once or twice, shook his head now and again and asked a few questions. When I was done, he spoke.

"You greedy sod," says he. "It's all money with you, ain't it? Damned if I know why I like you." But he grinned. "I'll do what I can for you. Can't have the lower deck thinking you was that close to the enemy. But if you ask me, it's a race between how fast Braun learns English, and us finding Lord Howe! 'Cos then we'll all have other things to worry about. The Frogs, for one thing."

In the event the race was a close one. Cutler knew where Howe intended to be during the month of May – ploughing north and south across the Bay of Biscay. But that's a needle in a haystack without a definite rendez-vous. So it was probably as much by luck as judgement that we sighted one of Howe's frigates on 25th May and finally encountered the Channel Fleet itself on the 26th.

And that's how I came to see one of the great fleet actions of the age, but at least I was free of gossip about my doings aboard *Declaration*. That's what I thought, anyway.

Chapter 21

ITEM: *Lady Sarah.*
QUESTION: *How much is true?*
SUBJECT: *Unnatural relations between & with her sons?*
Plot by son Alexander to murder FP. Murders by son Victor?
ACTION: *Decide further involvement of self*
(Transliteration of shorthand notes from
Samuel Slym's memorandum book for
26th September 1793.)

*

Just after dark on the evening of 26th Septmber 1793, Mr Samuel Slym was admitted, by the front door, to Admiral Lord Williams's modest terrace house in Greenwich. It was not much to look at: a ground floor and a first floor with casement windows, a garret above for the servants to sleep in and a basement below for the kitchens. To give some pretension to elegance each two adjoining houses shared a pitched roof seemingly supported on cheap imitation pillars of painted brick. The house had no special merit to it, but Slym's heart was beating as if he were being received by King George at St James's Palace. He was consumed with curiosity and excitement. Always previously she had come to him.

"Mr Slym?" said the servant girl who opened the door. "You are expected, sir." She took his hat and indicated a door. "This way, if you please, sir." Instinctively he glanced round, noting the cheap furnishings of the hall, the carpetless stair and the peeling wallpaper of the first floor, just visible in the light of the girl's candle. It looked as if there was little money in the house. As always, he checked his escape, should one be needed: three doors plus the front door, led from the hall, with a stairway up and one down to the basement. Slym's business depended on his taking care in such matters.

Just as he passed into the brightly lit room with the girl standing politely aside, his acute senses detected three things and swiftly drew his conclusions. From upstairs a faint wheedling voice was being hushed by a strong, female voice, like a mother scolding a child. And there was a thin stench of sickness too. So! Not a child, an invalid. An old man. That would be the old Admiral. Slym had made enquiries about Lord Williams and he'd not been seen abroad for months.

But then the door was closing behind him and he was alone with Lady Sarah. She was draped across a chaise longue in a thin gown that displayed her figure to perfection. Her hair was loose and her arms bare. She played with a pair of tiny embroidered slippers, dipping her toes in and out of them like inquisitive little fishes.

"My dear Mr Slym," she said with a smile that would have buckled the knees of a bronze statue (given only that it were male). She held out one hand, and before Slym knew what he was doing, he was kneeling to take the pink, dainty fingers and kiss them reverently. He'd never done the like in all his life. But then he'd never met a woman like her.

She smiled again and he was stunned to realise how deep the harpoon had gone in. He was an intensely private man that ran his personal affairs with the same ruthless care that he applied to the dazzling blacking of his boots or the starching of his linen. Samuel Slym was forty years old and had thought that he was fixed in his ways, but now he was out of control.

In the same instant, in the same man, the heart soared to heaven, and the cold powerful brain filled up with doubt and fear. All the careful questions he had intended to ask were thrown into a jumble, and control of the interview passed irretrievably from him.

Lady Sarah noted all this and had to pinch her thigh cruelly with her left hand in order to stop the laughter that welled up within her. Her single imperfection in the art of bewitching men was a terrible desire to laugh at their ridiculous behaviour when the spell fell heavily upon them: the fatuous, wide-eyed wonder as if they were the first it had ever happened to, and the pathetic eagerness to please. But to laugh at that moment would shatter the magic like a wine glass dropped on stone.

"Do sit down, Mr Slym," she said, indicating a chair, conveniently close to her chaise longue. Slym sat, noting the threadbare upholstery on what had been an expensive chair. "Now," she said, "what have you to tell me? I have read your letter but I should prefer to hear everything from your own . . . lips." The slight pause before that last word, and the relishing of it as she spoke it, put Slym in a further confusion. But the force of habit came to his rescue. He drew out his memorandum book and made his report, as many times before he had done to other clients.

"Ma'am," said he.

"Ma'am?" she mocked.

"Ma'am?" he repeated.

"I have a name . . ."

"Ah! Yes," said Slym, furious with himself for being capable of being played with like this. He was far too sharp not to see her game. But he was like a rabbit in a snare. The harder he fought, the tighter the hold. "Lady Sarah . . ." said he.

"Lady Sarah," said she, satisfied for the moment. "Do continue, Mr Slym, I await your report with no little anticipation."

"You know from my letter of my interviews with Lieutenant Salisbury and the girl Kate Booth. I will therefore be brief and list the salient items." He ticked off a list with his pencil: "One," he said, "the man Fletcher is in London, having vowed never to go to sea again. He is trying to set up in business. Two – the girl Booth is in love with him and she believes he reciprocates this sentiment . . ."

"This *sentiment?*" mocked Lady Sarah. "You classify love as a sentiment, Mr Slym?"

"Ah!" said Slym, thrown off course. "Er, why, er . . . yes. A sentiment. What else?"

"Pray tell me, sir?" she said, and produced a pretty painted fan that she proceeded to flicker across her face. Slym bit his lip. They were alone in the room. He was being made a bloody fool of. But they were alone, and he dared to hope that . . ."God dammit!" he thought to himself. "Damn! Damn! Damn!"

"*Three,*" he said with emphasis, "and this is the most important of all – I suspect, though cannot prove, that the man Fletcher committed murder while aboard the Press Tender *Bullfrog.*"

"Tell me what you know," said Lady Sarah. She'd stopped playing games for the moment, and Slym was surprised at the quick turn in her manner. "Tell me everything," she said. Slym meticulously recounted every word of his conversations with Kate Booth. He had an excellent memory and gave a clear, pertinent account. He saw the bright joy shine in Lady Sarah's eye at this deadly weakness in her enemy's position.

"So," she said, "you suspect that he threw this Bosun Dixon over the side?"

"Yes, ma'am . . . Lady Sarah," he said. "He appears well capable of it. The girl Booth says he's a giant. Enormously strong."

"Is he?" said Lady Sarah. "I'd heard that from my son Alexander." Her face darkened at the memory of the death of her favourite. "Alexander was an officer in Fletcher's ship. But my son was killed trying to quell a mutiny."

Slym paused before he spoke.

"Lady Sarah," said he, "I am sorry to be the one to bring you this news. The girl Booth had it from Fletcher himself. Your son did not die in fighting mutineers. That was a fiction invented by Captain Bollington of *Phiandra* because he believed your son was trying to murder Jacob Fletcher for the Coignwood inheritance. Bollington wanted no scandal to spoil his victory at Passage d'Aron. The truth is that your son was killed aboard the prize-ship *Bonne Femme Yvette*. It was Fletcher that killed him."

Slym's flesh crept and his hair stood on end at the howl of anguish Lady Sarah let out. It was an animal sound of rage and grief. Tears flooded down her cheeks, she leapt to her feet, she ground her teeth, she clenched her fists, she stamped and cursed and threw over the furniture of the room. The servant girl appeared at the door, in fright and shock at the din, and ran for her life with a footstool shattering on the door behind her, and a tirade of filthy abuse ringing in her ears. Slym's whole life had been spent among the lowest creatures in the land. But even he had never heard such putrid obscenity and vicious curses as his beautiful companion poured out.

"Well, bugger me blind!" said he when the torrent finally ceased.

He glared contemptuously at Lady Sarah, where she sat panting and besmeared with tears, twisting the cushions of the chaise longue between her fingers. "I'll not ask you to pardon my French, missus, 'cos I've never heard the like of *yours*, not from a pair of Billingsgate fishwives on Saturday night!" He stood up, tucked his memorandum book into his pocket, carefully replaced his pencil in its neat little silver tube with its cap on a fine chain, and put that away too. He brushed imagined dust from his coat, and flicked at his boots with a handkerchief.

"Lady Sarah," said he, "I ain't particular in who I work for. Leastways, I didn't think I was, but I'm a straight man, and always have been. But you and your family, why you're too rich a brew for me, what with your plots and double-dealing. You've been trying to murder this Fletcher, haven't you? And what about your doings up in Lonborough? It was either you or your other bleeding son that shot a man dead in Coignwood Hall. But that's not all. I didn't – no, I wouldn't – believe what that prick-louse Salisbury said about you. Not from him, I wouldn't! But judging from the performance you've just given, missus, I think that dancing the blanket hornpipe with your own sons is the least you're capable of!" She never even blinked at this. Instead the vestiges of the enormous temper-tantrum drained away as she saw the great mistake she had made and set about retrieving what she could. There was still a very important part for Slym to play in her plans.

"Poor boy!" she said with bitter sarcasm. "Are you then disappointed in me? Have all your plans of self-betterment been dashed? Have you then given up all hope of becoming a gentleman, moving in society with a great lady on your arm?"

The stab went home. Slym had never guessed that she knew so much of his secret desires. He stopped in his tracks on his way to the door.

"And who are you to pass judgement on my private life, Mr thief-taker Samuel Slym? What are you but a hangman's pimp? How many poor souls have you sent to be strangled and piss their britches with their mothers hanging on their legs to end it quicker? And have you ever wondered whether any of them were actually guilty? And guilty of what? Stealing a loaf of bread when they were starving?"

"Bah!" said Slym. "I don't bother with cheap trash like that. You know the sort I bring in. Those that nobody else dares go after!"

"True," she said, "but only because those have the highest prices on their heads; so do not give yourself airs. And do not you *dare* to think yourself better than me!" She stood and walked towards him. She walked slowly, swaying her hips, and stopped an inch from him. She looked up into his eyes. "Do you think I do not know what you want?" she said.

Slym struggled with himself. It was the same battle he'd been fighting ever since he'd first met her. He knew exactly what she was. He'd guessed it early on, and the facts he'd uncovered had only served to underline what was written in his mind. But . . . but . . . the temper and anger were gone. If anything, she looked more enchanting than before. Her long dark hair was fallen out of its pinnings and hung in curls about her face and shoulders. By accident or artifice, her gown was slipped from one shoulder and the little buttons at the neck were parted so the thin material gaped open, half-revealing the plump breasts within.

"My Slym," she whispered, "I have things to tell you that you do not know. Things that bring the Coignwood fortune within my grasp. Soon I shall be the richest woman in England. I shall live in splendour and I shall enjoy the society of the noblest families in the land. I shall have estates in the country, a noble town house, a box at the opera, and I shall be received at Court."

Slym listened, fascinated, as she pulled the strings that more effectively than any other most powerfully moved his heart.

"Mr Slym," she said, "I offer you the entrée to that society. You will never have a better chance to become a gentleman. That is the second thing that I offer you."

"The second?" said Slym, and the blood thundered in his veins. "And what's the first?"

"This," she said, and went back to the chaise longue. Without a word, she rearranged the cushions into a pile at the head end of the couch. Then she stood, stretching to her full height and slowly raised her hands to the shoulders of her gown. She tugged at something with either hand, and the whole thing fell cascading to the floor in a shower of muslin.

Slym realised that the thing had been prepared. Ladies' gowns didn't behave like that. She'd dressed for the occasion in something special and he was being very professionally seduced. But he didn't care. He was gazing at the magnificent naked body, shining in the candlelight. She lifted her long hair in her hands and let it tumble back over her shoulders.

"Well, Mr Slym," she said, "shall you continue to act in my interest, or shall you leave now? I will of course meet your reasonable expenses up to this evening . . ."

"Reasonable expenses be damned!" said Slym, and

threw off his coat without even bothering to fold it. Then he dropped into a chair and tugged his boots off.

"I take it that you will be staying, sir?" she said, but Slym was busy with his waistcoat and shirt, which he had halfway over his head in his eagerness.

She smiled to herself and placed herself carefully on the chaise longue. The position was a favourite of hers, based upon Francois Boucher's famous nude portrait of Louise O'Murphy, the sixteen-year-old Irish girl who'd been the mistress of Louis XV. Lady Sarah lay face down with the pile of cushions beneath her breast, so that her back sloped upward with her head erect. Her legs were parted and bent slightly at the knee, inviting the gentleman of the moment to enter her from behind, at the delicious junction of plump thighs and rounded buttocks.

Slym nearly choked when he saw that. He'd had his share of women, but his experience had been that of a man who gulps water after a week in the desert. A release of pent-up lust on the body of some Covent Garden tart. The sophisticated arts of the courtesan were beyond him.

Lady Sarah looked at his broad, square body. He was down to his breeches now, and knotted muscles bulged up and down his torso. He was not a specially tall man and was wide in the loins. He did not taper down to a narrow waist. But to her surprise, she found herself aroused. She hated slack bodies and fat bellies in men, and Slym was muscle and bone from top to toe. She liked that and was pleased to realise that the encounter might involve delight as well as duty. In any case, she'd not had a man for months. Not a proper man, anyway.

And Samuel Slym was a proper man. In more ways than Lady Sarah had expected, too. She was resigned to being rammed and boarded all at once, while Slym took his pleasure. But Samuel was a fastidious and discriminating man. He recognised the difference between a fine wine and a cheap one. And so gave the act the attention that it was due.

He took one rounded thigh in either hand and kissed her rump with fervour. He ran his lips up and down her thighs and he kissed steadily all the way up her back to the nape of her neck. Lady Sarah sighed in unexpected pleasure.

"Again, again!" she said, and Slym obliged until the urgent pushing of her buttocks against his body told him that the time was right to slide himself deep into her body. After that, it would be nonsense to pretend that either of them was in conscious control of what happened next. It was more like a wild feast by hungry savages. But over the next hour or two, a bond was forged between Samuel Slym and Lady Sarah Coignwood that was stronger than anything either had known before. For if ever a man and woman had been made for each other, it was those two.

*

Hours later, Slym and Lady Sarah lay together in her bed, having made their way there for greater comfort after their furious love-making. They were cosily at ease in each other's company, and making plans.

"Do you think we shall learn more from Miss Booth?" said Lady Sarah.

"I don't know," said Slym, "we shall have to tread careful. If she guesses what we've got in mind for her Mr Fletcher, she'll shut up tight."

"My dear Sam," said Lady Sarah, "bring her to me in this house, and I promise you I'll make her tell me everything she knows and then rack her brains to find more to tell!"

"Huh!" said Slym, and stroked her cheek. "My pretty! Yes, you would an' all, wouldn't you! All right. It'd save me days of pussyfooting with her. I'll bring her across tomorrow. She's at Wheeler's Hotel in Denmark Street." He frowned, and took Lady Sarah's chin between his finger and thumb. "Just leave her in one piece, that's all. And no marks that can't be explained."

"I'll leave no marks," said Lady Sarah, "but you take care to bring her after dark and in a closed carriage. Nobody must see her."

"What about your servants?" he said.

Lady Sarah laughed. "They are mine to command. There's the girl and Mrs Collins, that's the woman who looks after my uncle. They'll do as I say. I know things about both of them."

"Oh?" said Slym.

"Oh, yes!" she said. "Mrs Collins procures abortions and the girl is her assistant. I could have both of them hung if I wished."

"Huh!" said Slym. "A very proper house you keep, ma'am!"

"A very safe house," she retorted.

"What does your uncle know?" he asked.

"Nothing. He's in his dotage. He was broken by the death of my son, Alexander."

"Truly?"

"Yes." Slym felt the anger rising within her, as she thought how her elder son had died. He thought it best to change the subject.

"You said you had things to tell me, ma'am," he said, "things about the Coignwood money . . ."

"Oh, yes," she said, as one does when some happy thought is brought to the front of the mind. "But first I must persuade you to cease to call me ma'am."

She rolled on top of him and raised herself on her arms so that the points of her breasts brushed softly across his lips. "Tell me, Sam," she said, "just how intimate must our connection be before you shall call me by my name?"

"Sarah," he said, with a smile.

"Sarah!" she said. "Well done! Now wait while I fetch my news." She swung herself upright, threw back the bedclothes and walked across the bedroom. Slym shook his head in wonderment. He'd never met a woman so totally at ease in her nakedness.

"Here!" she said, and jumped back into bed with a newspaper. It was the *Clarion of the North*, Lonborough's principal newspaper. The edition of 25th September 1793.

"How'd you get this?" said Slym. "D'you have it sent special?"

"Yes," she said. "It comes down on the Mail and is delivered to me here, by courier."

"Why take such trouble to obtain a provincial newspaper?" he said.

"Look!" she insisted, with the happy smile of a child perceiving some particular treat. "Read this article."

Slym looked where she pointed. There between the personal advertisements ("One pound shall be paid to any person bearing news of a small lost dog, white in one ear, black in the other, which answers to the name . . .") and the notices of local market days was a heavy-typed headline:

Bold and Iniquitous Attempt at the Murder of a Prominent Citizen by the Infamous Mr Victor Coignwood, Younger Son of the Late Sir Henry.

Slym sat up with a jerk. He held up the newspaper for a better light from the bedside lamp.

"My God!" he said, as he swiftly scanned the article. "He's took! And he's near dead to judge from this . . ." And then, as he saw the contented smile on the lovely

John Drake

face of his companion, a cold shudder ran down his back. "Sarah," said he, "'tis your son. Your Victor! Why did you not tell me this? What the hell was he trying to do?"

She laid a hand upon his lips.

"Do not say 'trying', my love," she said, "for that suggests failure. And my son has *not failed.*"

Chapter 22

I'd seen the Channel Fleet before, anchored at Spithead, when Captain Bollington brought *Phiandra* in with the captured French frigate *Thermidor* following meekly astern of him. But that was the fleet at anchor and the ships asleep. To see them under way, out on the broad Atlantic and five hundred miles from the nearest land, was something else again, for this was England's elite and the Navy's pride. No other fleet in the world could match the Channel Fleet for seamanship and drill. Lord Hood's Mediterranean Fleet might run them close, and the Dutch weren't half bad seamen, and the Yankees had no fleet anyway, but it was beyond doubt that the Fleets of France, Spain, Russia and other still lower forms of humanity couldn't be compared with them.

First we came upon the screen of frigates spread out

far ahead, searching for the enemy, and even as their topmasts hove in sight above the horizon, *Fydor* was challenged by a hoist of flags from the distant *Pegasus*, 28 guns, Captain Robert Barlow. A long exchange of signals followed as Cutler explained our mission, and *Pegasus* passed on the news to the main fleet, dozens of miles away, under the horizon.

Cutler's Signals Midshipman was pressed to his limits by this. With the eyes of the whole quarterdeck upon him, he grew red-faced and flustered, fumbling through the code book, fast as he could, trying to keep up with the speed of the signals coming from *Pegasus*. The poor wretch twice dropped the book in his anxiety. But you could hardly blame him. The Channel Fleet was mustard hot for signalling in those days.

Within an hour the big ships themselves were in sight. And a fine sight they were too, plunging majestically forward under their pyramids of bulging sails. They were as regular in their station-keeping as a line of rail-road carriages running behind a steam locomotive. Only a seaman can understand just how hard it was to achieve that level of fleet seamanship, so I won't bore you with long explanations. But take it from me that it weren't done easy.

Cutler took *Fydor* down the line of heavy ships, and tacked her smartly to bring her around on to the same course as the flagship, *Queen Charlotte*. With the whole fleet looking on, this was a nervous moment for Cutler.

One spar carried away, or sail split, could blight his reputation. And worst of all, should *Fydor fail* to come through the wind, and be thrown all aback, in irons – then he might as well go down to his cabin and blow out his brains.

But he was a good enough seaman and his men were sharp. Soon, they were hoisting out Cutler's barge and manning her for the brief pull across to the flagship. His barge crew had puce jackets with black piping and red caps with tassels. I remember that for the vile bad taste of it. I was ordered to collect my traps (which was little enough) and accompany Cutler into the illustrious presence of the Admiral. So down the side I went, and carefully timed my final jump into the heaving boat that bucked up and down ten feet with each passing wave. It was one of those occasions when my strength was no help and my weight against me.

A bloody awful business it is too, getting into a boat at sea. It's really hard to do without falling into the sea or breaking a bone, but nobody thinks the least of you if you do it right, while they all sneer if you do it wrong. But that's a seaman's lot, and one reason why I preferred dry land.

As soon as Cutler joined me (in his full dress) his men set their teeth and tried to split themselves with the maniac force of their rowing. They were on their mettle every bit as much as Cutler had been. It wouldn't do for the fleet to mutter that *Fydor*'s barge-crew were a set of slack-handed idlers, and that's what they'd be called if they didn't sweat actual blood.

So, on 26th May 1794, I set foot aboard *Queen Charlotte*, flagship of the Channel Fleet, a 100-gun, first-rate line-of-battle ship and one of the biggest vessels in His Majesty's Royal Navy. To give you some idea of just how big she was, I would remind you that a good-sized, ocean-going merchantman in those times, was a 300-tonner, like *Bednal Green*. A large frigate like *Fydor* was near a thousand tons' burden, while the main fighting ship of the fleet battle-line was the 74-gun ship, which was a vessel of 1,800 tons, give or take a few hundred.

But a first-rate, my boys, was of another class entirely. *Queen Charlotte* was a beast of near 2,500 tons.

[Fletcher gives tonnages by the ancient reckoning of "burthen" the supposed carrying capacity of the ship achieved by complex calculation. Modern calculations of displacement, give a higher figure, thus Queen Charlotte may have been a ship of some 3,500 tons displacement. S.P.]

Forests of oaks had been felled to build her and she towered up in majestic height, of deck upon deck, with three full rows of great guns glaring out of her ports, ready to pulverise any lesser thing that dared to come within her reach: 32-pounders on the lowest gun-deck, 24-pounders on the middle deck, and 18-pounders on the upper gun-deck, not to mention the lesser ordinance on her quarterdeck and fo'c'sle.

There were never very many first-rates because

they'were so fearfully expensive to build, and on that particular occasion, of the twenty-six ships in the Channel Fleet, nineteen were 74- or 80-gun third-rates, four were second-rates of 98 guns, and only three were first-rates: *Queen Charlotte* herself, plus *Royal George* and *Royal Sovereign*.

Generally they weren't fast or nimble sailers, 'cos they were built first and foremost as gun-platforms, and stood so high out of the water that they made a lot of leeway. But nothing on the face of the earth or the waters could match their enormous fire-power. You should think of a first-rate as a great, dense-packed fortress, bristling with guns, and given the magical ability to move at will and direct its fire wherever it chose.

And dense-packed they were too! *Queen Charlotte* had 900 souls embarked. Starting from the bottom up, there were 100 Marines, under their own Captain, Lieutenants, sergeants and corporals. There were fifty ships' boys and 600 seamen. There were half-a-dozen women who weren't supposed to be there at all and who the Navy pretended were *not* there at all. There were shoals of Warrant Officers, craftsmen and specialists. Every trade was present from barber to Bosun, cooper to clerk, sailmaker to surgeon, and cook to chaplain.

There were dozens of busy midshipmen and six, lofty Sea-Service Lieutenants. There were *two* Post Captains, both noble Knights: the Fleet Captain, Sir Roger Curtis (who was a sort of "Admiral's mate") and the actual, the executive, ship-commanding Captain, Sir Andrew Snape-Douglas.

So that was *Queen Charlotte* and the fleet that she led. But what then of the man who stood in command of all this? The man who wielded such power as was beyond the dreams of Alexander the Great or Julius Caesar? The man who stood above every Captain in the fleet and the two Captains aboard his own ship? That man was Admiral of The Fleet, Richard Lord Howe.

He stood by the weather bulwark of the quarterdeck, glittering in gold lace, with his minions and followers in attendance upon him. I recognised him at once from a hundred prints and portraits. The scowling heavy brows, the big lower lip and the swarthy face that had earned him the lower-deck nickname of "Black Dick".

He was sixty-eight years old, a seaman from the age of fourteen and of a seniority and experience that beggared belief. He had actually been a bloody *Admiral* longer than I'd been alive, for he'd achieved flag rank in 1770, five years before I was born.

So when their Lordships of the Admiralty were wondering to whom they should give this choicest appointment of all those that they had within their gift, they naturally thought of Black Dick.

They thought of him for his courage and skill and his fathomless experience afloat. But there was something else too. For Howe's mother was the illegitimate daughter of King George I. So Black Dick was King George III's cousin, and His Majesty always acknowledged Howe as such.

As a bastard myself, I must say I approve of this. I only wish my own relatives had been half so kindly as King George. But then he was only a lunatic, while my kin (my half-brothers Alexander and Victor) were bloody maniacs.

*

Once they'd piped the side for Captain Cutler, he and I were ushered into the presence of our noble Admiral and allowed to make our bows. I'd begged a hat from *Fydor*'s gunner so I could doff it as I came aboard the flagship, for it's important to take account of these trifles. The Navy sets great store by its ceremonies and, civilian as I was, I wanted to show respect. And this is no light matter. It costs not a penny to show good manners, while you can deliver a mortal insult by neglecting them, and that's pig ignorant, plain stupid, and bad business.

As soon as Cutler and I came within range of his Lordship, my hat was off again and so was Cutler's. After all, and for all the various reasons I've given you, Black Dick was one of the greatest men in the Kingdom.

"Good day, my Lord!" says Cutler, and drew himself up, laden with self-importance, "Cutler of *Fydor*, my Lord, very much at your service. I bring news of the utmost importance to England!" Black Dick's eyebrows twitched and a stir ran through the crowd of gleaming officers that surrounded us.

Out of the corner of my eye I noted the dazzling white decks, the shimmering metalwork, the marionette-like perfection of the Marines. I think I may have said elsewhere that Cooper's *John Stark* was smart as a flagship. Well, that was poppycock. Not compared with the spit and polish of the real thing, it wasn't.

"So," said Howe, "you claim you have the rendezvous where Villaret Joyeuse is to find the Grain Convoy?" He knew this from the signals relayed from *Pegasus*.

"Indeed, my Lord!" says Cutler eagerly. "I have incontrovertible evidence thanks to this gentleman's efforts." And he introduced me. "May I present Mr Jacob Fletcher, my Lord," says he, "an English gentleman of independent means, who risked his very life to obtain the inestimably valuable information now in his possession."

Well, that was handsomely said and no mistake. There were plenty of officers afloat in those days who'd have bust their breeches trying to prise some of the credit off of me. But Cutler wasn't one of them.

"My Lord," says I, bowing low.

"Fletcher?" says Howe, and his black brows creased halfway down his nose. "Jacob Fletcher? Your name rings familiar, sir. But I don't know you . . ." He frowned again and looked at the easy way I swayed with the heaving deck. It's instinctive after a while. "And you have the look of a seaman about you. Are you in the King's service?"

"No, my Lord," says I, "though I had the honour to serve aboard *Phiandra* under Captain Bollington, who I believe is known to your Lordship."

Howe nodded ponderously. "Bollington," said he. "The Victor of Passage d'Aron. Fine seaman. Fine fellow!"

"And as for my name, my Lord," says I, "that was put before the public in the newspaper reports of the circumstances of my inheritance . . ."

"Ah!" says Howe, in sudden recollection. "You're Fletcher the Coignwood heir!" He grinned like a boy and shook his head. It was a startling thing to see in a man of such sombre appearance and enormous seniority. "You're a rare bird, Fletcher," says he. "Don't you know there's men who'd wade through the blood of their own children for the fortune you've set aside."

"I know it only too well, my Lord," says I, stung to annoyance, "for some of them have done their utmost to wade through mine!" Now that was a saucy reply to give to an Admiral aboard his flagship. But it came from the heart, for it was God's truth, and I was fed up with being told what a fool I was to turn my back on the Coignwood money.

Every man and the ship's cat had said that aboard *Fydor*, and they needn't have bothered because I already knew it. All I wanted to do was step ashore at Portsmouth and claim the money.

But Howe slapped his thigh and laughed loudly, and his staff grinned and nodded to one another like the good courtiers that they were. I do believe that the old boy was sharp enough to guess some of my thoughts. But whatever his reasons, he took a liking to me from that moment.

In fact, to be completely accurate, Black Dick took a liking to me from a later moment about five minutes afterwards, when he and a group of favoured acolytes (plus myself and Cutler) repaired to the Master's day cabin, beneath the poop deck, to study his charts of the Bay of Biscay.

We crammed into the small cabin, and a chart was pulled from its pigeon hole, unrolled and flattened on the chart table with round chart weights that fitted snugly into the brass-railed corners of the table to hold the chart still.

Howe had Cooper's secret orders in his hand and himself read them aloud for all to hear. By the time he came to the rendezvous – 47 degrees 48 minutes north, 15 degrees 17 minutes west of Paris – they were hanging open-mouthed on his words. As Howe read out the latitude and longitude, every head bent over the chart and the Master made some swift calculations to render the unnatural, Froggish, Paris-based longitude into the Greenwich longitude that the Lord God had intended decent men to use. He made a neat pencil cross at the rendezvous point and we all gasped to see how far south of it we were.

"Mr Fletcher," says Howe, "England is in your debt!" He turned to Snape-Douglas, the flagship's Captain. "Sir Andrew," says he, "I'll have the fleet alter course immediately to close with the enemy!"

"Aye, aye, my Lord!" says Snape-Douglas and disappeared at once.

"See the size of the problem we faced!" says Howe. "Attempting to cover every French port from Calais to Bordeaux, with even the possibility that the rogues might pass through the Straits of Gibraltar to become the lawful prey of my Lord Hood and the Mediterranean Fleet." He paused and looked solemnly at our faces. "At least we now know that this latter and ultimate disaster shall not occur!"

We all laughed at his joke, but you could see the impossibility of the task he'd been given. Now, you might think it an easy thing to find a fleet of a hundred ships. Especially when you've a string of lively frigates spread out over the ocean, all in communication with one another and signalling back to the flagship. But it ain't like that.

Under ideal conditions, from a ship's masthead, the horizon could be twenty miles away. So a ship could spy another ship anywhere within a circle of radius twenty miles, and diameter forty miles. But that's ideal conditions. The weather can close down your line of sight to no more than the end of your nose if it chooses. And at night even the best-drilled ships can lose contact if they're unlucky. And you can't move fast, either, not when you've to keep a fleet together. It's an ancient axiom but I'll repeat it for those that may not know it: the best speed of a fleet is that of its slowest, worst-sailing member.

So what had been happening in those early days of May '94 was a stately blundering dance of three great fleets manoeuvring across the Atlantic like three fat, deaf, blindfolded duchesses trying to find one another by touch, starting each from a separate corner of an empty ballroom: Howe, with the Channel Fleet out of Portsmouth, Villaret Joyeuse with the Frog Atlantic Fleet out of Brest, and of course, Vanstable with the Grain Convoy out of Norfolk, Virginia. The rules of the dance were as follows: The Grain Convoy sailed in terror of meeting the Channel Fleet and was trying to rendezvous with the Brest Fleet. The Brest Fleet was trying to rendezvous with the Grain Convoy and to avoid the Channel Fleet, since the Frogs hadn't the bottom for a fight.

[*In typical disdain for the French, Fletcher fails to mention that the commanders of the Grain Convoy and Brest Fleet had been promised the guillotine, by their government, should they fail to bring home the Grain convoy, inevitably persuading them to preserve their ships rather than seek battle. S.P.*]

The Channel Fleet, meanwhile, was straining to catch either of the other two, and was happily content to deliver the same desperate violence to either or both, separately or together, and entirely without prejudice.

And just to prove, if you haven't realised it, that truth

is stranger than any fiction, on the 17th May, the Channel Fleet and the Brest Fleet had actually passed through one another in thick fog. They heard each other's bells sounding and the signal guns firing, but they couldn't see one another. And on the following day when the fog lifted, they'd lost each other again.

But now *Queen Charlotte* was heeling over on to a new tack and the fleet was following her lead. The Master grabbed one of the chart weights as it slid across the table. He missed it and the fat porcelain lump ended up smashed on the deck.

"Never mind, gentlemen!" says Howe. "We'll break more than that before we're done!" and to my great surprise he added, "Mr Fletcher, a turn about the deck with you, if you please."

Now that was condescension. Poor old Cutler got fobbed off with Curtis, the Fleet Captain, and was hustled off back to his ship. Howe had taken *Fydor* under his command, as no Admiral could have too many frigates and he wanted her among the rest, out in front of the fleet.

And meanwhile I got half an hour of the undivided attention of Black Dick himself. He made me go over my tale, from *Bednal Green* to *John Stark* to *Declaration* and my escape with Cooper's orders in my pocket. He listened without interruption, except once. I got to the point where I was claiming to have joined the Yankee Navy as a sort of unofficial spy (I damn near believed it myself by then) and I was about to explain my patriotic motives for doing this. But he raised his hand and looked at me down his nose.

"Mr Fletcher," says he, "I'll have you know that I execrate espionage in any of its forms." But then he grinned and waved Cooper's orders at me. "'Tis enough that I have this in my hand. Pray continue, but spy me no more spies!"

When I was done, he nodded and he questioned me about the Coignwood money and who my friends were ashore.

In fact, I had no friends – not in the way he meant, at least. For what he was doing was feeling out where I stood in a political sense. As a great nobleman and a relative of the King, he was a Tory among Tories and was probing for any taint of Whiggery, nonconformism or the like diseases. Of course, I'd none of that nonsense about me. Indeed, I'd no taste for religion or politics at all (still don't, neither, though like any man of business I've always been an Anglican Tory. That's just plain common sense).

So Howe nodded wisely at my replies.

"Well, young Fletcher," says he, "I'm pleased with you! So I shall keep you here with me aboard *Queen Charlotte* and if, as seems likely, you become the means of my seizing the Grain Convoy, or of bringing Villaret Joyeuse to battle, then you may look upon me as a friend." He looked at me to judge my reactions. "I'll see you presented at Court," says he, "and you may look to me for other favours."

"Thank you, my Lord," says I, "I am conscious of the honour you do me."

And indeed I was. I was conscious of the honour and wondering what the price might be. I was right to wonder, too. For I didn't know at that time just how enormous my father's fortune was. And nor did I know that he'd been a sort of banker to the Tory interest, which accounts for why Lord Howe was being so solicitous to the heir of that fortune, for wouldn't it have been bloody tragic should I take all that money across to the rival camp?

So I didn't have all the facts, but I guessed some of it. Because if Black Dick wanted me as a chum, that meant that he saw me as an asset to whatever faction he drank his claret with when he was in London. He that was King George's cousin! That meant . . . it meant . . . My God! It meant I was not only rich, but that I could move among the nobility. I could get myself a title: Sir Jacob Fletcher! Lord Fletcher of Polmouth! I could have a house in town, one in the country, a string of juicy mistresses and a nobleman's snow-white, trembling virgin daughter, for my wife.

I smiled happily to myself, utterly dazzled, and for the first and only time in my life I let go of my lifelong desire to earn my own money. It's interesting to note that in that moment, I thought of Kate Booth for the first time since the Boston prison.

I thought what a splendid thing it would be to seek her out and set her up in a nice little house somewhere, where I could visit her whenever I wanted.

In short, therefore, I believed that I was about to ascend to Olympus to sup with the gods.

Chapter 23

MISS KATE BOOTH *begs* MR JACOB FLETCHER *to* apply *to The Blue Boar Inn, Aldgate High Street, where he will learn of the perilous circumstances in which she is placed and from which only* MR FLETCHER *may bring her dear. In the event of* MR FLETCHER's *being unable to come forward, she undertakes to pay the sum* of FIVE GUINEAS IN GOLD *to any person providing true information as to the whereabouts of* MR FLETCHER. (Advertisement placed *in The Times, Globe, Morning Post* and several other London newspapers between 28th September and 8th October 1793.)

*

After midnight on the night of 27th September 1793, a hackney carriage drew up outside No. 208 Maze Hill,

Greenwich. The sashes were drawn up and improvised curtains, that recently had been a black cloak belonging to Mr Samuel Slym, covered the windows (the curtains originally belonging to them having long since rotted into uselessness).

As the half-ruined horses stood tired and wretched in their harness, too worn out even to toss their heads, Slym himself got out from the vehicle and addressed the driver. He pointed straight down the road.

"You keep your eyes down there, Benny Riley," said he, "or I'll knock 'em out of your bleedin' head."

The driver hunched deeper into his overcoat and his heavy shawl. He pulled his hat over his eyes and bit his lip. But he said nothing and did as he was bid, for this was a man deep in Slym's power. The great archive of information on the neat little cards in Slym's office provided all sorts of useful strings and levers.

Slym checked once more that nobody else was about and pulled open the carriage door.

Nobody saw the small female form bundled up in its heavy coat. Nobody saw the door of No. 208 silently open. Nobody saw her go in. Slym turned back to the carriage and pulled out the lady's bag. He looked up at the driver once more.

"If anyone asks . . . Where've you been tonight, Benny Riley?" he said.

"Indoors with the missus, Mr Slym," said Riley, staring fixedly ahead.

"All night?" said Slym.

"All fucking night, Mr Slym," said Riley.

"Filthy tongue you've got, Benny," said Slym. "Just you remember when to hold it."

"Didn't stir out all night, sir," said Riley, urgently, frightened that he'd given offence. "Not all night, sir. The missus'll witness to it, Mr Slym."

"Good night, Benny Riley," said Slym. "Whip 'em up, now!"

"Go-on!" said Riley and flicked his whip. And Slym entered the house as the carriage rattled away into the dark night.

Inside, Kate Booth was waiting, looking with disfavour at the dirty hall and at the grubby servant girl who had a look of sly amusement on her face.

"What is this house?" said Kate.

"A property owned by Mrs Manton, ma'am," said he. "Uncomfortable, perhaps, but safe. There are pervasive interests ranged against us. There could even be danger for you, if it were known that you are in London." He took her arm and led her forward before she could ponder too much on the matter. "This way, ma'am," he said. "Mrs Manton is expecting you," and so into the drawing room where Lady Sarah was waiting.

He almost gasped when he saw her. He knew some of her talents already, but obviously not all. Lady Sarah was sitting reading, but as they entered she stood and smiled. But it was miraculous. Slym shook his head in respect. The woman had put on a new manner. A new soul. What an actress she'd have made! She was still a lovely woman but it was like meeting your maiden aunt. And all she'd done was put on a plain gown and a lace cap. The transformation was all within her self. No make-up. Not so much as a pair of spectacles which a lesser performer would have thought an obvious stage property for the part she was playing.

"Mr Slym!" said Lady Sarah. "Do come in." She smiled sweetly at Kate. "My dear," she said, "you must be Miss Booth. I do so much sympathise with all that you have been put to by the demands of a cruel world, and equally, I so much share your anticipation of the happier times that now lie before you."

The words were simple enough, but Lady Sarah's delivery of them turned them into something near magic, and Kate Booth was instantly put at her ease. She became one of the many whose first impressions of Lady Sarah were false. Alone, among strangers, in the dead of night and in a strange and unhealthy place, Kate was much relieved to meet so charming a lady.

The past few days in an excellent hotel had reassured her a little, but Slym had brought a cold chill in with him every day when he came to "report" to her. On those occasions he'd given her such a complexity of detail to describe the progress of his campaign that it left her wondering what in fact was going on, and even whether he was not just inventing it to keep her bemused.

But she knew that the die was cast and that she must follow on where Slym led. For the present, anyway. Certainly there was no going back to Mrs Simpson's. There'd been threats and shouting when Kate left.

But now this sweet and kindly lady, who had every authentic mark of position and good breeding, was treating her as an equal. "All that you have been put to, by the demands of a cruel world," she had said, and "The happier times that now lie before you." Kate dared to hope the great hope of her profession that she might cross the gulf between the whore and the lady. And then there was Fletcher himself. A kind man and a generous one. She'd thought a lot about him. He'd wanted to marry her.

Lady Sarah noticed a sudden look of worry on Kate's face.

"What is it, my dear?" said Lady Sarah, with all the warmth and solicitude of a mother. It flicked through her mind that it was a pity that her son Victor was otherwise engaged, for it was great sport to see the envy on his pretty little face when she extended to some stranger the kindness that she had withheld from him.

She crushed her dangerous tendency to laugh at the wrong moment and threw an arm around Kate and drew her to a comfortable armchair, by the fire.

"Poor child!" she said. "You are frozen! Let me help you with your bonnet and coat." She turned to Slym who'd been hovering in the background. "Mr Slym," she said reproachfully, "did you not have wraps and blankets in the carriage? Were there no hot bricks nor foot-warmers? This poor creature is near dead with cold!"

"No time, ma'am," said Slym. "Our business is urgent, as you know . . ."

"Bah!" she said, and waved her hand at him. "Leave us at once, sir!" She caught Kate's eye and smiled, as between confidantes. "Miss Booth and I will do all the better without your intrusive presence."

She kissed Kate's cheek and chafed her hands to warm them. At that moment Kate Booth, clever woman though she was, was utterly deceived. She even smiled.

"Begone, sir!" said Lady Sarah, as Slym hesitated. "Leave us to talk without a man to interfere!"

So Slym did as he was told. As he left the room he turned and looked at the two ladies for a second. They were both so lovely in their very different ways. Sarah was stroking the moll's hair and charming her like the witch she was. Christ! He thought of some of the things she'd done to him in bed! What a woman! Now the two were talking like sisters. The girl was tiny and slender. It fascinated Slym that she always sat so straight-backed and neat. He liked neat things. A twinge of guilt tickled him, a pain like a tooth just starting to complain of decay.

"Huh!" he said to himself and shut the door and stumped off to find somewhere to wait in this decrepit and miserable house. He chose the kitchen, in the basement. There'd be a fire there. As he entered, the two servants stood up from the table with surly half-hearted respect, disturbed from their gin and playing cards. He saw that they'd not been chosen for their good manners. Nor cleanliness, neither.

The girl he already knew, but the other, Mrs Collins the abortionist, he'd not met before. She was a thick, heavy woman, of about fifty years, with big red arms and a well-developed moustache.

"Sit down!" he said. "I'll wait here." He sat at the other end of their table.

Mrs Collins nudged the girl sharply. "Harsk the gennelman hif 'e wants to partake hov some refreshment," she said. The girl wiped her hands on her apron and shoved the gin towards Slym.

"No," he said. And that was as much conversation as passed between the three of them over the next couple of hours until one of the bells high up on the kitchen wall summoned the servant girl to the drawing room. A minute later she was back.

"Mistress says, would the gennelman join herself in the with-drawin' room." She gave Slym a perfunctory curtsy, and turned to Mrs Collins. "And there's a room to be made up for the other lady, and a fire lit in it and the sheets aired." Slym left the two of them grumbling over this unprecedented extension of their duties.

In the withdrawing room, Sarah was playing the same game, and Miss Booth looked tired. But each looked happy and it was clear that Kate had accepted whatever tale Sarah had told her, and would stay in the house willingly. That was one objective achieved. Slym was burning with curiosity to know if Lady Sarah had found out more than he had, but he was far too experienced to clump heavy footed into the matter. So he followed Sarah's lead and talked of nothing in particular until the girl came to say that Miss Booth's room was ready.

"It is upstairs, under the roof, my dear," said Lady Sarah, "but the best we can provide here, and there is a good fire."

"That is perfectly adequate," said Kate, making the best of the inevitable. "Thank you, ma'am, and you Mr Slym, for all that you have done." She offered him her hand and he shook it carefully. Lady Sarah kissed her and she was led upstairs by Mrs Collins and the girl, holding a candle.

"Now then!" says Slym as the drawing-room door closed behind the procession.

"Wait!" said Lady Sarah, and poured herself a glass of wine. "Ahhh!" she said and sank back on to her chaise longue, shedding her assumed persona, as a snake slides out of its old skin. She drained the glass as Slym sat down beside her.

"What does she know?" said Sim. "What happened abroad that blasted Press Tender? Did Fletcher do for that bloody Bosun or did he not?" She took a moment to think, then sighed and shrugged her shoulders.

"Sam," she said, "I don't think you realise how determined a creature is our little Miss Booth. She looks like an angel but she's lived aboard ship as a common sailor's tart, which I imagine to be a hard school dealing rough knocks."

"Hmm," he said. As usual, Sarah had hit the nail on the head. The fact was that Kate Booth had such an air of gentility about her, and the speech and manners to go with it, that even Slym tended to forget where she'd come from. "What the hell is she?" he said.

"It's obvious!" said Lady Sarah, and smiled mockingly at him. "Can't you guess? How does a girl of her sort come to be a whore?"

"Well," he said, "she's been ruined, I'd say. Some well-born girl that's been seduced and abandoned."

"And so she is," said Lady Sarah, "but not a word did I get from her as to her family or parents."

"And what about Fletcher?" he said.

"She loves him. She thinks he loves her. She says he's kind and generous . . ." she paused and frowned in disbelief, "and . . . and she says he didn't want the Coignwood money!" She stared at Slym. "Can you believe such a thing?"

"I *told* you that!" said Slym. "I found that out! Now what about Fletcher and that Bosun?"

"I learned no more than you," she admitted. "Fletcher did something that she won't talk about, but that is all I learned." She smiled and leaned across to nestle comfortably against Slym. She slid an arm around his neck and ran her fingertips through his hair. "Though of course," she said, "I could have it out of her if I chose . . ."

"Well, why didn't you?" he said, irritated.

"Because I'm tired," she said. "It's late. I don't want to go to the trouble tonight."

"What do you mean?" said Slym.

"Well," she said, "I have two methods in mind. I had Mrs Collins find me a large barrel and place it in the cellar – she's stronger than most men, you know. A useful assistant for work of this kind. What I had supposed was that we might fill the barrel with water and give Miss Booth a bath. But first we'd bind her to keep her from struggling, so that I might the more easily push her head below the water and lift it out when I chose. I imagine that would be most persuasive."

"Good God!" said Slym, staggered at the casual way in which these words were delivered. "You can't do that, you'll kill her!"

"Yes," she said, "that could be a danger. We shouldn't want to lose her before she'd told her tale, should we? But we might not actually have to put her to it. Drowning is so horrid a thing that the threat of it might be enough!" She looked into his eyes. "Did you know, Sam, that when Galileo was before the Holy Inquisition, they took him to the torture chamber and simply showed him the instruments, and he, like a sensible fellow, immediately did what they wanted. Perhaps Miss Booth would do the same?"

"Good God!" said Slym.

"Must you repeat yourself, my dear?" she said, and continued, "The second course would be simpler and although it would lack the former's special capacity to inspire horror, it would have the advantage of there being no possibility of an unintentional death." She smiled. "And that would be a simple flogging." She leaned closer still, whispering the words and sliding her tongue into his ear. "I'd have her stripped naked and tied to her bed: one limb to each corner, and then I'd take a riding whip and give her the finest thrashing she's ever had in all her life." Slym shuddered with peculiarly mixed feelings. "You might like to watch, my dear," she breathed, "many gentlemen find it most stimulating to see one woman whip another."

"But, but," said Slym, far out of his depth and clutching at straws, "we can't do it . . ."

"Of course we can, my love," she said, "these are practical possibilities. The first leaves no marks at all and so long as we keep the girl here until she's healed, then neither does the second. Miss Booth could prove nothing against us. She's no more than a street-walker, in any case. Who'd believe her? She is in our power to do with as we will."

"None the less, hold your hand," he said, finally. "We know Fletcher did something she's frightened of, and

I'm damn sure I know what it was. So what's to gain by her telling what it was? She'd never testify against him, that's for sure."

"Hmm," said Lady Sarah. "I think you are rationalising, my dear Sam."

"Sarah," said he, taking both her hands in his and glaring at her, "keep her here. Keep her safe. And leave me to chase Mr Fletcher. If I get nowhere then you can have your way with her. But just having her here gives us an advantage over Mr Fletcher, and gives me an idea. I'm going to put advertisements in all the papers for Mr Fletcher to see. We'll use Miss Booth as bait to catch him. That's what you want, isn't it? To get your hands on him?"

"Oh, yes!" she said. "Oh, yes indeed."

Chapter 24

One good thing about a three-decker is that there's plenty of cabins aboard for supernumaries like myself. At least there is if the Admiral himself has instructed that a cabin must be found and someone turned out on his ear if need be. Even so, rank has its honours in the Navy, and it was only the most junior Lieutenant who had to give up his cabin for me. But a Lieutenant is a Lieutenant none the less, so he took the Master's Mate's cabin, who took the Bosun's cabin, who took the Gunner's Mate's cabin, who kicked the arses of the lower-deck hands until everyone was perfectly happy again.

In addition, I was found shirts, shoes, razors, tooth powder and brush, bedding, and other things I stood in dire need of (I also got a horn snuff-box that I've kept to this day and which I never needed at all). All these things were kindly paid for by my mighty patron, Admiral

Lord Howe. But the best thing he did was to endorse my status as a gentleman. That meant I dined with the wardroom, I had absolutely nothing to do, and I could walk the quarterdeck and generally nose around and see what went on. It was the closest thing I'd ever had to a holiday, for there was plenty to see, plenty of good company and all the food and drink I could take aboard.

There was one other thing I was given and which had to do with my being a gentleman. In fact it was a pair of things. Black Dick sent me a brace of horseman's holster-pistols, a spare pair of his own, by Griffin & Tow of Bond Street. Twenty years old and a bit battered, but fine pieces with good, fast-acting locks. He put a little note in with them, in his own hand.

My dear Fletcher,

You have not the look of a manufacturer about you, but rather that of a warrior. You may find these of use should we get aboard of the enemy.

Howe.

And there's another little insight into human nature. Howe liked me, and so he supposed that I must be like him, and thirsting to kill Frenchmen. He must also have thought it a kindness to help me escape my base roots in trade. But if you've read this far of my memoirs, you'll know which I consider the better between a warrior and a tradesman.

But there was no sending them back, and the implication was obvious. Should it come to hand-to-hand work, then I couldn't slip below and find a quiet spot.

None the less, I suppose I should be thankful (though I'm not) for the unrivalled opportunity that I was given to see the events of the next few days. For the great battle that I was about to witness was really a scrambling chase over the five days of 28th May 1794 to 1st June 1794.

From 26th May to sunrise on 28th May, the Channel Fleet cracked on sail and lumbered northwards towards the Frog rendezvous point. The screen of frigates ranged out ahead and the formidable line-of-battle ships came on behind them. There was considerable contact with other ships during these few days, including the recapture of elements of a Dutch convoy, out of Lisbon, that had been made prizes by the Froggy Fleet. The Hollanders were overjoyed to be free and passed on all sorts of information on Villaret de Joyeuse's Fleet. This included the welcome news (to every man in the British Fleet with one exception) that the Frogs were determined upon close action and a fierce encounter.

But what a puff that was! On the 28th, at half-past six in the morning, our frigates finally caught sight of enemy sail. It wasn't the Grain Convoy but the Brest Fleet itself. And they didn't want to fight! The Frogs were to windward of us, which gave them the easy choice of joining action, for in a sea fight under sail, the windward fleet can easily bear down upon the enemy, but has to beat into the wind to escape. Whereas the leeward fleet can easily run downwind, but must beat into the wind to attack.

It helps to think of upwind and downwind as uphill and downhill. A ship running downwind is like a man running downhill. A ship running upwind is the opposite. For a great clumsy fleet of square-riggers you should think in terms of a very steep hill, and of men burdened with heavy packs. So in trying to close with the French on that morning, Howe's ships were struggling "uphill", and much dependent on the French choosing to come down to us.

By ten o'clock that morning, the fleets were in sight of one another and the Frogs seemed to be bearing up bravely towards us. Spirits rose aboard *Queen Charlotte* and everyone hoped for action before supper time.

Leaving aside their five frigates, since frigates take no part in a fleet action, the Frogs were twenty-six strong, exactly the same as ourselves, but some of their ships were bigger than ours and most were better sailers, which is to say that despite the poor seamanship of their Froggy crews, the ships themselves were better built. And Villaret de Joyeuse's flagship *Montagne* was a colossus of 120 guns, a truly magnificent ship that was the envy of every British officer who set eyes on her. Furthermore, the Frogs had another three more first-rates besides, each of 110 guns, to oppose our total of three 100-gun first-rates. Not only that, but ships nominally equivalent in number of guns were not equal. On our side the heaviest gun was the 32-pounder, while the Frogs' equivalent was the 36-pounder *French* measure which fired a shot of 38 British pounds! There are many more comparisons of this kind, all to the favour of Monseer le Crapaud, but those I've listed are quite enough to give you the idea.

Just after ten, when the Frogs were nine or ten miles from us, they hauled to the wind on the larboard tack and lay to. Thunderous cheers echoed through the British Fleet as it was seen that the French were forming their battle line.

Imagine a string of pearls laid on a table. Pull the string from each end until it lies in a straight line. Now imagine that each ship is a two-decker or three-decker, and you know what a battle line is. Fleets had to fight like that because each ship's firepower is almost entirely on the broadside.

The classic fleet action consisted in two lines of pearls manoeuvring alongside of each other so that each pearl had a partner in the other line to pound into blood-stained, smoke-blackened wreckage.

Battles exactly like that had taken place many times over the centuries. Particularly against the Dutch in the 1600s and early 1700s, for the Dutch are a valiant and seamanly people who never hang back from a fight. And if the Yankees had had a battle fleet, I don't doubt they'd laid their ships alongside ours in just the same way. Finally, to give the Frogs their due (not a thing I often do, for they haven't got much due to them) the old Royal French Navy had also known its business in this respect. But the Red Republican Frogs were another matter.

On 28th May 1794 there'd not yet been any engagement between a British and a French Fleet since the war began in the previous year. On our side every man from Lord Howe down to the snottiest-nosed ship's boy was just aching to get at the French. It's true, I was there. I saw it with my own eyes. And so, when the French took up their battle formation, joy was unbounded.

But the Frogs never did come down upon us. They backed and filled and shuffled their line while we strained every spar to come up with them. Howe paced about growling at everything and at half-past one, he sent a flying squadron of his fastest ships ahead of the fleet to do what they could. Finally, an hour later, when it was obvious that the rogues were inclined to make off, he gave the signal for general chase.

Gunfire was exchanged with the rearmost Frogs at about three in the afternoon, and at about six o'clock the most furious engagement took place between our *Bellerephon*, 74, and the great three-decker *Revolutionnaire*. With a strong wind and lively sea the powder smoke cleared rapidly and we could see everything from *Queen Charlotte*. Having no duties I could please myself and got up into the mizzen top for a better view. By George it was exciting! *Bellerephon* went at the big Frog hammer and tongs. But the Frenchies were firing well too and by my reckoning the rate of fire was three British to two French broadsides. *Bellerephon* fired ripple broadsides, and the Frogs salvoes by sections. Then *Revolutionnaire*'s mizzenmast went over the side and we thought she was ours. But poor *Bellerephon* was too cut about in the rigging to take her and could not follow when her huge opponent wore and ran downwind like a beaten dog. But that wasn't the end of her troubles by any means.

Several of our ships fired at *Revolutionnaire* as she tried to escape, though at long range and without visible effect. Then at just after nine in the evening *Audacious*, another of our 74's, managed to get under her lee quarter (that is downwind and "downhill" so she couldn't run away) and gave her the close-range battering she so richly deserved. It was like nothing so much as a bulldog sinking its teeth into a mastif and hanging on for dear life.

Within half an hour the Frog three-decker was a beaten ship. I'd borrowed a glass by then and I could see that besides her mizzenmast, she'd lost her fore and main yards and the maintop-sail yard too. Finally, at about quarter to ten, I saw her colours come down in surrender. Immediately *Audacious* ceased firing and we heard the delighted cheers of her people.

But then, contrary to all the rules of war, the Frog got herself under way with her foretopsail drawing and managed to slip under *Audacious*'s stern, and so run downwind as she'd wanted to in the first place, while poor *Audacious* was so cut about in her own rigging that she could do nothing to prevent it. This dastardly abuse of surrender – strildng their colours to gain respite, and then carrying on the fight afterwards – was a feature of French behaviour throughout the engagement and only goes to prove what I've always said, which is that you can never trust the bastards.

[Again Fletcher does not tell the whole story. French captains were under threat of death should they surrender their ships: a policy reflecting shame upon those who made it, but which would explain why a French captain might hoist colours again, having struck them. S.P.]

Eventually, the Frogs had to take *Revolutionnaire* in tow of one of their frigates and she played no further part in the action, while *Audacious* was so badly damaged that she was last seen running to leeward under reduced sail, unable to rejoin the fleet.

So that was the first day of the battle. Sunset found both fleets on the starboard tack, a few miles from each other and steering parallel courses. Each had lost a capital ship. But they were down a 110-gun first-rate while we'd lost a 74.

And so we pranced about for the next three days. Twenty-five ships in each fleet: thousands of heavy guns, tens of thousands of men, each Admiral trying to gain advantage over the other.

Daylight on the 29th brought stronger winds and

heavy seas, with the French clear in sight, a forest of masts and a cloud of sails, six miles off. Howe tried mightily to trap their rear and failed, and all the while *Queen Charlotte*'s pumps were going, for her lower-deck gun-ports were no more than four and a half feet from the sea and she was shipping it badly on the lee side. This was another problem endemic to three-deckers, and caused by the designer's need to sacrifice sea-keeping qualities to the cramming in of the utmost artillery.

That night we were losing the Frogs if anything and each fleet was on the larboard tack some ten miles apart. On the 30th we could do little as a fog closed down upon us. Howe signalled for the fleet to form two columns as the long battle line meant a greater chance of ships losing contact. On the 31st we thought we'd got them. The fog began to lift at about nine in the morning and by midday we could see the Brest Fleet once more, which was a relief, since we feared they'd got free of us.

Excitement rose as, at about two in the afternoon, the Frogs formed battle line, still on the larboard tack. They were eight or nine miles away, to the north-west of us, and this time we had the weather gauge. That meant we could run "downhill" upon them. Accordingly, at three-thirty, Howe formed our battle line and signalled to engage them van, centre, and rear. There was a huge swell of enthusiasm at this in the British Fleet. Bands played, cheers echoed, and the men danced hornpipes at their guns: "the hotter the war, the sooner the peace" was what the lower deck believed.

To fall upon the enemy and yet maintain our line, our ships sailed slantwise fashion, neither quite in line astern nor in line abeam, but something between the two; "lasking" this was called. But it all came to disappointment once more, when the Frogs edged off and slipped away to leeward when our ships got close. It was infuriating, and despite angry signalling from Black Dick to maintain the battle line, our faster ships began to haul away from the slower.

Confusion reigned and our splendid formation degenerated to a shuffling herd as every Captain raced to put his ship in action before all the others. Howe was unsafe to be near at this time. He blistered the paintwork and cursed God. Some said that his famous nickname had more to do with his temper than his swarthy looks, and I could see the truth in this.

"Damn your eyes and bones, you slovenly nincompoop!" says he to his Signals Lieutenant. "Can you not make known my wishes to the fleet? Look, sir! Exercise your bloody eyes in this direction! Are you blind as well as bloody stupid?" He stabbed his finger furiously at *Brunswick*, under full sail and plunging bravely out ahead of the fleet with her Captain, John Harvey, waving his hat in the air to encourage his men to their work. "Tell that bloody bugger Harvey to shorten bloody sail this instant, or I'll break the bugger!"

Then he clapped his glass to his eye and studied the French flagship.

"Disgraceful!" says he. "Villaret de bloody Joyeuse? Huh! Will you not give battle, sir? Bah! In King Louis' time the lubber would have been strung up by his own bollocks to his own yardarm, and the punishment too bloody good for him!"

But it was no good, and at about seven in the evening and faced with the likelihood of a piecemeal engagement at night, with all the dangers of mistaken identification and British ships firing into each other, Howe was forced to give up. He signalled the fleet to fall off and prepare for battle tomorrow.

At sunrise on 1st June 1794, the wind was still south-westerly, but was only a moderate breeze and the sea was smooth. The French were six miles off to leeward, still in battle formation, still on the larboard tack. At six in the morning Howe tried again, and our ships bore up together, steering north to engage the enemy. This time the French did not start to waver and it was soon clear that they'd found their courage at last. At quarter-past seven Howe signalled that he would pass through the enemy centre and attack their flagship from leeward. This would prevent her being able to run. Each other ship of our fleet was to act similarly. It was a manoeuvre long planned by Howe, which his Captains were familiar with. In theory, at least.

By eight o'clock Howe was so sure that the French

would not run that he ordered the fleet to heave-to so that the men could have their breakfast. This sometimes causes landsmen to smile as if it were a trivial matter, or an affectation like Drake's playing bowls as the Armada bore down. The facts here were different.

Hardly a man in our fleet had slept properly for days, and with the ships cleared for action life was uncomfortable aboard them. And if it did come to a general engagement, then the men would be asked to perform the heavy labour of manning the guns for hour after hour. So all in all, a quarter of an hour spent issuing food to the hands was time well spent, for they'd soon need every scrap of strength that they'd got.

With breakfast over, we filled and bore down on the French. To accommodate Howe's plan to cut their line at every point, our ships came on in line abeam, which meant we approached all the faster, but had few guns to bear on the enemy.

Every ship in both fleets was now under battle-canvas, with no more than single-reefed topsails. The French were drawn out in their line, east to west, and closed up with as little space between as they could manage. We came up from the south-west at a steady five knots, which is a painful slow rate of progression when you're expecting the broadsides of an enemy line and all you can reply with is your bow chasers.

At twenty-four minutes past nine, the ships at the head of the French line opened up on ours. It was like rolling thunder, as so many guns fired as to blur the distinction of the individual detonations.

Soon after, we aboard *Queen Charlotte* came under fire, at first from *Montagne* the French flagship and then from the three ships astern of *Jacobin*, 80, *Achille*, 74, and especially *Vengeur*, 74. It was poorly directed but *Queen Charlotte* shuddered as heavy shot crashed into her timbers. At that moment, we had hardly a gun to bear on *Montagne* but our starboard battery had a good sight of *Vengeur* and Black Dick gave this ship the honour of receiving our first fire.

"Sir Andrew," says he to Snape-Douglas, *Queen Charlotte*'s Captain, and pointed at *Vengeur*, "be so good as to return the fire of that ship before it becomes a nuisance. Upper deck and quarterdeck batteries only, if you please. I wish to reserve our heavy guns for *Montagne* as we break the line."

You'll notice that Black Dick was polite as could be once battle had been joined. What's more, he didn't even object when *Queen Charlotte*'s gunners disobeyed his orders. For it was too much to ask of our middle deck and lower deck to hear the guns above them in action and yet hold their fire while *Vengeur* was large in their sights and firing at us. So the whole starboard side *of Queen Charlotte* vanished in jets of flame, banks of smoke and ear-splitting bellows as our whole battery set to work.

We were very, very close to the French by then and their line stretched away on either hand, thundering away at ours. Howe was stamping up and down in delight with *Queen Charlotte*'s being the first of our ships to break the Frog line. There was no chance now of their getting away and we were about to pass under *Montagne*'s stern and ahead of *Jacobin* immediately astern.

Now the great 120-gunner was mere yards off our larboard bow. We were so close that the great ensign waving at her stern flagpost actually swept against our main shrouds as we passed under her stern. Musketry from her tops was banging away and bullets cracked and whined about the quarterdeck. You could see faces, uniforms, hats, every detail of the Frogs, right down to the hammocks stowed in the bulwark nettings. I could see what was coming and checked the priming of the pistols his Lordship had given me. I had a cutlass too. Someone had offered me a more gentlemanly fighting sword, but it felt like a twig in my hands.

Then at no more than twenty-feet range, our larboard gunners blazed away into *Montagne*'s stern, straight in through the stern windows and down the length of her decks. A torrent of shot smashing and tearing its way from end to end of her. The very heaviest blow we could deliver, and upon the very weakest part of the enemy. Immediately, we put down our helm to take up the position Black Dick wanted, close alongside *Montagne* and in her lee.

Half deafened by our gunfire, I saw Snape-Douglas yelling into Howe's ear and pointing. *Jacobin* had made sail to reach ahead of *Montagne* and to leeward of her. It was an intelligent move, for it anticipated our intentions and would catch us between the fire of two ships. I couldn't hear what Howe said, but he shook his head vehemently and pointed at *Montagne*.

Snape-Douglas smiled and saluted. Then he yelled in the ears of his Sailing Master who yelled in the ears of the quartermasters at the ship's wheel. The result was that *Queen Charlotte* held her course. Nothing in the world now would stop Black Dick from placing his ship broadside to broadside with Villaret de Joyeuse. But he was going into deadly peril.

Both French ships had seen the opportunity to trap *Queen Charlotte* and for once they were co-operating well. *Montagne* shortened sail to fall alongside of us and her gun-ports opened as her crews ran across from the larboard guns, which previously had been in action, to run out the starboard guns which now bore upon us. Simultaneously *Jacobin* put down her helm and bore down upon us to nip *Queen Charlotte* between herself and her consort. But she overdid the thing, and there came a deep, groaning rumble as our bowsprit tore into her mainmast shrouds and our bows ground against her hull. *Queen Charlotte* was the bigger ship and we struck *Jacobin* amidships, throwing her over so the seas came aboard in the waist. Men were cast over the side and gun tackles parted under the shock.

But *Montagne* opened a heavy fire into our larboard

side, and as she righted, *Jacobin*'s gunners joined it too. Our larboard guns gave as good as they got and more into *Montagne*, but *Jacobin* had us caught in a jam of rigging and was placed to rake us by the bows. Worse still, a yelling horde of boarders was pouring on to our fo'c'sle and cutting down every man that stood before them.

"Hands to repel boarders!" bellowed a voice beside me, God knows who it was, and there was a rush towards the bow, led by a Marine Officer in his scarlet coat. I hadn't the wit not to join in, so I drew my cutlass, took a pistol in my left hand and charged like a fool with the rest.

There were fifty Frogs on the fo'c'sle, armed to the teeth and screaming for blood. But there was nothing for it but to let fly, and wade in hacking left and right.

[When Fletcher pretends unwillingness to fight, he strikes a ludicrous pose. By all accounts he was a formidable adversary and the fury of his temper was a tangible fact to all who knew him. S.P.]

Chapter 25

It is further reported that shortly before the engagement, his Lordship had taken into his flagship Mr Jacob Fletcher, a private gentleman recently become heir to the estate of a noted Staffordshire manufacturer, the said Mr Fletcher having been of invaluable assistance to his Lordship in revealing the whereabouts of the French Fleet.

(Extract from a despatch by Captain William Parker, of *Audacious*, 74, published in a special edition of the *London Gazette* on 5th June 1794.)

*

Just after ten o'clock on the evening of 28th May 1794, His Majesty's Ship *Audacious*, 74, with shattered rigging, powder-stained timbers and guns still hot from her fight with *Revolutionnaire*, was in imminent danger of falling upon the French line-of-battle, which lay no more than half a mile downwind, an endless succession of crossed yards, bulging canvas and chequered stripes of menacing gun-ports.

Captain William Parker had just seen his surgeon's report which listed only three dead and nineteen wounded (three seriously and expected not to live). That was good, for he'd stake his commission he'd inflicted ten times that on the cowardly three-decker that had hauled out of the fight. But it was all of a piece. The French had fired high from the start. All they'd wanted to do was smash his spars and rip his sails so they could get away, and that's why the butcher's bill had been so light.

"Wear ship, mister!" he said to his First Lieutenant, stuffing the piece of paper into his pocket. "We must bring her clear of that herd." He pointed at the French Fleet, and lifted his voice for the men to hear, "One first-rate is nothing to this ship, but there's another three hiding from us in there!"

They cheered him for that, as well they might, but it was some time before *Audacious* could effect the manoeuvre, for her damage aloft was even worse than it had first seemed.

By nightfall, *Audacious* had weathered the French line and her people worked on through the night to put their ship in a condition to rejoin the fleet. But daylight brought two disappointments. First, it seemed that nothing short of a dockyard refit would put her right. And second, although they'd escaped the Brest Fleet, by an evil chance an entirely different French formation was no more than three miles off to windward. There were two 74's, two frigates and a vast shoal of merchantmen. It was the Grain Convoy itself. Alone of the entire Channel Fleet, *Audacious* had found this incalculably important prize, and the tragedy of it was that hopelessly outnumbered and unable to manoeuvre, there was nothing *Audacious* could do other than exert herself to escape.

And even that was dangerously close. As daylight came, *Audacious* was halfway through bending fresh sails to replace those shredded in the action. Her foresail and three topsails were unbent – the main topsail was actually on its way up, with the hands hauling away, as the French were sighted. With no more than main-and fore-topmast staysails set, Parker put his ship before the wind and limped away, and it was only the luck of a haze of fog descending on the ocean that enabled the crippled 74 to make good her escape.

Given the respite of invisibility, Captain Parker and his men set to with redoubled energy. If only they could get their ship properly under sail, they might still enable Lord Howe to intercept the Grain Convoy. But there was little they could do. Masts were gouged and weakened by shot, the standing rigging was barely secured by their efforts, and any attempt to bear up into the wind would put such a strain on her as to tear her wounded, weakened rigging into pieces.

That left only one course of action, and it was bitter hard for Parker to accept it. For one thing, he knew there were those who would now accuse him of cowardice.

"Portsmouth, mister!" he said, to his First Lieutenant. "Wind's steady south by west. We must take her in. We can do no more."

"Aye, aye, sir," said the First Lieutenant, as miserable as if he'd been ordered to murder his mother.

Five days later, on the morning of 3rd June 1794, *Audacious* dropped anchor in Plymouth Sound. She was growing steadily more unseaworthy and Parker deemed it best to make landfall as soon as possible.

By the afternoon of 3rd June, Parker was on his way to London with the Mail, via Ashburton, Exeter, Collumpton, Wellington, Taunton, Bridgwater, Wells, Bath, Devizes, Marlborough, Hungerford, Newbury, Reading, Maidenhead, Hounslow and so to the main terminus at the Swan Inn, Lad Lane, in the heart of the Metropolis. He brought with him his own account of the actions of 28th May, plus letters from the Senior Naval Officer, Plymouth, plus certificates from the dock-yard officials particularising the damage sustained by *Audacious*.

Already spent by his exertions aboard ship, Parker was numbed by the twenty-hour overland journey. When he climbed out of the coach in the courtyard of the Swan, with his hat and his papers under his arm, he was like a man in an opium-trance: he actually didn't know whether he were tired or not tired, hungry or not hungry. He made his way through the press of travellers, servants, porters touting for business, and got roundly cursed by the drivers of the gleaming outbound Mails for not getting out of their way quick enough.

Fortunately, a sharp-eyed hackney coachman, hovering like a hawk after pigeons, caught sight of his uniform and took him up, just as he emerged into the street.

"Whitehall, Captain?" said the coachman, for here was a Naval officer fresh off the West Country Mail, unshaven, with no luggage, but guarding a bundle of despatches.

Half an hour later, and having been charged approximately twice the legal fare, Parker staggered through the Admiralty Arch, up the stairs into the building and entered into the very heart, liver and brains of the service to which he'd given most of his life.

He was lucky. They were so delighted that Howe was in contact with the Brest Fleet, and so sure that a great victory must follow, that they believed his (true) story of the fight with *Revolutionnaire* and the unquestionable propriety of his subsequent actions. He was congratulated, employed constantly thereafter, and received a medal for gallantry, at Lord Howe's command.

On 5th June, a special "Gazette" was issued, containing Parker's report verbatim. It caused great excitement and was avidly read and discussed. However, some people who read the despatch noted one little point of detail that Parker had included. And those who did note it, did so with a savage and ecstatic delight. This was the fact that a Mr Jacob Fletcher, gentleman, was aboard Lord Howe's flagship.

With this information, any persons wishing to contact Mr Fletcher, for whatever reasons, needed only await the fleet's return in order to be sure of finding him.

Chapter 26

It was bloody murder on *Queen Charlotte*'s fo'c'sle with dead tars sprawled underfoot and the decks wet and slippery. The Frogs had themselves well organised. Boarding is something they always put special effort into, in their methodical logical style of thinking.

There were two teams of them at work. One was up on our bowsprit and in their rigging, busily making fast the one to the other, so we couldn't get clear. That would give their gunners down below their best chance to go on pounding us through the bow and down the length of our decks. The other team, which was growing all the time, came aboard by the bowsprit, using it as a gangplank. They had clumps of pikemen out in front, trained to act together, like a hedgehog of spikes with each man protecting his mates. And behind the pikes came grenade men with slow matches and a bag full of black iron balls, the size of a man's fist, filled with powder and musket balls and set off by a fuse that gave a few seconds' grace after it was lit.

A grenade is a frightful weapon, for it scorches and mutilates. And it's bloody dangerous aboard ship for its capacity to start fires. In short, a typical Frenchman's idea of a weapon. The only good thing about them is they're so bloody dangerous to the grenadier. He's only got to make one mistake and he's up in smoke.

So that's what I blundered into with about twenty or thirty others, officers and men from *Queen Charlotte*'s own boarders. And it was pistol and cutlass against pike and grenade.

There's no time to think in such a melee, and I galloped forward in the crowd, bellowing madly and trying to keep my arms free of the men on either side of me. Bang! I let fly with one of Black Dick's pistols into the mass of French faces behind their glittering pike-heads. One man screeched, dropped his pike and clutched at his face. Blood sprayed between his fingers and he was down. I hurled the empty pistol at the head of another man, then, boom! A grenade went off with a deafening roar, somewhere just behind me. My ears rang, the hot blast sizzled the hair on the back of my head and two men collapsed around me, clutching at my coat tails trying to keep their feet as the shrapnel thudded into them. Boom! Another grenade, not so close but well into the thick of the British charge. The scarlet Marine Officer turned and bawled at his men, as still more grenades went off and our bold rush wavered and lost heart.

The Frogs immediately to my front cheered and pushed forward with their pikes, a dozen of them working as a team, stamping their feet in time as they advanced and jabbing the fearsome points forward in short, controlled lunges. They'd learned it as a drill, it was plain to see. I fell back, fumbling for the second pistol, which was stuck somehow in my belt and wouldn't be drawn.

They skewered the Marine before my eyes, even as he was waving his sword in the air, calling his men onward. He groaned and died as two steel-tipped ash staves squelched into his lungs. He must have been a popular officer, for a couple of our tars hurled themselves forward in a screaming rage. One got caught on the pikes, but I didn't see what happened to the other because I was leaping in beside him.

I wrenched out the second pistol at last (snapping my belt, though I never noticed) and blazed away into the belly of the nearest pikeman, while beating my way through the pike hedge with my cutlass.

Once inside the reach of the pikes, it was faces, hands and elbows on every side, and I staggered as the Frenchmen swayed to and fro. One man dropped his pike and had at me with a dirk, but I caught him with a swing of my heavy cutlass, just above the ear. *Queen Charlotte*'s armourer must have done a good job with his grindstone, 'cos the three-foot blade was wickedly sharp and took the top right off the bugger's head. I distinctly saw the sliced brains inside and the dome of scalp and bone fly away with the hair fluttering.

That cleared some ground around me and I laid on furiously, left and right at anything that looked French. Our men came up all around in support and we began to shove them back. But another dozen pikemen fell upon us with a Frog officer in command.

Then I saw a grenade man among them, actually holding one of the sodding things, fizzing in his hand as he looked for a target. The Frog officer screeched at him to throw it and it went sailing up in the air, over my head to burst uselessly in the air. Bullets spattered down, doing as much harm to the French as to us, and another beastly, vicious struggle took place.

My cutlass broke on something, God knows what, and I was left with the steel guard and a couple of inches of blade, so I swung it like an iron glove and clouted the first Frog I could get hold of. But three or four of them got me on my own, with some behind the some in front, and I really thought I was going to die in that moment. The officer was one of them and he drew a pistol from his belt, while the others had the foot-long dirks that seemed to be their secondary weapon. I was shrivelled with terror and I fought like a madman in that dire extreme with my life not worth a bent farthing.

I flung the useless cutlass hilt into the officer's face, grabbed him by his belt and collar, and swung him off his feet like a doll. In a frantic burst of strength, I hoist him quickly over my head and hurled him at those in front of me with all my might.

(The secret of it is sheer strength and should you ever be placed as I was, then you should not attempt to do the like but should scream loudly, fall down, and play dead.)

That left two of them, with expressions of gawping disbelief on their faces. But they went for me with their dirks and one of 'em got his blade into my side just as I caught the pair of their heads and cracked them smartly together and knocked them senseless. Strength again, d'you see? And speed too. It was all a matter of seconds and then our men were swarming forward to finish the thing, even as I dropped my two Frogs on the deck.

And that was the end of the French attempt to board *Queen Charlotte*'s fo'c'sle. Of course, mine wasn't the only fight that took place in those few dreadful minutes. Nearly a hundred men fought that battle and there were a dozen struggles like mine going on simultaneously and tumbling all over one another. But, as you'll imagine, I hadn't time to pay attention to them. Unfortunately that wasn't the end of my part in the greater battle between *Jacobin*, *Montagne* and *Queen Charlotte*. Our bowsprit was still jammed into *Jacobin*'s rigging, *Jacobin*'s 36-pounders were hammering us end to end, and we must soon either break free or be battered to pieces. Then up comes *Queen*

Charlotte's *First* Lieutenant with a couple of dozen men, fresh from the guns below.

"Away boarders!" he cried. "Axe men with me!" and he instantly led a charge up the bowsprit to cut away the French lashings so we could pull clear. At least he tried to, and I took a discarded cutlass and went with them, but it was no use. *Queen Charlotte*'s bowsprit, the big jutting spar that rose diagonally up and forward from her bow, was a monster of near four feet in diameter, but even so there was room for only one man at a time, and we had to scramble up in single file. What's more, with the two ships heaving and grinding against each other, and trembling with gunfire, the bowsprit was shifting alarmingly and you couldn't go at a rush for fear of falling off.

Jacobin had the advantage of us, you see, for with their ship broadside on to ours, all three of their fighting tops could fire down on our fo'c'sle while only our foretopmen could fire back. The fighting tops in a three-decker are big platforms fixed to the masts, just above the lower yards, about eighty feet from the deck. In action these are filled with sharpshooters whose job it is to fire down upon the enemy: quarterdeck officers being a particularly favoured target. That's how Nelson was killed, as you know (and if you didn't know that then I don't see how you can call yourself British).

Well, *Jacobin* had made regular little forts of her tops with timber barricades to give cover, and they were bristling with musketeers.

First they'd killed or wounded everyone in our foretop, then they'd cleared our fo'c'sle for their boarders, and when the First Lieutenant's men tried to go up the bowsprit, they had the easy target of a line of men all coming up the same path and they fairly showered us with bullets. I saw three men at least struck down and go into the sea between the two ships. I felt shot go through my coat and we were all of us crouching low with our arms raised over our heads in a futile, instinctive gesture to ward off the musket balls as if they were rain. It was a death-trap and we had to fall back.

But the First Lieutenant knew his business and with the bullets splintering the planks all around him he bawled at us to bring one of the fo'c'sle 12-pounders into action.

"Canister!" he cried and shook his fist at the Frog maintop. "We must clear out the nest of 'em!" says he. So we fell upon the gun and hauled it round, nine or ten of us, by brute strength to point forward towards *Jacobin*'s mainmast. Stumbling over each other in the rush, someone found a cartridge, and another a round of canister from a nearby shot-locker. We got the gun loaded, primed and ready. But French bullets were pouring among us, and grouped round the gun we made another fine target. Soon there were only five of us left besides the Lieutenant and the rest were laid out around us, stone dead or writhing with plain.

"The coign! The coign!" cried the Lieutenant. I

understood fastest and found a handspike to lever up the breech so the elevating wedge could be drawn out from beneath it. But the gun was laid for point blank, with the coign lashed in place, so one of the tars had to out with his knife and slash it free. Thump! I let fall the breech and up rose the muzzle. But it was useless. We got no more than five or six degrees of elevation. The old wooden carriages on their squat wheels just weren't meant to point at the sky.

"Up with . . ." cries the Lieutenant, and choked off in surprise as something hit him. He staggered back and sat down heavily on the deck. There was blood all over his face and he couldn't see. The other men gawped at this and stared at one another. There's only so much even brave men can do and they were on the point of running.

But a French bullet banged into the fat black breech of the gun, whizzed off and shot across my thigh. Christ, but it frightened me! And it hurt like the cat-o'-nine-tails. I think I was already half mad with battle and that shoved me over the brink completely.

"You!" says I, to the nearest man, "get something to put under the forrard end of her." He dithered, for I was nobody that he knew, so why should he take my orders? But I took him by his collar and hurled him on his way and turned to the others. "You! And you! Get the bloody stern wheels off her and the rest of you go and help *him*!" I pointed at the first man, who was struggling with half of a shattered gun-carriage, split apart by French shot.

More men came up and joined in as we worked, and some Marines too, for there were muskets banging away at the Frogs, while I built my crazy pile of wreckage under the long 12-pounder. But I was transported with a furious energy and a consuming madness. I threw off my coat and shirt and the sweat ran off me like water as I hauled and shoved and levered and yelled at the others to get the front end of the gun up, inch by inch. The trick was to lever her up, slip another lump of wreckage beneath and let her fall. With the rear wheels struck off the carriage, it couldn't roll back (not quite, anyway) and so on and so on until the whole gun was pointing crazily upward at an impossible angle and the seven-foot, twenty-one hundredweight barrel was finally lined up on *Jacobin*'s maintop.

I shoved everyone else clear and took up the lanyard to the firelock trigger. I peered over the sights, but couldn't see a bloody thing for the sweat in my eyes and my gasping breathing. I was like a horse that's just won the Derby. Then somebody in a blue coat with gold lace was handing me a handkerchief. I snatched it and wiped my eyes. It was another Lieutenant come from somewhere. I'd no idea who he was. But I took another sight and saw the damn thing was aimed off.

"Point!" I yelled. "Point!" And at least twenty men seemed to be shoving to my direction, red Marines and blue tars together. I glared over the sights and saw the barrel inch and slither on to target. "Well!" I roared. "Stand clear!"

Jacobin's maintopmen could see what was coming now, and some of them were scurrying down the shrouds to escape, while from her fore and mizzentop, which were not directly threatened, there came a redoubled crackle of musketry, instantly answered from all around me. There were Marines all around me by then blazing away, as we fought for advantage in this crucial moment.

"Stand clear," I roared, once more and at the top of my voice. Then I jerked the lanyard and jumped out of the way myself.

Boom! The gun leapt from the improvised bed of loose timbers, spun ponderously round in its own swirling smoke, and thundered down in a massive crunch upon the deck, smashing its carriage and tearing its trunnions out of their capsquares. But one full round of canister, two hundred musket balls, blasted into *Jacobin*'s maintop, leaving not a man alive of those who'd not got out of the way.

There was a savage cheer from our side and the tars positively fought to be first up the bowsprit. A horde of them were up in *Jacobin*'s rigging and knives, cutlasses and boarding axes were rising and falling in a cascade to cut us free from the enemy's imprisoning hold. While this went on our Marines blasted away at remaining French topmen, but you could see that they'd lost heart.

Soon, the new Lieutenant (the one with the handker-chief) was calling back his men, as *Queen Charlotte* and *Jacobin* began to tear free of one another. Lines snapped viciously and our bow rumbled sternwards against the Frenchman's hull, snapping and ripping gun-ports away and dismounting half a dozen guns that were caught with muzzles protruding.

We were barely moving, for we seemed to have taken a pounding aloft, but *Jacobin* close-hauled on the larboard tack was gathering way and inching clear of us. I looked around for *Montagne*, the huge French flagship, and saw that she too was pulling away, somewhat on our larboard quarter. While I'd fought my campaign on the fo'c'sle, there'd been the most tremendous gunnery duel with *Montagne*. Neither of our main batteries had been able to find *Jacobin*, but by training hard on the stern, our larboard broadside had been able to vent their fury on *Montagne*, and by Jove they did so too. Even with raking fire coming down the gun decks from *Jacobin*.

The results of *Queen Charlotte*'s steady fire into *Montagne* had been to extinguish any fighting spirit that might have been lurking in the enormous French three-decker, and persuaded her she'd be better off out of our company. She even slammed her gun-ports and ceased firing as she went.

Free of our close embrace by *Jacobin*, *Queen Charlotte* slowly began to gather way, and as soon as she'd answered her rudder, Black Dick brought her round so her starboard guns could take their revenge upon *Jacobin*. But that was as much as I saw of the battle, for I'd come over most peculiar.

You'll have noticed I didn't scamper up the bowsprit with the rest to help cut us free. Well, the reason was that I simply hadn't the strength. I wouldn't say I hoist that 12-pounder up alone – even I hadn't the strength for that – but I probably did three mens' share of the work, and I had nothing more to give at that particular moment. I was utterly spent.

And then the Lieutenant with the handkerchief, whose face was sliding in and out of focus before my eyes, pointed at the deck beneath my, feet. He said something that I didn't properly hear and I looked down. I was standing in a pool of blood and my clothes were wet from the waist down. It was one of those rascals whose heads I'd clapped together. He had got his dirk into me after all. He'd opened me up a treat, and when I realised what had happened I suddenly felt the ache of the wound and the gush of blood.

The Lieutenant was shouting again, and two men took hold of me and led me away. Down into the waist we went, then down more steep companionways, down to the upper gun-deck, to the middle gun-deck, the lower gun-deck, and so down and down to the orlop, below the water-line. It was a fine chance to see a first-rate going about her business: deck after deck with its rows of huge guns lined up on either beam, thundering and bellowing, and bounding back in recoil, the hundreds and hundreds of skilled men to serve them, the enveloping smoke and, above and beyond all else, the appalling, agonising din. It's said that the devil himself invented gunpowder. Well, if so, then Old Nick would have just loved the middle gun-deck of *Queen Charlotte*, by George he would! For on the middle gun-deck guns are working on either hand, *and* above your head, *and* beneath your feet. It was like Hell on a bad day.

But I wasn't on a tour of the guns, and I can't say I paid them much attention. I was carried down the last companionway (God knows how they did it, considering the size of me) and even before my blurred eyes could see where we were, I knew we'd found the surgeons, by the groans and screams and particularly by the hot stink of dozens of candles. The first thing a surgeon does when a ship goes into action is get as many lights burning as can be.

I'm pleased to say my memories of my visit to *Queen Charlotte's* cockpit are limited. There were bodies laid out in rows, the living kept apart from the dead, there were folded, bloodied sails draped over barrels to form benches for the operators to work on. There were buckets and sponges and lint and bandages. There were two surgeons with bared arms and their long brown linen aprons, two similarly attired surgeon's mates, the Chaplain, the Purser, two women lending a hand and a dozen or so wounded men awaiting their turn.

All this in a low, shadowy wooden cavern with five feet of headroom, and the massive transverse beams that supported the deck above waiting to brain you if you didn't crouch and duck as you moved.

And finally, there were the neat sets of shining instruments, laid out ready for use, the very sight of which could make a man squirt his bowels on the spot.

Not very nice, my jolly boys, was it? But here's a thought for you. This was *luxury* compared with what soldiers suffered. At least our tars got their wounds tended. They were treated promptly, and down on the orlop they were safe from the enemy's shot. Now compare this with what happened to a wounded soldier. He might lie on the field of battle for days, and nobody to come to get him. And what with cavalry and horse artillery charging about, even if his wounds didn't kill him, there was every chance of getting his chest smashed in by a hoof or a wheel, 'cos they certainly didn't stop to look what they were riding over. I know, for I've been there!

On this occasion, by the grace of God, I can't recall what they did to me down there, for I passed out just after they rolled me over and set to work on my side, where the knife had gone in.

So I missed the rest of the action and woke up bandaged tight as a mummy, in my cot in the Sixth Lieutenant's cabin. They'd put a servant to look after me, and later in the day, Black Dick himself, no less, came down to see me. He was pleased as punch with himself and the world and with me as one item in it.

"Well, Mr Fletcher," says he, taking a seat in my tiny cabin, while his ever-present minions hovered about, "how d'ye do, sir?" and pressed on, bursting with satisfaction, before I could reply. "D'ye know how we beat the rogues? Eleven prizes, sir! And some of them the finest ships ever built by the hand of man! I only regret that so few of my Captains managed to penetrate their line as we did!" He shook his head ponderously. "For that has allowed that unspeakable coward Villaret de Joyeuse to skulk off with most of his fleet. They couldn't face us and wouldn't face us, sir! All firing ceased by a quarter-past one because the enemy had fled."

Then he smiled and looked down at me. "I hear well of you, Mr Fletcher," says he; "I find it hard to believe that a man who fights like a lion should seek a career in commerce. Should ever you wish to enter the Sea Service, you may call upon me."

Now that was an offer that thousands of men would have sold their souls for. Howe was so God-Almighty powerful in the Navy that his patronage was a sure and unrivalled ladder to advancement. It was an offer too good to refuse. At least, not without the deepest consideration. And so, despite all my contrary inclinations, I thought it best to keep this particular choice alive.

"You are too kind, my Lord," says I, carefully. "I am deeply grateful."

He grinned and nodded.

"Come to me when you are well," says he. "The surgeons say you'll be a whole man in a week or two. You are a young man with luck on your side!"

*

And that, children, is how your Uncle Jacob fought for his country at the battle of THE GLORIOUS FIRST OF JUNE. I suppose I was lucky. On the British side, about three hundred were killed and nine hundred wounded. On the French side, some three thousand were killed or mortally wounded, and about another three thousand taken prisoner.

Despite his victory, Black Dick's Fleet was in such a knocked-about state, and the captured French ships so much worse (one of them, *Vengeur*, actually sank) that we didn't get under way until nearly five o'clock in the afternoon of 3rd June, when we steered north-east for England.

For the next ten days, while my wounds healed and I slowly got myself out of bed, the damaged ships limped along at a snail's pace and it wasn't until eleven o'clock on the morning of 13th June 1794 that the Channel Fleet anchored at Spithead. There we found the most colossal host assembled to greet us. It was later estimated that some three hundred thousand people had poured into Portsmouth to see England's premier battle-fleet come home in victory.

You'll notice incidentally that nobody paid much attention to the fact that Lord Howe had failed in his strategic objective of intercepting the Grain Convoy, which finally reached Brest on 12th June. And the reason for that was simple. Without the Grain Convoy, the French might or might not have starved – who could tell? Maybe they'd have scraped along without it. But if England once lost command of the Channel approaches, then the Frogs could invade us and we'd be finished beyond doubt. And Howe had re-established our command of the Channel by not only beating, but comprehensively humiliating the main battle-fleet of our ancient enemy.

So Howe was England's darling, and the Royal Family descended as a tribe upon Portsmouth and on 26th June the King held a Royal Levee aboard *Queen Charlotte* and presented his cousin with a diamond-studded sword of £3,000 value, plus a large medal on a gold chain to go round his neck.

But I didn't see that. I was elsewhere because something very nasty happened to me at Spithead and a very old, and very deep wound was opened.

Chapter 27

. . . Between 10th February and 16th February 1793 the said Jacob Fletcher did strike down the said Boatswain Dixon with a club or other such weapon and did cause the said Boatswain Dixon to fall from the bows of His Majesty's Ship Bullfrog in such manner as to be lost and drowned in the sea, the aforesaid act of the said Jacob Fletcher being wilful and deliberate murder.

(Extract from an affidavit sworn and signed on 2nd October 1793 by Mr Solomon Oakes, Mariner, before Mr Donald Fry, Solicitor and Commissioner for Oaths of Aldgate High Street.)

*

Late in the afternoon of 1st October 1793, a fierce, spiteful argument was taking place in a garret bedroom underneath the roof of Admiral Lord Williams's house in Maze Hill, Greenwich.

"You're a damned liar, madam!" cried Kate Booth.

"And you, miss, are a whore that served a whole ship's crew for sixpence!" said Lady Sarah. She smiled nastily and added, "Tell me, ma'am, for I've often wondered about these practical details, did a hundred of them form a queue and have you in turn, or did they throw dice?"

Kate Booth sneered, "At least I never practised filthy incest!" she said. "Your son Alexander let that out in his filthy letters. Jacob read them and he told me." Lady Sarah frowned at the mention of her favourite, and Kate saw she'd landed a blow. "Yes," she continued, "we read your son's letters aboard *Phiandra*," she shouted in fury, "after Jacob had killed him."

"Bitch!" screamed Lady Sarah.

"Monster!" cried Kate. "Let me go! You cannot hold me against my will!" She pulled on the long chain that held her by a steel anklet to a ring-bolt firmly driven into one of the rafters.

"No?" said Lady Sarah. "And why not, pray?"

"Because of the Law! The Law forbids it!" said Kate, though even as she said the words her voice failed. Lady Sarah sneered with amusement.

"The Law?" she said. "The Law is not for such as you, miss! Do you not know that yet? Why, girls like you are held in houses all over London for the pleasure of gentleman customers." The complete truth of this unpleasant fact knocked the fight out of Kate for the moment and she fell silent.

Lady Sarah sat beside her on her narrow bed, this was *her* advantage, and she pursued it. "In fact," she said, "one of a number of unpleasant things that I might do with you when I've finished with you is sell you to one of them. I know of several establishments that would take you. You're young and you're very pretty."

Kate remained silent, so Lady Sarah tried another tack. She stroked Kate's hair and softened her voice. When she wanted to be, Lady Sarah could seem selflessly kind, and she was so beautiful that even other women usually succumbed to her charm – as Kate herself had done at first.

"My dear girl," she said, "cannot we settle this matter as sensible women? Mr Fletcher has abandoned you. You owe him nothing, while I am ready to advance a sum of money that would enable you to live in luxury for the rest of your life. I can return you to the respectable society in which you belong. And all you have to do is tell me what was this thing that *he* did aboard the ship *Bullfrog* . . ."

Sarah Coignwood was never more persuasive in all her life. She touched on every chord that might shift Kate's determination. For even in her own heart, Kate didn't know for sure who had left whom, her Jacob or Jacob her.

Lady Sarah saw her confusion and put an arm around Kate's neck, and kissed her cheek, gently, as a sister might.

"Kate," she said, "cannot we be friends?" Kate's lips parted. She was about to say something, but Lady Sarah's own character and appetites betrayed her. Kate was such a pretty little thing that instead of listening, she moved closer and kissed her properly. A lover's kiss, and not a sister's.

Kate had done many things to earn her keep. She was beyond being shocked by the devious pleasures of men or of women. But the cynical hypocrisy of Lady Sarah's behaviour roused her to anger. Here and now she was being offered money and friendship, perhaps something more, and only this morning they'd taken her down to the cellar, Mrs Collins hanging on one arm and Lady Sarah on the other. They'd shown her the great wooden tub, brim full of cold water, and Lady Sarah had explained how they proposed to use it. There had also been various other domestic devices, ingeniously improvised for equally terrible purposes.

Kate pushed Lady Sarah off and struck at her, landing a blow squarely on the side of her face.

"Filthy creature!" she cried, "I'll tell you nothing!"

There was a quick, savage fight, which despite her temper, Lady Sarah got much the worst of. She pulled free and leapt back beyond the reach of Kate's chain, the long coils of which were tied up short so she couldn't move too far. She was frightened and hurt and so reverted to type.

"Have it your own way, miss!" she snarled. "I'm done playing with you. I'll have Mrs Collins bring you down below *now this instant!* And we'll see how pert you are when we've done some of the things that I have planned for you." She leaned forward with an ugly expression contorting her features. "I should warn you that my son Victor has an extensive library on the subject of torture, and I have consulted it fully!"

Lady Sarah slammed out of the little room, bolted the door behind her and flounced down the stairs, calling for Mrs Collins at the top of her voice. If she'd done what was in her mind at that instant, then whatever Kate Booth might or might not have been forced to divulge, it is highly improbable that she would have survived.

But the test was never made. Even as Lady Sarah reached the ground floor and found her two servants gawping at her, there came a heavy knock at the front door. The three of them jumped. Lady Sarah received no visitors and it was possible that this could mean that she was discovered and an officer of police was outside with a warrant for her arrest. But the servants knew their work, and the old, mad, gibbering Admiral was upstairs in his bed, kept alive for just such moments as this, when he could be displayed as the master of the house and its sole occupant besides "his" servants.

But it was not Sheriff's Officers or the Parish Constable

who were at the door. It was Sam Slym, accompanied by two grubby men in sailors' clothes. As Slym led them into the withdrawing room, they snatched off their round, tarred hats and bent half double with respect, knuckling their brows to the elegant lady before them. They looked uncomfortable, but had an air of crafty greed about them.

"Good day to you, ma'am!" said Slym, bowing to Lady Sarah. She could see he was pleased with himself. A man like Sam Slym could never be described as "bursting with excitement", he was far too cold a fish for that, but he was somewhat along the path that, in lesser men, led to this condition.

"Good day to you, sir!" she snapped, still flushed with anger. Slym raised his eyebrows, but said nothing. He deduced that Miss Booth was still uncooperative.

"Now then," said Slym, prodding his companions with his stick, "this is the lady I told you about. Your every hope of the reward lies in her gift. So you stand there till you're told to move, you step up when you're told, you tell your tale when you're told, and you shut yer gobs afterwards, right?"

"Aye-aye, sir!" said the two in unison, and Lady Sarah smiled, despite herself, at the quaint way they saluted him: raising the right hand to the brow and stamping simultaneously with the right foot. She'd seen players do that on the stage when imitating sailors, and was amused to see that the pretence, for once, reflected reality.

"Ma'am," said Slym, sweeping his coat-tails forward and settling into a chair, "the advertisements that I placed in the newspapers have borne fruit."

She glanced at the two seamen, who were listening to every word and shifting awkwardly from one foot to the other. She looked at Slym questioningly.

"No," he said, "never mind them, ma'am, there's no men in all the world that knows better than these two what a villain is Mr Jacob Fletcher!" He smiled, for he was deliberately building the tension before making his disclosure, and that was something very unusual for him. Her heart suddenly beat faster as she guessed that Slym had found out something of great importance.

"As you know, ma'am," he continued, "we placed them advertisements in the hope of drawing forward Mr Fletcher himself, but we added the promise of a reward for any who could tell us his true whereabouts."

"Yes," she said. "Do come to the point, sir!"

"I'm coming to it, ma'am," he said, and positively chuckled. "You there!" he said, pointing to the nearer of the two seamen. "Step up and give your story!"

"Aye-aye, sir!" says the first little man and took a step forward. He had a sickly look about him and coughed continuously. He cleared his throat, licked his lips and ran a hand over his head, nervously smoothing the tight-drawn hair which was pulled into a long pigtail at the base of his neck.

"Beggin' yer pardon, mum, but I dunno where to begin . . ."

"Bah!" said Slym. "Get on with it! Give it just as you did to me in the Blue Boar this morning."

"Aye-aye, sir!" said he, and saluted again. "Solomon Oakes, lately able seaman in His Majesty's Fleet, at your service, ma'am!" he jerked a thumb at his companion, "and this here's my messmate Charlie Pegg, foretopman before he ruptured hisself — begging yer pardon, ma'am — he done hisself so bad this time that the surgeon couldn't truss him up fit for to serve. And so he and I was discharged the service, what with his rupture and my consumptive fever, which is cruel hard, ma'am, on account of our . . ."

"Never mind that," said Slym, interrupting, "get to the *Bullfrog*, tell the lady what you saw."

"Aye-aye, sir! Well . . . him and me, Charlie, we was took this Febr'y, ma'am, during the hot press when the war started. And so we was under hatches in the old *Bullfrog* bound for Portsmouth. And every morning they had us up on deck for exercise, a few at a time, so's we couldn't take the ship . . ."

By now, Lady Sarah was on the edge of her chair. She was burning with anticipation. She had a very good idea indeed of what was coming, and a thrilling hope was rising within her like an ascending skylark.

". . . and so there we was, ma'am, me and Charlie and another man by the name of Polperro, also a seaman, we was standin' on the fo'c'sle one morning, when we see the old Bosun, Mr Dixon, we see him go forward to the heads."

"That's the bows, ma'am," said Slym, seeing her puzzlement, "in the very front of the ship, where there is a little platform under the bowsprit. It is where the men ease the calls of nature, ma'am."

"Aye," said Oakes grateful for not having to make this explanation himself. "Well, ma'am, we see the old Bosun go forrard, and we see that swab Fletcher . . ."

"FLETCHER!" she cried. "JACOB FLETCHER?" One hand, clenched into knuckles, was at her mouth while the other drove its sharp-nailed fingers deep into the upholstery of her couch.

"Aye-aye, ma'am," said Oakes and paused, unsure of her reactions.

"GET ON WITH IT!" she cried.

"Well . . . well . . ." said Oakes, "that Fletcher, why he hit the old Bosun on the head and he knocked him down and kicked him into the sea. Murdered him, he did." He turned to his mate, "Ain't that right, Charlie?"

"Aye!" said Pegg. "And no matter what the Bosun done, he didn't oughter have done that to him."

"Ahhhhhh!" said Lady Sarah, and sank back into her cushions, full of the same sensations as accompany the conclusion of a particularly luscious sexual encounter. "And you're sure of this?" she said. "The man was Jacob Fletcher?"

"Aye-aye, ma'am," said Oakes, "the same Fletcher what got made heir to a fortune."

"And you will testify to this?" said Lady Sarah. "In court?"

Oakes and Pegg looked sideways at Slym and said nothing.

"These excellent fellows are now penniless, ma'am," said Slym, "and I took it upon myself to promise them all reasonable expenses from now until Mr Fletcher's case might come to trial."

"Of course," she smiled. "You see to it, Mr Slym, but I would ask that each of these good fellows should receive five guineas in gold, at once, on account."

Oakes and Pegg grinned like monkeys.

"Testify before any court in the land, we would!" said Oakes.

"An' it's no more'n the truth, ma'am," said Pegg. "It's him what done it. That Jacob Fletcher."

"Thank you, Oakes! Thank you, Pegg!" said Slym. "Be so good as to leave us now. If you go to the kitchen, I'm sure Mrs Collins will find you something to keep body and soul together."

The two shabby broken seamen saluted again and shuffled out, happy as could be. They wouldn't have to starve on the shore, after all. And they could get blinding drunk on five guineas each.

As the door closed behind them, Lady Sarah was up from her couch and leapt upon Sam Slym where he sat

primly upright in his chair. She dropped into his lap with
skirts round her waist and her long legs coiled around
the back of his chair. She threw her arms round his neck
and kissed him as if he were the last man in the world.
Her tongue was working halfway down his throat and
he could hardly breathe. But he didn't complain.

"My darling Sam!" she said at last. "Where did you
find them?"

"They found me," he said. "They came to the Blue
Boar, just like the advertisements said. And the landlord
sent for me. They were nervous at first, 'cos they don't
know *where* he is, which is what the advertisement asked,
but they had something better, didn't they?"

"If they saw the Brat kill this Bosun, then why have
they kept silent so long?" she said.

"'Cos seamen don't 'peach on one another," he said,
"and the third man, who witnessed the murder, this
Polperro fellow, persuaded Oakes and Pegg that the
Bosun deserved it. It seems the Bosun was a little free
with his chastisement of the crew, and they all hated
him."

"Do you know what this means, my love?" said Lady
Sarah. "Yes," said he, "you've got the last thing you
need."

"Yes! Yes! Yes!" she said and reached down to unbuckle
Slym's breeches.

"Will you throw yourself on the mercy of the law
now, as you said?" he asked.

"Yes!" she said, pulling at his shirt and waistcoat to throw them open so she could feel his naked flesh.

"But the risk?" he said. "How can you be sure you'll win?"

Briefly she stopped burrowing her hands inside his clothes.

"Sam," she said, "I will accept nothing less than my late husband's house, his title, and all his money. I will not live in the shadows and in fear of arrest. And there is no other route to those things than through the courts. I have told you how I will crush the charges laid against me, and I have only delayed going forward while we either found and killed the Brat or found . . ." and she smiled and busied herself again, "until we found what you found today, my love . . . Ouch!" she gasped. "Have a care with that buckle . . . Help me out of these!" she said, trying to peel off a pair of skin-tight, flesh-coloured pantalettes, while remaining in the saddle.

"What in God's name are those?" said Slym, holding the filmy leggings in his broad, hairy hand.

"The latest from Paris, my love." she said. "Are they not the most elegant things? They are of knitted silk." She sighed and settled her naked behind into his lap.

"Paris?" he gasped. "But there's a bloody war with the French, isn't there?"

He got no answer, for she'd wriggled herself on to his spike and was bouncing her hips to and fro with her head thrown back and her eyes closed. Slym himself lost interest in the conversation at that point.

*

However, Lady Sarah did not present herself into a magistrate's charge immediately. There were many things still to do, of a practical and minor nature, as well as one very important and major matter. So several days of busy activity followed until Sam Slym hired a post-chaise to take them both northwards to the next stage of Lady Sarah's campaign. For her son Victor had been left dangerously injured by his disastrous attempt on the life of the Taylor family, and it was vital that something should be done about this to make sure that Victor's own position was secured.

*

Public servant though he was, Mr Magistrate Gardiner flatly refused to have Victor Coignwood under his roof during a prolonged convalescence. So shortly after Victor underwent surgery, he was removed upon his front street door to the Charity Hospital next to the Parish Workhouse. As a concession to his rank, a private room was found him, and Mr Wallace the surgeon visited him daily.

There, he was guarded, day and night in watches, by the Plowright brothers: Adam, the Parish Constable proper, by Noah, the Parish Constable (acting), and by their younger brother Abram. Adam had been entrusted with his share of the duty only after solemnly swearing on the Bible to Mr Gardiner that he would not strangle Victor if left alone with him.

*

And so, late in the evening of 6th October 1793, when Victor received two unexpected visitors, it was Adam himself, still awkward on his fine, new wooden leg, that received them.

Victor's room was normally the Hospital Clerk's office and was located just off the entrance lobby on the ground floor. It was spacious, easy of access, and had the valuable asset of barred windows. These normally served to keep the public out, and away from the clerk's strong-box, but now they helped to keep Mr Coignwood in. Not that he was in any fit state to escape.

At night, when the hospital doors were locked, the porter was allowed a fire in the lobby, which was high and draughty and stone-flagged. Normally he went his rounds through the night and returned from time to *time to* warm himself, and to take a drop of the bottle he kept in his own little cubicle. But he'd got used now to keeping company with whichever Plowright brother was on duty and they'd sit and chat and smoke a pipe or two beside the fire. This was a congenial practice which all enjoyed and agreed was superior to normal duties.

But that night, the porter and Adam Plowright were disturbed by the sharp clatter of a stick battered against the door. Grumbling and muttering, the porter drew the heavy bolts and pulled open one half of the big double doors.

A man and woman entered, clearly gentry, and Adam Plow-right hauled himself up from his chair and doffed his hat in respect. He peered at the couple, who were somewhat out of the light from the fire or the porter's lantern. The man was a gentleman from the crown of his smart round hat with its up-curling brim, to the multiple capes of his travelling coat, to the toes of his gleaming boots. The lady was all smothered in a cloak, and so could not be seen.

"Good evening!" said the man, a Londoner by his voice. "My name is Slym, and I have urgent business with Mr Victor Coignwood. I am told he is here."

"Arr . . ." said the porter, unsure of what to do. "That'd be Mr Plowright's affair: our Constable. That's he by the fire."

At the mention of Plowright's name, the lady caught the gentleman's arm and whispered urgently in his ear. They exchanged a few private words, and finally Plowright heard the gentleman say: "If you are sure you can do it . . . only if you are sure."

"Yes," said the lady distinctly and threw back her hood. Plow-right staggered on his wooden pin. Even in the half-light he knew her. No man who once set eyes on her ever forgot that face.

"'Tis *her*!" he gasped. "Lady Sarah Coignwood," but

she was already gliding towards him and working her craft upon him. The soft folds of the hood about her neck and the firelight on her face played a part, but Slym had to shake his head in amazement to see the change come over the stolid, middle-aged, thick-set man that received the full blast of her charm. The poor devil hadn't a chance. He went from hatred to worship in about ten seconds.

"My dear Mr Plowright," she said, "you are a much-wronged man and the hurt you suffered is constantly in my prayers. I am come to appeal to your charity as a God-fearing Englishman . . ."

"Oh! Arrr!" said Plowright, and shuffled to and fro in bewilderment.

"I am come to Lonborough to throw myself upon the mercy of the Law," she said, "I who am as wronged and as wounded in this affair as is your brave self, Mr Plowright – perhaps even more so!"

"Arrr?" said Plowright.

"Indeed," said she. "Soon you shall hear the full story, my dear sir, but first I beg a favour of you in the name of the dear mother that bore you, and whose memory I know you cherish. The dear mother whose tears bathed you when you suffered hurt, and kissed your wounds away."

Plowright gulped with emotion.

"My . . . my . . . my old ma?" said he, his voice quavering and tears welling in his eyes. The porter sniffed loudly and even Sam Slym thought back to his childhood.

"Yes," she said, "I ask to spend a last moment with my son Victor, before I am taken to prison. I ask what any mother would."

Plowright produced a large, multicoloured handkerchief and blew his nose loudly.

"God bless yer sweet soul, ma'am!" said he, profoundly moved. "You shall see him this instant, and devil take whomsoever stands in yer way!"

With great respect, he ushered Lady Sarah to a door which he instantly unlocked and threw open. Inside, a single candle was burning on a little table beside a camp bed. Victor Coignwood, awakened by the noise outside, sat up in his nightshirt, hollow-cheeked, yellow-faced, with huge shadows beneath his eyes, and his skull swathed in bloody bandages.

"My boy!" she breathed. "Oh, my son!" She flew to him, arms outstretched, fell on her knees beside the bed and embraced him.

Plowright and the porter sobbed with emotion and stood back to respect the privacy of the moment. They saw the fond embrace, they saw the gentle lady smooth her child's brow. They saw everything but heard nothing. She spoke too softly for that.

"My boy!" she said.

"Mother!" said he. "I have failed."

"No, dear, you have done all that I wished."

"But you sent me to kill the Taylors."

"Oh, yes."

"And I was caught! Look what they did to me!"

"Never fear, my love! Listen to me now."

"Yes, Mother."

"Do you remember my list?"

Secretly, so nobody else could see, she unfolded a scrap of paper. It was a copy of the list she'd made in August:

> Fletcher
> Mr Forster the magistrate
> Mr Pendennis the Polmouth merchant
> Mr Taylor the bookseller (and wife)
> Mr Forster's Constable
> The Constable's two brothers.

*

"And now," she said, "Fletcher is in my power, Forster was good enough to kill himself, Pendennis will say what I tell him, Taylor does not matter, and the Constable is a fool. His brothers will be the same." Victor was puzzled.

"But Taylor," he said, "he saw me kill Lucey the solicitor."

"It does not matter, my love," she insisted, and so absolute was Victor's faith in his mother that the dreadful fear and guilt (especially guilt) that had been his constant companions these last few weeks began to recede. Victor's mind had never been one of the healthiest, and he'd wandered dangerously close to the abyss of insanity.

"So what shall you do, dearest?" he said, pathetic in his relief and eagerness. "How shall you deal with the Taylors?"

"I can explain everything with two words," she said. "There was a name missing from the list."

"Yes?" he said, expectantly.

"Shall I tell it you?" she said.

"Yes," he said.

"Are you listening, my dear?"

"Yes."

"The name of my remaining enemy is . . . Victor Coignwood."

*

Even Sam Slym was shocked at the fearful shrieks that burst from the sick room. Even his toughened hide shuddered at the sight of the foaming, spitting, clawing lunatic tearing at his mother's face and howling like a damned soul. The two simple Staffordshiremen who were with him never shook off the horror of it as long as they lived and would never talk of it, except when safely drunk and late at night, supported by a company of stout men and the comfort of a good fire.

Slym led the rush and dragged Victor off Lady Sarah.

Her cheek was scratched and her hair torn, but she'd taken no real harm. He got her out, seemingly limp and fainting, but she hissed fiercely into his ear.

"Get back in there! I want him *alive*!"

He was not a second too soon. They had Victor on the floor and Plowright was throttling him while the porter laid in with his heavy boots.

"You *soddin'* bastard!" cried Plowright, over and over again. Slym hauled him off and threw Victor back on to his bed. He peered at him carefully, felt for a heartbeat, and turned and nodded at Lady Sarah, standing in the doorway. Only Sam Slym saw the satisfied little smile for a job well done. He shuddered again.

Chapter 28

Lo! Sweet Venus comes to trial,
And England fawns upon her.
For those that said they'd tell her sins,
Give witness to her honour!
The Sorceress weeps a sparkling tear,
And weaves her spell as Circe.
The Jury are become her hogs,
To grunt and snort for mercy!
Thus jury, Judge and Lawyers too,
Have made THE LAW *a farce.*
And raced like runners for the prize,
To kiss La C*******d's a**e!

> *(Scurrilous verse beneath a Gillray cartoon depicting*
> *Lady Sarah Coignwood's trial, entitled,*
> *"The tri(UMPH)al of Venus". First published by*
> *H. Humphrey of St James's as a coloured print on*

Fletcher's Glorious 1ˢᵗ of June

14th May 1794, it was an enormous success, with many
subsequent editions and pirate copies.)

*

From 10th May to 13 May 1794, there was one topic of
conversation alone, among all classes of society in
London. Similarly, all matters of the war with the French,
of Parliamentary debate, or of any other kind whatsoever,
were driven from their former places of prominence in
the London newspapers, to make way for the ONE
GREAT EVENT of Lady Sarah Coignwood's trial, on
a charge of murder, at the Old Bailey.

Lady Sarah was already well known to the elegant
world as the outstanding beauty of the day. She was a
leader of fashion and kept the most glittering and spec-
tacular salon in London. Her house in Dulwich Square
was one of the hubs around which society revolved.

Or at least these things were almost true. There had
always been a powerful undercurrent of rumour about
the Coignwoods: Lady Sarah and her sons Alexander
and Victor.

Even the rake-hell society of London in the 1790s
had its limits and the solid rock of respectability had
always groaned and rumbled beneath the Coignwoods,
like the slopes of a volcano that slept uneasily.

Thus the family. Now the lady herself. All superlatives
failed where Lady Sarah Coignwood was concerned.

Charles James Fox, the great Whig statesman and reputedly one of her many lovers, said of her:

"No man who gets into the same room with her can bear to let her out, and no man's wife who gets her out of the room can bear to let her back in." In another version of that famous quotation, the word "bed" takes the place of "room".

But as with her sons, particularly Alexander, there was the scent of a carefully hidden corruption. Men, and women too, were blinded by her beauty when in her presence, and could think no ill of her. But they weren't complete fools and when one prurient story piled upon another, they began to wonder.

So when, in early August of 1793, the world learned of Lady Sarah's disappearance, together with Victor, fleeing a charge of murder, and the mysterious disappearance of Jacob Fletcher, Sir Henry's illegitimate heir, the world nodded its head, smirked wisely at itself, and said that it always knew Lady Sarah would come to no good. And when in October '93 Lady Sarah gave herself up in charge of Mr Hector Gardiner, Magistrate of Lonborough in Staffordshire, the sensation produced by this news was greater than anything since the fall of Quebec to the British in 1759.

So intense was the interest in the case that powerful influences were brought to bear to ensure that Lady Sarah's trial should take place not in Staffordshire, but in London, so that the spectacle could be enjoyed by the

Great and the Good of the Land, without the horrors of having to toil north into the unknown wastes beyond civilisation.

The Prince of Wales himself was undoubtedly involved in this *despite* (or perhaps because of) the fact that Lady Sarah had once snubbed him cruelly at the end of a brief liaison they had shared. But some things are beyond the influence even of princes. The law of England would not be hurried, and it was not until seven months later that London society got its treat and the case came to trial at the Old Bailey, before the Master of the Rolls, Lord Lairing. In the meantime, Lady Sarah was supposedly held in Newgate Prison, though in reality, and for the usual "fees" to her gaolers, she was allowed to live in Dulwich Square, provided she presented herself each Monday morning at Newgate to prove that she had not fled.

It was obvious at this time that Lady Sarah was awash with credit. Fletcher, the supposed heir to the Coignwood fortune, was still missing, and legal opinions were swinging behind Lady Sarah as rightful heir to her husband's bottomless moneybags.

Consequently, Dulwich Square became a centre of pilgrimage for not only the fashionable, but the nosy, the curious and the mob. In the week before the trial the disturbances outside Lady Sarah's house grew so great that troops were called out to seal off the Square. London duly noted that the regiment entrusted with this duty was the 10th Hussars: "The Prince of Wales's Own".

Finally on the morning of 10th May 1794, the longed-for entertainment commenced. Twelve jurymen, solid, respectable tradesmen to a man, sat shoulder to shoulder in three neat tiers of banked wooden pews, with a closed gate shutting them in. Immediately in front of them was a sort of orchestra pit in which important witnesses would be stored and kept waiting the pleasure of the court. Beyond that, on a raised bench of their own, were representatives of the newspapers, given the privilege in a free England to report the proceedings.

To the left of the jury, uprose the dock itself, the focus of every man and woman's gaze. Still empty, as yet, of the lovely creature that all had come to see.

Immediately above and behind the jury box, there rose a high wooden screen, like a giant, turned-up coat collar. This effectively blocked off the jury from the public gallery above, where a choice selection of England's ruling class was on display.

To the right of the jury box was a huge half-moon shaped table with a green baize cloth and several dozen lawyers, black-robed and white-wigged. Among them were Sir Anthony Beaufort who appeared for the Crown, and Sir Patrick Joyce the brilliant, witty Irishman – one of the finest advocates in the kingdom – who appeared for the defence. These two at least had work to do, but most of the others were shuffling papers and trying to look important, for far more of them had claimed the privilege of attending than necessity really demanded.

Further right, fitting snugly against the round side of the table, arose the high panelling of the bench, behind which, and at a commanding height, Lord Lairing would survey the court. Above his seat, there was mounted upon the wall a great sword of justice surmounted by the crown which represented the King's Majesty.

At half-past nine there came a sudden buzz of expectation, a simultaneous falling silent of the hundreds crammed into the court room, then a communal gasp of wonder. Between two officers of the court, Lady Sarah was ascending into the dock.

She wore a flowing gown of soft shimmering lilac silk with a full skirt, long tight sleeves, and a sash tied in a huge bow at the back to nip it in at the waist. Her long hair tumbled in a cascade of curls from under an enormous hat decorated with voluminous ribbons to match those at her throat. She was breathtakingly lovely, and left every other woman in London trailing in her wake.

She glanced briefly around the court room, nodded graciously to her champion, Sir Patrick, and sat straight-backed on the chair they gave her, with her head high and her hands folded in her lap. She looked sweet and natural, and those who knew her sighed in admiration and muttered to one another that a change had come over her. Usually, she lounged with the languid fluidity of a lazy cat. Only Lady Sarah knew that her bearing was consciously modelled on that of Miss Kate Booth, still chained in her attic room in Greenwich. Lady Sarah was ready to learn from anyone; all that mattered was winning.

Compared with Lady Sarah's entry, the arrival of Lord Lairing to the stentorian bellowing of a court usher was an anticlimax, but all stood while he heaved his bulk into the Judge's chair and his active, busy eyes, half-hidden in folds of flesh, swept around the court. His Lordship was vastly fat and his red face and wheezing breath advertised the impoverished state of his health. But the swollen body housed a quick, penetrating brain and he alone of all the men in court that day smiled in amusement at Lady Sarah's affectation of girlish innocence, rather than being stirred and aroused by it.

With all the players assembled, the game began. There was an hour or so of formality as the jury were sworn in, the lovely accused duly pleaded "Not Guilty" and still more bodies managed to squeeze themselves into the court room. Later, Sir Anthony addressed the court to list the divers murders and deadly assaults of which Lady Sarah and her son Victor stood accused. This amounted to the following:

1. The murder of Arnold Burroughs, Coachman to the late Mr Cecil Forster, Magistrate, of Lonborough.
2. The murder of Richard Lucey, Solicitor, of Lonborough.
3. Assault with grievous bodily harm upon the person of Mr Adam Plowright, Parish Constable, of Lonborough.
4. Assault with grievous bodily harm upon the person of Mr Edward Lucey, Solicitor, of Lonborough.

Of this total, charges (2) and (4) were rapidly struck out as far as Lady Sarah was concerned. Mr John Taylor, bookseller of 38 Market Street, Lonborough, was called by the Prosecution and told the court in a clear and angry voice how he and his wife had seen Victor Coignwood emerge from No. 39 Market Street, opposite his own house, on the night of 19th July 1793, with a sword in his hand, before running off up the street. No. 39 immediately took fire and the wounded Mr Edward Lucey emerged, dragging the body of his father.

"Thank you, Mr Taylor," said Sir Anthony. "My Lord," said he, "I now produce affidavits from Mr Edward Lucey, attesting to the fact that the deadly attack upon himself and his father was carried out by Mr Victor Coignwood."

"Sir Anthony," said Lord Lairing, "is Mr Edward Lucey not in court?"

"No, my Lord," said Beaufort, "he is ill and unable to travel. I have certificates from two physicians . . ."

"No doubt," said Lairing dismissively, "but you have not yet advanced evidence of the involvement of the accused in the assaults upon either Mr Lucey. Do you not propose to do so?"

"No, my Lord," said Beaufort, "but I hope to show . . ."

"Sir Anthony," said Lairing, "you have shown that Mr Victor Coignwood committed these assaults, have you not?"

"Yes, my Lord."

"The same Mr Victor Coignwood now confined in a straight waistcoat, insane and unable to plead, in the Charity Hospital, Lonborough?"

"Yes, my Lord."

"Then what have the assaults upon the Luceys to do with the accused?"

"It is my contention, my Lord, that Mr Victor Coignwood committed these crimes under her influence."

"Have you evidence of this?"

"The totality of my case permits of no other interpretation, my Lord."

"I repeat, Sir Anthony, have you evidence of this?"

Sir Anthony was stopped in his tracks. Whispers flew round the court and there was a brief silence.

"In that case, Sir Anthony, I will ask you to confine yourself to those charges for which you are able to present evidence of the involvement of the accused!"

Sir Patrick Joyce smirked, and turned to smile at Lady Sarah. She nodded to acknowledge him and returned to the serious business of staring in adoration at Lord Lairing.

Sir Anthony was rattled, but shifted quickly to the events of 30th July 1793 when Mr Magistrate Forster had led a party of men to arrest Lady Sarah and her son at Coignwood Hall. Of this company, Forster's coachman had been shot dead, and Forster himself had later died in his hunting accident.

But five witnesses remained alive: Mr Nathan Pendennis, Lord Mayor of Polmouth; Mr Adam Plowright, lately Parish Constable of Lonborough, and his two brothers who went with Forster's party on that fell occasion.

So much time had gone on the earlier formalities and on Mr Taylor's testimony that no further business was conducted in court that day.

On the 11th, the court reassembled. Lady Sarah wore an entirely different and still more stunning outfit. Actual fights broke out among those queuing to gain entry to the public gallery and places were sold for huge sums of money.

Excitement was intense as Mr Pendennis took his place before the bench, to give his evidence. The jury stirred with anticipation, and readied themselves to give most especial weight to a man who was the very embodiment of all that any tradesman could aspire to in his bearing or his unquestionable honesty. True, Mr Pendennis was nervous and sweating, but the court was hot with the press of bodies and who would not be nervous in such a position?

Sir Anthony led Pendennis through the events preceding the arrival of Mr Forster's party at Coignwood Hall. He led Pendennis to the central point of his case and approached the question that would put a rope around Lady Sarah's adorable neck.

"And how were Lady Sarah and her son situated at that moment?" said Sir Anthony.

"Side by side, my Lord," said Pendennis, looking up at Lairing.

"And how were they armed?"

"Victor Coignwood had a double pistol in either hand, and more in his belt."

"And Lady Sarah?" asked Sir Anthony, with a frown. "How was she armed?"

"She was not armed," said Pendennis, sweating furiously. "*Not* armed?" said Sir Anthony, surprised.

"No."

"Are you sure?"

"Yes."

"I remind you, sir, that you are on oath and must answer truly on peril of your immortal soul! Now, sir, was Lady Sarah armed?"

"No, my Lord," said Pendennis looking straight at Lord Lairing.

"Then what did Lady Sarah say to her son?" asked Sir Anthony. "What did she say when he threatened Mr Forster's company with his pistols?"

"Nothing, my Lord," said Pendennis.

"What?" said Sir Anthony, searching through his notes. "Did she not say – 'Show them, pick any one you wish'? And later did she not warn her son not to kill the Magistrate because it would provoke the wrath of the Law but to kill any other that he chose? And . . ."

"Sir Anthony," intervened Lord Lairing, "do you entertain hopes of further advancement in your profession?"

"Ah, er, yes, my Lord."

"Then why are you attempting to lead your witness in this naive fashion?"

Sir Anthony begged the court's pardon and turned upon Pendennis with all his considerable skill.

But Pendennis could not be shaken and Sir Patrick declined even to question the witness when given the opportunity. So far Sir Patrick had earned his huge fee by doing next to nothing.

Next the prosecution put up the three Plowright brothers. Of these Adam Plowright, with his wooden leg, token of the mutilation inflicted upon him by Victor Coignwood, was by far the most impressive, though his evidence was long and rambling. It was soon clear that he was deep under the spell of Lady Sarah and was filled with a poisonous loathing of her son. He had constantly to be stopped from wandering off the point into a tirade of hatred against Victor Coignwood, accompanied by protestations of the lady's virtue and the cruel burden she bore in having such unnatural children.

These excursions drew a chorus of "Shame!" and "Infamy!" from the public gallery when they touched upon Victor Coignwood, and cries of "Here, here!" when they concerned La Belle Coignwood's motherly gentleness. Still more ominous for the prosecution's case were the sympathetic growls that arose from the jury box whenever Lady Sarah was named.

"Unfortunate lady!" said the foreman of the jury, more than once. Eventually the foreman was reprimanded for this by his Lordship, though those familiar with Lairing's career had known him give far more savage warnings for far less serious misbehaviour.

Overall, and in so far as a clear testimony could be got out of him, Adam Plowright denied that Lady Sarah had any responsibility for the crimes of the night of the 30th July, and blamed her son comprehensively.

When his brothers stood up, one after the other, the first real shadow of evidence seemed to appear against Lady Sarah. In varying degrees they appeared to agree that she *had* said the words that Sir Anthony had so utterly failed to draw forth from Nathan Pendennis. This gave Sir Patrick his first real exercise of his two days in court. He picked on the inconsistencies between the accounts given by the three brothers and so completely made fools of them that the court rocked with laughter and the jurymen shook their heads in contempt of these Staffordshire clods with their uncouth accents and thick boots.

There then followed a long and complicated series of efforts by Sir Anthony to bring forward witnesses to Lady Sarah's allegedly scandalous and depraved character. He had in fact made terrific efforts to delve into some of her more interesting pastimes and the list of allegations, and the persons whom he had waiting to be summoned, some of them trembling in fear, would have made a very interesting pamphlet for public titivation.

But now, Sir Patrick came into his own. To the intense disappointment of the public gallery, he succeeded one way or another of disqualifying or discrediting every witness that the prosecution advanced for this purpose. In this he was aided by Lord Lairing's scrupulous refusal to admit any evidence that did not bear directly on the charges the accused had to answer.

And so, the second day of the trial came to a close. All present went away buzzing with satisfaction and the newspapers again ran special editions for the benefit of the waiting multitudes that had failed to get into a court designed for a few hundred souls. None the less, on the third day, with the prospect of Lady Sarah herself being brought forward, the multitudes redoubled their efforts to get in. Fortunately, this had been anticipated and the 10th Hussars were out again, plus a battalion of foot-guards with bayonets fixed, to see fair play in the seething queues.

Once again Lady Sarah stunned her audience with a fresh and wonderful ensemble of clothes, and it was noted that as she took her place, the jury involuntarily rose to their feet in respect and were sharply told to sit down again by the indignant senior usher with his long staff of office.

With his Lordship mounted on the bench, and formalities concluded, Sir Anthony stood up and spoke brilliantly to conclude his case, and made some of the finest bricks without straw that the Old Bailey had ever known. Despite two days of interception or destruction of much of the Crown's evidence, and despite constant interruptions from Lord Lairing, he returned to his theme of a weak son dominated by a depraved mother and did his agile uttermost to insinuate the slurs against the accused, that his uncalled witnesses of yesterday would have proven. Eventually, he saw the jury nodding in response to his words: a most excellent sign.

After nearly two hours of nonstop oration, he sat down to murmurs of applause from all sides. He'd done very well and he knew it. Sir Patrick caught his eye and gave a tiny bow to acknowledge him. He could afford to be gracious because he was about to call Lady Sarah to give evidence.

The silence of the tomb fell upon the court as the

slim, beautiful figure made her elegant way down from the dock and went forward to stand before the bench. The very rustle of her gown, her soft footfalls, could be heard.

The architect who designed the court room had intended to give advantage to the Judge and the Law's mighty power in placing his Lordship up above the place where witnesses stood.

Also, the imposing robes of a Judge and his minions were meant to add to his terrible dignity, and imbue lesser mortals with a proper respect for the proceedings.

But these factors, so effective when the accused was a man, rebounded catastrophically when she was a lovely woman on trial for her life. The great bloated, red-caped Judge glowering down upon her; the surrounding lawyers in their sinister, swirling black; the mere fact that a lady of such imperial elegance was forced to stand while all around her "gentlemen" sat at their ease – all these things combined to give Lady Sarah the most enormous advantage in the eyes of the jury.

Especially it did when she exploited it so well. She was playing Kate Booth to the life. The brave little chin tilted up in pride, the straight back, the slight trembling of the limbs as if in barely mastered fear.

Her situation and bearing touched chords in the hearts of men that are deep and sonorous. There was not one man in that jury box that wouldn't have given his shop (stock, fittings, goodwill and all) to the nearest beggar if he could have ridden forward on a white horse to sweep the lady off her feet and thunder away into the setting sun. And that was before she'd even spoken.

Sir Patrick led her through her piece, prompting with minimal questions and carefully relegating himself to the supporting role. In five minutes she had annihilated Sir Anthony's account of her domination of her son Victor. In ten minutes the jurymen were ashamed they'd ever entertained it. And so it went on to the climax.

"Ma'am," said Sir Patrick, "the court has heard of the complete responsibility of your son Victor for all the crimes of which you are accused. I must ask you now why for so long you tolerated his presence in your house? Why did you not turn him out? Why did you not make known his crimes?"

"Because he held me in fear," she said. "He many times said that he would kill me if ever I betrayed him." She paused, lowered her head and a tear was seen to glisten on her cheek. "He was my son, my own child, but even from boyhood he was so strange . . ." For the first time she faltered. With great tenderness Sir Patrick drew out the sorry tale of Victor's life (much of it true). His sadistic cruelty to animals. His perverted habits, etc., etc. The court was agog with fascination. Here were some of the treats they'd been denied yesterday.

Having blacked Victor beyond redemption, and explained Lady Sarah's behaviour beyond question, Sir Anthony concluded with a stroke of genius.

"You are a widow, are you not, ma'am?" said he.

"I am, sir."

"And your elder son is dead, slain in his country's service?"

"Yes, sir."

"And your younger son, Victor, the perpetrator of all these crimes, is confined in the madhouse?"

"Yes, sir."

"Have you parents still alive?"

"Alas no, sir."

"Then whom have you left?"

"No one, sir."

"No one, ma'am? Is there no relative to give you comfort?" Sir Patrick paused, glanced towards the jury, whose faces were working with emotion, judged his moment and added, "Is there no man to protect you?"

"No," she said, "I am quite . . . alone." She sobbed softly and a massed groan rose from the court. Lord Lairing ordered proceedings to be suspended and a chair instantly found for the lady. His own fat-lidded eyes were red, and he who'd donned the black cap times beyond number was snivelling into his handkerchief.

Later, when Sir Anthony made his attempt to cross-examine, he saw such ferocious, unforgiving, hatred crackling in the eyes of the jury that he knew he was lost and gave it up as a bad job.

Lord Lairing's summing-up drove more nails into the coffin where the Prosecution's case already lay in state.

When commanded to consider their verdict, the jury simply looked to their foreman and nodded firmly at him. He nodded back and rose for his moment of glory.

"We shall not need to retire, my Lord," said he. "We find the defendant not guilty, a true and a cruelly ill-used lady!"

Cheers, wild demonstrations and confusion followed. Lairing cleared the court. All departed. The news sped through London like a stampede of wild horses. Lady Sarah's carriage was pulled through the streets to Dulwich Square, by the twelve jurymen, with the 10th Hussars in close attendance like a sovereign's escort. The mob lit bonfires and screamed in delight. The fashionable world sent their cards in congratulation and Lady Sarah rejoined their ranks not just in triumph, but in glory.

But one man was left isolated from the celebration. Sam Slym had watched the trial and marvelled at his lady's talents. He was pleased to see her free and satisfied with what she'd done so far to keep her promise to make a gentleman of him. In the false dawn of the months before the trial, he'd already enjoyed a way of life in Dulwich Square beyond his dreams.

He'd enjoyed *her* too. The trouble was, so had others. He was sure of it, and he was madly jealous. He was sure that now she had all that she wanted, with the lawyers promising to elbow Fletcher aside from the Coignwood money, and in any case now that they could dangle Fletcher from a rope, so soon as they found him, now that she had all that – what did she need him for?

In fact there was plenty of work yet for Sam Slym in Lady Sarah's plans, and the next task was presented to him a couple of weeks later, on 5th June 1794, when a Special Gazette gave news of the arrival in Portsmouth of *Audacious*, *74*.

Chapter 29

On 13th June 1794 I saw the Channel Fleet anchored at Spit-head like Grenadiers on parade. The long lines of great ships swung to their cables in unison, and the dozens of masts and hundreds of spars, now bare of canvas, gave the impression of a strange, rigid forest in which everything grew at right angles. A forest braced and stayed by thousands of straight black rigging lines, crossing, joining and converging in an uncountable profusion of sharp geometric patterns.

Howe's prizes were on display with British colours over French, anchored together for the world to see: as fine a collection of the shipbuilder's craft as any man could wish to see. Some of them were brand new ships incorporating the latest ideas in French shipbuilding. Our own dockyard people were already swarming over them, taking careful note of the beauty, and efficacy of French design while criticising it with an unquenchable spite because they hadn't thought of it first.

The fleet anchorage in the Solent is a mile or two south of Portsmouth itself, and on that day the whole shoreline from eastward of Southsea Castle to westward of the Haslar Hospital was lined with people. We could see them and hear them. Music, cheering and all the celebration of Howe's great victory over Villaret de Joyeuse. And of course, the town turned out in its boats to see the fleet. Every craft from wherries full of fresh bread, fruit and brandy, to tarts in smart-painted launches, to the Mayor and Corporation in a barge pulled by boatmen in craft-guild regalia.

Lord Howe took this in his stride. He'd been a sailor for more than half a century and had learned not to whine at disaster nor let success go to his head. In any case, he already enjoyed every advantage of wealth and rank that his country could give, so what was left to him, other than satisfaction of a job well done?

And then, late in the afternoon of the 13th, a boat bumped alongside *Queen Charlotte* with half-a-dozen passengers aboard who'd not come out to see the fleet, nor Lord Howe, at all. They'd come out for the particular purpose of meeting me: Mr Jacob Fletcher of Polmouth in Devon, entered into His Majesty's Navy by the Impress Service on 10th February 1793, subsequently rated Boatswain in H.M. Frigate *Phiandra*, 32, and honourably discharged from that ship, while lying at

Portsmouth, by Captain Sir Harry Bollington on 19th July 1793.

You see? They had all my service down to a paragraph. Somebody had gone to a lot of trouble to put all that together and they'd done it so there was no chance of their ending up with the wrong man.

I was down below when they came aboard, so I didn't see them until I was summoned before Black Dick by a midshipman. The lad was polite, and touched his hat to me just as if I were an officer. So I suspected no ill, and followed him past the Marine sentries, and into Howe's day cabin which was full of Clerks, Tradesmen, Mayors, Lieutenants and even Captains, all waiting their turn to pass into the inner sanctum of the Great Cabin, and the Admiral's presence.

The Mid whispered to another pair of sentries at the Admiral's door and stood back as the door was opened for me. I went in and found Howe standing with his back to the stern windows, Sir Roger Curtis, his Fleet Captain, was on one side of him and his Chief Clerk was on the other. There was a pronounced atmosphere of hostility in the room and Howe and his two chief confidants were glaring across the cabin at three men and a woman who'd just come aboard the ship.

One of the men was a big, middle-aged Sea-Service Lieutenant named Lloyd. He was grey, and muscular, running to fat but with hard eyes. He wore a cutlass on his hip and gripped it as if he was expecting imminent action. Standing with Lloyd, as if a companion, was an elderly gentleman who had lawyer written all over him, from his wig to his buckled shoes. This was a Mr Smithers, an Officer of the High Court of Admiralty. The third man was an odd creature. Probably the smartest and most immaculately turned-out man I've ever met in my life. His boots shone, his linen was dazzling and his coat fitted like a skin. He must have spent hours getting himself up like that.

In a man, such attention to appearances usually means he's in the fops' regiment of the bum brigade, but this gentleman was about as far from that as ever could be. He caught my eye as I entered the cabin and stared straight at me with a total confidence and a damn-you-to-hell expression that would have got him my fist in his face had we two been alone. Believe me, children, there weren't many men in 1794 who felt safe to look at your Uncle Jacob like that. This beauty was one Samuel Slime, a celebrated thief-taker.

[This notorious person famously spelt his name "Slym" but Fletcher insisted on "Slime" since that would be all that would be left of him, should ever Fletcher get hold of him. S.P.]

Now, I've run through the list of them and told you who they were. But I don't want to give you the impression I gave any of these three much more than a quick glance, because something else had caught my entire attention. And that was the lady standing with Mr Slime.

She was an absolute stunner. Not young but a

gorgeous, lovely woman. About five-and-half feet tall with long, heavy black hair and a sensual voluptuous look about her. By George, she really was something out of the ordinary! Like her pal Slime, she was dressed up to the eyeballs and in addition her manner proclaimed wealth and position.

The thought sprang to my mind that she seemed familiar and even as I was wrestling with this idea, I knew who she was! It hit me like a physical blow! This was Lady Sarah Coignwood, wife of my natural father, Sir Henry Coignwood. This was the woman who'd set her son Alexander to press-gang me into the Navy and try to kill me. It was the likeness to him, the vicious bastard, that had puzzled me. Well, I'd shoved a cutlass blade through his chest last July and thought that was the end of my troubles. But it wasn't 'cos here was the force that drove Alexander to his work.

So I stared at her and she at me. I could see that she was as fascinated as I, and startled too. She raised a hand to her mouth and gasped. She clutched at Slime's sleeve and backed away to place him between her and me. In fact, she wasn't just startled, she was *afraid*. Slime placed a hand on hers protectively, and glared at me with renewed venom.

Suddenly I began to feel very uneasy. Sarah Coignwood could only be my enemy, and a deadly enemy at that. She and her party had come seeking me and they couldn't mean me any good. But she'd come openly, so this must be some attack that was within the law: making use of the law, if Mr Lawyer Smithers was anything to go by. It couldn't be a simple matter of getting me out of the Coignwood will, for they'd not need to come aboard *Queen Charlotte* for that. I wondered what they could want, but the wondering was a lie to myself. I knew what was coming, and it drained the courage out of my boots.

"Mr Fletcher," said Lord Howe, after he'd made the introductions, "here's Mr Smithers on behalf of the High Court of Admiralty, with papers duly made out and in all respects correct." He glanced at his Clerk who had a sheaf of papers in his hand, and the Clerk nodded. "Papers obliging me to give you up in charge of Lieutenant Lloyd and his men, to be taken away, awaiting your trial on a charge of mutiny and murder." I felt sick and my legs went weak. Howe continued, "Mr Fletcher, I have told these gentlemen what you have done for your country in enabling me to bring my fleet into action with that of the French. I have furthermore told them that in the action, you yourself fought like a lion and even now are incompletely recovered from wounds inflicted upon you by the enemy."

In other words Black Dick was on my side and was seeking any just cause or reason that would support his throwing Mr Smithers and Lieutenant Lloyd into the Solent.

"Mr Fletcher," said Howe with his great black brows knit together, "I have a question for you. A question which shall resolve this matter, at least to my satisfaction. I charge you to answer truly upon your honour as an Englishman and a gentleman!"

"Aye-aye, my Lord," says I.

"Mr Fletcher," says he, solemnly, "did you murder Bosun Dixon of His Majesty's Brig *Bullfrog?*"

There it was. My worst fear made real. Shortly after I was pressed aboard the tender *Bullfrog in* February last year, I'd bludgeoned Dixon and thrown him over the side because he was a mindless moron who'd flogged me nearly out of my mind. Dixon was all the better for a drowning, and the Navy was better without a swab like Dixon. But the Navy would never agree with that, and the fear of retribution had been on me ever since.

And the fear was all the greater since I'd learned from my messmate, Norris Polperro, that he'd seen me kill Dixon, and so had two others. Norris had persuaded them to keep quiet, but for how long?

"Mr Fletcher," says Howe, frowning deeper, "I await your answer, sir!"

I didn't know what to say, and so said nothing. There was a long and unpleasant silence, broken at last by Lady Sarah. Even in that moment I noticed how beautiful was her voice.

"He is condemned, my Lord," says she. "His manner proclaims his guilt!"

Which, unfortunately, was the opinion of all those present. Smithers spoke up and gave a lot of legal detail.

Lloyd contributed that he would prefer for practical reasons not to take me off for a couple of days and he'd be grateful if I might be held aboard ship until then. Howe agreed, but there was some bickering over the precise circumstances under which I was to be secured, until Black Dick settled this with an outburst of temper.

"Lieutenant Lloyd," says he, "I'll not be lectured by one such as yourself! The prisoner shall be clapped in irons and he shall await your pleasure in this ship tomorrow morning. Is that good enough, sir? Or will you question my ability to keep my word?"

Lloyd blanched at this and backed off from giving further offence to so great a man. Shortly after that, they all trouped out and I was left alone with Howe, Sir Roger Curtis and Howe's Clerk.

"Well, sir," says Black Dick, "you disappoint me and that's a fact. What do you mean by standing there like a stuffed dummy, saying neither yes nor no?"

Once again I didn't know what to say.

"Good God, man," says Howe, "did you kill the fellow or didn't you?" But I was in a daze. It was just like my early days in the service when I was in daily fear of being hung for Dixon's murder.

"Bah!" says Howe, at last. "You're a bloody fool, Fletcher. But I'll help you if I can. I'm in your debt, sir, for my victory. Now then – who are your friends? To whom shall we send word that you might have their assistance to prepare a defence?"

And that, my jolly boys, was one of the worst moments of gloom in my entire life.

I thought hard about that. Who could I turn to for help? I had nobody to pull strings for me and work the levers of influence. The best I could do was mention the name of Mr Nathan Pendennis who'd been my employer in Polmouth. He was a powerful man on his own ground, but what weight he carried in London I did not know. And maybe he'd not put himself to trouble on my account, in any case. None the less, I gave his name.

"Pendennis?" says Howe's Clerk. "Mr Nathan Pendennis, Lord Mayor of Polmouth?"

"Yes," says I.

"He may prove an excellent ally," says the Clerk. "He is acting together with Lucey and Lucey, solicitors, as executors to the Coignwood estate, to which you, Mr Fletcher, are heir. I remember reading an article to that effect in the *Morning Post*, last year."

"Oh?" says I. I hadn't known that.

"Yes," says the Clerk.

"Write to him at once!" says Howe. "This day!"

"Yes, my Lord," says the Clerk.

I still had little hopes of action from Pendennis, but I supposed that he was better than nothing.

And as for real friends, my old shipmates, Kate Booth, Lucinda, Cooper and his Uncle Ezekiah (twisting sods the pair of them, those last two, but I'm sure they did actually like me after their fashion), not to mention a certain coal black African King and his five daughters – yes, I had friends all right, but either I'd left them, or they'd left me, or they were across the ocean and couldn't help anyway. So they weren't much use. All except one.

"And Sammy Bone," says I finally.

"What?" says the Clerk, looking up from his notes.

"I beg your pardon, Mr Fletcher," says the Clerk, realising he'd been rude, surprised by the plebeian nature of the name I'd just given him.

"Sammy Bone," says I. "He's a lower-deck hand who was taken out of *Phiandra* by Captain Cutler and entered into *Fydor*. I suppose he's still aboard her."

"A lower-deck hand?" says Howe. "And you regard him as a friend?" He turned over this unaccountable fact in his mind and produced the only possible explanation. "Ah!" says he. "I take it that Mr Bone is a gentleman swept in by the press. I have known such cases. Would you like me to investigate his circumstances, Mr Fletcher?"

"No, my Lord," says I, "but I'd like to see him if that can be arranged." Howe was deeply puzzled.

"But can this person be of assistance to you, in your plight?" says he.

"I don't think so, my Lord," says I, "but I'd still like to see him."

"As you wish," said Howe. "But is there no one else?"

"No, my Lord," says I.

"What an unaccountable fellow you are, Mr Fletcher,

but you have my promise of assistance," says he, and turned to Curtis. "See if this Mr Bone can be found, Sir Roger, and bring him aboard."

"Aye-aye, my Lord," says he, "I'll signal the fleet."

*

Half an hour later I was on the lower gun-deck secured by leg irons, like a drunken seaman awaiting the lash. But they rigged me up some canvas screens to form a little private cabin and I had an open gun-port for daylight and fresh air. A bored Marine with a drawn bayonet was set to guard me, so there was no chance of trying my strength on the irons, or the bolts that secured them to the deck.

I hadn't been down there very long when, much to my surprise, I received a visitor. It was Lady Sarah in company with a couple of *Queen Charlotte*'s Lieutenants. They gazed at her in wonderment, hung on her words and contorted themselves into knots to please her. They'd have made a spectacle of themselves before their men if the men hadn't been even worse: goggle-eyed, knuckling their brows, bowing half double, and grinning like half-wits.

She made a great play of surprise at coming across me and then somehow managed to manoeuvre things such that she was close enough to me to have a few private words while everybody else was busy casting off the lashings of a 32-pounder, ready to run it out for her.

The Lieutenants bawled and got in each other's way and the men hauled and struggled like madmen in their eagerness to please, and to show off.

She was outwardly calm, and cheerily encouraged the gun-crew and the Lieutenants. But I think there were very strong emotions surging within her.

"I've come to lay a ghost," she said.

"What?" says I.

"You are your father," says she. "Oh, well done, gentlemen! Haul away!" She clapped her hands for their benefit, but I could see she was nervous, darting little glances at me, as if to prove that I was really there. "My God!" says she. "It's witchcraft . . . you are *he!*"

"Aye," says I, "back from the grave to take my revenge, madam!" She shuddered as if confronted with a spider, for I'd correctly guessed what was bothering her. I'm the dead image of my natural father. Her blasted son Alexander told me that. Even he was unsettled by the likeness and I think with her it was worse. She actually lived with Sir Henry, after all.

"Capital! Capital!" she cried, laughing merrily. "You'll hang, you swine! I'll see the rope choke the life out of you and your legs kicking in the air, and then I'll spend your money!"

It was my turn to shudder now. It ain't nice to see that kind of spite come out of a beautiful woman.

"I never wanted your bloody money," says I, "not at first, anyway."

"Well, you shan't have it now, so you should be pleased." She sneered at me in hatred, and a sudden flash of bitterness swept through her. "By Christ, you filthy . . ." and such a stream of putrid oaths poured out that I was sickened. But she'd not done yet. "I have your little friend Miss Booth," says she, and I stirred at the name.

"Splendid! Oh, splendid!" she cried for the benefit of her other audience. "I see you know Miss Booth. She thinks she's in love with you, but I've told her you abandoned her. What shall I do with her?"

"Let her go, you creature!" says I, my ears still ringing from the assault of her putrid tongue. "She's nothing to do with you."

"Ah!" says she. "You care for her, do you?"

"Why should I tell you?" says I.

"You were lovers, were you not?" says she.

"Yes."

"Then I take it you'd have her back?"

"Yes," says I thinking of her pale, sweet little face. "I wanted her to come with me when I left *Phiandra* but she wouldn't."

"Ahhh! So it *was* her!"

"Yes."

"Then I shall give her back to you."

"What?"

"Which parts shall I send first?"

"*What?*"

"Hair? Fingernails? Ears? Or would you prefer larger

portions? If you won't choose then I'll make my own selection. Then I will send them for you to see before they hang you." The cold, lovely eyes bored straight into mine and she leaned close to make sure that I understood. "I shall do this. I promise on the sacred memory of my darling, my Alexander."

For a second I still didn't realise what she meant, but then it sunk in and Madame La Belle Coignwood got a very nasty fright.

I leapt from where I was sitting and went for her to wring her bloody neck. I was madder with anger even than I'd been in the action on *Queen Charlotte*'s fo'c'sle. My leg irons tightened and checked me, but she'd come too close for safety and I seized her with a roar of anger. I saw the fright contort her face and then my hands were round her neck and throttling. They couldn't hang me twice, and I was determined to take her with me. We crashed to the floor and she raked my face with her nails, trying to drive the thumb nails, sharp as a cat's, into my eyes. I screwed tight my eyes and shook my head from side to side and squeezed all the harder.

But it was no go. At least twenty men were on my back, battering and hammering with whatever heavy objects lay to hand: rammers, handspikes and the Marine joined in with his brass-capped musket butt.

God knows how I've survived some of the assaults I've suffered. This one was one of the worst beatings I ever took. And it was handed out by British tars, too.

When they'd rescued the "poor lady" and fussed her away, they threw a bucket of water over me to wash the blood off. They had two Marines there now, different men, with levelled muskets and ball cartridge loaded. I hurt all over and one eye was closed. I was bleeding from cuts to my head and coughing as if I'd bring my lungs up.

Later, when the fuss had died down and things were quiet again, one of the Marines had a little word with me, just to make sure I understood the new rules that were in force.

"Oi!" says he, prodding me with the long bayonet at the end of his musket. "Oi! Lissen, you baskit!" I raised my head and squinted through the good eye. "Our mate's gettin' two dozen tomorrow, on account o' you," says he, and he turned his musket to show me the lock – it was fully cocked awaiting only a touch on the trigger. "See this, you baskit? You try that again, what you did just now, and we'll shoot you fuckin' dead!"

I'd almost have preferred it if he had. And if I could have got myself out of the gun-port, I'd have dropped over the side and sunk without trace. I've had some bloody awful moments of misery in my life and that was one of them. I felt as if I hadn't a friend in the world and my enemies were taking their pleasure with me.

Chapter 30

I sat in my misery, hardly even touching the food I was given at tea-time, and simply stared out of the gun-port at the shifting waves. The double-notes of the ship's bell gave the time, and I thought of the early days of my service when I'd just been pressed and all seemed black. There seemed to be no way out at all.

Then at about ten o'clock with the summer light beginning to fade, I got another visitor. I was feeling so sorry for myself that I didn't even look up as footsteps approached. Then I heard his voice.

"Hallo, lad," says a Yorkshireman's voice, and I looked up to see Sammy Bone with his worldly goods over his shoulder in a canvas trug. He was dressed in his best, with round glazed hat, black ribbon in his long pigtail, coloured tapes sewn down the seams of his blue seaman's jacket, and a red and white striped shirt with a blue silk handkerchief at the neck. He even had silver buckles on his shoes.

"Black Dick sent for me," says he, grinning with pride: "Lord Howe, Admiral of The Fleet, who I sailed under in the American Wars! Sent for me to come alongside and come aboard. Asked for me by name, he did!"

There was a Lieutenant at Sammy's elbow. He stepped forward and touched his hat to me. Perhaps he was the Lieutenant with the handkerchief from the fight on the fo'c'sle, I don't know. But he had a civil word for me. "Sorry to see you circumstanced after this fashion, Mr Fletcher," says he, and gabbled at me in some gibberish that I took to be French. "Fortoon der lar gair," says he, which in the King's English means "Don't worry old fellow, it could happen to anyone," which was a kindly sentiment at that particular moment.

Then he turned to my two Marines.

"Mr Fletcher is to have private conversation with this good," says he indicating Sammy. "That is the wish of his Lordship."

"Sah!" says the two Marines and they stamped their boots and saluted with their muskets.

"And Bone," says the Lieutenant to Sammy, "you may ask for me outside the wardroom when your business is completed."

"Aye-aye, sir!" says Sammy, raising a hand to his hat. "Good day to you, Fletcher," says the Lieutenant, "and may you have better luck." And off he went.

My two guards backed off, and Sammy crouched down beside me.

"Stap me, Jacob," says he, "who did that to you, us or the French?" He was trying to joke, but I could see from the anxious look in his eyes that I was knocked about worse than I thought.

"Us," says I. He nodded and took his silk handkerchief from round his neck.

"Here," says he, "let's get the muck out of your eye." He looked around for something, "Hey! Jolly!" says he to the nearer of the two Marines, "get us some water, mate?"

"Fuck you, matelot," says the Marine, "I ain't your bleedin' skivvy!" Sammy stood up and stabbed his finger at the Marine. "You!" says he. "Lobster! What's your name?"

"Whatssat to you?" says the Marine.

"I want to know so's I can tell Lord Howe, that's why?"

"Garn!" says the Marine. "Lord Howe! Who might you be then?"

"Me?" says Sammy. "I'm Sammy Bone, I am. Sammy Bone that was signalled through the fleet to repair on board of the old *Queen Charlotte* to wait upon Lord Howe's pleasure . . . so if you don't get me some soddin' water I'll see you striped red, white and blue at the gratings! One word from me, my lad – that's all it takes!"

The two Marines looked at one another, nervously.

"Garn . . ." says the one Sammy had spoken to, but he gave his musket to his mate and went and got a bucket of fresh water.

"Let's clean you up, son," says Sammy and soaked his handkerchief before wiping the clotted blood out of my hair and eyes. I found I could see out of the closed eye when he had done. My eyelids had been stuck together.

I was something amazing glad to see Sammy. It reminded me of the happy days aboard *Phiandra with* him and my other messmates. I'd never had any sort of family and I'd been raised as an orphan. Sammy was much older than the rest of us and was the natural leader of the mess. And in Sammy's mess it'd been share and share alike. It's a good thing to have friends and desperate bad to be without them.

"They told me what's happened," says Sammy, when he'd finished cleaning me up. "It's that bugger Dixon, isn't it? The one you killed on the *Bullfrog?*"

"Yes," says I, "and her, Lady Sarah Coignwood. I've met her, Sammy. She was here."

"Her?" says he. "Your father's wife?"

"No," says I, "he's not my father. I can't think of him as that."

"No?" says he.

"No," says I, and I put my arm around his shoulders. "He ain't my Pa."

"Get off, you daft bugger!" says he, but he patted my

hand and made no effort to move away, and so we sat there for a bit without talking.

"So what're we going to do?" says Sammy, finally.

"I don't know," says I, then a thought struck me. "What about Norris?" says I. "Norris was there when those other two saw me kill Dixon. D'you think Norris would say Dixon attacked me first? Would he do that for me?"

Sammy sighed and shook his head.

"'Course he would lad, but he ain't able."

"Oh no!" says I. "He isn't dead?"

"No, lad," says he, "but he was bad wounded. Him and me was entered on board of the *Brunswick* as lower-deck gunners, and in the battle we was laid so close alongside of *Vengeur* that we had to fire through our own gun-ports, 'cos we couldn't get 'em up! And Norris got all mangled by the splinters off our own fire. He's taken ashore to the Haslar Hospital and God knows if he'll live." He looked at me and smiled sadly. "So here's you and me left of the lads from *Phiandra*, Jacob, and the old ship on the bottom of the sea."

"Oh," says I, "then I'm done for."

"Bollocks!" said he, fiercely. "By God, Jacob, you give up easy sometimes!"

"But I'm guilty," says I miserably. "It weighs on me, Sammy. I thought it didn't at first, but it does."

"You silly sod," says he, "you was killing Frenchmen like flies on the first of June, from what I hear, and that don't seem to bother you!"

"That was them or me," says I.

"Yes," says he, "and it was you or Dixon on the *Bullfrog*! The bugger was persecuting you."

"They'll hang me for it, just the same," says I.

"They've got to prove it first," says he.

"There's witnesses: Oakes and Pegg."

"So call 'em bloody liars!"

"But who'd believe me?"

"Every bugger! You're a rich man!"

"What difference does that make?"

"Every difference! Who's going to believe a couple of common, lower-deck hands against a gentleman who's heir to a fortune?" Sammy frowned and shook his head. "That ain't the way of the world, my lad, and I can't believe a fly young cove like you don't know it."

Sammy was right. And I knew he was right. But I couldn't find the heart for the fight. On most subjects I could lie with the best of 'em, but not this. Dixon's murder had struck at the roots of me and I knew that should I be brought to trial, then I couldn't face it out. I did my best to explain this to Sammy.

"You are a funny one and no mistake," says he when I'd done. He shrugged his shoulders and tipped his hat back on his head. "So be it, my boy!" says he. "Then we'll come about on another tack. Leave it to me. I'll find Mr Oakes and Mr Pegg and offer 'em fifty pounds a head to forget what they saw. Better still, make it a hundred. They'd swear they couldn't find their own arse-holes for that!"

That was better. Much better. And I perked up. But there was a practical problem.

"How can you find 'em?" says I. "They're gone ashore."

"I'll run," says Sammy. "Hop ship. But you'll have to slip me some gelt, Jacob. The lubbers'll need to sniff ready money to bring 'em around. Don't have to be the whole whack. Just enough to show 'em what's on offer. How much've you got?"

But I wasn't listening. Sammy had set my mind working.

I was trying to hold a dozen ideas together all at once. And it was hard, 'cos one thing kept slipping away just as I got the others nicely lined up. And it had to be all or none.

What Sammy had proposed was good. It was a way forward. And he'd cut the knots inside my head. But there were flaws. Maybe he could run, maybe not. Maybe he'd get a musket ball in the back from a Marine as he tried to steal a boat. Maybe he could find Oakes and Pegg, maybe not. Most likely Sarah Coignwood and her chum Slime would have their two witnesses safely locked away. And above all there was Kate Booth. I didn't know whether Sarah Coignwood's terrible threats were real or only said to torment me. But I thought of poor little Kate screaming as that monster sliced her with a knife and it made me sick: physically sick till my guts heaved.

"Jacob!" says Sammy, "what is it?" He turned to the two Marines. "Get the bloody surgeon!" says he. "My mate's havin' a fit!"

"No!" says I. "No, I'm not. Just let me think, Sammy."

"What is it, son?" says he peering at me anxiously. "Tell Sammy."

And then the light shone. It all dropped together. It still wasn't perfect and a lot depended on how much credit I still had with Black Dick. But it was better than waiting for them to hang me.

"You!" I cried in my best, hailing-the-masthead bellow, and half the lower deck jumped, never mind the two Marines I was yelling at. "Send word to the Admiral's Clerk and tell him I wish to take advantage of his Lordship's offer!"

It worked a treat. Marines are only automatons, after all. Bawl at 'em loud enough and they do as they're told. Sammy leaned back and grinned. Then I lowered my voice to a whisper and we talked for another hour.

At first light on the following day, 14th June, a boat cast off from *Queen Charlotte* and the four oarsmen pulled for Portsmouth Point. There was one passenger in the boat: Sammy Bone. After forty years' unbroken service as a man-o'-war's, Sammy was going ashore with a certificate of honourable discharge in his trug. The certificate was signed by Admiral Lord Howe himself.

Also, Sammy was carrying bills signed by the Admiral's clerk in the sum of three hundred pounds. One hundred was a pension for Sammy, discharged the Service as a favour to me, the rest was for Norris Polperro or his widow. All the money to be refunded to his Lordship by myself at such time as I was able. Black Dick was still on my side, thank God. So far, so good.

*

I was two days more aboard *Queen Charlotte*, for they didn't come to get me until the afternoon of the fifteenth. Mr Smithers, Lieutenant Lloyd and his men came out in a launch with a dozen oarsmen, all of them armed with cutlass and pistol. Lloyd had his crew lined up waiting for me on the quarterdeck when I was brought up from below. They were a fine collection of slack-bellied, broken-nosed old toughs borrowed for the day from the Impress service, and *Queen Charlotte*'s tars viewed them with contempt. I was brought out with my two Marines behind me, all smart in a suit of clothes I'd begged off the Admiral's Clerk. My face looked as if I'd gone fifty rounds with the boxing champion of all England, but I was a gentleman by my clothes.

The same Lieutenant who'd spoken politely to me before was standing alongside Lieutenant Lloyd.

"Ah!" says he as I approached. "Here's your man, Mr Lloyd," and he looked at me, and looked along the line of Lloyd's dozen, armed as if for a boarding action. "Are you entirely sure you have taken sufficient precautions? Allow me five minutes and I could muster the starboard watch to strengthen your party."

There was laughter from those of *Queen Charlotte*'s people who heard this, but Lloyd just sneered, said nothing and produced a set of leg and wrist irons linked with a few feet of chain.

"Of course!" said the other Lieutenant. "How wise! What a fine thing it is to see an expert go about his work."

But I was stunned to see the ironmongery.

"Sir," says I to the friendly Lieutenant, "I was firmly assured by his Lordship that there was no question of my being shackled. I am a gentleman and I demand to be treated as such." I was sweating and trying to hold my knees from shaking, for fear of what might happen next. If I couldn't get rid of those irons, I was finished.

"And so you shall, sir!" said he. "Mr Lloyd, I will vouch for this gentleman's honour."

"Mr Fletcher," says he to me, "will you give me your word as a gentleman not to attempt escape?"

"I will, sir, and I do," says I.

"Hm!" says Lloyd. "This 'er . . . gentleman is on a charge of mutiny and murder."

"Possibly," says the other, "but you'd not chain a French officer when you took him in charge and you'll not treat an Englishman less well than that!"

"Aye!" came a murmur from *Queen Charlotte*'s *people*,

and Lloyd's men began to shuffle their feet and look shamefaced.

Is it not bloody amazing what an appeal to unreason will do? If you look into what he was saying, it was rubbish. What did it matter if I was English, French or a Chinese washerman? If you ask me, Lloyd was right and all the rest wrong. I've been arrested dozens of times in my career and any arresting officer who'd had the slightest chance to look me over never came with less than six men at his back and some brought many more. I take it as a sort of compliment.

None the less, the Lieutenant, whose name I never learned, got me out of a hanging in all probability, for Lloyd's chains went back into a sack and were seen no more. And shortly after that Smithers appeared having duly signed receipt of my body and over the side we went. It reminded me strongly of being taken out of *John Stark* at Boston. Once again I was under arrest. But I got no cheers that time.

I was good as gold as we headed for the shore, and the launch rode the big slow waves. Smithers and Lloyd chattered a bit, and I flapped my ears to catch what was going on. I had a pretty good idea of their plans already, for I'd pumped Black Dick's clerk for all I was worth. Being the Admiral's man in all things, and the Admiral being favourable to me, the clerk had talked freely, so I knew that a closed carriage would be waiting on shore to carry me off to prison. Smithers and Lloyd were bickering over my lack of chains. It seemed Smithers had final responsibility for bringing me in, and was piqued that he'd not been consulted. I thought I'd better intervene.

"Gentlemen," says I, "please rest assured that I have given my word and that I am bound in honour with chains more formidable than any that a smith could forge."

"See?" says Lloyd. "What did I tell you?"

"Hmm," says Smithers, peering at me with sharp little eyes. "I suppose no harm shall come of it." He looked at the brawny arms of the twelve Impress men. "Yes," says he, "I suppose so."

After that, I did my level best to behave like an English gentleman, suffering nobly under the blows of cruel fate. I worked so hard at it that when the launch ground its bows into the pebbles on Portsmouth Point, I was allowed to climb out and make my way with Lloyd's men without anyone laying hands on me or sticking a pistol in my ribs. Crunch! Crunch! Crunch! Up the beach where generations of British seamen have passed before and will come after. And then there was the promised carriage.

My heart began to thump. My moment was coming. Already the guard of a dozen was down to eleven. Someone had to stay with the launch or the dear little boys that lived along the shore (bless their innocent hearts) would've had the oars and fittings out of her before you could cry thief.

When he came to the carriage there was a driver up on the box, room for one more beside him, and four inside. The rest of Lloyd's band were dismissed, and marched off to whatever press-gang rendezvous he'd got them from in the first place.

I climbed in and the carriage springs sagged under my weight, then swayed to and fro as the other three joined me: Lloyd and two of his men. I don't know where Smithers went but it wasn't with us. Unfortunately the two who came aboard with Lloyd were a couple of special toughs that I suppose he must have brought with him and not from the Impress service. Certainly the three of them knew one another, and the two tars were sharper and brighter by a long way than the old rogues we'd got rid of.

The coach swayed again as the driver flicked his whip over the horses and we set off. I had learned that we were going to the new Hilsea Barracks, a few miles outside Portsmouth along the London Road. What I had in mind had to be done within the walls of the town itself, which meant I'd about ten minutes in which to act. So I looked at my three companions and made the final adjustments to my plans.

Lloyd was sat beside me, on my left, with inches to spare between us since the coach was narrow inside and just had room for four. His two bruisers were sat opposite, in seaman's rig, each with cutlass scabbard awkwardly stuck down the side of his left leg, and a Sea-Service pistol clapped across his belly by its belt hook. Each pistol-butt sloped to its owner's right, so he could seize it quicker. Lloyd was armed exactly as his men: cutlass on the left hip and a pistol in his belt. I had to admit they looked three likely lads for a fight.

But in that nice, tight coach, they were all within reach of my arms, which is a very dangerous place to be for men who weren't my size and weren't anywhere near my strength. They weren't expecting trouble, neither. Not properly, not as they would have been if I hadn't been such a precious good boy and stepped out so neat and pretty in my clean, gentleman's clothes. In any case, by God for England and St George, I'd given my word, hadn't I?

None the less, I admit that this was the weak part of my plan. But I offer a further piece of advice, which is this: sometimes, my boys, there just ain't no clever way and you can't creep in safely round the back, but must charge in the front way. And in that case there's nothing for it but smash down the door and go at it just as hard and as fast as you can.

I waited until we were going up Warbleton Street and the coach was stopped in the busy traffic, and I hit the man in front of me a mighty blow, just beneath the tip of the jaw. There was a fat wallop and the odds were only three to one. I spun round to my left, leapt on the other two and stretched my arms to gather them in. A split second's fumbling, and my left hand caught Lloyd behind the neck, while the fingers of my right hand closed on the front of the third man's collar. I heaved with all my strength, jerking the pair of them out of their seats and driving Lloyd's forehead into the wide-open terrified mouth of the tar.

Then I was wrenching open the door and tumbling out into the cobbled road. I stumbled and fell, but was up at once and darted through the carts and wagons and was in among the people going to and fro by a row of shops. A shout went up from the coach, then another. Two voices at least, but I forced myself to walk steadily away without looking back. Sammy told me that. Left to myself I'd have run, and so would have instantly identified myself as a villain and a runaway, and encouraged some bloody fool to tackle me. But walking briskly away in my new suit of clothes, I didn't stand out any more from the crowd than my size makes inevitable.

"Stop that man!" screamed a voice. "The big 'un!" But I found a side street and turned sharp left and quickened my pace. I could see people looking about as a hue and cry developed around the corner, behind me, but aside from a porter with a side of beef on his shoulders, who looked at me queer then thought better of it as he saw the look in my eyes, nobody bothered me. Then there was a patter of feet and I knew someone was running after me and catching up fast.

I couldn't help but look back, and there was Lloyd with blood on his face and a naked blade in his hand.

He was ten yards away and mad with anger. He was out to kill, not capture, and practised fighting man that he was, he skidded to a halt to get a good balance before taking a cut at me. He was on me so fast I had no time to do more than raise my arms against the murderous slash of the heavy blade.

But then there was a sudden blur of movement from among the people around him and a vicious thud! And Lloyd went down with the iron hilt of his cutlass clattering out of his hand as he hit the flagstones, knocked out cold.

"Come along o' me!" says a voice at my side and Sammy Bone was taking me by the arm and leading me away. He was shoving something into his pocket. It was a neatly-sewn canvas cylinder about eighteen inches long, two or three inches wide, and packed with sand. A wrist-loop of plaited leather was worked into one end, all the better for it to be swung by. It had all the marks of Sammy's careful handiwork.

"Come on! Come on!" says Sammy. "Never mind them!" for folk were staring. "They won't do nothing," says he. And he was right. It was the beginning of my time as a fugitive from justice.

Chapter 31

One reports, with an incredulity bordering upon the sundering to their roots of all one's deepest convictions of that which is proper and polite, that the influence of La Belle S.C. has proved so overcomingly enormous as to persuade their Graces the LADIES OF THE COMMITTEE OF ALMACK'S *to admit as a member, into that august temple of society, a certain individual whom La Belle Madame has, these past months, been leading about the town despite his known connections in the* HEMP TRADE *and his facilitation of the art of* DANCING UPON AIR.

(From "Lady D'Arcey's Chatterbox", a society column, which appeared in *The Polite Monitor* of
1st July 1794.)

*

"But why d'you think he'll come after you?" said Slym.

"I do not think, I *know*," said Lady Sarah. "I've looked him in the eye and he's that old bastard come to life again!"

"Your husband?" said Slym.

"Yes, him!" she said. "Once he'd fixed his mind on a thing, nothing could shift him. How else could such a creature make so much money from nothing? He was one of twelve children. A bare-arsed brat out of a miner's hovel with an earth floor. He had none of this!" She waved her hand at her beautiful, exquisitely furnished salon, her favourite place in all the world. Her beautiful salon with the tall, graceful windows that looked out on Dulwich Square, with its private gardens and the most desirable houses in London.

Slym picked up one of the newspapers that were cast on the sumptuous carpets. He peered at it, and shrugged his shoulders.

"Sarah," said he, "he escaped from custody in Portsmouth. The cove . . ." he stopped and corrected himself quickly, for these days there were words that he was seeking to expunge from his vocabulary . . . "*the fellow*," said he, "is a mariner, and *all* my experience tells me he'll stay in Portsmouth among the things he knows. Why should he risk coming to London where he has nothing and knows nobody?"

"No," she said, "there are other considerations." Her eyes flickered away from his for an instant. Slym noted the evasiveness and frowned.

"Just what did you say to him when you were down below in that ship?" he questioned.

"I've told you," she said, "I provoked him into attacking me, and got him an excellent beating."

"Now where's the value in that?" said he, irritated by the pettiness of the reply. "You've got the evidence to hang the man, you've got the Coignwood gold – or as good as – so why bother with spite?"

"Because I am a spiteful person," she said, with a self-satisfied sneer, "as all those soon learn who are foolish enough to do me ill!"

"Bah!" said he, in disgust. "It won't do, ma'am. Your drawing-room games don't suit the case." It was his turn to sneer. "Your little bitches' secrets whispered behind another bitch's back, to do her down!" He took her arm, and glared at her. "You're playing a dangerous game and I'll not be put off . . . So! What did you say to him? What were your words?"

Lady Sarah looked at him thoughtfully. She had to be careful now, for the relationship was changing. She was still attracted to him, powerfully so, for he was the most virile and deadly man she had ever met. But she could never be faithful to a single man and the harmless little diversions she'd indulged in, since her triumphal return, would infuriate Mr Samuel Slym should he find out, and unfortunately there was no man in England more able to find out should he put his mind to the matter.

Then there was Slym's own attitude to herself. She

was almost sure that he was in love with her – actually in *love* in the sense that poets, young girls and other mental-deficients understood the expression.

In fact the only thing preventing her from embracing this incredible hypothesis was her underlying conviction that any such emotion, based as it was upon self-denial and the elevation of another's advantage over one's own, was simply impossible.

None the less, Slym was living in her house, sharing her bed and supposing himself to be a gentleman. Since she could snuff out these pleasures whenever she chose, and since he must know that she could, they put the reins in her hand and the bit in his mouth. At least, they did so long as she was careful and did not too obviously confront the infuriating scruples that he was beginning to display.

So: careful she must be! For she needed him badly. Personal inclinations in the matter were temporary and changeable, as well she knew, but the need to place Sam Slym between herself and Jacob Fletcher was absolute. Lady Sarah's salon was warm in the June sunshine flowing in through the big windows, but she shuddered at the thought of Jacob Fletcher.

Try as she might, and stupid though she knew it to be, Fletcher's likeness to his father was so great that she could not shake off the supernatural fear that Fletcher was Henry Coignwood returned from the grave to take vengeance for the hell she'd inflicted on him during their marriage. And then there was the shocking, animal energy of the man, leaping up from the deck, snapping his chains and seizing her with murder in his eyes.

"Sarah!" said Slym, shaking her by the shoulder. "What did you say to him?" She thought quickly.

"I told him we had Miss Booth," she said.

"And . . . ?" said he.

"And what?" said she.

"You never stopped at that! What else?"

"I said she was hostage for his good behaviour."

"Good behaviour?" said Slym, in patent disbelief. "Pig-shit, ma'am! If I know you, the least you threatened was to cut her throat!"

"And what if I did?" she snapped.

"What, ma'am?" said he, with the blood rising into his face, and the veins swelling. "Why! I'll tell you what! You can do it without me, that's what!"

Sarah Coignwood fought a mighty battle to deny a temper that was used to being nourished and indulged. Slym was a contradiction. He'd kill a man and never worry. He'd knock the teeth out of a suspect to get information. He'd sent hundreds to dance the Tyburn jig – women among them – and watched their judicial strangling as a matter of principle. But Miss Booth's pretty little face had managed to stir his moribund conscience. And Lady Sarah knew why. It was Kate Booth's amazing air of upright dignity, somehow preserved through her service as a common whore. As she recalled that even she, Sarah Coignwood, had consciously imitated Kate Booth during her trial, a shade of something perilous close to envy slid through Lady Sarah's mind for the faery-princess bearing that the girl displayed.

Envy of another woman was an unknown experience for Sarah Coignwood and her inward struggle reached its climax. She ground her teeth, drove her nails into the cushions of the vast sofa she was seated on, and smothered the eruption of fury that she was longing to unleash. She had to, for giving in to it would see Sam Slym out of her house and gone from her control for ever.

"Sam," she said, laying a soft hand on his, "I'm afraid. And if you won't stand by me, I'm lost. Who will defend me if I lose you?"

Slym saw the change come over the lovely face. He saw the anger quenched and the forced, conscious representation of tenderness begin. He knew her far too well by now not to recognise it. And he was far too acute an observer of mankind.

He knew all about the other lovers. There were detailed entries for each of them on his record cards in the office off Aldgate High Street. He knew precisely when each had been sneaked into the house and he knew who was current favourite. He knew Sarah would turn him out whenever she was done with him and he'd spotted enough sneers from her elegant friends to know that he could never enter into their world except as a curiosity, led in on a golden chain for their amusement.

He also knew what she and her perverted, maniac sons had done to that poor bastard Jacob Fletcher. The man was clean as a whistle. The Coignwood money was legally his and if he'd pitched Bosun Dixon into the sea, then it was self-defence 'cos of what Lieutenant Seymour and Bosun Dixon were doing to him.

He knew – for he'd seen it – what she'd done to her own son when it suited her and he knew what she'd do to Kate Booth given the chance. It was only his objections to some of her more creative ideas that had kept the girl in one piece. And it wasn't that Slym was finicky. He'd have clipped Miss Booth's dainty ear himself if that's what it took to help her memory along. That's why he'd brought her away from Mrs Simpson's in the first place. But the things Sarah wanted to do to the girl were different. And at bottom of it, and worst of all, he knew that it was only the fear of Fletcher that kept him, Sam Slym, in Dulwich Square.

But he listened while she lied that she'd never intended Kate Booth to be used for anything other than bait. And he listened while she explained what must be done to make sure that Fletcher would find the house in Maze Hill, and how he must arrange to receive Fletcher such that he got in, but never got out again.

Sam Slym listened and nodded, and added a few points of his own, and a plan of action was agreed even though he saw all her lies and could list her faults like the expert that he was. He knew she'd betray him the moment it suited her. But he would stand by her and fight for her, and die in her service if need be. In short he would deny himself and elevate her interests above his own, because he loved her.

Chapter 32

I escaped from the Admiralty's officers on 16th June. From then until the 24th I hid with Sammy in the lodgings he'd found for us in Fighting Cock Lane. With the money he'd got from Black Dick he could take his pick more or less, and so had been careful to find us somewhere in a quiet street, with its own front door, so I could be smuggled in when nobody was looking.

Sammy being ashore first, before my escape, was a vital part of our plan. For otherwise how would I have kept out of sight? I'm too big to hide and folk notice me, so once the hue and cry went up, then I'd have been taken or betrayed in no time. But as it was, we had a nice cosy hole to hide in, and Sammy could go out and bring in our food and drink while things got quiet enough for us to leave Portsmouth. And remember, that getting out of Portsmouth was no easy matter, for "Pompey" was the strongest place in the kingdom. A regular walled city with fortifications, earthworks, and guns bristling at the landward approaches to the eastward, and the sea to every other direction.

The only ways in and out were by sea or through gates which in wartime were guarded by armed Redcoats. So once the news of my escape was out, the soldiers were looking for me at the gates and the Navy was guarding every boat.

On the other hand, this was wartime, and the Army and Navy had too many things to do to give much attention to one absconded man. That's what we'd hoped and so it proved to be. Sammy kept a watch on the gates and we found that after a few days the guards grew slack and eventually they stopped turning over the contents of carts and waggons to see who was hiding inside, and the mails and coaches went through without even a check. But to be safe, we left it for eight days in all, and Sammy drove in and out of the town a few times in the cart he'd bought just to see if he'd be stopped.

The cart was another idea we'd had aboard *Queen Charlotte*. I could not possibly expect to walk out of Portsmouth. Even at night I'm just too big and too easy to spot. Even the dullest soldier would have challenged me. So that meant the cover of a vehicle. But any public conveyance would have risked the chance of my being discovered, so we had to have something of our own.

In that way, I could hide while Sammy drove and we wouldn't have to walk all the way to London once we were beyond the city walls.

The fact that Sammy knew nothing about horses or carts didn't bother him in the least.

"Can you drive, Sammy?" I'd asked.

"Aye!" says he, without hesitation.

"Have you ever driven?" says I, suspiciously.

"No!" says he.

"But how can you . . . ?"

"Jacob, lad," says he, "if I can strike a main t'gallant stuns'l in a gale of wind, I don't see as how I can't steer an 'osses arse!"

That was typical of bloody seamen. They were so pig-headed proud of what they could do, and so contemptuous of landsmen, that they thought they could do anything. And in fact one of the sights of any naval seaport was a party of seamen on shore-leave, with a commandeered public coach laden with tarts and grog, thundering up the turnpike at full gallop with a cheerful tar at the reins and the white-faced driver cowering beside him.

So Sammy bought a large dog-cart, with seating for two and a big box behind with slits for ventilation, for taking gun-dogs on a shooting expedition. He paid far too much to the villain that sold it him and he spent a day blundering round the town learning to say "Whoa!" instead of "Avast!" and "Walk on" instead of "Give way". But he got the hang of it soon enough, and by the time I came ashore he was driving like a man of twenty years' experience. Which I suppose proves his point.

He'd hung about Portsmouth Point with the cart on the day I was due ashore, and followed the coach with me and my captors inside. When I jumped out, he left the cart in charge of a crossing-sweeper and chased after me. He'd come prepared and the unfortunate Lieutenant Lloyd was not expecting an attack from behind.

The sand-bag was a careful thought too.

"It's heavy, you see?" says he. "But it's limp so it don't break bones. No point killing the sod, was there?"

So, on 24th June Sammy drove us out through the old St Thomas's Gate in the Landport Ravelin, picking a time when the traffic was busiest, and got through with nobody paying us the least attention. He was driving and I was crammed into the dog-box with my knees under my chin and feeling sorry for myself. For one thing it was deuced uncomfortable for a man of my size but worse than that I was worrying. I was worrying about what Sarah Coignwood might do to Kate Booth. Later on, when we got on to the open road and there were less people about, I got out of the box and talked it over with Sammy – for probably the hundredth time.

"D'you think she'll do what she said, Sammy?" says I.

"No, you daft bleeder!" says he. "I told you: she only said it 'cos she's a mad bitch."

"Yes, but if she *is* mad she might do it anyway."

"She ain't *that* mad. She come after you with the Law at her back, didn't she? That was clever work that was. A mad woman couldn't have done that."

"But she might do it for spite. She might . . ."

"Bugger me, Jacob," says Sammy, exasperated with my persistence, "clap a hitch on your jawing tackle, will you? Listen! If she was to . . ." Sammy paused, searching for words to say an unspeakable thing, "if she was to do . . . them things . . . what she said . . . then she'd do it for you to see, wouldn't she? It'd be done to get at you. And with you out of sight, there ain't no point in it, is there?"

"I suppose so," says I glumly.

"Any road," says he, "why've we got to go to London at all? We could get a ship in Bristol as easy as London, and then the wide world's ours!" He turned to look at me. "You got along without Miss Katy all these months, so why're you moping over her now?"

"No," says I, "I'm responsible. I wouldn't leave a dog in that creature's hands."

"Hmm," says Sammy and sighed deeply. "Suppose not," says he, "but Lady bleedin' Sarah ain't just going to give her up, you know."

"I know," says I. "D'you think your brother can help us?"

"Maybe," says he, and sighed heavily.

"Tell me about him again, Sammy," says I, partly because I wanted to know, but mainly because my worrying was getting Sammy more and more depressed – a state I'd never ever seen him in before.

Sammy liked to talk about his brother, and I thought that might cheer him up.

"Well," says he, "our Toby's a few years younger'n me and he went to London as a lad. He married Pen years ago and they got six or seven kids. I see him every few years when I get to London. He's got a boatyard down Wapping way, and he's a fly cove." Sammy grinned. "He's a sort of rescuer. That's what he is. Him and his mates they rescue all sorts o' tackle and gear out o' the ships in the London Docks."

I grinned too. This was a favourite subject of Sammy's. He was tremendously proud of his brother, whom he took to have really made something of himself.

"What sort of gear does he rescue?" says I.

"All sorts," says Sammy. "Bit o' rum and sugar out o' the West India Docks. Then there's spices, silk and the like out o' East Indiamen. Things that ain't too bulky."

"He rescues them, does he?" says I.

"Aye, lad!" says he.

"And he'll take us in, will he?" says I.

"That he will, lad!" says Sammy.

*

We were ten days on the road because we found it better to keep off main roads, which were too busy. That way I didn't have to scramble into the box to hide myself every *time* a coach went rattling past in a cloud of dust and the outside passengers gazing curiously down upon us. But side roads meant a circuitous route and getting lost frequently. We didn't dare try to change the horse, for that would have drawn attention. So we had to keep resting our one nag, and that slowed us down too. We camped at night in a little canvas tent and cooked our food over an open fire.

Sammy dealt with the practicalities with consummate ease. It really was true that seamen could master any craft. He was as good at making camp as an American frontiersman.

Finally we came into London, which you could smell before you saw it, just as you can today: coal fires and horses. Countless thousands of both. Once we were well into the throng of traffic I came out of the box and sat out boldly beside Sammy. There's no better place to hide in all the world than London. What's one man among those hordes?

And it didn't matter if I was a big 'un, neither. What might have stood out even in a town the size of Portsmouth was lost in London. I dare say even a man with two heads would find a dozen others like himself, and certainly once you got along Cheapside and Cornhill where trade was celebrated in its glory, then all the faces of mankind were on display: Turks, Chinese and wool-ly-headed negroes, let alone simple Englishmen who happened to be well grown.

You have to remember that in those days London was bigger than any other city in England (or in the world for that matter) to a degree that folk don't appreciate today. To strangers in 1794, London was simply dazzling. Boston was a fair city, as I've said in these pages, and Portsmouth was no mere village, but either of them would have been swallowed up in London and hardly noticed. In London, there were so very many people, there was so much unending noise, the crowds were so unimaginably large, and the streets so winding, and the whole place so precious complicated that Sammy and I, who neither of us really knew it, got lost far worse than ever we did on the road.

As anyone does in these circumstances, we fell out repeatedly and blamed one another for taking the wrong way. We got hot and bothered and even Sammy lost his temper. And when we asked directions, I had to hold him back from using his sand-bag on some of the bright Cockney wits with their pitying scorn for clod-hopping rustics who didn't know which way led to Wapping.

But eventually we made our way by Tower Wharf, past the ancient fortress, along Catherine Street by the Red Lion Brew-house and so to Wapping Street which ran on for miles, with the River Thames to our right. And always: people, people, people, all different. The endless succession of new faces – rich, poor and middling – that only London could present.

But now we were on the right road, and at last, with me leading the horse, which was staggering and not fit for its work, and Sammy walking beside me, and both of us in so foul a mood that we were no longer talking to one another, Sammy recognised landmarks and said we were nearly there. At about ten o'clock in the evening, with the sky still light, we found Bone's Wharf. It was on Wapping Street, facing the river, between King Edward Street and Warren Square, just down-river from New Wapping Stairs.

Bone's Wharf was set among a row of similar premises, each comprising a pair of heavy gates, barred against the street, and enclosing a yard to receive carts, a house, some sheds and a warehouse, a short pier running out into the river and a boathouse. Each pair of gates had its owner's sign hung on it or raised above it in an arch. There were half a dozen of them: a tight little squadron of busy enterprises, and it cheered me up just to look at them.

I led the horse across the road and got the cart out of the way of traffic, stopped before the gates of Bone's Wharf and Sammy hammered away on the woodwork with the butt end of the whip. Eventually a little hatchway, set into the gates, swung open and there was Sammy's brother, a little fellow just like Sammy himself, with the same sharp eyes and alert look about him, but a good deal younger than Sammy, with only a few streaks of grey in his hair. I'd say he was a man in his forties. And by Jove he was pleased to see Sammy!

As soon as his little spy hole swung open and he saw who was outside, he grinned and yelled back across his shoulder.

"Pen," says he, "it's our Sammy!" and he threw open the gates to let us in.

Well, I can't say there's many places where I've been made quite so welcome as Bone's Wharf. Toby Bone lived with his wife and two sons and three daughters. The lads were full grown, the eldest girls nearly so and the youngest a little 'un of six years. The whole crew of 'em came pouring out and brought us indoors as if we were royalty.

They unharnessed our horse and rubbed him down and stabled him nice and cosy alongside Toby's own horses and they parked our cart in the yard. Our bits and pieces of luggage were carried in, and Sammy and I were sat at the head of the table in the parlour and food and drink placed before us. Everyone talked at once and Sammy beamed with delight and kept looking at me and nodding. He was showing them off, you see, for he was proud of his family and proud of their generosity.

As for me, it was the first time in my whole life I'd ever seen a family – that is to say a family under way and in action: "with steam up" as we say today. Sammy and his brother were so alike, and you could see the likeness in the faces of the others.

Some looked like Toby, some looked like their Ma, and some were a mixture, which of course is the natural way of things, but I'd never seen it before. Not seated all round the same table and shouting and laughing and elbowing one another. I thought it was just like a mess table at dinner time. It was strange and familiar all at the same time, and it was probably the first time I realised how much I'd missed by being raised up as an orphan.

The other odd thing was feeling such a giant. I'm big even among normal folk, but Toby was the same size as Sammy, and his wife, Pen, was even smaller, and all the children took after their parents. The result was that I felt like Gulliver in Lilliput, and when I stood up I was looking down on a room full of tiny people. I felt that I must keep my arms folded and move carefully for fear of knocking them over.

The youngest daughter was like a pretty little doll with a bright china face and big blue eyes. To me she seemed unbelievably tiny and delicate. Being the youngest, she was the pet of the entire family and when they pushed her forward to my chair to be introduced she stood up straight with her hands behind her back, and turned her cheek towards me. I guessed that she was expecting a kiss but I was unsure how to behave. I didn't know how to treat children. I'd never met any before, aside from ship's boys, and my communication with them had usually been through the toe of my boot. So I looked quickly at Sammy and he nodded, and so I leaned forward and planted a kiss on her little face, hardly daring to touch her for fear of breaking something.

After we'd all been introduced, and Sammy and I had been fed, Toby took Sammy and me outside and across the yard to the loft over the stables where he had a sort of office looking out over the boathouse and the river. He kept a bottle of brandy up there and it was private so we could talk.

"Well then, our Sammy," says he, "I can see from the look on your face that something's going forward, so now the wife and the nippers is out of the way, you can tell me what it is."

And so Sammy explained. He told his brother everything about me, sparing nothing. I was uneasy at hearing so many of my secrets told, but I trusted Sammy and I had to trust his brother. For we could certainly not do all that I wanted without his help.

And by George there was plenty of help Toby Bone could give, too. He was clearly a man of far greater means than he seemed. During the next hour or so all sorts of things came out in his conversation: other properties up and down the river, quiet warehouses where goods of all kinds were safely hidden, river boatmen that he could call on to turn out armed for a fight, and when

Sammy asked if Toby weren't afraid of the Press taking his men (boatsmen being popular with the Press if they couldn't get real seamen) Toby just grinned.

"Lord Mayor's protection, Sammy," says he, and went over to a cupboard and took out a box of big brass badges to show that the wearer was a Livery Company boatman, and so immune from the Press. Now that *can't* have been legal. Not with the line of business Toby was engaged in, and not with him having a stark of badges to hand out. So by what greasing of palms Toby could wield the mighty name of the Lord Mayor of London, I didn't know and chose not to ask.

Finally when Sammy and Toby had talked me over to their hearts' content, they turned to me.

"So there you are, our Toby," says Sammy. "That's the tale. But what I want to know now is, what're we gonna do with this bugger?" He jabbed his thumb at me. "'Cos if you ask me, I don't think he knows what to do with *himself*!"

They both looked at me, the two acute intelligent faces, one older, one younger, but two peas in a pod really. They even frowned with the same creases on their brows. They made me uncomfortable. The trouble was, Sammy was right. I knew the Navy'd hang me if I stood trial for Bosun Dixon, and so I'd escaped. But didn't know what I was doing in London other than following a deep and consuming feeling that I would not leave Kate Booth at the mercy of Sarah Coignwood.

That was clear enough, but after that all was fire and smoke. I only had to think of that monster Sarah Coignwood to send me off into fantasies of murder and revenge. She was the one at the bottom of it all. I'd had my hands round her neck once and if I got them there again, then God help her.

"I want Kate Booth," says I; "I want to find her and bring her out safe, from wherever she is."

"What about your stepmother?" says Sammy, peering at me hard. "What's your course in that respect?"

I thought hard about that but couldn't give a proper answer. Finally, Toby filled the silence with a practical remark.

"Let's worry about that all in good time," says he. "First you got to find your Miss Booth. I'll have a word with some of my pals tomorrow and get some questions asked. Lady Sarah Coignwood's one o' the bright and beautiful and her doings is well known. I'll get some questions asked of her servants in Dulwich Square to find out who's living in the house. I'll spread the word that Toby Bone wants to know."

We talked some more after that, and then we went to bed. They gave Sammy and me a nice little room which two of the daughters had been turned out of. It had pretty wallpaper with little flowers and songbirds. Sammy and I were both very tired and we didn't talk much before falling asleep, but Sammy was worrying over me and Sarah Coignwood.

"What'll you do if you find her?" says he. "A fight's one thing, leastways it is against a man, but you can't just hunt her down and . . ." He fell silent. "Bugger it," says he, "what's in your mind, lad?" I didn't answer him because I didn't know.

Chapter 33

COIGNWOOD & SONS

butchers and purveyors of choice meats to the carriage
trade, beg to announce a unique and special sale of

JAMBON KATERINE a la BOOTH

at their Premises at

208 MAZE HILL, GREENWICH

They assure their customers of the exquisite tenderness of
the meat which will be sliced while still

ENTIRELY FRESH

The carving to commence at 12 o'clock 10th 1140

PROMPT. *Those who might wish to purchase the meat*
intact are warned to arrive early since otherwise the
proprietors will be obliged to cut it entirely into small pieces.

(Handbill circulated in large numbers in Wapping
during the period 6th to 10th July 1794.)

*

A footman in elaborate livery – snowy wig, scarlet coat, gold frogging, satin breeches, silk stockings and silver-buckled shoes – opened the door of Lady Sarah's house in Dulwich Square. Sam Slym pushed past him, shoving hat and stick into the minion's hands.

"Sarah!" he roared. "News!" He turned to the servant. "Where's your mistress?" he said.

"Her Ladyship is upstairs, in her dressing room, sir. She is receiving . . ."

Slym was already halfway up to the first floor with his gleaming top-boots taking the stairs three at a time. He darted along a corridor past elaborate mirrors, luscious paintings in ornate gilt frames, glittering sconces of candles, French side tables with dainty bronzes and every other sign of the opulent style in which Lady Sarah lived.

"Sarah!" he cried and wrenched open the door into her dressing room.

Inside two figures jolted with shock and pulled still further apart than the few seconds' prior warning had enabled them to manage.

Sarah Coignwood's dressing room was an inner sanctum to which she admitted only a handful of chosen intimates. Next door to her bedroom, it was really a small sitting room, elaborately furnished with upholstered French furniture. A single big window looked out over the Square, but it was heavily draped with silk and muslin curtains to give light and privacy at the same time.

"Huh!" said Slym as he saw who was being "received". It was the pretty-faced boy who was her current pet: up to the eyes in fashion, heir to millions, less than half her age, and all the brains of a carrot. Just the type she preferred. They licked her toes like spaniels and imagined she was adorable.

Sarah was sat comfortably on a sofa, with a tiny coffee cup in her hand, and smiling at Slym as calm as you please, while the lad, looking distinctly pale, was jammed into a chair that looked to have just been shoved against the wall furthest from her.

Slym said nothing, but took the boy by the collar of his coat, heaved him out of his chair and dragged him to the top of the stairs. The footman was gaping up the stairs with round eyes and open mouth.

"This gentleman is just leaving," said Slym, and gave him a hefty shove and turned on his heel. The sounds of the young gentleman making his way downstairs came faintly to his ears as he closed the dressing-room door.

She had that look on her face again. The look of a tempest being held back by force of will. He almost wished she'd open fire and not hold back. At least that would have been straight.

"Never mind none o' that!" he said. "I've got news." He paused, for this was too important to deliver offhand.

"Fletcher and his pal," said he, "they're in London. I know it for sure and I think they're in Wapping. I've been out and about for a couple of days – that's why you ain't seen me – and I've had people asking questions. Fletcher's mate's called Bone and I think they're hiding at Bone's Wharf in Wapping. Toby Bone must be a brother and helping out."

He saw the fear in her eyes and his own feeling for her overwhelmed him completely. They overwhelmed even the sound of the front door closing on the rival he had just thrown out. Slym sat beside her and put his arms around her.

"Never fear," said he, and fumbled for endearments in a cobwebbed, empty vocabulary, "my girl, my brave girl." For an instant she leaned her head on his shoulder in as near to a genuine act of trust and submission and a seeking for comfort in the arms of another person that Sarah Coignwood could ever be capable of. Sam Slym was flooded and sunk with joy.

"Never you fear, my girl!" said he. "I'll see to him. I'll get a dozen good men together and burn the bastard out. I'll not play games with him, I'll . . ."

"No!" said she. "Not that way." The first shock was receding and she was able to think clearly. "It must be done quietly," she said. "There is much the world must not know. I want him brought to me."

"Here?" said Slym.

"No," she said, "not here. He must go to Greenwich. To my uncle's house. I absolutely forbid that any of this business should take place in Dulwich Square."

"Well, yes," said Slym, unsure of exactly what she wanted, "if he's to be brought to Maze Hill, my girl, then I'm your man. But he's a bloody big cove by all accounts and he'll take some bringing!"

"That won't be necessary," she said and smiled sweetly at him. Sam felt the chill of what was coming even before she said it. He knew her very well now. He knew that such a happy smile in the face of all her fears of Jacob Fletcher could only mean some bloody vicious plan was hatching in her mind.

And he was absolutely right. His warm happiness in her acceptance of his comforting arms was frozen rigid by the detail of her plan to make Jacob Fletcher walk into 208 Maze Hill of his own accord. Naturally, she insisted that everything was a bluff. But he knew better.

None the less he went to the printer's and ordered five gross of her handbills. And he had them given out and posted up all over Wapping. Especially round about Bone's Wharf.

Chapter 34

They looked after us well at Bone's Wharf. Toby's wife, Pen, took a fancy to me as women often will and the daughters did too. They were bright enough little things, if a bit tiny by my standards. And they obviously thought me a figure of romance. As I'd found with Lucinda, there's nothing that gets the lust going in a woman like the knowledge that they've got a noble warrior in their power: one word from them being capable of sending him to his doom. Of course, the girls weren't supposed to know what was going on, but such secrets don't last long in a family.

All in all, I had to behave myself while I was under Toby's roof, what with the two girls following about behind me making big eyes and giggling to one another. It would have been poor thanks for Toby's hospitality to please myself the way I had in Boston.

For a few days Sammy and I did nothing but eat, sleep and idle our time away. Pen looked after the cuts and bruises that were still on me from the beating I'd got aboard *Queen Charlotte* and I suppose this quiet time helped me get back to my full strength, which is just as well, all things considered.

And then on 7th July, two things happened at once. Georgie Bone, the middle son, came rattling into the yard under the "Bone's Wharf" sign in a one-horse gig. He leapt down, tied up the horse and yelled for his Pa.

We had another meeting in the office overlooking the river and young George told us what was up.

"They're looking for you, Mr Fletcher," says he, "and Uncle Sammy too."

"Who is?" says Toby.

"Slimy Sam and his pals," says George. "Sam Slym the thief-taker," he added, seeing my look of puzzlement. "He's Lady Sarah's latest. Goes all round the town with her."

"I know him," says I. "Hard-faced man, about forty, dressed like a tailor's dummy?"

"How d'ye know it's Slimy that's looking for 'em?" said Toby. "Did you see him asking questions?"

"No," says George, "that's the odd part of it. It was one of his regulars, that goes nosing round for him, and this cove asked me if I knew of a big seaman and a little one, on the hop from the Navy. And he had your names too."

"That's nothing particular," says I. "It was in the news-papers that I'd escaped."

"Yes," says George, "but this cove he let on it was Slimy he was asking around for. He did it on purpose, to make sure I knew what was going forward; that Slimy was working for Lady Sarah Coignwood. He said Slimy wanted it known." He fumbled in a coat pocket and produced a handbill. He held it out to me. "And he said since I'm from Wapping, I should have one of these. He said Slimy's men are handing 'em out all over the docks."

I unfolded the paper and read it through and sat down feeling sick. Then I had to listen to it all over again as Toby read it aloud for Sammy who, like most lower-deck seamen, could not read. It was a ghastly thing, masquer-ading as a tradesman's bill but really a threat to kill Kate horribly, inch by inch, as Sarah Coignwood had threat-ened.

"This is for you, lad, isn't it?" says Sammy.

"Yes," says I.

"They say they're going to do it on the 10th," says Toby, "and today's the 7th."

"I'm going this instant," says I, standing up.

"What?" says Sammy. "Where?" I took the paper back from Toby and looked at the address.

"208 Maze Hill, Greenwich," says I. "That's where they've got her, and I'm going to take her from them."

"Avast there!" says Sammy. "You're going right now, are you, lad?"

"Aye!" says I. "I'll not leave her a second longer with that bitch. I'm going now!"

"Just as you are?" says Sammy. "Unarmed? What'll you do? Knock at the door and ask for her?" He jabbed me in the ribs and looked up at me with a frown. "This is a trap, lad! This is your bloody stepmother's work. It's bleedin' obvious! They'll have that place crawling with men and you'll be cut down or pistolled the moment you step inside the door."

Toby stepped forward and placed a hand on my arm. "See here, Jacob," says he, "this bill says you've got until noon on the 10th, so I say take the bloody thing at its face value, which means we've time to do the thing proper, which means we take a good look at No. 208 and when we go, we go prepared!"

"Aye!" says Sammy. "Listen to our Toby. We ain't letting you go, Jaocb, not like this!"

Eventually they prevailed. They were so obviously right that they managed to calm me down and make me wait. But it was a bad time and I didn't sleep very well over the next few days.

Toby sent George and his other two sons to look over No. 208. This incidentally was something they were well used to doing, and the fluent ease with which they described the approaches to the house, and its various defences against forced entry, revealed the tradesman discussing his craft.

"Three floors and a basement," says Georgie, "spiked

railings and an area at the front: eight feet across and a twelve-foot drop, so there's no getting at the front windows, the which are shuttered heavily on the inside in addition."

Toby nodded thoughtfully.

"What about the back?" says he.

"No good, Pa," says Georgie, shaking his head.

"But Maze Hill backs on to Vanburgh's Fields, doesn't it?" says Toby. "That's open parkland! That must be good."

"No," says Georgie. "Ten-foot wall at the back, with shevow-derfreeze on the top: all nice new ironwork, greased and sharpened. And there's a heavy gate with a good lock."

"Hmm," says Toby. "Difficult, I would agree, but I've known active men get round problems like that."

"No," says Georgie, again, "it's a rum go, Pa, the place is busy."

"Ah!" says Toby, and looked thoughtful.

"What does that mean?" says I.

"Busy," says Toby, "that means there's men on guard."

"Men at the upstairs windows," says Georgie, "big kiddies: milling coves. Trying to keep out of sight. I counted five different faces."

"What about servants?" says Toby. "Any way there?"

"No," says Georgie, "there's no opening there neither. Leaving aside the bruisers, there's two proper servants. One's an old cow with a face fit to frighten the French. The servants from the next door houses say she helps out ladies what get themselves 'embarrassed'. But she don't talk to nobody. And the other one's a little slut that don't do nothing at all 'less cow-face tells her to!" He shook his head. "I'm sorry, gents, but it's the tightest drum I ever saw."

There was a gloomy silence in the room. Toby sighed, his sons shuffled their feet and looked uncomfortable as if it were their fault that the house was impregnable, and I began to lose my temper.

"So what's it to be?" says I. "Sit on our backsides and let that bitch have her way? You can all please yourselves but I'm going tonight, and if I have to do it myself, then I will." They looked back at me with a mixture of guilt for their own lack of courage and pity for my crass stupidity. I might as well have told them I was planning to blow my brains out. Toby tried to explain.

"Look, son," says he, "them coves'll be armed and they'll be waiting for you. They'll . . ."

"I don't give a damn," says I, for I was full up with anger and half-a-dozen other emotions all mixed up. I just *couldn't* let Kate be killed for that creature's pleasure, and I was burning for revenge on my own account. I don't pretend for a minute I was acting sensibly, but that's how you are when you're young and the blood is up. I was just drawing breath for another speech when Sammy spoke up.

"This paper," says he, waving the handbill. "It's an invite to all-comers, ain't it?"

"What're you talking about?" says Toby.

"*What* if they all turned out?" says Sammy.

"Meaning what?" says Toby.

"Meaning, my lad," says Sammy, "that I think I can see our way through the shoals and safe ashore. But we'll have to be guided by you, Toby, for you're the master of this trade."

And so began a very long and very remarkable discussion.

Chapter 35

ITEM: *Own circumstances.*
QUESTION: *To proceed?*
SUBJECT: *Booth* & *Fletcher.*
ACTION:?

(Transliteration of shorthand notes from
Samuel Slym's memorandum book for
9th July 1794.)

*

Sam Slym posted one man at the front and one at the back and called the other ten into the big kitchen at 208 Maze Hill. The past week had been very uncomfortable in the house, with so many men under the roof, not to mention the two servants, the mad old Admiral still clinging to life in his squalid bedroom, the girl Booth chained in the attic, and her Ladyship who'd insisted in sharing every moment of it, despite all Sam Slym's pleas.

The men stood respectfully as Slym entered the room, Danny and Jimmy to the front as his lieutenants. Slym's eyes narrowed as he looked at each man. He looked for any signs of drink or slackness or personal dirtiness (which of all things he was constitutionally unable to tolerate). In fact he glared at them like a hawk, for it was not his way to do things by halves and this little meeting, one of many over the last ten days, was as formal an inspection as the Duke of York could make of the troops on Horse Guards Parade.

"Arms!" he snapped, and there was a rustle of movement up and down the room as each man drew a short, brass-hilted hanger and a brand shiny-new Tower horse pistol – the new carbine-bored model with the steel rammer fixed by a swivel so it couldn't be dropped. Not all the regulars had those yet. He went among the men, looking for notches on the blades that would show they'd been playing about fencing one another, as idiots will do unless they are prevented, and he carefully checked the priming of each pistol.

"Well enough," says he, and turned to Danny. "What're your duties?" he snapped.

"Go the rounds and check each man's at his post," says Danny, promptly. "Each man to do a one-hour turn and one hour off. Watches to be posted through the night. No drink in the house, and no naked lights after eight o'clock."

"What're your duties?" said Slym, picking a man at random. The fellow was less ready than Danny, perhaps embarrassed at speaking out before his mates. But after he'd swallowed a few times he spoke up well enough.

"Keep an eye on the street from the first floor front and pass the word at once on sight of any unusually big man, especially if he looks like a sailor."

"When d'you use this?" said Slym tapping the man's pistol. "Only when told by you, Captain," said he.

"What if you let it off without orders?"

"Dismissed without pay, Captain."

And so it went on for five minutes or so. The ten men, carefully chosen for steadiness and reliability, from those Slym had used for many years, knew exactly what was expected of them, and could be relied upon to do Sam Slym's bidding when it came to a fight. He'd picked them and drilled them and he'd done it very well. In fact anyone who'd seen Sam Slym at this work would have agreed that it was tragedy on the face of the earth that he'd never become a soldier, for he'd have made such a sergeant-major as colonels dream upon.

"Now then," said he, when he was done, "pay attention. Today is the 9th of June. Tomorrow is the last day of this business. We've had no sight so far of those we're looking for, and so tonight after dark is the most likely time for them to come. You will therefore, all of you, every man of you, pay the most special attention to your duties this night. And I'll remind you: it's five guineas a man, come what may, for all who see the thing through. Should it come to a fight, it's ten guineas a man, and then my usual terms for wounds and widows. You all know that."

"Yes, Captain," they said. Sam Slym would crack your head like an egg just for peeing in the corner when you couldn't be bothered with the privy, but he'd see your family squared if the worst happened.

Afterwards he sent them to their posts and as he went up to the ground floor, from the basement, Lady Sarah came out from the drawing room, and the men respectfully touched their hats as they went past. Slym gulped as he saw her. She was a remarkable sight. She'd got herself up in some sort of riding costume with a tight jacket and pantaloons like a man's, complete with riding boots. And her hair was pulled back from her face and tightly bound into a silk handkerchief. She looked devilish smart and the perversity of her being attired as a man played on just that chord in Slym that had always been drawn to her unmatchable sophistication.

She smiled at him and presented herself for his inspection like an actress on the stage. "Ready for action against the enemy, sir!" she said and bowed like a man. The pantaloons showed every inch of her legs from waist to knee and were so tight about her backside as to be positively indecent. But didn't they just suit her!

"What the hell are you doing, Sarah?" said he in her ear, so the men shouldn't hear. She laughed.

"I told you, I'm ready for action. Did you think I should hide in a corner when my enemy comes?"

"Yes!" said he. "This sort of work is not for you."

"Oh?" said she and produced a hunting knife.

"Dammit, woman," said he, "just keep in your room when the thing begins."

"Will it be tonight?" she said, and some of the bounce went out of her.

"Yes," said he, "if it's to happen at all. It'll be tonight or not at all."

"Good," she said, "I'll not wait longer."

"What if they don't come?" he said.

"Then you can release little Miss Booth, find Fletcher and give him to the Navy. That's your trade, is it people?"

"Yes," said he, "my trade." He hesitated and the girl goes free?"

"I've said so, my love," she said. "You cannot believe I ever meant all those things." She moved close, looked up at him and pressed her lips to his.

Slym shuddered with pleasure at the wriggling tongue searching deep into his mouth, and at the same time was acutely embarrassed at the knowledge of this taking place in full view of half a dozen of his men.

"In fact, my love," said she, when she was done, "I'll go and tell our prisoner that, one way or the other, her term is nearly at an end."

"Yes," said he, comprehensively confused. "Tell her."
And he stood with his men gaping at the tight white
rump and round thighs swaying up the stairs towards
the attic.

The little prison where Kate was held had one narrow
window and was at the very top of the house, under the
rafters. She was safely secured by her chain, but to make
doubly sure, during this final and crucial stage of the
operation, either Mrs Collins or the girl had been required
to stand guard with instructions to talk to nobody. Not
to Slym's men (who knew but a tiny fraction of what
was going on) and certainly not to Miss Booth herself.
It was tiresome in the extreme, with hours sat on a little
chair on the landing outside the attic room, but what
did that matter? As far as Lady Sarah was concerned,
either creature could and would and *must* do as she was
told or suffer certain extremely unpleasant consequences.

It was Mrs Collins's spell of duty at that particular
moment, and the heavy, pie-faced woman with her broad,
red arms rose at sight of her mistress and unlocked the
door without a word. Sarah Coignwood went inside and
smiled sweetly at Kate, closing the door behind her.

"How are you, my dear?" said she. "I do hope you
have received every attention from my servants."

Kate sat up on the bed where she had been lying,
bored almost to madness. It was the first time she had
seen Lady Sarah for some days and she knew as little of
what was happening as Sam Slym's hired pugs. Kate had

been nine months in this dirty little room and was not even afraid any more. Nothing had happened to her, despite Lady Sarah's ferocious threats.

But now something *was* happening in the house. Nobody talked to her, but Kate had heard the heavy feet on the stairs, and the sounds of men's voices. Even Sarah Coignwood's expression told a tale.

And now here was Lady Sarah herself, dressed up like something from the tableaux vivants that they performed at Mrs Simpson's house in Gosport. Sarah Coignwood noted the glance at her clothes.

"Fetching, is it not?" she said, waving a hand expressively at her neat and immaculate outfit.

"Yes," said Kate, "in a whore."

"Well, my dear," said Sarah with a narrow smile, "you would be the judge of that, of course." She looked at the bedraggled garments Kate was wearing – mostly what she'd had on her back when she entered the house last September. "Just as your elegance enables you to pass judgement upon mine."

"Bitch!" said Kate.

"Slut!" said Sarah.

And there followed a rapid exchange of epithets which Sarah Coignwood won with practised ease, smoothly drawing on the vast stores of filth in her enormous repertoire. Kate Booth was amazed and somewhat educated by the experience. Even tarts and sailors never cursed like that.

"There, then!" said Lady Sarah. "Are we all quite done?" Kate said nothing but sat up on the bed judging the distance to Sarah Coignwood. She'd eased herself closer while the woman was spitting out oaths and Kate thought she was just within reach.

"Now," said Lady Sarah, "I have brought you something, my dear Kate," she said. "It is a little puzzle to amuse you. I want . . ."

Kate leapt in that instant, but Sarah Coignwood was too quick. She jumped out of range and the iron ring bit viciously into Kate's ankle as the chain stretched to its limit. Kate fell heavily and measured her length upon the bare boards.

"Would you, though?" said Lady Sarah and sneered down at Kate. "Listen to me, miss," she said, "I have set a trap for your Mr Fletcher, and you are the bait! But more important, I want you to know that what I have promised shall be carried out to literal effect whether he comes for you or whether he does not. Perhaps you would like to see the details?"

And Sarah Coignwood handed Kate Booth a copy of the printer's handbill.

Chapter 36

The level of violence against individuals and the extent of crimes against property, so casually recounted by Fletcher in what follows, together with an implicit assumption that there would be no attempt to interfere with the commission of these crimes by the forces of Law and Order, demand an explanation. The case is that in 1794 London had no police as the word is understood today, Sir Robert Peel's Metropolitan Police Service did not come into being until thirty-five years later in 1829. Until then there was no intermediary between the ineffectual parish watchman and the mailed fist of the military. Only fourteen years before the events described in this chapter, the notorious Gordon Riots took place in London, between 2nd June and 9th June 1780. Tens of thousands were on the streets with criminal intent. The prisons were broken open and the inmates released, and houses of noblemen were looted and fired, and the night sky burned red as great areas of the city were destroyed. Only the Army, firing volleys into the people as if upon the field of battle, was able to quell this, the greatest civil disturbance of the century. The Gordon Riots were unusual only in their extensiveness, being otherwise typical of many similar occurrences. Such was the lawless condition of the times. Such was the power of the London Mob. S.P.

*

Just after ten o'clock on 9th July, and with the sky darkening, a launch forged steadily downriver with fifty men aboard: myself, Sammy, Toby, and a fine collection of gentry hired for the night's work. Some of these didn't smell too sweet and none of them were pretty, but they chuckled and muttered merrily and those manning the oars pulled with a will. Just astern of us were two more launches similarly packed with dark figures.

Every man was armed, though with no weapon more formidable than a stave or a cudgel. Toby had been very particular about that. He specifically forbade the bringing of firearms or pikes, particularly the latter which had red revolutionary connotations. Personally I'd have issued all hands with musket, bayonet and sixty rounds, and I'd've taken along a pack of artillery. But I wasn't the Captain that night. Toby Bone was.

The river was crammed with anchored merchantmen and the Isle of Dogs with its line of big windmills was sliding past on our larboard beam as we headed down towards Greenwich Reach.

"Shut up there!" hissed Toby as somewhere in the boat a man laughed.

"God-love-ye!" says the voice, "'tis shut up that I am!" There was more laughter.

"Stap me, Toby," says Sammy quietly, "are you sure about them heathen Irish?"

"Yes," says Toby, "they're just the kiddies for the work. The buggers'd charge down the muzzle of a cannon for a shilling and a bottle of gin."

"Aye," says Sammy, "I know that right enough, but can you hold the bleeders back when the work's done?" He pointed at the mass of figures in the dark boat. "This lot'd burn bloody London down, given the chance."

"Sammy," says Toby, "I'd not tell you how to tie a bowline, would I? So leave my trade to me!"

"Aye," says Sammy, "but . . ."

"Stow it, Sammy!" says I. "You know what's to be done. Who'd you think we'd get for this, the Royal Marines?" None the less I shoved forward down the boat and reached out for the man who I thought had laughed the most. (It didn't matter really, any one will do on these occasions.) I caught him by the throat and shook him a bit to rattle his windpipe, for you can't knock a man down in a crowded boat for fear of upsetting her. "Shut it!" says I. "Next man that speaks out of turn can swim home with no pay!"

That kept down the chatter for a bit, though I had to wipe my hand on my breeches after the feel of his greasy neck.

Soon we were past Deptford Creek and the splendid frontage of the Greenwich Hospital lay on our starboard beam.

But we pulled on past that, for there were too many prying eyes, and official eyes at that, in and around the great naval hospital, to risk a landing at Greenwich Stairs.

When Toby finally swung the tiller and brought us in on the Greenwich side, the chatter in the boat rose up again. And when the next two launches joined us, and over a hundred and fifty men had landed, half of them Irish – labourers, chair-men, porters and coal-heavers – there was just no stopping them.

There was a sudden waving of cudgels and a kindling of torches from the boat lanterns. The drink came out too, and they began to roar and sing and festoon their hats with the white ribbons that Toby had given them so's to make the thing proper – it being an established principle of London street fighting that factions should know one another by the colour of their ribbons. How else would a man know who to cudgel?

"No point holdin''em back now!" says Toby, yelling in my ear. "In fact it's time to gee 'em on a bit!" Toby's eyes were wide with excitement and I could see that while he'd arranged this night's proceedings on my behalf, it was by no means a thing against his inclinations.

"Now, me boys!" cries Toby, climbing up on a box

that he'd brought for the purpose. "Are we going to see Admiral Williams murdered by the French?"

"No!" they roared.

"Shall we let the bloody French rule London?"

"No!"

"Are we true-born Britons, or are we bloody traitors?"

"Yes!" they cried, and "No!" depending on their understanding of the question (especially in the case of the Irish). But it didn't matter. All that mattered was noise and the thrill of the game that was afoot. They'd turned out at half-a-crown a head (a huge sum) and all the gin they could drink. The cause, as it had been explained to them, was to rescue Admiral Williams from the combination of traitors, Levellers and French spies, that had the old hero imprisoned in his house. They'd fight for that, all right. That and a bit of looting.

So off we trotted bawling and singing, with most of the brethren already well drunk and sweating red-faced in the torchlight.

By George it was devil's work, I can tell you. There's a combination of night-time, torches and marching feet that nourishes deep and dangerous sentiments in a crowd of men. We headed south with the river at our backs, struck out across Vanburgh's Fields, with silly fools falling into ditches and hauling one another out, we found Maze Hill with Greenwich Park on one side and the street of houses on the other and headed for No. 208.

Just as we turned into Maze Hill, the howling mob

behind us saw the one thing that would screw them up to a still higher pitch of excitement.

Up the street from the other direction came Toby's sons and the landward "pincer" of our expedition. Three hundred more, just the same as ourselves: white ribbons, torches flaring and sticks raised in the air. A tremendous cheer broke from each mob as they surged together and embraced one another as if brothers: brothers once parted but now reunited in their joy. They hopped and capered, they yelled and laughed, they drank from each other's bottles, they fraternised lovingly. For it's a true and singular characteristic of mobs that when one encounters another bent on the same errand, the thrill of reinforcement plus the warm confirmation of the righteousness of the common cause work a magic stronger than drink, which sends them onward, merciless and utterly determined.

It does that and more besides. For one thing it robs a mob of what little wit it started out with, and the specific hate for the "anarchists" and "traitors" in No. 208 was now broadening to envelop all of Maze Hill. Stones and clods were flying and the windows were going in all up and down the street.

"Save the Admiral!" cried Toby, and Sammy and I and Toby's fads took up the cry. "On to 208, lads!" he cried, and enough of our thugs took heed for the mob to roll forward. And there it was, the centre of a short terrace of three houses, on three floors and a basement, facing the park. 208 was dignified by an extra storey with a pitched roof. Already some glass was out of the windows, and BANG! BANG! BANG! *as I* got there, pistol fire came down from the first floor and men dropped wriggling on the ground.

"Ahhhh!" screeched one, right at my feet, "Mother! Mother!" says he, tearing his clothes to find the wound.

He had a hole in his belly and was a dead man. He groaned and wept, his white-ribboned hat had been trampled in the street beside him, and blood and gin vomited up from his torn stomach. "Urrrgh!" he heaved violently. "Ah, me mother, me mother . . ." But the hundreds of men around roared with anger and I fought my way to the front as the thunder of feet swept onward and forward towards the front street door of No. 208.

There I was jammed against the woodwork with mad Irishmen up to my armpits and fists and sticks coming down from all directions in a battering hail upon the stubborn door.

The good thing about my position in that moment was that I was out of sight to the pistol-men steadily blazing away from the first floor. It was a vicious fight now between them with their firearms and the mob with its cobblestones and brick-ends. But the bad thing was a stout oaken door and no obvious way to break it down. And I was mad myself by that time, mad to get inside and get on with the thing.

*

Slym ran up the stairs in answer to the warning shout. In the first-floor front sitting room, half a dozen of his men were craning their necks trying to see what was coming up the street. Little pools of light came from the row of street lamps but they did little more than mark out the line of the pavement, while a dull red glow and a deep low roar of voices told them something big and menacing was coming.

"Get away!" said Slym, pushing to the front. He threw up the sash and leaned out to look down the street. "Dammit," said he, "the mob's out! Now what could that be for?"

He leaned back inside and saw the anxious faces of his men. "Don't have to be nothing to do with us, boys," he said. "Just keep back from the windows and let the buggers pass. God knows what they're after." He shoved one man firmly towards the door. "This ain't your station, my boy!" says he. "Get back where your duties are." He snarled at the rest of them. "Damn your bloody eyes! What's the matter with you? Never seen the mob before?" He laid on with his blackthorn stick. Not hard, but enough to liven them up and chivvy them back to their proper places. Once he'd done that he looked for Sarah.

She was on her way up the stairs, looking excited but still calm. "What is it?" she said. The bawling of the mob could be heard clearly now, even inside the house. He shrugged his shoulders. "I don't know," said he, "but keep away from the windows."

"Could it be him?" she said. "Fletcher?"

"I doubt it," he said. "Don't see how he could raise the mob. He's got no friends here."

"None the less," she said, "I shall go to our prisoner and take her in charge personally. If we need to bargain with her, then I want her under my own hand."

"Sarah," he said suddenly, "get out the back way, now! I'll look after this place. If you're quick you can be away across the fields before they get here. Take old mother Collins with you, she's as good as a man."

She looked at him, puzzled, for a moment.

"You'd stay here?" she said. "Why?"

"Never mind that," said he. "Run for it – *now!*"

"But you said it's not him."

"Yes, but I'm not sure."

"Then why do we not both run?"

"Sarah," said he, for he could see that she was playing with him, even now. "I want you to go. I'll stay here and keep 'em busy. That way they'll not look to chase anybody."

"Would I not be safer here?" she said.

"No," he said, "they'll have the door in or they'll fire the house. There's hundreds of them, and I'd planned for one or two."

"But if I run and you stay, what will happen to you?"

"That's my business," said he, "and my pleasure." With the baying of the mob growing louder, he cast off the last restraint. "I know what you think of me, my girl, but no man shall harm a hair of your head while Sam Slym lives."

"*Beau chevalier, sans peur, sans reproche,*" she said, and kissed him on the cheek. Sam Slym had no French and for once could not read the expression on her face.

"Don't mock me, girl," said he, angrily. "Just get out while you can."

"No," she said, "not even if I could, and I think it is now too late. I want you to kill Jacob Fletcher and I want to see you do it."

"Oh Christ!" he said as there came a clash of breaking glass. "Get upstairs!" he said. "Guard your hostage if you must, but keep out of this!"

BANG! a pistol went off. Then half a dozen more. The men were in fear of their lives now, and nothing would stop them firing. He'd have ordered them to, in any case. A howl of rage came from the mob and more glass was smashed out of the windows. "Go on!" he cried and pushed her bodily up the stairs. She laughed and ran off, up to the attic.

Sam darted into the living room, now swirling with powder smoke. Men were loading and ramming for another volley, all around him. Outside, the street was a mass of heaving heads and shoulders and bellowing mouths. Torches flared in the night, and one or two were tossed forward to curve in a roaring arc, trailing smoke and sparks and crunch against the front of the house. Fire! That was the mob's weapon *par excellence*. Burn, loot, smash – but never forget to burn! Slym ran downstairs and yelled at his men to fill buckets with water from the pump in the kitchen, but even as he did so, a more immediate danger presented. The front door, which was holding back the mob, suddenly boomed and split as something struck it a tremendous blow from outside.

"Danny! Jimmy!" he cried. "And all the rest of you! To me, downstairs – they're breaking in!" Slym threw aside his precious blackthorn and drew his hanger, trying the edge of the two-foot curved blade on his thumb.

CRASH! The front door shuddered again. Dust and flakes of paint leapt from it and began to settle. CRASH! And the butt-end of something black and soil-encrusted drove through a hole in the middle of the door. A cheer came from the mob and the planks and panels of the door burst inward under the pressure of a dozen bodies. Men tumbled over one another fighting to get inside, Sam Slym gripped his short sword and stood ready to fight, with Danny, Jimmy and those of his men who'd the stomach for it behind him.

Among the press, and well to the front, Slym saw a very big man. He recognised Jacob Fletcher and ran forward with the fixed determination of killing him.

I could see very little crammed against the front door of 208 Maze Hill, but I noticed that while most of the mob was busy here, its outermost arms were attacking the houses on either side. It looked like a lively night in that quarter of London.

Then there was a swirl in the crowd and a dozen wild-eyed figures were pressing forward with a cast-iron lamppost, torn up by the roots to serve as a battering ram. In their eagerness they hadn't even extinguished the lamp, which guttered and spluttered as it bounced along, sprinkling burning oil over those at the lamp end of the iron column. They didn't seem to mind though, and pressed on with their coats singed and smoking. Thus the ponderous instrument drove forward, braining one poor dolt for not getting his head out of the way quick enough. Down he went under the heels of the twenty or thirty men struggling at the front door of 208, crammed into the narrow railed steps that bridged the drop down to the basement area and the basement windows.

"ONE!" we yelled, swinging our ram against the door – CRASH! It ground home, demolishing the doorknob which dropped off and rolled away. "TWO!" and the door split from top to bottom. "THREE!" and the woodwork surrendered and shivered into ruin. At once we tore our way through the shards and splinters, dropping the lamppost which clanged on the stone steps and bounded up again, knocking men off their feet. Bodies poured through the doorway and I stumbled over those who'd fallen in front of me. By George! It was just like one of Wellington's ghastly sieges in Spain in the early 1800s, with the mad Irish first through the breach in the wall.

Then there was a shouting from within the house and four or five lost men rushed at us with short, curved swords like cut-down cutlasses. One was Mr Samuel Slime and the bastard went straight after me. He'd have split my skull to the chin if I hadn't got my cudgel up in time. CLUNK! The blade bit hard and I reeled back from the blow, hauled my cudgel clear and took a swing at his head.

Ahhh! Someone screamed at my side and a pair of men fell into me, the one shoving a blade into the other's guts. They knocked me off my stroke and got between me and Slime. I basted the swordsman hard across the back of his head, since he had no white ribbons, and shoved through the press to get at Slime.

Swish! Slime's sword sliced the air over my head as I ducked. Then we were driven into each other's arms as the hundreds without tried to heave themselves in, and filled the hallway with angry, fighting men.

Fighting among themselves, that is. The dozen or so defenders were overwhelmed by sheer numbers so there was little opposition. But the English among our mob were already fallen out with the Irish.

Meanwhile, I had my hands full with Mr Slime. He was a vicious swine, hard and skilful, who'd learned his fighting in the gutters of Whitechapel. He bit me, the rogue, full on the chin, which was all he could get at, and he jammed his knee hard up into my groin. I bellowed in pain and got my fists working into his ribs. But he wriggled like a greasy pig to turn the blows, and I never got a good one home. Then he dropped his sword, which there wasn't room to use, and dived a hand into his coat pocket. I grabbed the hand which for sure was after something nasty, and took a leaf out of his book by clamping my teeth on his ear and jerking back my head to detach a good chunk.

Not that that stopped him! He never even flinched but pulled his hand free and whipped out the pistol he'd been after. Bang! Sizzle! The blasted thing went off, burning the pair of us with its flash and drilling the carpet underfoot. But he couldn't concentrate on two things at once and I managed to catch him a good one in the bread basket, while he was fumbling for the second shot from his pistol, which was a double.

He staggered at the blow, and I cracked my cudgel across his pistol hand, knocking the weapon flying. Instantly he was on me like a bloody tiger. He grabbed the cudgel with both hands and we fought for it furiously. But once again, bodies rolled between us as the wild struggle went on all around. I lost my cudgel, more guns went off, blades flashed, sticks whirred and the noise was deafening. And over the surging heads and shoulders there was Slime's cold, angry face glaring at me with the blood running down his face from the torn ear. He was just burning to finish it between us.

Well, so too was I. And I knocked men down left and right to get at him. Once we were face to face we went at it with our fists.

He was older than me and not so strong, but by George he was a devil to fight! I don't know to this day if I'd have got the better of him or not, for Sammy came pounding up at that moment, with Toby and the lads and those of our people still inclined to obey orders.

They piled into Slime at once and he went down under a storm of boots and cudgels.

"Search the house!" yelled Sammy.

"Save the Admiral!" cried Toby, sticking to his tale, and still more men piled in through the shattered doorway. They were mad drunk by now, with fighting and with gin, though all resistance had ceased when Slime went down to join the rest of his men, dead or unconscious on the floor.

"Jacob," says Sammy, "find Kate! Get her out, quick!" He pointed to a grinning monkey trying to set the wallpaper alight with his torch. "This place'll be up in smoke in a trice!"

"Come on!" says I, and pushed open the nearest door. It was a sitting room, rapidly being emptied by busy hands. I saw Toby's lads (stone cold sober the pair of 'em) leaving with the silver candlesticks and a fine bracket clock off the mantelpiece. The curtains were well alight and men were merrily swinging chairs over their heads to smash them on the floor, for sticks to feed the blaze. The smoke was choking already.

"No good!" says Sammy. "Outside." And as we turned

to go out, I heard a thing that chilled me with fear and horror. It was a girl's scream, piercing and high with terror.

"God Almighty!" I roared. "Kate!" and I threw men bodily aside in my furious haste to get to the source of that dreadful sound.

Chapter 37

The scream came from the kitchen downstairs. I kicked in the door which was hanging on its hinges and saw the room full of staggering men emptying every bottle in sight and smashing open the cupboards to get the pickles and raisins and any other delicacies. On the kitchen table, in the middle of the room was a grubby servant girl, shrieking and dancing up and down as a dozen men grabbed at her skirts and ran their hands up her legs. Just now they were only playing, but you could see the hot, wet faces and the slobbering tongues, and the girl was terrified.

I knocked a couple of them down to clear the way and let 'em know I was there. Then I grabbed the girl, swung her off her feet and down to the ground. She looked up at me from the depths of terror.

"After you, Cap'n darlin'," says a loud Irish voice.

"Officers forst, as always, but kindly leave a piece for us when you's done!" This brought cheers and a roar of laughter, and more screams from the girl, who struggled fiercely. But I hung on to her and yelled with my best sea-going bellow.

"Belay that squawking!" says I. "I'm a gentleman and I promise no harm shall come to you! Stop it at once, I say!" That calmed her down enough so's she'd pay attention. "Now then," says I, "where's Kate Booth?" The girl's eyes widened and I could see that she knew. Fear and anger rose within me. "Where is she?" says I, but she was either too frightened or too stupid to speak. "Damn you!" says I, "tell me this instant . . . or I'll give you to them!" and I held her out at arm's length to my Irish colleagues, bringing a roar of approbation.

"Come, sweetheart, come!" says one of 'em and the girl gabbled hysterically, "She's upstairs!" says she. "Right up the top!"

"Sammy," says I, shoving the girl at him, "get her out! I'm going for Kate!"

Up in the hallway the smoke was thick, and red flame roared inside the sitting room as I ran up the stairs.

Toby's son George passed me, going down with a bulging sack over his shoulder, and on the first floor I had to struggle through a fierce battle between the Irish and the English for possession of a yellow old man, dragged out on a day-bed from one of the bedrooms. He looked up at me grinning vacantly and stirring his blankets with one foot. It was grotesque. They'd found his sword and shoved it in his hand, and a couple of dolts were fighting for the privilege of shoving his thin arms into the sleeves of a gold-laced, full-dress Admiral's coat looted from a wardrobe.

"Here's his honour's hat!" cries a big Irishman, hauling a sea officer's cocked hat out of its leather case as he ran forward to jam it on the old grey head.

"Giss that 'at, you Irish turd!" says an English rival. "You ain't fit to serve a' Hinglish gennelman!"

"Fock you, Cockney!"

"Fuck *you*, bog-trotter!"

"Fock the King!"

"Fuck the Pope!"

SMACK! THUMP! SMASH! And a pile of 'em pitched into one another as the smoke rolled up the stairs and the roar of flame grew angry below.

I pushed through and ran forward for the last flight of stairs, but as I turned to go up them, I stopped off short and a cold fear took my heart. I hope to God that you who read this should never have such an experience, but that's what it feels like. As if the Devil's claw, made of ice, had got inside your breast to pluck the life from you.

At the very top of the stairs, a door stood open to a little room. In the doorway was a big squat woman with a face like a toad, and she had Kate Booth held clutched against her, with her thick, muscular arms around Kate's waist, pinning her arms as Kate kicked and struggled furiously. Next to them, in a bizarre costume like a postilion or a hussar, with preposterous white breeches, was Sarah Coignwood, about to put a knife to Kate's throat.

"Kate!" says I.

"Jacob!" says she, and I charged forward to tear Sarah Coignwood limb from limb. I was halfway up the stairs when she screamed in fury.

"No!" she shrieked. "Not on her *life*!" She slid her knife a fraction, and I saw the blood swell on Kate's neck.

"No!" I cried and stopped in my rush, grabbing the banister to steady myself.

"Then stand aside!" says Lady Sarah. "Stand aside and let me pass."

"Jacob!" says Kate. "Kill her!"

"I'll kill *her* first!" screams Lady Sarah.

"Beware, you bitch!" says I. "For God Almighty won't save you if you do!"

"Collins!" says she, grabbing Kate. "Unlock the chain and bring her." The gross woman fumbled for a key and leaned down to unlock a padlock securing the anklet on Kate's foot. But Kate kicked and stamped and caught her a clout in the chops with the heavy steel, and laid her back on her haunches, stunned. But it was no good, for Lady Sarah shrieked in rage and pulled the girl close with the knife blade glittering. Kate shuddered as the cold steel pressed into her throat.

And then there was a commotion on the stairs and Sammy and Toby came running up. Sammy'd got a pistol from somewhere, a big service weapon with a swivel rammer.

"Now then, missus," says Sammy, to Lady Sarah, "it won't do!" He levelled the pistol at twenty-foot range. "Put down the knife or I'll blow your soddin' guts out!"

"Hold your fire, Sammy!" says I, afraid he'd miss, for she'd got herself behind Kate now, with the knife sitting in the blood on Kate's neck. Sammy was a famous gunner, but I didn't know what he might be capable of with a smooth-bore pistol, and Sammy wasn't sure either, for I saw the weapon waver in his hand.

As Sammy hesitated, there came a roar of flame from the sitting room on the ground floor and a shocking blast of hot air shot up the stair-well. You could feel all the hairs on that side of your body crisping at their ends.

"Jacob!" says Sammy. "Do something smartish, mate, or we're all done. We can't stand here talking!" But every avenue was blocked. I dared not advance on Lady Sarah, not with her knife already drawing blood from Kate's throat. Sammy dared not fire for fear of hitting the wrong one, and Sarah Coignwood herself most certainly wasn't coming down those stairs past me.

"Let me pass," she spat, like a cornered alley-cat, "or I'll slit your little friend from ear to ear."

"No!" says I. "Let her go, and I'll let *you* go."

"I'm not that stupid!" she snapped. "D'you think I'd trust a whore's bastard like you?"

"I'm not asking for trust," says I bargaining for my life, and Kate's life too. I always did think I was good at that, didn't I? Well now was the time to show it. "I'm asking you to come to terms," says I.

"Jacob," says Sammy, urgently, "there's no time, the bloody stairs are going . . . look!" And down below there was a stampeding of men to get out of the house. The carpets were smouldering, flame was pouring out of the sitting room, and the paint on the staircase was bubbling and cracking in the intense heat. The whole stair-well glowed red like the mouth of hell.

"Listen to me, you bitch!" says I.

"Run for it, Toby lad," says Sammy.

"Get out of my way," screams Lady Sarah.

"This ain't your fight, Toby," says Sammy.

"We can come to terms!" says I.

"What terms?" says she.

"What about you, Sammy?" says Toby.

"Run, you silly bugger!"

"Give me Kate and I'll let you pass . . ."

"Good luck, Sammy!" says Toby and sped away.

"You'll kill me once I let her go."

"No," says I, "you can call off the Law. You can stop them, trying me for killing Dixon. I need you alive and free for that. I promise to let you go if you give Kate to me."

"No! No! No!" she screamed in hysterical rage, with

her temper in full flood. "Get out of my way! I'll count to three . . . One!"

"Wait!" says I, casting about for anything to say, to make some advantage. "We've got all your men outside. I'll kill the lot of 'em . . ."

"Kill them!" she cried. "Two!" and Kate shuddered as the knife deepened its first cut over the pulsing artery.

"We've got your lover!" says I. "Slym! If you hurt Kate I'll wring his neck!"

"Him?" she screamed. "That common little man? He's served his purpose! He's nothing to me!" Her face twisted in contempt and fury. "Three!" says she and tensed her arm for the sweeping cut as a pistol went off thunderously close by.

*

The heat from the blazing sitting room woke Sam Slym despite his injuries. The blast of hot air cut through the stupor and roused some protective instinct. Slym's jaw was broken, his head was thick from the battering of fists and boots, a couple of ribs had been stamped in, and one knee was agony to walk with. But he dragged himself to his feet, leaning against the wall to steady himself, only to be knocked spinning by fleeing men, desperate to escape before the house came in on them. He coughed in the smoke, half blinded with tears, and stumbled forward with the herd, as best he could, one hand against the wall.

He was nearly at the door when he heard voices yelling from upstairs, over the roaring of the flames. One of them was hers – Sarah Coignwood's. Slym turned at once and fought his way to the staircase. Toby Bone, fleeing at Sammy's command, rushed past Slym and out of the front door with the two hardly noticing one another. Slym craned his neck to see what was happening upstairs, and he groaned and he damned, and knew he could not run.

Immediately, he cast about for a weapon and by blind chance found his own pistol with the second barrel still unfired. He tried to cock it but found the thumb of his right hand was dislocated and pointed back up his forearm at a sickening angle and it made him impossibly clumsy. As best he could, Slym stuck the pistol in a pocket and, taking the thumb deliberately in his left hand, he jerked it sharply back into place. The pain would have floored most men, and even Slym screwed up his eyes and wept tears that were not of the smoke's making, but he drew out the pistol again, cocked it methodically and went up the stairs as fast as he could go.

He held the pistol in front of him, ready to fire, for he feared they'd see him every second. But the smoke and noise of the fire hid him, and anyway they were engrossed in their own drama. Just before the run of the last flight, where they were all standing, the landing ran off into a little side passage where Slym could hide and peer round the corner to see without being seen.

Fletcher's broad back was six feet away. The little white-haired sailor was beside him with a pistol aimed up the stairs. Away at the top of the stairs, Sarah had the girl Booth by the throat, with a knife under her chin. Mrs Collins was sat on the floor with her head in her hands. They still hadn't seen him and Fletcher was begging for the girl's life.

Slym raised his pistol and aimed at the back of Fletcher's head, just underneath the white-ribboned hat. The weapon was small, but it had rifled barrels and sights. Normally, in Slym's hands it was dead accurate. He took up the first pressure on the trigger, but the smoke stung his eyes so he couldn't see. He dashed the tears away, and tried again. Sarah was screaming something at the top of her voice. Aiming up the stairs at a steep angle, Slym found that Sarah's face, half hidden behind Kate Booth's, was directly in line with Fletcher. Indeed, the trembling of his injured hand shook the pistol from side to side, so first Fletcher, then Sarah and then the girl came into its sights. Slym pressed his arm hard against the wall to keep a steady aim.

Fletcher yelled at Sarah.

"We've got all your men outside," he said, an obvious lie. "I'll kill the lot of them . . ."

Slym held his breath and squinted over the sights but the pain in his thumb was so bad that he couldn't keep his hand still. "Kill them!" cried Sarah . . . "Two!"

Slym concentrated hard and brought Fletcher's head

large into his sights. He began to squeeze the trigger again.

"We've got your lover!" cried Fletcher. "Slime!" and Slym jumped to hear himself so named, and the pistol wandered off target. He groaned with effort and faces swam before him.

"Him?" screamed Sarah. "That common little man? He's served his purpose! He's nothing to me!"

Slym cried aloud in pain, and achieved his personal redemption by aiming squarely between Sarah Coignwood's eyes and deliberately squeezing the trigger.

*

In the same instant, a number of things happened. Kate kicked hard backwards at Sarah Coignwood.

Sarah tried to cut Kate's throat, missed her footing and fell forward, as Slym, who was supposed to be her poodle, put a bullet into her. She dropped like a stone, Sammy spun round and shot Slym and I leapt up the stairs to catch Kate who'd stumbled and was about to fall. She was so bloody angry she even tried to fight me off at first. Meanwhile, the pug-ugly old troll of a servant woke up and tried to snatch Kate from out of my arms, but I caught her a good one with my fist and sent her back on her fat arse beside her mistress.

"Come on, Jacob!" says Sammy and started down the stairs, but in that instant the entire woodwork of the first and second flights, that had been nicely baking away these past five minutes, went up in flame. It was an inferno and there was no going back that way.

"In here!" says I, darting into the little attic room, now bright lit by the flames from the stair-well. I could see a window and thought to escape that way. Sammy grabbed a chair and put it under the window. He smashed a catch with his pistol butt and threw open the window. He was out in a second and leaning back in to help me with Kate, who was unsteady on her feet after her long imprisonment.

"Hand her up, lad!" says he and I tried to pass her to him, but something jerked at her leg and held her back.

"The chain!" she cried. "Get me free!" She was secured by an anklet and a long chain ending in a big ring-bolt driven into one of the rafters.

I set Kate on the bed as I took a turn of the chain around my body and threw my weight on it. It was no good. The links were as thick as a man's finger. But I tried and tried again till my muscles cracked.

"You'll never break that!" says Sammy dropping beside me.

"The key!" says Kate. "The old woman's got it!" As I heaved at the chain, Sammy darted towards the woman where she sat with her arms round Lady Sarah's body. But the bitch had been listening, for she held up a key for us to see . . . and then deliberately threw it down the blazing stairs!

"Christ!" says Sammy, aiming a savage kick at the

malevolent old cow and dashing back to Kate. "See if we can get the bloody thing off her foot!" says he.

Gasping with effort, I let go the chain for an instant and knelt with Sammy to see if we could get the anklet off Kate's foot. Out in the stairway the flames roared louder. Sammy cursed horribly. It was no good. The thick band was clamped tight over Kate's slender ankle. There was blood there already from our pulling at it.

Sammy looked at the fire and looked at me.

"Jacob, lad," says he, "we ain't got long and she'll die for sure if we leave her . . ." He produced a seaman's knife and looked at Kate. She stared at the knife, wide-eyed, then nodded at me, screwed her eyes shut and clutched at my arm for support.

"No!" I cried and threw the heavy chain round my body once more. I took it in both hands, got as close to the ring-bolt as I could, and threw myself down so I could brace both feet against the timber and heave with all my heart, soul, mind and strength. I screamed with the effort of it and hauled till the chains bit through my skin. I pulled and pulled and pulled, mad with the terrible thing we'd have to do if I couldn't break the chain. And then, suddenly, I was skidding backwards as the ring-bolt tore out bodily from its seating, like a stubborn cork out of a bottle.

But I was up at once and the three of us were scrambling out through the attic window. Kate still needed a lot of help, what with the state of her and having to trail twenty feet of chain.

We clambered over the roof to the next house, but that was ablaze too, and we had to go on to the next. And then we had to break our way in, for the people were gone: fled from the riot and fire, leaving their house to be ransacked and every door broke open and left swinging in the wind.

As we stepped out, at last, into the street the mob was roaring off towards Greenwich in a procession with what looked like a bed carried aloft at the head. The street reeked of flame and three houses were cracking and blazing merrily. We were filthy and tattered, with eyes red with smoke. And Kate was too weak to walk. But that was no problem at all. I carried her in my arms like a child. And do you know, she didn't even thank me!

"Come on, lad," says Sammy. "Toby and the lads'll be waiting for us with the boats. Let's get down to the river."

Chapter 38

OUTRAGEOUS DISTURBANCES IN
GREENWICH AND WHITEHALL.

The scale and outrageous character of the disturbances of the night of 9th July, must bring again into question the means whereby the metropolis is defended against the forces of anarchy and dissent. Once again the unopposed and impertinent fury of the mob has been permitted to take its unholy pleasures even with the persons of noblemen.

(From *The Times* of 11th July 1794.)

*

In the face of all precedent, the English and the Irish reached a compromise. The English took the right-hand side of Admiral Williams's bed and the Irish took the left. Blind drunk, triumphant, and with the moral satisfaction of good fellows who'd done a tremendous night's work, they bore their hero through the streets of London, breaking windows all the way and sending the Watchmen about their business with eyes blacked and lanterns smashed.

In his uniform, with his sword by his side, and confused by the swaying motion and the raucous noise, the old Admiral's mind finally slipped its moorings and he fancied himself once more in command of a King's ship. In his mind's eye he took his squadron down upon the enemy in the sweltering heat off Barbados, reliving the battle which had won him a peerage.

"Steady, Mister Raine!" says he, to a long-dead quartermaster. "You'll lay this ship alongside of Admiral Torres de La Cruz's or I'll see the backbone of you at the gratings tomorrow!"

But the sick body could not stand the shock of this adventure and halfway up St James's Street (even as his ship trembled to the thunder of her guns and stern-faced he gazed across at the Spanish Admiral who at once raised his hat with the courtly manners of the Dons) he sank back to breathe no more.

The learned doctors of a later age would have recognised the massive infarction, consequent upon left ventricular hypertrophy and congestive heart failure. But they would have missed a more important point.

"Look, boys!" said one of the pall-bearers. "The old bugger's dead."

"Ah, but he died happy!" said another.

They conferred boozily and decided to take the corpse to the Admiralty Building in Whitehall, to present it to the proper authorities. However, when they arrived, swollen to nearly five hundred souls with pie-men, whores, gin-sellers and urchins, their motives were misinterpreted. A company of Marines turned out to the urgent rattle of a drum, and levelled their muskets in defence of the Sacred Halls of their Masters. And so, Admiral Williams of Barbados was dumped safely out of range, in the middle of Horse Guards Parade. A sad end for a Naval Officer.

Chapter 39

Extraordinary expenses 9th-10th July 1794
To Passage for 3 in The Lady Jane *outward bound of*
Shadwell basin – £30
To discretion of Shipmaster and Crew – £20
To ditto Dockyard Officials – £10
To ditto Excise – £30
To ditto Navy Convoy Officials – £30
TOTAL – *£120*

> (Extract from Personal Account books of
> Mr Toby Bone, esq., Waterman and
> Warehouseman of Wapping, London.)

*

In the small hours of the morning of 10th July 1794,
Toby Bone was alone in his office over the river. Tired

as he was, he was casting up his accounts. Experience had taught him that the task must not be neglected but must be done now, with the memory fresh. After all, the goods concerned were already on their way to further destinations. The work had to be done at once or things would be lost track of.

"Debit," he wrote: "To hire of participatory agents: 347 head at 2/6d per head – say £44. To gin for same, 350 bottles at 1/- per bottle – say £18. To hire of boatmen to stay sober: 12 head at 1 guinea per head – say £13. Total £75."

"Credit," he wrote: "Item: 1 pair candlesticks, silver 39 ounces, Hallmark 1756 by John Cafe of London – say £12 cash. Item: Clock, 8-day, striking and repeating the hour, verge escapement, ebony case with brass handle, by Francis Dorell of London (glass broken) – say £20 cash."

And so the list went on. It was long and authoritative. It revealed the discrimination of a connoisseur and the precision of a clerk. Jacob Fletcher would have approved right heartily. At the end of the list came a most gratifying total.

Toby sat back in his chair and sighed, wondering when next he'd see his brother. After some thought and with considerable reluctance he drew a line under his accounts and added a list of extraordinary expenses.

It was painful to see it in black and white. That was why Toby had hesitated. It knocked back his profits to a sizeable amount. But this was a family matter, after all, and there would have been no point in any of it if he hadn't got Sammy and his young friend, and his young friend's lady, safe out of England for a while.

And of course, Toby could never have taken money from Sammy. And what with young Fletcher being such a pal of Sammy's, why, he couldn't take from him neither. Still, Toby was well ahead on the night and he was fond of his elder brother.

He put away his papers, made all secure, blew out the candles and went to bed.

Chapter 40

With contrary winds we were nearly three months in *The Lady Jane*. Sammy, who could never be idle, insisted on working, despite being a paying passenger. Mr Cloud, the Master, was only too happy to oblige him once he learned what sort of a seaman Sammy was, but he insisted on rating Sammy as Third Mate. That flummoxed him at first, since he'd never had official rank over men, not in all his years at sea, and he said he didn't want it. But it was that or nothing and he made the best of it.

Kate got better from the harm she'd taken at the hands of that vile woman and she soon lost the thin, grey look that she'd had when we found her. And she was able to cut a bit of a dash, since Pen Bone had given her some of her daughters' clothes which, what with their Pa being a well-heeled man, were of the best. Kate set these off a treat. She always turned out on deck looking like a lady and the crew all fell in love with her, and went out of their way to do things for her – rigging hammocks in the nicest places for the shade and the breeze, and so on.

I suppose this was not surprising really, since she was the only woman aboard, but she was such a neat, pretty little thing, and so nicely turned out in her hats and gowns, that she'd have stood out among a thousand. God knows what *Lady Jane*'s people would have thought if they'd learned what Katie had done on her last voyage, though.

I suppose I fell in love with her too. No doubt of that. How could I not, all things considered? And when the sun began to shine, she smiled a bit and took to me. At least she did well enough for us to pick up where we'd left off aboard *Phiandra*. We let it be known we were married, for decency's sake aboard ship, but she'd not let the Captain marry us in reality, however many times I asked.

None the less, when we reached our destination she graciously condescended to let me provide for her, which was the next best thing.

Bloody woman. The trouble she's caused me! But at least she never had to go back to her old trade again.

We finally reached Jamaica at the end of September 1794, avoiding Kingston and Port Royal and anchoring up in the north-west of the island, near Pedro Point: not a good anchorage, but private and suiting both Mr Cloud's business and mine.

I was now just about as far from the Coignwood inheritance as it was possible to be. I was an ocean away, and outside of the Law. Worse still, since becoming identified as Bosun Dixon's murderer, and having escaped lawful authority by the use of violence, I had made an enemy of the only institution known to mankind that exercised its power across the entire globe: the Royal Navy.

On the other hand, Sammy, Kate and I had nearly a hundred pounds between us, in gold, and Jamaica was busy with trade of all kinds in those days. If I couldn't make a fortune for the three of us out of that, then my name wasn't Jacob Fletcher.

And of course, I did have the enormous satisfaction of knowing that Lady Sarah bloody Coignwood was dead and burned to ashes in the ruins of 208 Maze Hill.

Chapter 41

The Town, nay the World, rejoices to learn of La Belle Coignwood's delivery from the flames by a faithful servant. It further rejoices that the wicked wound inflicted upon La Belle by the hand of a POPISH RIOTER *has not only failed to prove mortal, but has equally failed to harm something more important by far than her life, viz:* HER BEAUTY! *We learn that the wound is confined entirely to the upper bones of the skull where the famed and lustrous tresses of* LONDON'S FOREMOST BEAUTY *provide a complete and entire screen. Furthermore,* EVENT *succeeds* ADVENTURE *for* LA BELLA DONNA *who, although thankful for her narrow escape, may be more sanguine in her sentiments as regards the recent escape from* DOCTOR CRICK'S INSANE ASYLUM *in Staffordshire of her son, Victor who is reputedly become a* MALICIOUS MURDEROUS MANIAC.

Fletcher's Glorious 1st of June

Post Scriptum: La Belle's pet ape, Mr S.S. the black-thorn-wielding skull-cracker, likewise escaped from peril. Though wounded, he yet lives, and he thrives in animal vigour.

(Extract from "Lady D'Arcy's Chatterbox" of 15th July 1794, *in The Polite Monitor.*)

ENDEAVOUR INK

Endeavour Ink is an imprint of Endeavour Press.

If you enjoyed *Fletcher's Glorious 1ˢᵗ of June* check out Endeavour Press's eBooks here:
www.endeavourpress.com

For weekly updates on our free and discounted eBooks sign up to our newsletter:
www.endeavourpress.com

Follow us on Twitter:
@EndeavourPress